Roll.

Tap.

Tap.

Tap.

THE MARBURY LENS

LENS

ANDREW SMITH

SQUARE
FISH

FEIWEL AND FRIENDS
NEW YORK

For Liz Szabla

SQUARE FISH

An Imprint of Macmillan

THE MARBURY LENS. Copyright © 2010 by Andrew Smith.
All rights reserved. Printed in the United States of America by
R. R. Donnelley & Sons Company, Harrisonburg, Virginia. For information,
address Square Fish, 175 Fifth Avenue, New York, NY 10010.

Square Fish and the Square Fish logo are trademarks of Macmillan and
are used by Feiwel and Friends under license from Macmillan.

Library of Congress Cataloging-in-Publication Data

Smith, Andrew (Andrew Anselmo),
The Marbury lens / Andrew Smith.
   p. cm.
Summary: After being kidnapped and barely escaping, sixteen-year-old Jack goes to
London with his best friend Connor, where someone gives him a pair of glasses that
send him to an alternate universe where war is raging, he is responsible for the survival
of two younger boys, and Connor is trying to kill them all.
ISBN: 978-1-250-01027-8
[1. Emotional problems—Fiction.   2. Kidnapping—Fiction.   3. Survival—
Fiction.   4. London (England)—Fiction.   5. Horror stories.]   I. Title.
PZ7.S64257Mar 2010
[Fic]—dc22   2010013007

Originally published in the United States by Feiwel and Friends
First Square Fish Edition: October 2012
Square Fish logo designed by Filomena Tuosto
macteenbooks.com

10 9 8 7 6 5 4 3 2 1

AR: 4.4 / LEXILE: HL720L

part one

THE
AMETHYST
HOUR

I guess in the old days, in other places, boys like me usually ended up twisting and kicking in the empty air beneath gallows.

It's no wonder I became a monster, too.

I mean, what would you expect, anyway?

And all the guys I know — all the guys I ever knew — can look at their lives and point to the one defining moment that made them who they were, no question about it. Usually those moments involved things like hitting baseballs, or their dads showing them how to gap spark plugs or bait a hook. Stuff like that.

My defining moment came last summer, when I was sixteen.

That's when I got kidnapped.

one

I am going to build something big for you.

It's like one of those Russian dolls that you open up, and open up again. And each layer becomes something else.

On the outside is the universe, painted dark purple, decorated with planets and comets, stars. Then you open it, and you see the Earth, and when that comes apart, there's Marbury, a place that's kind of like here, except none of the horrible things in Marbury are invisible. They're painted right there on the surface where you can plainly see them.

The next layer is Henry Hewitt, the man with the glasses, and when you twist him in half, there's my best friend, Conner Kirk, painted to look like some kind of Hindu god, arms like snakes, shirtless, radiant.

When you open him up, you'll find Nickie Stromberg, the most beautiful girl I've ever seen, and maybe the only person in this world, besides Conner, who ever really loved me.

Now it's getting smaller, and inside is Freddie Horvath. That's the man who kidnapped me.

Next, there's the pale form of the boy, Seth, a ghost from Marbury who found me, and helped me. I guess he was looking for me for a long time. And the last thing on the inside is me. John Wynn Whitmore.

They call me Jack.

But then I open up, too, and what you'll find there is something small and black and shriveled.

The center of the universe.

Fun game, wasn't it?

I don't know if the things I see and what I do in Marbury are in the future or from the past. Maybe everything's really happening at the same time. But I do know that once I started going to Marbury, I couldn't stop myself. I know it sounds crazy, but Marbury began to feel safer, at least more predictable, than the here and now.

I need to explain.

two

Smoke.

Everything smells like cigarettes.

The stink helps me get my head focused so I can will my eyes open. I don't know where I am, but I can tell there are cigarettes. The smoke turns my stomach, but at least it is something I can connect to — like an anchor, I guess, and it keeps my head from floating away again.

I want to move.

My arms are telephone poles.

I'm lying on my back, right?

Wasn't I supposed to be leaving soon?

My eyes are open. I am sure I felt the paste between the lids giving way, but it's like trying to see in a swimming pool. A yellow and gray swimming pool, where I can make out the shape of a window and the outline of Freddie Horvath standing there.

Smoke.

I fall to sleep again.

My whole first day is like this.

Five seconds long.

three

Let me back up a bit.

I lived in my grandparents' house then. Wynn and Stella. I guess it's kind of a stupid thing to say, because I'd never lived anywhere else.

It was one of the biggest houses in Glenbrook. Wynn built it when my mother was just a kid. It sat on over four hundred acres of some of the best grape-growing land in Central California, and that's how Wynn and Stella made all their money.

I was born on the kitchen floor.

Stella said I couldn't wait to get here. That's why I came out between my mother's blood-spattered feet, right on Wynn and Stella's nice wood kitchen floor, while Amy leaned over the breakfast table grunting, her legs locked in the only contraction she'd had.

She was seventeen.

I've only seen her one time that I can remember, and I always dreaded the two times per year I'd feel forced to say awkward hellos by telephone.

Sometimes, okay, a lot of times, I'd stare at that spot on the floor — Stella drew imaginary circles around it with her fingers whenever she'd retell the story — and I'd wish that Amy had been standing at the top of a ladder or something so Little Jack would have hit his head just hard enough that he'd never know any world could ever exist outside the lukewarm nothing of the amnesiac womb.

It was the first weekend of summer, and just about everyone I knew was going to be at Conner Kirk's house getting drunk that night to celebrate twelve weeks with no school. Of course, I was going to be there, too. That's what kids do.

But mostly all I cared about was getting away. Wynn and Stella promised to send me to England for two weeks, and my flight was in just five more days. Wynn decided he wanted me to visit his old school — a "grammar school" in Kent — to take a tour. He told me if I liked it enough, he'd send me there for my junior year. And I already knew I'd like it enough, that there was something itching inside that made me want to get as far away as possible from that invisible circle on the kitchen floor. Conner was going to come, too. His parents had enough money that they made the same offer to Conner about attending St. Atticus. *If* we both liked it. So it was like this fantastic opportunity for me and my best friend to do something together we'd probably never get a chance to do again.

I could say it was going to be the trip of a lifetime, but that's just because I can't clearly remember what it was like slipping around naked and wet, gasping for my first breaths on the kitchen floor while Amy screamed and cursed, "The goddamned baby! The goddamned baby!" At least, that's how I always imagined it happened.

In the end, Conner and I both ended up getting more than we bargained for there, I guess.

But that one Saturday morning at the start of the summer when I woke up, things felt changed — different. It was already so hot, and I could tell it was going to be the most hellacious boring and long day. I got right up from bed and looked out the window like I always do, snaked into a T-shirt and basketball shorts, grabbed an armload of extra clothes so I could spend a night or two at Conner's, and I didn't even say much more than *hey* to Stella or Wynn as I passed them in the kitchen.

I'm not exactly certain what made me such a loner around them. It wasn't that I hated Wynn and Stella, but I think I probably expected them to abandon me, too, so I made it as easy as possible for them to assume I wasn't even there.

"I'm going to be at Conner's till Monday. His parents are gone for the weekend."

Wynn nudged his glasses higher and looked me over. It made me feel like I'd forgotten to get dressed or something. I squeezed the bundle of clothes tighter under my arm.

"He could stay here if he wants," Wynn said.

Oh, yeah. That would be real fun, Wynn.

I shrugged. "I have my phone."

Stella said, "Have a nice time. We love you, Jack."

"See you Monday sometime."

I pushed the screen door open and walked across the wet lawn to my truck, thinking I'd go over the pass and head down to the beach. And I ended up in the other direction for no reason I can recall, driving, instead, toward Paso Robles out along the dirt roads that cut perfect squares through my grandfather's vineyards.

I called Conner on my cell phone. I knew there was no way he'd be awake at seven thirty on a Saturday, and I got ready to shut it off if I heard his annoying voice mail greeting.

He answered. Just a grunt.

"Hey, Con."

"What's up, Jack? Damn." I could hear him moving around in his bed. "Seven in the morning. Are you in jail or something?"

"I was going to go to the beach. I was bored. I ended up driving out across the fields toward Paso. I don't know why."

"Maybe it's because you never know where the hell you are," Conner said.

"Want to go to the beach?"

I steered with my knee and held my phone in one hand while I shifted gears.

Conner grunted again.

It sounded like *no*.

"I'm coming over. Okay?"

"Wake me up," Conner said. "Bring me a Starbucks."

Conner's house was part of a walled-in tract of enormous stucco homes with no yards and fake tile roofs. Honestly, they were built so close together Conner said if his neighbors kept their bathroom window open wide enough, he could take a piss across the gap into their toilet. Good thing they liked their central air. I'm sure Conner would have tried it. And I swear there was never any sunlight that hit the ground between some of those tall houses, but most people in California like living like that nowadays.

Burning my fingers on two paper coffee cups, my bundle of clothes tucked under an arm, I pushed his front door open with an elbow and made my way upstairs to Conner's room. I knew I'd find him sleeping.

I dropped my clothes on his desk chair and put the cups down on the stand next to his bed.

"Coffee's here."

Conner pulled the sheet down from over his head and sat up. He looked at me, nodded, fumbled with his cell phone to check his missed calls, then dropped it on the bed next to him, and took a sip from the coffee.

"Thanks, man." Conner scratched his armpit and yawned. "Looks like we've got a nonstop party for, like, the next couple weeks or so."

My trip to England would be just over two weeks long — a few

9

days shorter for Conner, because I'd be leaving before him and meeting him over there. I'll admit I was pretty nervous about being on my own without anyone I knew there, too, but there was no way I'd say that to Conner or my grandparents. But it was just how the whole thing got set up by Wynn and Stella, and Conner couldn't leave the same day because his brother was coming home from Cal. Family stuff. Like I'd know anything about that.

When I think about it now, it was like everyone involved in the whole thing was playing chicken — seeing who'd be the first to blink.

"I don't have to be back home until Monday or so, just enough time to get my stuff together to leave," I said.

"You want to go get something to eat?" Conner asked. "I don't want to mess up downstairs before tonight."

"Sure."

"Lauren Willis is going to come," he said. "Maybe she'll give you the same going-away present Dana's giving me, so I don't have to hang out for two weeks in the same room with a frustrated virgin who only pretends to never think about sex."

He knew I thought Lauren was hot, even if I didn't really care much about the whole boyfriend-girlfriend thing.

"You think about it enough for both of us," I said.

Conner got out of bed, hair crazy, wearing nothing but stretched-out red shorts. He grabbed his coffee, barefoot-stepped around the glass ice-block wall that separated his bathroom, and turned on the shower.

"Give me a minute," he said.

four

Everyone was at Conner's party, even people we didn't like. That's how parties are, anyway, once the word gets out. While most of the kids started their drinking games early, I tried to stay straight-headed, at least for a little while.

I liked to think that one day Lauren and I would actually go out on a date or something. Some people believed we would, too — even some of the guys who were always calling me "gay." I'm not gay. Not that it matters. But sometimes it felt like even Conner was testing me on that, and I mostly just wanted people to leave me alone. Because I might be weird, but I really didn't care about sex. To be honest, I was kind of scared of it, even if I did think Lauren was incredible.

So when she showed up with a couple other girls from Glenbrook, I watched her as she walked across the Kirks' tiny front lawn, and I smiled as I greeted her at the door.

When we walked through the living room, Brian Fields saw me and yelled, "Jack and Lauren, sit down and play!"

Brian was a friend of ours. We were all on the cross-country team together: Conner, Lauren, Dana, and me; and he was sitting with five other kids on a big pit couch. There must have been twenty cans of beer on the round table in front of him, so I knew they were playing a drinking game.

I looked at Lauren.

She said, "Okay!"

And that was it for Jack. We got a little overly competitive in Brian's game of Tower, something involving five stacked shot glasses of beer, held up with cardboard coasters between them, and one die.

I didn't realize it, but at some point Lauren had gotten up from the couch and didn't come back.

Conner and Dana blurred through the living room and waved at me.

Nobody was really playing the game anymore, and I suddenly had to get up.

The house was so crowded and hot.

I knew I'd had too much to drink, and was feeling a little sick. I needed to pee, too, which didn't help. But there was a line of girls waiting outside the downstairs bathroom.

Most guys at parties would just pee in the backyard, but I didn't want to go out there, either. I could see Brian and some of the other boys from school sitting in a circle, smoking pot, and I didn't want to get invited into that game, too.

So I went upstairs to Conner's room. I was fully intending to use his bathroom and then just put myself to sleep.

I practically tripped on my own feet making my way down the hall, trailing my hand along on the wall just to steady myself. I pushed his door open and went inside. The lights in Conner's bathroom were on, so the room was dim, framed in the smearing swirl of the yellow glow through ice block.

"Lock the door behind you, numbnuts."

It was Conner.

I just stood there, my back pressed to the door, my hand closed around the latch.

Conner was on his bed, with Dana. He was lying on his back and Dana was straddling his hips, facing away from him, her hands gripping his knees as she rocked back and forth, up and down into him, or Conner into her. She smiled at me, her eyes half-closed.

Neither of them had anything on. Their clothes were scattered everywhere; and Conner just watched me, grinning confidently, his arms folded behind his head like he was lounging in a hammock. He said, "Are you going to just stand there and watch, or do you want to hop in here and have some fun with us? Dana's totally cool with that."

It was one of those situations when there really is no right answer.

Dana kept sliding against Conner, moaning.

They both had their eyes on me.

"I'm sorry, Con. I . . . I was just looking for a place to . . ."

I turned around and squeezed back out into the hallway. I locked the door before I shut it behind me; and I could hear Conner calling after me, "Jack! Hey! Come on, don't be such a loser!"

I rubbed my eyes and turned back to the door. And I thought, *What's wrong with me?*

I didn't know what to do. Maybe I should have gone back in there, just to get all this crap over with and prove I was someone other than the person everyone thought they saw — so people like my best friend would just leave me alone about stuff. But I was relieved that I'd locked myself out, too; and as I turned and stumbled down the hall toward the stairway, I could hear Dana on the other side of the door, and Conner called my name one more time.

And I practically fell down the stairs, thinking, *I should have stayed in there with them.*

I wanted to leave.

And I'd locked my keys and phone upstairs in Conner's room.

But that was probably a good thing.

Downstairs, the music blared so loud I could feel it buzzing up through my legs. The drinking game had evolved into Tip the Cups, and I saw Lauren curled up in the corner of the couch, sleeping.

"Jack! Jack!" someone called. "Come dance. No boys want to dance."

It was one of the girls Lauren came in with. I didn't even know her name. I think it was Ellen or Eileen, or something.

"I'll be right back. I need to pee," I said, and I headed away from the noise and out the front door.

It was good to get out of the stuffiness of the party. There were a couple other guys peeing on the side of the house. No big deal. I knew I wouldn't go back inside. The ground seemed to come up to my feet each time I took a step. I saw my truck parked on the street and wanted to go home, but it took me a few minutes to remember I'd left my keys up in Conner's room with the clothes I'd brought over that morning. I tried to shake the image of Conner and Dana from my head.

"Hey, Jack, want a beer?"

The kid who was peeing next to me pulled a can of beer from his back pocket.

"Sure."

I took the beer and walked across the lawn, drinking as I staggered down the sidewalk in the direction of my home, six miles from Conner's place. The night was so warm, and I was sweating a little, even though I was only wearing a T-shirt and some baggy shorts.

And I don't know where that beer ended up, but I do know where I did. I didn't even make it two miles. I fell to sleep on a bench in Steckel Park.

five

"Hey, kid."

I felt a hand on my shoulder, shaking me.

"Kid. Are you okay?"

A face leaned in close to mine. I could feel the warmth of breath.

"Do you need any help? Are you hurt or something?"

"Huh?" I put my hand up to my eyes. My head hurt. The guy was looking right into my eyes, like he was trying to see if anyone was really home.

"Did you take anything tonight, kid?"

I wasn't sure where I was, had to think, remember. The man in front of me smelled like cigarettes and coffee. He was dressed all in green, a doctor or something. I thought I must have been in the hospital, but it was too dark.

"Where are we?"

"Yeah," he said. I heard him sniff at me. "How much did you drink?"

"Huh?"

"Can you sit up?"

"I'm drunk."

The man pulled me up. His hands felt warm, careful. When I sat up, everything in front of me spun like a compass needle in a hallway of magnets.

"Do you know where you are?"

No.

"I was at a party. I was trying to go home."

The man looked over both shoulders. I thought he was trying to see if there were any other kids there, that maybe they'd know what to do with me. I could hear music coming from somewhere. I remembered, the park was in front of Java and Jazz. I heard jazz.

The man was still looking right into my eyes.

"Are you going to throw up?"

"No."

"Where do you live?"

"Glenbrook."

I tried standing, but it felt like there was no blood in my head. I fell back onto the bench.

"I'm a doctor at Regional. I'm headed that way. I can take you home, if you want."

The man pulled me up from my armpit. "But you have to promise not to throw up in my car."

"No. I'll be okay," I said. "It'll be okay for me to walk."

He let go of me. "Are you sure? It's no problem."

"I'll be okay," I repeated.

The man turned away. I fell down, caught myself on the pavement, and landed on my hands and knees.

He turned back. "I think I'd better call someone."

He started to unclip a phone from the waist of his loose green pants.

"No," I said. "Do you think you could drop me off?"

He smiled. He helped steady me on my feet. "Sure."

He said his name was Freddie Horvath. He even gave me his card, which, I guess, was supposed to prove something. I didn't know what to do with a doctor's business card. I slipped it into my wallet, which I dropped when I tried putting it back in my pocket. Freddie laughed and picked it up, handing it to me.

"I remember what it was like, being a kid, too. You'll be all right."

He was nice, and I trusted him. But I was drunk and stupid.

I fell asleep again in Freddie's Mercedes. I woke up when my head snapped forward. The car stopped somewhere. I couldn't recognize the place, and had to think, again, about where I was, piece together the blurry sequence of disjointed events from the party: walking in on Conner and Dana, and ending up, somehow, asleep in this car that was now parked in front of a dark ranch-style house that I had never seen before.

"Stupid," Freddie said. "I left my ID badge at home. I'll be right back."

He pushed his door open. I could have sworn he was wearing an ID badge when he found me on that park bench.

"Where are we?"

"Don't worry," he said. "We're probably less than a mile from your house. I'll be right back. Can I get you some water or something? You look like you could use it."

My head pounded. My mouth was paper.

"Thanks," I said.

He closed the driver door and walked around beside the car. I watched him as he came up and pulled my door open.

"Want to come in?"

I knew I was stupid, should have never accepted his help. But I rationalized that he was a doctor. Still, all I really wanted was to get home; and I wanted to speed him along, too.

"It's okay," I said. "I'll wait here."

Freddie smiled. "I'll be right back, John."

John?

I never told him my name. At least, I don't think I did. I figured he must have looked at my driver's license when I dropped my wallet in the park, because I'd never say my name was *John*.

17

I felt in my pocket. My wallet was still there.

I nodded and said, "Thanks."

Freddie came back out in a minute, a plastic badge dangling from his breast pocket and a bottle of drinking water in his hand. He got in and started the car and passed the water to me.

"Are you going to be okay?" he asked.

I was so thirsty. "Yeah. Thanks."

I opened the bottle and drank.

I was unconscious before we made it out of Freddie's driveway.

SIX

That's how I ended up in that smoky room.

Freddie smoked constantly.

And it wasn't until maybe a full twenty-four hours had dissolved invisibly past me — Sunday night — when I started to soberly realize that I was in a situation that seemed unreal, like something you'd only see on TV, something that would never happen to me.

But it was real.

Something hurts on my foot.

That's the first really clear thought I have: *Something hurts.*

I sit up. There is a constricting tightness around my ankle, cutting into me if I pull against it too much. That's what holds me there. I'm lying on a bed. There are no sheets on it. I can feel the swirling grooves stitched into the mattress.

My hands are free. I sit up and rub my ankle. The binding feels like one of those heavy-duty zip ties, the kind cops use. That's what it is. I feel the trap mouth where the toothed band has been fed through.

I see a slit of light along the floor. A door.

I run my hands over my body. Check everything. I don't feel like I've been hurt. I don't feel like he did anything to me. He didn't. I am sure of that. But I'm lying there, stripped of everything I remember wearing, except for my boxer briefs, the same ones I put on when I got dressed for Conner's party.

How long ago was that?

I try to think, feel around the bed to see if I might find my clothes, my wallet, something I can use to cut this goddamned strap off my leg.

Nothing. I track my fingers along the edge of the bed as far as I can, my hands blindly squeeze between the mattress and the foundation, probe the cool bare floor underneath. It is clean, but I can reach pretty far. I push my hand up inside the box spring. Something metal is there. I slide my fingers behind it and begin pulling.

Black shadow moves beneath the door.

Someone is out there.

I flip myself back up onto the bed. My ankle burns. Just that moment of exertion leaves me gasping for breath. I am sweating, my eyes wide; and I watch the light at the door's edge.

It opens.

I shut my eyes.

I heard him walk up to the edge of the bed. He put his hand flat on my chest.

"I know you're awake, John."

I opened my eyes.

"How are you feeling?"

And I thought, *What an idiot. How do you think I feel?* I wanted to scream, howl, but I kept my mouth shut. Mostly, I had questions. I kept hearing them over and over, but I didn't want to say them.

What the fuck are you trying to do to me?

"I bet you're thirsty," Freddie said.

I was.

"Would you like a drink of water, John? Do they call you Johnny, or just John?"

Jack, asshole.

"I promise it's only water this time."

He walked out the door, leaving it open. My eyes adjusted to the light. He was wearing those same doctor's scrubs. I saw the name badge, too. He didn't even try to lie about his name. That was bad, I thought. And he looked big, like I'd never be able to fight him, even if I was pretty strong.

In a minute Freddie Horvath came back through the doorway, pushing one of those adjustable rolling desk chairs in front of him. There were some plastic bins on the seat that had things in them — I couldn't tell what they were — and a bottle of water, the same brand he'd given me the night before.

A cigarette pointed at me from his mouth. The smoke curled back through the uncombed hair that hung down over one eye. I tried to take in as many details about him as I could, but looked away every time his eyes landed on mine. I thought he was maybe about thirty. Maybe younger than that. His mouth and eyes looked dead, like he was bored.

He took the things from the chair and put them down on the floor beside the bed. He took a drag from the cigarette and pulled it away from his lips, exhaling streams of gray from his nostrils.

"I know." He smiled. "A doctor who smokes."

He held the water bottle in front of him and sat down.

I could reach your fucking throat.

"Thirsty?"

I put my hand out, but Freddie jerked the bottle away.

"First lesson, John." He drew another hit from his cigarette and said, through the smoke, "You have to ask me."

I looked at him, his name badge, the water.

He sat back in the chair.

"Ask me for it."

"Can I please have some water?" My voice sounded sick, far away from my body.

"That's nice," he said. "That's how you do it."

He handed the bottle to me.

"See?" Freddie said. "It's sealed. No tricks."

I drank, and spilled some of the water down my neck onto the mattress.

"What did you do to me?" I said.

"I didn't do anything. You did it to yourself."

I capped the bottle.

If that's what you think, asshole.

"This thing really hurts my ankle." I thought about what he'd do. I wanted to be careful. "Will you take it off, please?"

Freddie leaned over the bed. He put one hand beneath my heel and the other on top of my foot. The way he turned my foot in his hands and looked at me told me he really was a doctor.

"Stop pulling against it," he said. "I can put something on it so you don't get an infection. Tomorrow, maybe I can switch it to the other side if you want."

I wondered if he was going to make me ask for that, too. He reached down to the floor. I heard him moving things around, the sound of a plastic lid being pulled open. He took the cigarette from his lips and tilted it toward me.

"Smoke?"

I looked away.

"Didn't think so. You sure can drink, though."

He put the cigarette down somewhere. I couldn't see. He squeezed clear, greasy cream from a silver tube onto the tips of his fingers and wiped them around the burning cut on my ankle. Gently. I looked at the window, wondered what was out there.

"Does that feel better?"

I didn't say anything. I took another drink and recapped the bottle.

"You need to pee? I bet you need to pee, John."

I needed to piss so bad, it felt like I was going to burst.

"My name's Jack."

I looked right at him, trying to see if he'd have any reaction to that. I couldn't tell anything from his eyes. He scared me. I knew I'd have to play along with him so he wouldn't hurt me, but I wanted to lash out and hit him as hard as I could. The only way he'd think my name was John was if he'd looked through my wallet. I wondered what he did with it, with my clothes. How he got me into this room. I knew what I'd done to myself to get here, and I realized nobody would even miss me yet.

Conner probably thought I was mad at him or something.

I should have stayed in there with him and Dana when he asked me to.

I felt sick.

"Will you let me up so I can take a piss?"

Freddie bent forward and picked something from the floor. He held up a milky white plastic container with a wide angled mouth on it and red rubber stopper held on by a band that looped around its handle. He pried the cap off, and I could see his cigarette butt curled up inside the bottle.

"Male urinal," he said. "From the hospital. I'm sure you can figure it out." He stuck his finger into the mouth and tipped it downward. "Like this. Use it."

My stomach turned. He handed the urinal out and teasingly pulled his hand back when I reached for it.

"Ask me."

I started thinking about him hurting me. How bad it would feel. I wondered if he was going to kill me. When.

"Can I please use that?" I said.

"Nice."

He gave me the bottle. I really didn't want to use it there in front of him, but there was nothing I could do. I knew that this had to be some weird game of his to make me act like some kind of fucking animal in a trap, but just thinking about it made me feel like I was about to piss myself, and I really didn't want to do that in front of him, either.

I tried not to look at him watching me as I lay there on my back, peeing into that plastic thing. I tried to make myself go away, even if I couldn't.

Freddie lit another cigarette, watching me as I filled that bottle.

"Are your parents hippies or something, Jack?"

I was so nervous, I couldn't say anything. I didn't know what he was getting at.

He nodded his cigarette at my hands. "You know. You weren't circumcised."

I stopped, pulled my underwear back over me. I swallowed. "I was born on the floor. I've never been in a hospital in my life."

I didn't finish right. There was a fist-size circle of piss on the front of my boxer briefs. I tried to cover it with one of my hands. I was afraid he'd get mad at me. I started to shake. I'd never done that before from being scared. It was like I was studying myself: I'd heard that people could shake uncontrollably when they were scared, but I didn't really believe it. Until now.

Freddie took the bottle from me. He replaced the cap and held it up, swirling it, more than half-filled. I could see the black curl of his cigarette butt floating inside. He scanned me like he was measuring me for a box or something. "Now you'll need to take a bath in the morning. And I'll wash your shorts out for you, too. If you behave yourself. And if you ask me to."

He pushed the chair back from the edge of the bed and stood up. He put the sloshing urinal on the seat and picked up the plastic box he'd placed on the floor. Then he set another clean urinal, a full water bottle, and a plastic bedpan down on the bed next to me.

"Can I have my clothes?"

"Why? Are you cold?"

I was sweating. He knew I wasn't cold. I didn't answer.

"Please?"

"I'm going to go now, Jack. But you'll see me soon, I promise. Don't do anything stupid. Don't try to make any noise because nobody will hear you. Well, if anyone does hear you, it will be me. And you don't want to make me mad. You've been a nice boy so far, Jack Wynn Whitmore, who just turned sixteen in April. Nice kid. Stay that way."

I was shaking so bad. Freddie had to notice how scared I was, but he looked like he didn't care at all. And I could tell — I knew — he'd seen this before, too.

"Do you want me to give you something to relax you?"

"No. Please don't."

I had to force the words out of my throat, my jaw was frozen.

"I could," he said.

24

He turned and began wheeling his chair toward the doorway.

And I screamed, "Fuck you, sonofabitch!" and threw the full bottle of water at him. I couldn't stop myself from doing it. It hit him square between his shoulders and bounced back to the floor.

Freddie froze, then spun around. He picked up something from the chair, something black and shiny.

A stun gun.

And Freddie said, "You made it longer than most till we got to this part, Jack."

I tried to twist away, but the metal ends of that thing were pressed right into my belly before I could do anything.

It felt like being stabbed by a thousand knives at once. And as I attempted to scream and thrash, mute and unmoving, I could hear Freddie shouting above the surge of pain that swelled in my ears, "I'll fucking kill you right now if that's what you want! Is that what you want? Just ask me! Just ask me, Jack!"

He stopped.

My body wanted to shut down.

I felt the wet of tears running from my eyes as my lungs tried to refill against the spasms from the shock.

Jack doesn't cry, though.

Never has.

I squeezed my eyes shut. Then Freddie put the prod up inside my armpit and shocked me a second time, longer.

I thought it was going to kill me.

When he stopped, I was trying my hardest not to cry. He put the gun back onto the chair and said, like he was offering me a gift, "Do you want me to kill you now, Jack?"

"No."

"Ask me."

"Please don't kill me, Doctor."

I heard him make a clicking sound with his mouth, like he didn't want me to call him that. Then I heard him push the chair out the door.

I kept my eyes shut. I was so scared. But I could almost feel his shadow on me when he came back and stood in the doorway. I looked at him. He held a syringe in his hand, the stun gun was sticking out from his front pocket.

"Then I'll tell you what we're going to do, Jack."

He came to the bed.

I shook.

He put his palm on my thigh and pulled the leg of my underwear up high. A cool swab of alcohol on my skin.

I turned away and felt the sting as he stabbed the needle into the muscle.

"Don't worry," he said. "It's just going to make you calm down. That's all. Just calm down."

He pulled the needle out and rubbed his finger over the spot where he'd injected me. Then he licked my leg, slowly, and I felt like I would throw up when I felt his teeth and tongue against my skin, but there was nothing in me.

I heard him swallow.

"Try to calm down, Jack."

He put his hand on my forehead, then felt my heart.

He brushed my hair with his fingers.

I shut my eyes, turning my face away.

He began pulling my shoulder up, trying to get me to turn over. "I need you to roll onto your stomach now. Do that."

I could already feel the shot taking effect. It felt warm, soft. Funny.

"No. Leave me alone."

"Jack?"

He stroked the stun gun across my throat.

I couldn't take that again. My chest heaved, frozen hiccups. It was strange, but I started not caring about anything. It was all a joke, anyway. And I felt like I was melting. I began to turn over on the bed, and he pushed me flat, facedown, and held me there with his hand pressing between my shoulder blades. I tried to pretend this wasn't happening, that I was outside, somewhere else. It felt like that anyway. Then his other hand slid down my back, and pulled my underwear away.

When he got them down over my feet so I could feel the soft weight of them hanging loose on the connected chain of zip ties, he pushed my knees apart. Something cold and slick — like jelly — squeezing out onto my thighs. His hand slid up between my legs and rubbed. I tried crawling away from his hand, but I was stuck there. I didn't care anymore. It was my fault. I felt myself drifting away, and a phone began ringing.

He pulled his hand away. I could hear him wiping it on the mattress.

"Shit. You made me late."

He twisted his fingers around in my hair and shoved my face into the bed.

The door closed.

seven

A television came on somewhere in the house. Sounds of one of those nonstop shopping channels. *The Amethyst Hour.* I felt fuzzy, good. The bed was comfortable. I couldn't feel the hurt in my foot. I tried pulling my underwear back up.

Don't go to sleep, Jack.

Don't.

It seemed like I lay there staring at the curtained window, feeling the buzzing beneath my skin, inside me like humming insects, soft wings caressing, not blinking, so relaxed, so relaxed, for hours. It may have only been moments. The voice from the television seemed to repeat the same sentence over and over.

I heard something different. It sounded like it was under the bed. I pictured some little kid rolling a wooden ball along the floor, then tapping it down.

Roll.

Tap. Tap. Tap.

I thought I was hearing things. But there was a familiar quality to the sound, a message I somehow understood but couldn't bring to the surface, irritating me like a trapped sneeze.

You're losing your fucking mind, Jack.

Move.

Get up.

You need to get out of here, Jack.

Roll. Tap. Tap. Tap.

I think the bastard is gone.

Sitting up was difficult. I nearly fell off the side of the bed. I rolled over and pushed my hands up through the gauzy batting on the underside of the box spring. I remembered there was a reason I wanted to go there. I'd felt something metallic inside the foundation.

A bit of a spring or a fastener of some kind. The top of my head was on the floor and I was trying to look under the bed, but I couldn't see anything but the upside-down black. And my fingers didn't work properly. I felt a meaty tugging against my ankle.

There.

Got it.

Something I could bend. Back and forth. Back and forth. I cut my hand. It didn't hurt. I could feel the blood trickling down my wrist, getting heavy where it would ball up before sending a thick drop onto Freddie's floor.

Just like being born again.

I made it longer than most.

He did this before. What happened to them? Why didn't they fight back? How does this asshole get away with it?

What happened to them?

I felt myself blacking out. I let go of the spring and pushed myself back up onto the bed. Too much blood in my head. I had to move, did sit-ups. I felt stupid and ridiculous, not because I was doing sit-ups, tied to a bed in my underwear, but for what I did to end up here in the first place. I knocked the urinal and the bedpan to the floor and rolled over and worked at the spring again.

Snap.

He was stupid.

He should have left me alone at the park.

With that little piece of metal, I had that nylon zip tie off my foot in five seconds.

There was blood all over the end of the bed, from my hand, my leg. I must have looked like a murderer, if anyone could see me. I hadn't realized how much that thing cut into my ankle.

I stood, listened.

Making no sound, I felt my way around the room. It was completely empty except for the bed. There was a sliding double door to what I guessed was a closet, and the one door with the light on the other side. I got on my belly on the cold floor and tried to look under that door. I couldn't see anything, just floor and the reflection of incandescent light. I felt myself slipping toward sleep and pushed myself up onto my knees.

Dizzy.

Wait.

I pulled the curtain back from the window. There was an outside, on the other side of the pane, and it was night there, too. I looked out over a tiled roof. The room he kept me in was on the second floor. In the gray light, I saw a front yard with a white railed fence, a mailbox, oak trees, and lights atop pillars of brick at the end of a driveway.

I knew I had to get out of there, that I wasn't going to chance going through the house. That was where Freddie came from, where he'd wheeled that chair, where *The Amethyst Hour* was still going on.

I leaned my face against the coolness of the glass. I tried to think. I wanted my clothes, my truck, my phone.

I wished I could ask Conner to help me.

I hoped he wondered if I was okay, if maybe he, or anybody, had tried to call me.

Get out.

I felt myself wanting to cry, to lie down on that bed and be scared.

But Jack doesn't cry.

30

Maybe.

I slid the closet door open, pushed my hand across the bar. Nothing. Not enough light here. I got onto my knees and felt around on the floor. Cloth. Maybe a rag, nothing else. I picked it up and went to the window.

Pale green scrubs, just the pants. Dark smears of blood down one leg. It was from my own hand.

I tried not to think about who'd worn them as I slid them on and tied the drawstring tight.

I undid the catch on the window and bent the screen away.

The tiles felt good under my bare feet.

When I jumped from the roof, I couldn't tell where the ground was. I hit hard. One of my knees went into my chin and I got dizzy again and had to sit down in his grass. I looked at my blood on his pants, and at the driveway where he'd parked and gone inside to get me a bottle of water.

The driveway was empty.

I was the only one there.

From the end of his driveway, I followed the street toward my right.

The closest house was maybe a quarter mile away. I didn't want to see anyone, didn't want to be seen.

Off in the distance, the dull lights and fuzzy hum of Highway 101.

eight

I almost wanted to yell when I saw my Toyota truck still parked where I'd left it in front of Conner's house. I was so relieved, like I had stepped back into my real world. Like I crawled out of some really bad dream.

Barefoot, shirtless, drugged as I was, I'd walked back to my best friend's house before the sunrise. And every step of the way I thought Freddie would come after me, so I'd hide when headlights flickered near. And I wondered, too, if maybe I was dead and it was just my ghost wandering back along the outskirts of Paso Robles in that summer night to find a place to rest.

I pounded on the door until Conner came down from his bedroom wearing only boxers and carrying a baseball bat.

"Jack." Conner put the bat down and opened the door wide. "What the fuck happened to you?"

"Something bad, Con."

"What?"

I stepped inside and sat down on the stairs. I put my head between my knees, looked at the blood smeared on the tattered cuff of the right pant leg.

"I don't know. I need to take a shower. I need some clean clothes. Let me sleep."

"Okay, Jack. Okay."

I slept in his bed. I made Conner promise he'd stay in there with me until I woke up, made him promise not to talk to me or ask me any questions until I could sleep my head straight.

He said he would.

In the night, I opened my eyes one time, panicked. I felt down between the sheets to see if I was dreaming, if my leg was still trapped, and I threw the covers off me and looked around frantically to be sure where I was, and found Conner had crawled onto the bed and fallen asleep beside me.

When I woke up, there were two large cups of black coffee from Starbucks sitting on the nightstand. I guess I stared at them for a long time. Conner was watching me, sitting in his desk chair with his feet on the bed. He tapped his foot into mine.

"I had them delivered," he said. "I had to pay the guy fifty bucks to do it."

I shifted my eyes onto him.

"I'm not lying," Conner said. "I told you I wouldn't leave. Here."

He stood and took one of the coffees and held it out for me.

I sat up and scooted my back against the wall so I could drink.

"What time is it?"

"Three," Conner said. "My parents are supposed to be back before midnight. Everyone's been calling for you. Your phone's battery's dead."

"Everyone?"

"Well, not everyone. Your grandparents."

"What did you tell them?"

"I told them your battery's dead. I told them you'd be home after my folks get back. Everything's okay. You know, they trust you and stuff."

Conner sat down on the bed next to me. "Are you in trouble for something?"

"No."

He leaned toward me, like he was confessing or something, almost whispering. "Are you mad at me? For what happened at the party? You know. I was just being . . . I don't know. Sorry if I pissed you off for doing that, Jack."

"I'm not mad at you, Con."

He sat up straight, exhaling. "Okay. Because I just . . . you know, I don't want it to creep you out or nothing before we leave for England. But, dude, I am going to see to it that you get laid before you come back from summer."

33

He smiled, but his expression was uneasy.

Conner sipped from his coffee and jerked it away from his mouth. "This goddamned stuff never cools off." He smiled stiffly. "So. Jack. What happened to you?"

nine

"Let's kill the fucker," Conner said.

I knew he wasn't serious. Conner was never really serious about anything. That's why he didn't even flinch the night of the party when I walked in on him and Dana having sex. Everything was a game to him, and he was always just trying to see if I'd play along.

So I told him what happened to me, as clearly as I could remember it, from when I took that beer from some kid I didn't even know after we peed on the side of the house, to when I showed up back at his doorstep. And Conner just shook his head when I told him about the things Freddie did, like it was hard to believe. I could hardly believe it myself, even though the words were coming from my mouth.

Once, Conner asked, "Did he . . . you know, make you . . . did he fuck with you?"

"No," I said. I stopped, waited, tried to swallow. "Not really. He was going to, though, after he gave me a shot. He started to try it and then his phone rang and he got pissed off and that's when he left. I had to fight from blacking out then. That's when I twisted a piece of metal from the bottom of the bed and got out of that shit." I swallowed. "He was all in this weird power trip of trying to make me ask him for everything."

I showed Conner the marks where the stun gun had left blisters on my skin — on my belly and under my arm. I showed him the needle mark, too.

"He still has my clothes and my wallet. And the shoes I just bought."

"You should go to the cops or something."

"No," I said. "I'm not going to say anything to anyone but you, Con. What would they do, anyway? I'd just end up in trouble for being drunk and on drugs. I don't want everyone to know how stupid I was. Especially Wynn and Stella. I'm leaving on Thursday, Conner, and I don't want this to mess things up. I just want to forget about it."

"But what if he does it to someone else?"

"I wasn't the first," I said. "He's going to get caught. Just, let's not mess up the summer over this, Con. I was stupid and it was my fault."

Conner shrugged. "You could at least scare the shit out of him."

"Don't tell anyone, okay?" I asked.

"No worries," Conner said. "Everyone already thinks you're gay, anyway."

Conner could tell by my expression I didn't think his joke was funny.

He kicked my foot. "Hey. I'm just kidding. It's going to be okay, Jack. Let's forget about it, if that's what you want. I don't think I could tell anyone if some guy did shit like that to me, either. No one except you. Damn."

ten

"Did you have a good time at Conner's?" Stella kissed me on the cheek when I tried sneaking in through the front door, barefoot, wearing the same basketball shorts and T-shirt I had on when I said good-bye to her Saturday morning.

I knew I looked terrible, guilty, like someone stuck me inside a sandwich board that said *Jack did something really bad* on one side, and *Can you tell Jack was drugged and almost raped?* on the other.

I could see Wynn down the hallway, sitting on the couch in the living room, watching a baseball game. He glanced over toward the entry and waved at me.

I nodded back, looked down.

"Yeah," I said. "It was fun."

I almost choked.

And Stella had her hands on my shoulders and looked me up and down and said, "What are we going to do around here when you're gone, Jack? I was so lonely and missing you this weekend."

"Oh, leave the boy alone and let him grow up, Stella. He's done fine, so far!" Wynn called out from the living room.

"Please keep your phone charged when you're in England, Jack," she begged.

"I promise I will, Stella. Sorry about that." I tried to make my way past her so I could get up to my room.

"Dinner will be ready in an hour," she said.

I started up the stairs.

"Me and Conner are going out," I said. "I need to buy some more clothes for the trip."

I stopped. "Oh. I lost my wallet. I need a new credit card, I guess."

"Some job of growing up." Stella tried to say it loud enough that my grandfather would hear. He didn't.

"Sorry, Stella."

I turned.

"Jack, honey. What happened to your foot?"

I froze. I've never been a good liar, and Stella knew it. And I wasn't even thinking about how I'd have to answer that.

"I got tangled up in something," I said. "On a run. With Conner."

"It looks like you stepped in a bear trap."

I felt myself turning red, hoped it was dark enough that she wouldn't notice.

"Well, put something on it so it doesn't get an infection," she said.

"I did."

"Do you want to see a doctor?"

"No."

I went upstairs.

When I was alone inside my room, I sat down on a corner of the bed and stared at myself in the narrow mirror on my closet door. It was the first time I'd really been alone since I got away from Freddie. I can't honestly count the staggering hike to Conner's house as being "alone" because that was a swim through pure drugged panic, where I felt like Freddie was with me every step of the way.

And I never cry. What I did at Freddie's house wasn't crying, it was more like my body just getting ready to die, I reasoned.

Because I believed I was going to die.

I looked at my ankle. It was messed up.

I pulled my shirt off and threw it at the door. The marks on my belly had turned into small purple bruises, like I'd been snake-bitten.

My hair was a mess. My eyes had black smears under them, and I looked like I'd lost ten pounds. I could see my ribs.

I slipped my shorts off and untied the drawstring from their waistband, pulling the length of it free, out through one side. I threw my shorts away and sat there in my underwear. It was like watching a sick movie, looking into the mirror as I wound that string around the cuts on my ankle.

Tight.

The pain felt good, a release.

I tied my foot to the bed frame and just sat there, looking at my pathetic reflection. I pulled and kicked against the string until I almost had to scream from the pain.

But I didn't cry.

Why did he do that?

What did he want me for?

I know this is going to sound insane, and I'm sorry for it, but a part of me wanted to go back to Freddie's house. Like there was something I'd left behind that I could only have if I went back to that room and went back to my place on that bed.

Like I belonged there.

Like I deserved it.

I sat there until it was too dark for me to see the sick, undressed, and dirty kid in my goddamned mirror.

It was the first time in my life I wanted to kill myself.

"What the fuck, kid? What the fuck?" Conner's voice came in an urgent whisper as he squeezed through my door and pressed it shut behind him with his back.

I was still sitting there, and his voice was like a rope that pulled me up from the bottom of an empty well.

"Jack." Conner flipped the light switch. The movie in the mirror began again.

"Oh. Fuck. Conner. Sorry." I shook my head, put my hand over my eyes.

"Get this shit off." Conner began pulling at the knotted line around my ankle. My foot had turned purple, and I was bleeding again. "Dude. You need help. You gotta cut this shit out."

I lay back on my bed as Conner unwound the stained cord from around my leg. He threw it down and went to the door.

"I'm going to get something to wrap that with."

I put my arm across my eyes.

"You better cut this shit out, Jack, or I'm going to have to tell someone. I should get Stella."

"No!"

He went out into the hallway.

I didn't realize how much time had gone by. Maybe I was still drugged, but I forgot all about going out with Conner that night.

He came back from the bathroom with a first aid kit in his hands.

Conner kneeled at the foot of the bed. He squeezed antibiotic goo over the cuts, spreading it carefully with his fingertips, like it burned him to touch me; or maybe I was toxic. Then he wrapped gauze around my ankle and taped the end, smoothing it down tight beneath his thumbs. I didn't say anything to him while he worked.

"You want to go get some help, Jack? I'll go with you. I think you should."

"No. I just . . . I don't know." I sat up and looked at him. I know my eyes must have looked messed up. "I think those drugs he gave me are making me crazy. And I haven't eaten anything for two days. I'll be okay, Con. Thanks."

"Come on. Get up and get dressed. Let's go get some food."

He pulled me up so I could stand.

I kept my eyes away from the mirror.

eleven

Stella called about my credit card. She gave me cash — she always had cash for me — and Conner and I had dinner at a brew pub that served pizza and burgers. I started to feel better, I guess, but couldn't stop myself feeling empty. Like something had been taken out of me and now there was nothing there.

The center of the universe.

While we sat there in the pub, I found myself staring off, past Conner, and images of what had happened to me replayed, so unreal. And Conner caught it happening and said, "Snap out of it, Jack. You sure you don't want to tell anyone about it?"

We hung out at the mall until it closed, at ten; and I bought some more clothes and shoes, but they didn't really make up for what Freddie Horvath had taken from me. I kept telling myself to stop thinking about it. I kept telling myself, but I couldn't do it.

And as Conner was taking me back home, we drove past Java and Jazz. I saw Freddie's convertible Mercedes parked in an alleyway on the side, between the coffee place and the high chain-link fence around the basketball courts in Steckel Park.

I had a feeling there was some reason for Conner coming this way; he kept looking over at me as he got us closer to the park. And when we finally drove by Java and Jazz, I said, "The guy who did that to me's here. That's his Mercedes right there."

Conner stopped his pickup right there in the middle of the street and looked where I was pointing. The car behind us nearly ran into us. I heard a squeal of brakes, and as the car swerved around us, middle fingers flared out the windows on both sides.

"Fuck you, too!" Conner said.

"What are you doing?"

"Dude, let's fuck with him."

"No."

But Conner wasn't listening. I could tell by the look on his face. We'd been best friends since before we started kindergarten, and I could always read that competitive look on Conner Kirk. It said he just wasn't going to give up until he won the game. He reached down beside his seat and pulled up a knife.

He flicked it open.

I felt suddenly sick again, and Conner said, "Knife versus tires equals unfair fight."

"Don't, Conner."

"Dude. You have to. It's what you need." And he added, "Knife versus ragtop Benz equals lambs to the slaughter."

Conner laughed.

I began to sweat.

"Con. Stop it."

He turned the headlights off and pulled around behind Freddie's car.

"Fuck that, Jack. I've got a stake in this, too. Nobody fucks with us. Ever."

He opened his door and left the truck idling.

"Now come on, Jack. It's time for a little payback."

My head rushed when I stood beside Conner, looking at that car. And he didn't waste any time, either, as he raised the knife and plunged it straight through the canvas top of the Mercedes. I kind of jumped, like I could feel the stab, and I heard the ripping sound as Conner shredded open gashes above the passenger side.

"That's my stuff in there," I said.

Conner stopped what he was doing.

I could see my clothes through the Mercedes' window: shorts, socks, the T-shirt I had on at his party, balled up and rumpled on top of the new Vans I'd only worn one time. Conner climbed onto the hood, snaked his arm down through the tattered top and unlocked a door. No alarm. The car must have been thirty years old, at least.

I began to pant when we opened the door. I could tell Conner was scared, too, and I'm sure it was because there was some part of him that didn't entirely believe everything I'd told him — maybe he was afraid to think those things really happened to regular kids like us — but, seeing my clothes there on the passenger seat brought that whole twisted world into focus.

"Take it back," Conner said.

It almost made me sick to touch my own clothes and shoes. I opened my wallet. Everything was there, but out of order.

Just like Jack.

When I picked up my clothes, I uncovered a familiar plastic box.

"Look at this, Con," I whispered.

Inside were a handful of the same zip ties Freddie had used on me. Conner picked two of them up, rolling the thick, glossy black straps with sharp edges between his fingers. The box also contained Freddie's stun gun, and a blister pack of pills. And there were some capped hypodermic needles and a bottle of clear liquid with its label blacked out by slashes of permanent marker pen.

"Fuck." Conner sounded like we'd unearthed a tomb. He picked up the stun gun, flicked its switch twice, then tucked it into the pocket on his shorts. "This guy's sick. Roofies." He held the pills so they just caught the faint light from over the courts.

"That's what he put in the water he gave me that first night," I said.

"And this is probably the shit he shot you up with." Conner turned the bottle in his fingers.

"Let's get out of here."

"I want to see him."

My heart felt like it would pound its way through my rib cage.

"Con," I began.

"Just point him out through the window," he said. "I need to see him."

"I'm scared."

"I know. That's why I want you to do it. 'Cause you don't need to be scared anymore, Jack. Let me have a look at that sonofabitch."

I didn't say anything. I walked back to Conner's truck and got in, holding my clothes on my lap, not looking at them, just staring straight down the alley toward the light of the street. I shut the door and Conner leaned his head in the window.

He sighed. "Okay, Jack. Let's get out of here, then."

Then he must have seen the change in my eyes as I stared straight ahead to the street corner.

Freddie Horvath was walking toward us, carrying a cup of coffee, dressed like he was heading to work for another night.

"He's coming."

Conner dropped down between the cars, hiding from the man who didn't seem to notice us sitting there in the dark. I began shaking as Freddie got closer. I was certain he would see me, even if it was

43

next to impossible in the shadows of the alleyway. Still, I couldn't overcome the thought that he would feel my presence.

"Come on, Conner," I whispered. My foot twitched. I thought Conner would have already made his way around to the driver's side, but as soon as Freddie got to his car and paused, seeing what had happened to it, Conner jumped up and shouted something as he pressed the stun gun into Freddie's neck.

The coffee flew from Freddie's hand, splashing across the hood of Conner's truck, and Freddie collapsed, striking his head against the Mercedes' door handle on his way down.

Conner kneeled. I couldn't see what he was doing, and I was terrified and just wanted us to get the hell out of there.

"Conner."

"Come here."

"Con, let's go."

"Come help me."

I sat there for a minute, wondering what to do. Everything was so quiet and dark. Finally, I put my clothes and shoes down on the floor between my feet.

I opened the door and stepped out into the alley.

Conner had bound Freddie's hands and feet with double loops of those black zip ties. Freddie's eyes were closed and there was a jagged cut on his forehead, a small circle of blood on the pavement next to the Mercedes' front tire. And Conner had opened that package of pills and was using his thumb to force one down into Freddie's throat.

"Conner, quit it."

"Too late," Conner whispered. "He swallowed it. Now come help me."

"How bad is he hurt?"

"He's not hurt. He's just knocked out, I think," Conner said. He wiped the spit off his thumb onto his T-shirt. "Well, he's going to be knocked out now, that's for sure."

Conner looked at me and smiled. He had that familiar expression of his: He was winning the game. I lowered my eyes to Freddie Horvath. He looked sick and weak, nothing like the monster I kept imagining since I'd gotten away from him.

I kicked him in the ribs as hard as I could. His eyes came open for a brief second, like he was a water balloon and the pressure of my kick nearly popped him open.

"Hell yeah!" Conner said.

I kicked Freddie again and a faint moaning wheeze fluttered from his lips. Then I spit on him.

I was breathing hard, excited and nervous. I looked quickly in both directions, up and down the alley, but I suddenly felt more awake and energized than I had since the night of Conner's party.

I dropped to my knee, hiding next to Conner between the cars. I whispered, "What do we do with him now?"

"You remember where he lives?"

"I walked home from there. I'd never forget it. He lives out in Dos Vientos Ranch Estates."

"Jack, we're going to load him in the bed of the truck and dump his ass at his house. Then let's call the cops so they can find all the sick shit he's got going on in there."

I said, "Do we have to say who we are?"

"No. I told you I wouldn't tell. This way, he gets caught and we get even." Conner slid the plastic box away from Freddie and picked it up. Then he took his T-shirt off and began wiping down the places where he'd touched the car. He looked at me quickly, handed me the box, and said, "You drive."

I turned Conner's truck around and backed up to where Freddie had collapsed in the alley. Then Conner lowered the tailgate and each of us looped our hands under Freddie's arms and tugged him up into the bed. I'd never lifted a body before, and Freddie Horvath was so difficult to move. We even dropped him once and he landed square on his face. I think it broke his nose.

Nobody saw.

Nobody knew.

He didn't care about me, and I didn't care about him — that's how it works.

And while we did it, I could hear the music from the coffee place.

After we closed the gate on the truck, I slid in behind the wheel. I left the headlights off and drove out slowly around the back side of Steckel Park and made my way up through the rolling hillsides east of Highway 101 toward the home where Freddie had taken me.

We had our windows down. Conner played music videos on his drop-down DVD screen. The music was loud and wild and it made me feel so free. Conner was pumped, too — he sang along, hanging his arm out the window. I smiled as we drove.

"Fuck yeah," Conner said. "This is the way we take care of shit."

I held out my right hand for a high five and Conner squeezed it so hard it hurt, but I wasn't going to let go. I tested his grip by squeezing back just as tight as I could.

I was glad we did it, convinced in the rush I was feeling that Conner was the greatest friend I would ever have, because I knew he would do anything for me and I wouldn't even have to ask him.

It wasn't until I'd turned around to back Conner's truck into that sick bastard's driveway in Dos Vientos Ranch that we both noticed the truck bed was empty.

Freddie Horvath was gone.

Conner said, "Oh Jesus Christ."

We backtracked.

What looked like a pile of old blankets lying discarded on the asphalt in the middle of the darkest stretch of Nacimiento Road turned out to be Freddie Horvath.

I turned the headlights off and pulled Conner's truck onto the dirt shoulder and parked it beneath a towering black oak tree.

"Oh, fuck," Conner said. He laughed nervously.

"He must have gotten up somehow," I said.

"Do you think he's dead?"

"Shit, Con."

We sat there in the dark for no more than a minute. Neither of us said anything. Didn't have to. We were scared, and we both knew it.

I opened my door.

Conner and I crept across the blacktop to where Freddie was lying. His hands and feet were still bound, and he was resting with the side of his face against an orange reflector that was stuck down in the middle of the roadway. His feet were turned around backwards and his dull eye and a black puddle of blood around his head reflected the nighttime stars. He exhaled once, that was all. Then there was nothing.

"Jesus, Conner," I whispered. "We killed him."

"We didn't do anything to him. He did it to himself."

"What are we going to do with him?"

"Don't touch him, Jack," Conner said. "We need to get out of here before someone else comes."

I stood over Freddie, my mouth hanging open, frozen.

Conner grabbed my shoulder. "Give me my keys and get in the truck."

And as he pulled away from the spot where we'd left Freddie

Horvath's body, heading back down Nacimiento Road toward Glenbrook — nobody else on the road at all — Conner turned to me and said, "Don't even think about it, Jack. It wasn't our fault, so forget it. No one's ever going to know."

Except us.

twelve

Stella assumed the reason I was so mopey around the house for the next couple days had to do with me being nervous about going on the trip. By Wednesday, the night before I was supposed to leave, the newspapers and television stations began running stories about the doctor who'd been murdered and dumped in the middle of the road; and how the search of his home turned up items that linked him to a fourteen-year-old boy who'd been missing since the summer before. They suspected there were others, too, but I already knew that.

Conner kind of gloated over it. Even though he was every bit as scared as I was that we might end up in trouble over what we did, he whispered to me how we were actually heroes for ending the career of one sick bastard. It scared me to think about it, though, because I felt like a hunted animal, so I just begged him not to talk about it anymore.

But I didn't sleep at all for those next three nights after what we did to Freddie Horvath; so I must have looked like a walking dead kid Thursday morning when Conner and my grandparents drove me up to San Francisco Airport. The whole ride there, I felt so torn: I didn't really want to go, but I sure as hell didn't want to stay anywhere near the place where Conner and I had accidentally killed someone. Even if that someone was a murderer himself.

Stella and Wynn asked me to wait with them before leaving for my departure gate.

"Let's find a place to get some coffee," Stella said.

"I want to try to sleep on the plane." It was my way of trying to push them all away from me, like they were holding me back from falling off a cliff and I wanted them to just let go.

"Coffee sounds good," Wynn said.

I pulled out my cell phone to check the time.

Two hours to go.

"I need to go to the bathroom first," I said. "I'll be right back."

"I'll go with you," Conner offered.

I sighed. "Whatever."

I left my small black carry-on at Stella's feet, and Conner and I pushed our way through the hundreds of anonymous people who were coming and going. And I felt like every one of them was watching us, like they knew what we'd done.

"I'm going to be sick." I leaned over the sink and splashed cold water on my face.

Conner stood behind and watched me in the mirror.

"It's going to be okay, Jack. The more distance and time we put between us and Monday night . . ." His voice trailed off. "We're going to be okay. I know it."

I shrugged and pulled some paper towels from the steel dispenser on the wall.

I didn't want to look at my friend, and he could tell. Conner grabbed my shoulders and shook me a little.

"Look. Let's try and have the greatest time we can when I get over there with you. Let's try, Jack. I'll be there in just a few days."

"I don't know if I can do this, Con. I can't sleep thinking about it."

We didn't notice, but a man with a gray jacket folded over one arm had come out from a stall and just stood there, silently watching us. Conner looked at me, then at the man, and he smiled at me and said, "Yeah? So, we're gay. Do you have a problem with that, creep?"

The man glanced down at the floor, embarrassed, and hurried away.

I gave Conner a push.

"You're messed up."

Conner laughed. "You can't honestly say that wasn't funny, Jack. Did you see how that guy was looking at us?"

I tried to smile back at him.

I balled up a wad of soggy towels and tossed them into the metal bin on the way out to find Wynn and Stella.

I've never walked on a frozen lake. I can only imagine what it would feel like — wondering if the next time I plant my foot would bring me plunging down between knife-sharp, icy edges into a smothering black, to fight against the cold, the dark, straining to find a way back to the surface so I could take another doubtful step forward.

Because I felt exactly like that when I walked away from Conner and my grandparents to pass through the first checkpoint on my way to the plane.

No turning back.

Even the crew on the plane who greeted me as I entered, holding my ticket in a shaking hand, looked like they knew who I was, as though they had whispered to one another while I made my way down the boarding chute, "Look, here's the kid who killed Dr. Horvath."

I felt myself turning pale.

I stowed my bag beneath the seat and wedged a pillow between my shoulder and the foggy plastic window. I looked out at the California sky, caught in the between-worlds nowhere of an airplane that would take me into a different day.

Then the man who had been watching me and Conner in the restroom said hello, stuffed his jacket in the overhead bin, and took the seat right next to me.

It was going to be like this, wasn't it?

I tried telling myself that it was crazy to think that everyone else in the world knew, they were all following and watching me. I felt myself struggling to catch my breath; I was sweating and felt sick again.

"Traveling by yourself?" he said.

I turned my eyes toward him, trying to give him a look that said leave me alone. He smelled like a lavatory soap dispenser and looked like any other middle-aged, plastic-mannequin business guy who you'd see on an airplane.

"Going to London all alone?" he persisted.

"I'm on my way to school. In Kent." My voice sounded detached, like someone else was answering for me.

"Oh," he said. "Your friend's not coming along?"

"Next Monday."

Go away.

I looked around, hoping for an empty seat there in business class. All of them were taken. I pretended I was trying to sleep.

"Well, you guys are going to have a lot of fun."

Something about the way he'd said it made me start to feel angry. I knew what he was getting at.

He went on, "I have an office in London. If it's your first time there, I'd be happy to show you around to all the exciting spots this weekend." He stuck his hand out. "My name's Gary."

51

I didn't shake his hand.

He leaned closer, half-whispered, "I know the best clubs. You know what I mean."

I whispered back, "Leave me the fuck alone." I plugged my headphones into my cell phone, turned away from *Gary*, and shut my eyes.

It was going to be a long flight.

I woke up four hours later when the flight attendant asked me what I wanted for dinner. Gary had his hand under my blanket, rubbing my leg. He'd been trying to unbutton my fly.

And I thought, *Why is this happening to me?* I wasn't sure what the attendant had asked me, so I just said a quick yes, and then I lowered my tray, looked Gary straight in the face, and said clearly enough for the closest ten people to hear: "If you don't get your goddamned hand off my crotch, I'll fucking kill you."

Gary jerked his hand out and turned his eyes forward, pretending he didn't know anything about what was going on. The stewardess looked worried, maybe a little scared. She backed away from her cart without serving either of us any food, and went to the front of the cabin, taking a quick look through the curtain that separated us from first class.

Gary cleared his throat and fidgeted nervously with his tray.

If I could have jumped out the window, I would have done it. I tried thinking about Conner, about meeting him in a few days, about having fun again; but I kept running myself back to Freddie's house, tied to that bed — and then seeing him all twisted up in the middle of the road.

Panic.

I felt like I was going to black out, do something really crazy. I remember shrinking back into the corner of my seat, wondering why the hell I'd gotten on this goddamned plane in the first place, convinced I would never make it through the next two weeks. Gary pushed the serving cart up the aisle and retreated behind me to the toilet. I watched the red OCCUPIED sign light up above the bulkhead.

The flight attendant came back. Her eyes were soft and focused on me.

"Sweetie, there's an empty seat up in first class," she said. "Let's grab your things and you come up there with me. Would that be okay?"

I nodded.

"Okay."

For the entire flight, it felt like I was still on those drugs Freddie gave me. I didn't watch the movies; and slept a couple of times through the shortened night and into the next morning.

I never dreamed.

I never saw Gary again, either. The flight crew managed to get me off the airplane ahead of everyone else and I raced down the endless corridors at Heathrow so I could disappear into the masses of people waiting to get passport stamps in the enormous arrivals hall.

And after I'd picked up my backpack, I had to walk through the customs area, a gauntlet of eyes where uniformed men watched me, maybe looking for the telltale indication that something wasn't right about this pale kid showing up all alone. And how could they miss it? I felt so lost, like nothing made sense, so I kept my eyes fixed on a yellow sign with an arrow on it that said WAY OUT TO TRAINS, and concentrated on making my feet move toward it, afraid to look back, afraid to stop.

God, I felt so sick.

This is when it started falling apart.

I know that now.

thirteen

I checked my cell phone. It was the next day, and I was on the other side of the planet. I really felt like I'd been torn from my world, even if there was still that lingering emptiness — like I had to wait for the rest of me to catch up.

If it ever would.

The train into London was empty, at least where I sat. Wynn insisted on buying a first class ticket on the Heathrow Express, and I realized that most travelers simply opted for less expensive methods of getting into the city. So I felt like I was inside an egg or something; and shifted my attention constantly between the news reporter on the television screen in front of me and the strangeness of the gray and green world that rushed backwards on the other side of the window glass.

My grandparents had already paid for a room for me and Conner at one of the nicer hotels in the city. It sat overlooking Regent's Park, just a few hundred yards from the Tube station at Great Portland Street, so it was easy to find, even if I hadn't ever been there before.

When I got in to the room, I threw my pack down on the bed. My back was sweating from having carried it in the humid summer heat. The room was nice, I guess, but not really much like the places I'd stayed at in America. It seemed so small, claustrophobic.

And there was only one enormous bed, covered with a thick comforter and a ridge of pillows, a headboard as high as I stood tall with a circular mirror in its center. I thought, *Just great, I get to share a bed with Conner.* With a computer desk, an armoire containing a flat-panel TV, a stuffed chair, dressing mirror, and two nightstands, there was hardly any floor at all. I kicked off my shoes — the same Vans I wore the night Freddie Horvath kidnapped me. The guy we killed.

Quit it, Jack.

I looked in the bathroom. Equally small. I found that I couldn't even open the shower door unless the bathroom door was open — or else I had to step over a tub that was nearly three feet deep, just to get a leg up into it.

Strange.

I filled a glass of water from the tap. It tasted thick and oily.

I checked the time zones on my phone. It was still too early to call Conner, and I didn't want to talk to Stella yet.

I went to the window.

There was something about the sky in London that seemed so flat and smothering. I was too used to the hills and rises of California. So the skyline in London made me feel like I was under a lens. But the air seemed so clear, too. It definitely didn't smell like California.

The park across from the hotel was surrounded by hedges and a tall fence. What I could see of it looked unnaturally perfect by the standards of home. Everything was manicured, green, alive. I saw groups of runners entering and leaving through the iron gates.

Good idea.

I opened my backpack. I was tired enough that I could have gone to sleep, but decided to try and stay awake until nighttime so I could begin to adjust to the time change. I took out my running gear and stripped off my clothes. For just a second, I sat on the edge of the bed and watched myself in the dressing mirror, but then I shook my head — like a wet dog — and laced up my running flats.

If I could do that, I told myself, I must be getting better.

The hotel's lobby was like a terraced cave. I had to walk down a short flight of stairs from the elevator to the crowded main, circular room. Everyone there looked like they were dressed to attend some kind of formal event. So I tried to tell myself that they were all looking at me because nobody would expect to see a tired-looking, skinny kid with uneven hair that hung over his eyes, wearing only running shorts and a holey T-shirt in a place like this.

Then I realized that without pockets, I didn't have anywhere to keep my room key. It made me nervous to think about leaving it with anyone. I looked over to the front desk. The guy behind the counter was staring at me, smiling. He seemed to catch on to what I was thinking. I slipped the key card into the liner of my shorts, hoping it wouldn't fall out. Not very comfortable. He watched me do it.

I made my way toward the uniformed men who stood at the entrance. I tried keeping my eyes down on the floor. Dark wood. Just like where I was born, I thought. I was so embarrassed for some reason, I felt like my skin was burning under all the attention.

Stop fucking looking at me.

The doormen stood ready, their gloved hands poised to let me out.

I passed the lobby bar.

Something made me stop.

That was the first time I saw the man with the purple glasses.

And I didn't realize it at that moment, but that was the first time I had a flash of the other side, too.

I guess I need to slow down here and try to remember exactly what happened.

How things began falling apart for Jack.

fourteen

There was something about the man wearing the purple glasses that scared and relaxed me at the same time. It's hard to explain, but it was kind of the same way I'd felt about Freddie Horvath, too.

He stood there, obviously watching me, and when I looked at him, he didn't glance away. He just kept watching me through those glasses, with a hint of a smile on his face like he'd been expecting me.

And, considering where we were, he looked as out of place in that lobby as I did: He was wearing a long, dull-colored traveling coat and sweater, despite the heat of the day, and he held a rumpled hat in one hand. He seemed young, maybe in his twenties, but he also looked very tired, like he'd been on the road for months. The uneven, sand-colored stubble on his face made him look too young to grow a full beard, and it seemed he hadn't been in front of a bathroom sink in at least a week. When I passed by, he stood up from the stool at the bar where he'd been drinking a glass of beer and quickly pulled the glasses away from his eyes, jolted, as if he recognized me, but I told myself I was just being ridiculously paranoid about people, and wondered if I would ever let myself relax and trust anyone again.

But the thing that was most intense about him — and I know this now after what I've been through, even if I shrugged it off at the time — were his purple eyeglasses. Because they weren't just purple, there was something else about them, and when I caught him staring at me and looked right at him, I swear that just for a blinking instant I could see something on the other side of the lenses.

Something that was all white and gray, with edges and folds.

Something like two deep holes that stretched farther and deeper than anything I'd ever seen before. Really big, like cracking a layer on one of those stacking Russian dolls and finding something you'd never expect could fit inside.

And I swear that for that smallest of moments, I could see people on the other side of the lenses, too.

All week long, I'd kept thinking about how the drugs Freddie Horvath gave me must have ruined something in my brain.

I gave the man a dirty look. I was sick of people staring at me.

That shit in his glasses had to be nothing more than the reflection of all those creepy old people hanging around in the lobby.

Nothing else.

Fuck this place.

The doormen pushed open the heavy glass doors.

I think I started running before I was even out of the hotel.

fifteen

I ran.

My ankle hurt. I thought it was probably bleeding inside my sock. I didn't look. It just wasn't healing well.

Yeah, I remember you, Freddie.

Fuck you, too.

As soon as I forget about you, you really will be dead.

I ran fast. Sweat dripped from my chin and elbows. Sometimes, I'd look back to see where it left dark coins trailing my direction along the pathway.

The park seemed to stretch forever beside an expanse of lawn where men in white played cricket, and blankets made red or yellow rectangles in the sun where lovers lay tangled, sleeping off the drowsy contents of emptied wine bottles.

Conner and Dana.

And everyone seemed to be looking at me.

Quit it, Jack.

A towering stone building on the other side of the trees to my left supported an immense clock on its highest peak. Five o'clock. I had to think about what time that really was to me.

I kept running, over a bridge and along the shore of a lake where an old man stood throwing crumbs to the birds that came out onto the grass between the water and the path. Behind the zoo, I made a circle around what I guessed was the perimeter of the park, clockwise, back toward the entrance.

Clockwise.

I stopped in a narrow garden that was walled in on both sides by tall hedges and lined with intensely bright flowers along the gravel of the pathway. I was drenched. My shirt was plastered to my skin. I took it off and held it to my face, bent forward, resting one hand on my knee.

"Are you hurt?"

Startled, I let the shirt fall. I straightened up.

An old man with a moustache bent toward me. A cricket player. He smelled like tobacco.

Smoke.

"Huh?"

"Your foot," he said. "Do you need some help?"

My sock was soaked through with blood where my shoe rubbed against what was left of the mark Freddie Horvath had left on me. I hadn't even noticed.

"Oh." I felt myself reddening, picked up my shirt. "I did that a while ago. I thought it was gone now."

"Mind that, then," he said. "Cheers."

And he walked off.

I found my way back to the park's entrance and turned right onto Marylebone Road.

The man with the glasses was waiting for me there.

He stood with his back to the park's iron fence and watched me while I pulled my soaked T-shirt back over my head. He wasn't wearing the glasses, though, and I thought it was odd, since we were outside and they seemed to be so dark. But he still had that expression like he knew me, or at least wanted to say something to me.

My stomach knotted. I was convinced that somehow I was being followed for what Conner and I had done.

I gave him another dirty look, turned my chin in the direction of the hotel's entrance, and jogged past him.

I took off my shoes and socks. I opened the window, peeled out of my wet shirt, and hung it from the casement hinge. I stretched out on the bed.

My cell phone showed I had a missed call, from Conner. It made me feel good to see his name.

He didn't say hello or anything. "Jack. How the hell is it over there?"

"Hey, Con. I don't know. I just got here. It's pretty cool, I guess. Just everything is different. Strange. It's real easy to get around. I just got in from about an eight mile run through the park. And wait till you see the room they put us in. It's kind of weird, too."

"Like what?"

"Well, there's only one bed."

"Don't tell Dana. You know she totally thinks you're queer, anyway."

"You didn't say anything, did you? About what happened to me?"

"Oh, come on, Jack. You know I wouldn't do that."

I sighed and sat up on the bed, like I was looking around the room with Conner's eyes. "And you have to leave the bathroom door open just to get into the shower."

"Nice. Super gay."

"And the water tastes like fish."

Conner laughed.

"But other than that, and all the weird people, I think we're going to have fun. And I'm going to be there on Monday at the airport when you get here."

"So, you're all okay, then, Jack?"

"Con, it feels like someone's following me."

There was silence after I said it.

I looked out the window, my wet shirt hanging there, convinced, now, that maybe somebody had heard what I said.

Quit it, Jack.

Conner made a joke out of it. "You? You'd have to pay someone to follow your skinny ass around."

I thought about that man in the restroom. Gary.

"I feel a little tripped out about things," I said. I inhaled. "But I think being over here is going to be good for me. You too. I've been making myself stay awake so I can get used to it. I'm going to take a shower now and go out and get some dinner."

"Dude. Don't get stuck behind the funky doorway. And go out and get a beer."

We both had fake American IDs from Idaho, like anyone here

61

would know what an Idaho ID card looked like. But we'd heard how easy it was to get served beer here, too.

"Yeah. Sure." I said it like I didn't want one, but it actually sounded good. "Oh, and Con? I need you to do something for me, okay?"

"What?"

"I forgot the charger for my cell phone. Stella's going to want to kill me about that. Can you go to my house and pick it up for me?"

"Damn. You've really been losing it, Jack."

"I know."

"Well, call me again before your battery runs out."

"Okay."

"And Jack? Everything's okay now. Really."

sixteen

I left the television turned on while I took a shower. I still couldn't figure out how they'd designed this place because there really was no way you could get in or out of the tub with the bathroom door shut, unless you crawled beneath the open glass shower door. And that was too weird to do, I thought. But it was possible to watch a left-handed version of the televised soccer match in the bathroom mirror and take a shower at the same time, so that was kind of cool.

By the time I dressed and got off the phone with Stella, it was dark. Of course she complained about how I forgot the phone charger, and I could hear Wynn in the background repeating, "Remind Jack they're expecting him and Conner at St. Atticus on Thursday." But at least I could make an excuse for ending the call quickly, since I wanted to save my battery as long as possible.

I walked east from the hotel that night and stopped at a place near Warren Street called The Prince of Wales, a pub where there were groups of kids who looked about my age, having dinner and drinking beer.

I realized how hungry I was, and how free it felt to be in a place that would actually serve beer to me, so I went inside.

It was a little awkward being there alone, and I had to sit at a long table with a group of noisy young people who laughed and drank beers. I ate a sandwich and chips, then got my nerve up and finally ordered a beer, which, one of the girls down the table explained patiently, had to be specified by name or I'd look like a tourist.

The kids said hello, asked if I was from California because of my shorts, then ignored me after offering generic well wishes for my "holiday." They left while I was on my second beer and finally feeling relaxed, almost happy, after the long ordeal of just getting here.

I wanted to call Conner and tell him what I was doing, but I dropped my phone on the floor when I tried taking it out of my pocket. I had to practically crawl under the table to get my hands on it. As I looked across the floor, I could see that the man with those purple glasses had come in to the pub and was standing at the bar across from me.

And he was watching me.

I sat up and put my phone in my pocket. As soon as I did, he took the glasses away from his face. I was sure he'd been following me, and now I was trapped. It was like being caught doing everything horrible and wrong I'd ever done, and I couldn't help thinking that maybe this guy knew about what I did to Freddie Horvath, that maybe he was going to do something even worse to me.

I felt like I was going to throw up.

I pulled some money out and left it beside my plate. When I

started sliding out from the bench I'd been sitting on, the man carried his beer over and stood across the table from me.

It was suddenly so quiet.

"Hello." His voice had a friendly sound to it, an English accent. Then he said, "Mind if I sit down, Jack?"

My heart almost stopped when he said my name.

What could I do?

I felt myself sliding back against the wall, wishing I could somehow sink into it.

The man sat down and placed his beer on the table between us. He smiled at me, as if he expected me to recognize him. But, except for those couple times earlier that day, I'd never seen him before.

"You know me?" I swirled my beer glass around on the table. Clockwise. It was empty.

He glanced over his shoulder at the bar. "Will you have another beer?"

"No."

Panic choked at me; my heart raced and my throat constricted in an invisible grip. It felt like I was tied down again. I thought about running.

"I only wanted to see if you knew me," he said. "I didn't mean to bother you."

I looked at him. I could see something human in his eyes, not like Freddie's. Freddie Horvath's eyes had no caring in them at all.

"I don't know who you are," I said. "Why are you following me?"

He took a drink.

I thought I was about to be arrested or something.

"I apologize if I've been rude," he said. "I really didn't intend to scare you." Then he stuck his hand out across the table and introduced himself. "My name is Henry Hewitt."

64

It was like falling from a cliff. I shook his hand.

"But really," he continued, "you seem frightened of me. I can assure you . . ."

"How do you know me?" I asked. I stared straight into his eyes and I tried to look like I was ready to fight.

Henry leaned forward. "I've known you for a very long time, Jack. Not from here, though. From Marbury. Then I saw you — I finally saw you — at Heathrow today, and I knew it was you."

And I thought, This must be some kind of weird coincidence — that he knows someone who looks like me from somewhere else.

"I think you're wrong," I said. "I've never been anywhere called that."

"Marbury?"

"Yeah. Where is it?"

"You're sure, then?"

"Yes. You must be thinking of someone else named Jack."

"You are named Jack." He said it as though he were asking the question to prove to himself who I was. Or maybe to convince me. And he said, "Jack Whitmore."

My eyes watered. I stifled a yawn and slapped my hand lightly down on the table. "Look. I'm really tired. I've been on an airplane all day. I should leave. I'm sorry, but you're wrong. Really."

I started to get up, and Henry pulled his glasses out from the breast pocket on his coat. When I saw the shine of the lens, the light seemed to move and shift inside them.

Henry put the glasses on for just a second, looking at me like he was snapping a picture, then he immediately folded them closed and lay them on the table between us without saying anything.

He emptied his beer.

I glanced at the glasses, and then at the man sitting across from me.

65

"Take care about looking at your friends there, Jack. I mean, in Marbury."

"I told you I've never been where you're talking about."

"Look," he said, and he leaned forward. "Are you certain you won't have another glass of beer with me, then?"

I was already buzzing. I wanted to sleep, but there was something that kept me there talking to him.

"No. But thank you, anyway."

"I'll just have one more, I think," Henry said, then spun around in his seat to go to the bar.

I stared at the glasses. There was definitely something odd about them. There was something moving inside them. I could see it, but I was afraid to look. I wanted to touch them, unfold them, but I knew that would be rude. Still, there was something that was so unique and attractive about them — and they just sat there on the table in front of me, as though Henry was tempting me with them.

I looked up at the bar.

And Henry Hewitt was gone.

A full glass of beer sat on the bar in front of the taps, and the bartender stood, his arms locked straight where he leaned against his counter, watching me.

I got up. I felt dizzy. The place seemed suddenly empty. There were two older men sitting in a dark corner near the toilets at back of the pub, but that was all.

I said to the bartender, "The man who ordered the beer. Do you know where he went?"

The bartender raised his chin. "He paid for the pint for you, mate."

He pushed the beer toward me. It made a slick trail of moisture on the wood of the bar top. Like a snail.

66

A business card had been pinched down by its corner beneath the glass.

I went to the door and looked both directions along the street, but Henry was nowhere in sight.

I turned back into the pub.

The bartender said, "Do you want the beer?"

I picked the card out from under the glass. It was blank, but someone had scrawled with black ink, in all capital letters that smeared from the condensation: DON'T LOOK FOR ME, JACK. TAKE CARE. MIND WHAT I TOLD YOU. — H.H.

"No, thank you."

Then I went back to my table, slipped Henry's glasses into the pocket of my shorts, and walked back to the hotel.

I didn't get it.

He knew who I was, said he'd known me for a long time. From somewhere called Marbury. But I'd never even heard of that place. He had to be wrong.

He'd followed me around all day. It couldn't have been an accident that he left those glasses sitting there on my table. It all seemed too intentional, too planned out. But I couldn't figure out what his messages meant, either. Was this all some kind of perverted joke? Was I on hidden camera or something?

I must be drunk, I thought.

Freddie Horvath did something to my brain.

Sometimes, I know it was just me, but I could almost hear his voice telling me things, trying to scare me.

You haven't gotten away.

seventeen

Midnight.

It was cool, so I shut the window. I left the drapes pulled back, then I undressed and got into bed. I lay there looking around the room that almost glowed in the gray moonlight filtered through the uneven, ancient glass of the window.

And in the night, something moved inside my room.

At first, I heard a rolling sound coming from beneath the bed.

Just like Freddie's bed.

You better see what's under there, Jack.

Something wooden and small, round — like maybe an empty spool of thread; maybe a nut. It rolled, and I could measure the distance it covered by the sound it made, across the width of the bed. Roll. Then stop. Then three taps; and it rolled back in the opposite direction.

He did something to my brain.

You better look, Jack.

Roll. Three taps. Right across the floor, an equator through the center of my belly.

Silence.

Roll. Tap.

Tap.

Tap.

Like someone knocking, but I was certain it was right there on the floor beneath my bed.

I pushed back the covers and turned on the lamp next to me. And I know it was compulsive and dumb, but the first thing I did

68

was to look at my foot to see if I was trapped again. I rubbed my hands around my ankle, and then I bent down to look under the bed.

What are you looking for, Jack? Something to get away with?

Don't fool yourself, Jack. You haven't gotten away from anything.

I couldn't see anything, just black. I reached up and tipped the lamp downward. It hung from the edge of the nightstand, swinging slowly. I lowered myself onto my hands and knees, the side of my face pressed to the floor.

Wood floor.

And I heard something, just a hushed whisper that sounded like someone said "shhhh" or maybe a word, like "soft." But it was real.

Did something to my brain.

There was nothing there.

Don't fool yourself.

You haven't gotten away from anything.

I sat on the floor. I was so tired. I got back into bed and switched off the lamp.

Then I went to sleep.

part two

THE
STRANGE
BOYS

eighteen

I think I never slept as soundly as I did that first night I spent in London. When I woke, I lay there on my back for a few minutes, pressed down into the softness of the bed by the weight of a heavy feathered comforter that seemed to be holding the pieces of me together, and looked out at the perfection of the day on the other side of the window.

The building must have mice, I thought. It didn't matter, once I fell to sleep I never heard anything at all. I didn't even dream.

I got up from bed and opened the window.

And later on, after I ate breakfast downstairs and went out for my run, while I fumbled around with putting on clothes so I could get out of the hotel and begin to explore the city, as I shook out the shorts I'd tossed on the floor the night before to see if my cell phone was still alive, Henry Hewitt's glasses fell right out onto the folds of the sheets I'd slept in.

I took them up into my hands and sat on the edge of the bed. They were so old and frail, made from such a thin gauge of braided gold wire that had serpentine patterns of black etched into the surface. And the lenses themselves felt so heavy in my hand, like they were polished discs of stone crystal. One of them was chipped on its edge, and unevenly tinted a kind of purple that faded, clear and milky in some spots, and dark as gemstones in others.

THE AMETHYST HOUR.

Quit it, Jack.

I unfolded the glasses and held them up at arm's length so I could see through them by the light from the window.

And then I heard the rolling sound again, but this time it was louder.

But when I looked through the lenses, something happened that was difficult to understand: I saw a bug — a big one — crawling downward, shiny, wet, black. I lowered the glasses. The rolling noise stopped.

So I thought that the glasses, held at a distance, acted as some sort of telescope. I wanted to find the magnified bug that must have been crawling on my windowpane.

But I'd left the window open.

Still, I thought, there must be a bug there. On the wall, the drapes, maybe.

I got up and went over to the window. I searched everywhere, shook out the drapes, but there was no bug. There had to have been one, I thought, because it was so huge. It couldn't have just disappeared.

It was there; I saw it.

I sat down again.

I held the glasses up.

I put them on.

You haven't gotten away from anything, Jack.

I don't even remember bringing my hands down from my face. Why would I remember it? I wasn't there anymore.

There was this bug.

The sky domed overhead like a vacant cathedral ceiling, white and hot.

I stood near a wall, watching the bug crawl out of a red-black hole the size of a soft rotten plum, breathing in the thick humid stench, sweet rot, fascinated by the hideous thing. If I grabbed it, the bug would have been bigger than both of my hands together. I'd never seen anything like it, not even in nightmares. I listened to it as it chewed a counterclockwise circle around the meaty rim of the crater it came from, making soft wet clicks. Then two more of the bugs crawled out from the same wet black hole. One of them dropped down next to my foot. I heard it thud onto the ground; and I took a step back.

That's when I realized the bugs were eating the meat from inside the eye socket on a human head.

Nothing more of the body was there; just the head. And it was nailed to the wall in front of me, held there as though in conversation, just at my eye level, by a thick wooden stake that had been driven into the masonry through the other eyeball.

"Fuck!" I backed up another step, felt vomit rising from my gut.

I tripped on something solid and soft, and fell back, catching myself in the dirt with my open hands. But I couldn't look away from that thing on the gray wall in front of me. One of the bugs, with its lacquer black, chitinous shell yawning open, began chewing up into a nostril. It made an electric buzzing with lime-colored wings. Blood angled, sprouting treelike outward from the neck where the body had been hewn free, forming pointed and glistening branches in the little creases on the shadowless wall.

Something moved across my hand.

One of those bugs.

I looked down, flailed. What the hell was I wearing? These weren't my clothes.

I recognized it.

The head on the wall was Henry Hewitt's.

I sat in gray-white dirt. The rest of Henry's body was next to me, my left hand, open, propping me upright, braced on his unmoving and hardened chest.

His hands had been hacked off, too. The sleeves of his coat were stained to the shoulders.

"Jack! Jack! We got to get the hell out of here! Now!"

I turned. I recognized the voice. Someone named Miller. Ben. I had to think, wasn't sure why I knew that name. I couldn't see where he was calling from.

A hiss, and three arrows with fletching the color of those monstrous bugs, glistening black, spattered into the wall just above me.

"Jack! Here! Jack!"

I turned over onto my hands and knees and crawled away from Hewitt's body. I looked back one time at that wall. It was covered with impaled heads and other dripping, black-rot body parts: hands, hearts, feet, ears, penises.

Where the fuck was this?

Welcome home, Jack.

You haven't gotten away from anything.

I scrabbled along the ground. More arrows whizzed over my head. I thought I was moving in the direction of Ben's voice, but I couldn't be certain. Everything here blended together: the white sky, the gray ground, no shadows, heat, fog, the smell, that back-and-forth rolling noise from under the bed.

"Here! This way!"

I lifted my head up, looked across the littered ground. There was the carcass of a horse, its belly split open and guts stretched across the pale ground. The lower body of a naked male had been stuffed up inside the rent in the dead horse, the obscene and final revelation of some gruesome vaudeville act.

He had one shoe and sock on his left foot.

Where was the rest of him?

Ben Miller stood in a pale-gray dustcoat that had been splattered with flecks of blood, holding two worn horses with his hand wound tightly through their halters, behind a breech where a landslide of fractured boulders from the dry mountain above had crushed down upon the strewn remnants of corpses and bones; the stones piled shoulder-high against the wall of the settlement.

I knew who he was, had a vague memory of where I was, too.

How did I know him?

I stood, began to run.

The arrow came, silent. It tore through my right side, just beneath my rib cage.

In.

Out.

And it buried its shaft in me up to the foul blackness of its feathers; and I watched my blood spit forward onto the colorless land like it was some kind of joke. But it hurt so bad. The stun gun in Freddie's prodding hand, magnified a thousand times and more.

You haven't gotten

I fell to my knees, tried to catch myself on my palms, but my face ended up in the dirt, sideways, watching one of those bugs coming toward me.

"Jack! Jack!"

The boy named Ben Miller was running toward me.

nineteen

I snapped my hands up, an electric jolt.

And there I was, shirtless, dripping wet, sitting on the edge of my bed and looking out the open window at one of my T-shirts moving, ghostlike on a cool breeze where it hung from the window's handle. I must have gone running. The shirt was soaked.

It was night.

My hand shook.

I looked at my side, cupped my palm over the skin and rubbed at the spot.

The purple glasses lay on the floor next to my foot. I braced my elbows against my knees and cradled my face. I was covered with sweat. It stung my eyes as I squeezed them shut.

Okay.

What the fuck was that, Jack?

Inventory time: What happened couldn't possibly have been real. Freddie Horvath did something to my brain.

Freddie Horvath did something to my brain and I need to get help.

I had to think. Put the pieces together.

I was thirsty for a beer. That was good. Real. I went to the minibar and opened a bottle. Wynn and Stella would find out. Stella would be mad. That was good, too. Wynn and Stella. They were real. I drank. It was hard to swallow.

Calm down, Jack.

I turned on every light in the small room, reaching from one to the next.

Here.

I was here.

This side: I was in England. It was nine o'clock in the evening. The last thing I remembered about being here was sitting down on the bed after breakfast, shaking out the curtains and looking for a bug.

Bugs.

That side: The worst things I'd ever seen in my life. Henry Hewitt's head staked into a wall. A wall of human butchery. Arrows. A boy named Ben Miller screaming to me, holding two horses behind a pile of rocks and corpses. And then me, getting shot through my side by a long black arrow. I could still feel it, the tickling vibration of the shaft sticking from my back as it quivered with each gasping breath and pulse of my blood, the pain, burning hot, stabbing every nerve in my body.

I ran to the toilet and threw up.

I sat on the edge of the bed. I had nothing on, just my underwear, and I was wet. I shut the window and took another gulp of warm, frothy beer. My hair dripped water on my shoulders and onto the wood floor. I went into the bathroom again, checked. I had taken a shower. A towel, my running shorts and socks, were thrown onto the floor. The clothes were damp and smelled like sweat. I must have gone for another run.

Why can't I remember?

Freddie Horvath did something to your brain and you better get help, Jack.

I checked the clothes I'd put on after breakfast, emptied the pockets of my jeans onto the bed.

The glasses. On the floor. I thought about the glasses. I didn't want to look at them, felt around with my palm, closed my hand around their bony frames, and slipped them inside one of my sweaty socks.

I didn't want to see those bugs again.

I could feel the beer. I wanted another one. I felt guilty about drinking it, but it felt good.

Fuck. Jack feels guilty about everything.

I opened another beer, went back to the bed.

My cell phone was dead. I wondered if I'd spoken to Conner, to anyone who could tell me I was really here today. Passport, money, folded slips of paper; and I found the smeared card Henry Hewitt had left for me in the pub lying on the bed under my digital camera.

I picked up the card and read it again while I took another gulp from the beer bottle. I rubbed my thumb over the black ink. I shook my head.

I must be going insane.

No, I am insane.

There was a yellow index card–size slip of paper tucked into my passport. It was a ticket for a Thames River sightseeing cruise, and it had been stamped earlier that afternoon.

Okay. Crazy Jack went on a boat, I guess.

I flipped my camera over and turned it on. I felt dizzy, like I was going to collapse. I dropped onto my knees, elbows on the bed like I was praying, holding the small screen of the camera up before my eyes. I played through the images: Marylebone Road in front of the park, a blurry image from the platform in a Tube station, boats on the river, the Houses of Parliament. Then there were pictures taken from a glass-canopied boat: the London Bridge, and, finally, a picture of me, smiling, standing in the sunlight, leaning against a red painted rail on the ship's deck, under a perfect, blue sky.

I think I stared at that picture for half an hour, studying every detail of it.

I looked happy, standing there in loose jeans and a white T-shirt that said GLENBROOK HIGH SCHOOL CROSS-COUNTRY, hands tucked into pockets, white baseball cap turned around backwards, hair blown across an eye on one side by a wind I thought I could remember feeling somehow, standing so relaxed. Smiling.

I wondered who took the picture.

I tried turning on my phone again, irrationally hoping the battery may have restored itself.

I pulled my jeans and T-shirt on. Then I tucked Henry's glasses, wrapped in my sock, into a back pocket and slid my bare feet into my Vans.

And then I went back to The Prince of Wales.

twenty

This is real.

My feet, inside my shoes.

Sounds of cars on the road.

I slip my hand up inside my T-shirt and feel my side.

This is real.

Henry's glasses are wrapped inside my sock and I know they're in my back pocket.

I haven't gotten away from anything.

Saturday night.

The pub was crowded with kids; and three guys had set up on a stage near the back and were playing folk music with a guitar, mandolin, and drum. I scanned the length of the bar, saw the same bartender who'd served me the night before, and just as I found a path to where he was pouring, I felt a hand on my shoulder.

A soft hand. It stopped me, turned me back.

"I didn't think you were going to come. I'd almost given up waiting for you."

I felt myself going white, like all the blood had just drained from my body, and my eyes met squarely with hers.

"It's Nickie, with an I-E," she had said, and spelled it out slowly. And now I remembered how I'd entered it into my cell phone, earlier, before it went dead. She was the one who took my picture after we met on the boat. I remembered it now, how she'd brushed my hand lightly while I was taking a picture and asked if I'd like her to take one of me, since I was alone, for my friends back home. Nickie.

Maybe.

What the hell is happening to me?

I exhaled, smiled. "I . . . I'm sorry. I don't know where the time went. Jet lag, I guess. I'll get over it."

She smiled back at me.

"Well, I'm pleased you're here now," she said, and added, "Jack."

Then she squeezed my hand.

I heard myself gulp. She was the most beautiful girl I'd ever talked to in my life, I think.

She wore those jeans that were so tight around her ankles and a pink sweater that clung to her waist with a wide, open neckline that showed her collarbone, the perfect smoothness of her skin. And she looked at me with the softest blue eyes — the slightest trace of a smile on her lips, and shining black hair that spilled down to her shoulders — like she was waiting for me to say something.

Nickie.

"Do you want to get something to drink? Something to eat?" I stuttered.

"It's very crowded in here, Jack," she said. "Can we go for a walk outside?"

I looked back at the bartender. He was watching us.

Everyone's watching you, Jack.

I took her hand. "Let's go."

When we were out on the street, Nickie slipped her arm in mine and I said, "Where to?"

Nickie smiled and said, "Come on. I'll show you."

And while we walked toward the Tube, I thought I'd better shut up and let her talk, because I didn't have any idea how a guy like me could get a girl like Nickie to wait for him anywhere.

Hey, Nickie, did I tell you about how I got kidnapped by this sick guy named Freddie Horvath? And how he shot me up with drugs and shocked me, and I thought I was going to die? And, oh yeah, how he tried to rape me, too?

But I got away from him.

YOU DIDN'T GET AWAY FROM ANYTHING, JACK.

Freddie Horvath did something to my brain.

And then me and my best friend, Conner, killed him. It was an accident, but we fucking killed him, just the same. Did I tell you that, Nickie? Or, did I tell you about how I can't even remember anything about meeting you today because I hallucinated some crazy shit about people getting hacked into pieces and eaten by bugs? Or how I got shot through my side with an arrow?

Did I tell you about that, Nickie?

Because I do remember that.

I reached around and felt those goddamned glasses there, still in my back pocket.

She took me to Hampstead, the part of the city where her family lived, and we ate Thai food at a café there and then rode on the Underground to Piccadilly.

She caught me staring at her on the subway. I wasn't really

83

staring, though, I was looking past her at the alternating blur and reflections in the window. I looked at myself, and sometimes I looked scared.

And Nickie said, "There's something about you, isn't there, Jack?"

That snapped me out of it.

I said, "I don't know. What do you think?"

"I think it's okay," she said.

She said it like she knew, like she could heal me. Maybe I was only hoping that was true, because I really didn't know what to believe anymore.

I said, "Thanks for having dinner with me, Nickie. I'm beginning to feel, well, not so alone."

It was warm, muggy, and we sat on the steps beneath the statue of Eros, looking out at the lights, the traffic. I felt so comfortable with her, but at the same time I felt like I wasn't completely there, too.

"What made you do it?" I said. "Ask if I wanted you to take that picture, I mean?"

Nickie sat right next to me, our legs touching.

"It was Rachel who dared me," she said.

I remembered. She had a friend with her. They wore dresses, uniforms, like they'd just come from school.

"Oh. Rachel."

"It was a lark, anyway." Nickie smiled. "I mean, we would never take a tour cruise on any other day. But when I saw you in the queue, I needed to follow you."

"You *followed* me?"

Everyone's following you.

"I was taken by you. I don't know why, but I had to see what you were doing there, all by yourself. We laughed as we watched you attempting to order coffee on the boat," she said. "When the server asked if you wanted filtered or Americano, you looked so confused and then you said, 'I'm American.' It really was, well . . ."

And her voice trailed off softly, blending in with the sounds of being there in that square, sitting beside her on a perfect evening in summer.

This is real.

Isn't it?

"Well, either way, it was horrible-tasting stuff," I remembered.

How can you remember the taste of the coffee, but nothing about Nickie?

Freddie Horvath did something to your brain.

You need help.

"So, I guess you thought I needed help or something."

"I said I thought you looked interesting," Nickie said. "And Rachel teased that I wasn't daring enough to say hello to you."

"Interesting?"

Nickie laughed. "You know," she said, "you had that way about you, I suppose. Well. Very handsome. When I finally did say hello, you were so charming and easy to talk to. And anyway, you certainly had no qualms about asking me for my telephone number."

"I couldn't help myself."

She put her hand over mine.

"Tomorrow, you should go buy a new charge cord for your phone, Jack."

I thought about it. "I don't want one. Too much of a connection to the other world back home. And Conner's bringing mine on Monday."

"If you'd like, you could call him with mine," she said. She looked at her watch. "It's afternoon there now. And I'm getting late."

She took her phone out and held it to me.

"Can we do something tomorrow?" I asked.

"I'm going to church with my parents in the morning. I could call your hotel in the afternoon."

"What time?"

I took her phone, flipped it open.

"Three," Nickie said.

"I'll make sure to be there."

"Don't stand me up again, Jack. Here, let me put in the code." Nickie's hand went to mine and she entered the dialing code for America. I looked at her face, and as I entered Conner's number, she leaned into me and her hair brushed my cheek.

"There," she said.

I almost forgot Conner's number.

"Hello?" he said.

"Hey, Con." I sounded choked, even to me.

"Jack! What happened? Don't tell me. Your phone's dead again."

"Yeah."

"I tried calling you. Is everything okay?"

"Yeah. Tell Wynn and Stella I'm fine. I'm calling from a friend's phone."

"A friend? Who?" Conner asked.

"I met a girl today."

"Dude," Conner said. "Did you get laid? Can I finally tell everyone you're officially not gay? I think Dana will be disappointed."

"Stop being a dick, Con." I held the phone away from my ear. "I'm putting you on speakerphone."

I held the phone in front of Nickie, and she tapped a button.

"Can you hear me?" I said.

"Yeah."

"Conner, this is Nickie."

"Hello, Conner," Nickie said. "I think you have a very nice friend."

"Wow," was all Conner said. Then, "Jack, take me off speaker."

I was embarrassed, I put the phone to my ear.

"What?"

"Dude," he said. "She sounds totally hot."

I felt myself going red as I looked at Nickie. She had to have known what he was saying.

"She is, Con."

"What's *wrong* with her? Is she missing an eye or something?"

"You're a dick. I'll see you Monday."

It was nearly midnight, and I'd walked Nickie to a taxi to take her back to Hampstead.

"I'll see you tomorrow, then," I said. I unlocked my arm from hers and stood in front of her before the open cab door.

I felt so awkward. I wanted to kiss her on the mouth, but I'd never done that before.

"Good night, Jack," she said.

I hugged her, and I watched her as we separated. I think we both looked disappointed. And when the taxi pulled away, I kicked the ground. I hated myself. I should have kissed her good night and now she'd probably never call me tomorrow.

twenty-one

I tried finding an Underground station, but the nearest one had already closed. I began following streets in no particular direction. And then I realized I had no idea where I was. I started walking back toward the statue where we sat earlier, or at least what I *thought* was the right direction, hoping to find an open Underground station, or maybe a taxi.

I didn't care. I finally felt happy. It was like the first time I actually knew relief.

Even if it wouldn't last.

The street I walked on stretched ahead of me, narrow and dark, with closely packed row houses that rose up, straight and gray-faced, behind low iron fences and emaciated trees. I couldn't see anyone else, and figured I must have turned the wrong way.

Then I heard a sound.

Faint, like a small wooden ball rolling across a plank floor.

I started running, hoping that the desperation of my breaths and the sounds of my footfalls would drown out the nagging *Why is this happening to me?* So I kept turning toward where I'd see lights, and I finally spilled out into a convergence of busy and crowded streets. A staircase leading down below the sidewalk, the Underground, people, noise.

You haven't gotten away from anything, Jack.

All the way back to my hotel, I kept a hand in my back pocket, fingers wrapped around the sock that contained the purple glasses. I thought about abandoning them in the train car, throwing them in the river, a thousand different ways of separating myself from them but it was already too late for that.

I needed them.

I needed them to prove that I wasn't losing my mind. Or maybe to relieve myself of worrying about what I saw on the other side of the lenses because I really *was* losing it.

I asked the clerk at the front desk if I could use his cellophane tape, and he looked at me as though wondering what kinds of drugs required the use of adhesives, but he gave me a roll anyway; and I promised I'd return it in the morning.

In my room, I shut the window and pulled the drapes across it. I kicked my shoes off and sat at the desk. I put the sock with the glasses in it on the corner of the bed and then took out the hotel stationery pad and began writing notes to myself:

> Jack: Do not leave the room.
> Jack: Remember Nickie is going to call at 3:00.
> Jack Wynn Whitmore

I taped all of them on the door at eye level.

The rolling sound again.

Something was going to happen.

Roll.

Tap.

Tap.

Tap.

Under the bed again.

I looked at the clock on the nightstand. I wrote down the time on another piece of paper:

> 12:31

Roll.

Tap.

I got on my hands and knees and looked under the bed.

I heard a voice. A whisper.

"Seth."

Seth.

Freddie Horvath did something to my brain and I need help.

Breathing hard, I pulled myself up onto the bed, sitting so my back rested against the headboard, barefoot, wearing jeans, and a T-shirt.

Then, on another piece of paper, I wrote down a list of the clothes I had on.

I grabbed the sock and put my fingers down into it. I felt the glasses in there.

I pulled them out.

Roll. Tap. Tap. Tap.

"Nothing's going to happen," I said.

You haven't gotten away from anything.

I put them on.

twenty-two

Pain.

It hurt so bad; and I was sick, felt the fever boiling inside me.

I opened my eyes and I was lying inside some sort of cave, wrapped in blankets that stunk and were soaked with my sweat. I could see the flat white sky beyond the jagged sash of the opening above my head, and I couldn't feel my legs. All I felt was the burning misery.

I turned my head so I could throw up.

I saw shadows, two others were in there with me. Kids. I knew who they were.

How could I know them? Everything about them: Ben and Griffin. Half brothers. Ben's father was killed at the start of the war, the beginning of the plague. A disease we couldn't catch. And Griffin was born after everything went dark.

Ben Miller sat beside me. He leaned forward when I moved. When I vomited, it felt like an animal clawing its way out from my side. I screamed.

"Hey! Shut him up!" I heard Griffin Goodrich moving toward us from where he was standing at the entrance.

"Shhh . . ." Ben wiped a wet cloth across my face. "It's okay, Jack."

And then I heard him say, "He's waking up."

"He's going to have to, Ben. Or I'm going to leave him here. Both of you. Two days in here is too long. We need to move."

"It'll be okay," Ben said.

"Not if they find us. You want to end up like Hewitt and the others, nailed to a fucking wall?"

The smell of puke in my face made me want to throw up again, but I held it back. My stomach convulsed, tearing my insides. I traced my hand down my chest toward my hip. It was wet and sticky and I remembered that black arrow, but now it was gone. My fingertip tracked across the bumps of haphazard knots where someone had sewn my body shut with what felt like a shoelace.

"What happened?"

"How you feeling, Jack?" Ben said.

I tried to sit up, couldn't. I answered with, "Uh."

Ben wiped my mouth off and slid his hands beneath my armpits. He looked at Griffin.

"I'm gonna try and move you away from that puke there, Jack. Try not to do that again if you can help it, bud."

He slid me around so my head was closer to the light coming in from the cave's entrance.

Griffin held a clear plastic bottle over my face.

"This is all we have left," he said.

He opened the bottle and poured a mouthful of cloudy warm water past my lips.

I swallowed.

"Thanks, Griff." I remembered how everyone — at least, what

was left of everyone — called the boy Griff. He was only twelve. Ben was fourteen. As far as any of us knew, that was all that was left. Just kids. And none of us had seen a girl in years. At least, not a live one. Or a human.

I knew where I was.

Marbury.

Griffin recapped the bottle and walked back to the cave's opening.

I struggled to prop myself onto my elbows.

"Let me see how bad it is, Ben."

Ben Miller stepped over me and squatted down at my side.

"It's not too bad," he said. He pulled the blanket down from my chest. "Just through where you could grab your fat, if you had any. But don't get mad at me. Griff's the one who sewed you up. You know I couldn't even look at it, Jack, I was so scared you were gonna die."

The wound puckered out like pouting lips, swollen and stitched shut with a winding of tawny thread. My skin was bruised black around it, the same on the back side as well.

"We had to take your shirt apart to get that thread. It was ruined, anyhow."

I fanned the blanket away from me. All I had on were pants, loose and torn open with vertical slashes on both legs. Nothing else, just pants. I could see a big straight-bladed knife lying on the ground beside my hip. I knew it was my knife.

"What happened?" I asked.

"You don't remember?"

"I'm having a hard time remembering anything," I said. I shut my eyes, tried to picture Conner, Nickie, London.

Conner and Dana on that bed the night of the party.

Freddie Horvath.

What the fuck was happening to me?

You haven't gotten away from anything, Jack.

"It was two days ago, outside the Bass-Hove Settlement. We found it. But they were waiting for us, knew we were coming. They got just about everyone." Then he lowered his voice to a whisper. "We're all that's left. Just us three."

Ben looked toward where Griffin was standing. "What are we going to do now, Jack? I'm scared. We don't have no place else to go."

"Fuck!" Griffin shouted. Then I heard the jarring sound of a heavy rock pounding against another.

Ben stood up quickly.

"The harvesters are coming," Griffin said. "I knew it. There's something dead in the cave back there. We should have looked better. They fucking know we're here now."

He lifted the rock he'd used and smashed it down again, crushing the large black bug that had crawled into our hiding place.

I knew that soon the bugs would come by the thousands. Millions. And I knew what would be following after them, too.

Ben said, "You're gonna have to ride, Jack. Get the horses, Griff."

Griffin slipped out from where he stood and disappeared into the white.

"Help me stand up."

I held my hand out for Ben.

"Stay there. Let me get your shoes, first."

They were work boots, splitting and mismatched; and Ben slipped them onto my bare feet and held each one straight between his knees while he laced them tight.

"Are you gonna be okay, Jack? I don't know what we'd do without you."

I propped myself into a sitting position.

It hurt.

"I think so."

Roll. Tap. Tap. Tap.

That sound.

Ben still had my foot wedged between his legs, but he turned around when he heard it, too.

Then I saw, standing at the back of the cave on the other side of Ben Miller, a pale and barefoot boy with sunken, dark eyes who looked like he couldn't have been any older than me.

And Ben said, "Goddamned ghost. That's all we need. No wonder that harvester found us so easy."

The boy sat down and hugged his knees in toward his chest. He looked scared.

I thought he might have been crying, but he sat there watching me; and I understood that he knew me, too, had been following me, waiting for something.

I could see right through him, the cracks in the stone wall behind him. Then he got lighter and just spilled out into a kind of fog that blanketed over the ground where he'd been sitting.

Ben looked at me. "I never did this before. I heard it works. Hewitt told us how he'd done it, remember?"

"No."

I couldn't remember things very well anymore.

And Ben turned his face to the back of the cave where that grayish fog sat low upon the hot ground and said, "Well if you can help him, then do it, boy. I figure you're the one what got us into this by being here in the first place, so it's the least you could do. The harvesters are gonna get you anyway if you don't."

The fog rolled up, like a blanket, and the boy was there again, now standing.

Roll. Tap.

He was barefoot and skinny, starved even, with neither shirt nor hat, wearing tattered pants held up onto his pale, naked waist with a fraying rope of some sort. He looked dirty and uncared for. His jagged and light-colored hair hung down past his eyebrows.

"Well?" Ben said with an edge of impatience. "Why the fuck were you following us to begin with if you're not going to help?"

The boy faded again, fogged over the ground once more. The cloud snaked along toward me, and the next thing I knew, it was slipping through the stitches in my side like wire-thin fingers, and getting inside me.

It was warm, and I could feel him like he was crawling into every part of my body. I knew who he was.

And I heard him say his name again.

"Seth."

twenty-three

My hand jerked to my side, rubbed.

No stitches.

The glasses lay open on the pillow beside me; the bed drenched in my sweat.

I needed to throw up, struggled to get my legs off the bed and onto the floor. I stumbled, saw the notes I'd taped to the door.

What the fuck is happening to me?

Gagging, I made it to the toilet just in time.

When I finished, I washed my face with cold water and went back to the bed.

I looked at the clock.

12:37

Not even one minute had passed since I put the glasses on.

This couldn't be real.

Freddie Horvath did something to my brain and I need to get help.

Okay, Jack, this is it. Get rid of those goddamned things.

Now.

I folded the glasses, put them back inside my sock, and stuffed the wad down into the bottom of my backpack. I needed time to think. I needed air. I opened the window and looked out at the lights passing below on the street.

Who was I fooling? There was no way I'd be able to give them up.

The panes of glass made smears of the lights over the park.

Smearing the light.

That had to be it, I thought. Maybe the glasses were some kind of filter that cut away everything we see here, that stripped off the surface, like opening one of those dolls, and showed what was going on in that other place.

Inside.

Marbury.

That had to be it.

The center of the universe.

You're out of your fucking mind.

And I wanted to look through them again, but stopped myself before I got my hand back on them.

I had to stop it.

This is fucking crazy, Jack.

I rushed back to the toilet and vomited again. I kneeled on the floor, cold and shaking in my sweat-soaked clothes. Resting my forehead on my crossed arms, I spit into the clouded water as I hung my face in the bowl.

Something rolled across the floor behind me. I heard it, and it passed so close I could feel its vibration tickling my bare feet.

Tap. Tap. Tap.

I pushed myself up. There was nothing.

If I looked worse to Conner that night when I came back from Freddie Horvath's than I did at that moment, standing in front of the bathroom mirror, wet, pale, stinking of puke, it would be hard to imagine. I was exhausted. I stared into my own eyes — I don't know for how long — and I said, "Seth?"

Something slammed angrily against the wall in the bedroom.

I whispered, "Are you here?"

I stepped through the doorway.

Click. Click.

Every light in the room turned off. Then my backpack fell over below the open window and something rolled out of it, across the floor, and stopped in front of my feet.

A wad of paper, crumpled tightly.

I opened the paper. It was the note I'd taped to the door — the one with my name on it. But scrawled on the page below my name, in nervously penciled, childish capital letters, were the words I AM SETH.

I waited. Everything became so still and quiet.

I smoothed the paper flat and laid it on the nightstand. Then I crawled under the bedcovers, shivering with all my clothes on, and waited through the silence until, exhausted, I finally fell to sleep.

The day stretched, an endless succession of doubt upon doubt, until it neared the time when Nickie was supposed to call me. Somewhere during my morning run, I'd decided I needed to get help, even if I had no idea how to go about asking for it.

Hey, Nickie, do you know any good psychiatrists? Because, I just thought I'd let you know that Jack has completely lost his mind and could possibly be a danger to you.

Just so you know.

Freddie Horvath did something, and I'm never going to get away from it.

Quit it, Jack.

I tried to force myself to stay away from my hotel room, afraid that I didn't have the backbone to keep my hands off those glasses. So I walked as far as I could, went to the Underground to buy tickets for the Express to Heathrow so I could meet Conner in the morning.

I wandered.

I tried to think about anything other than Marbury or Freddie Horvath, but I couldn't do it for more than a few seconds at most.

Finally, I went back to the hotel to take a shower. It was early in the afternoon, and the phone began ringing as soon as I stepped under the water.

I ran to grab it, padding wet tracks along the way and dripping all over the desk where I'd picked up the receiver. I tried to sound like I wasn't out of breath. I left the shower running. It sounded like rain.

"Hello?"

"Hello, Jack."

It wasn't Nickie.

"It's me. Henry."

I pulled the chair out and sat down. I looked at the water where it made twin puddles under my feet on the wood floor, dripping from my body.

Like being born.

"What?" I said.

"I was wondering. How are you getting on?" Henry said.

"Fucked."

I think he chuckled.

"I have something of yours. I think I need to give it back," I said.

"They wouldn't serve me any purpose now. You know that. Or haven't you been yet?"

"I've been there." I listened to the water, looked over at the gray steam fogging out from the open bathroom door. "I'm not going back."

"I can't tell you how many times I swore the same thing, Jack. But you'll have to."

"Why did you call me?"

"I told you. To see how you were getting on. But I wanted to ask you something, Jack."

"What?"

"Who's left?"

"Ben and Griffin. Nobody else."

"I'm sorry." I heard him exhale. A sigh, maybe. Or he was smoking a cigarette. "Be good, Jack. Oh . . . and Jack, I just want to be sure of one thing. Tell me what it looks like there. Marbury."

"A white desert."

"Okay."

"Henry?"

"Mmmm?"

"Is it real?"

"You know as much as I do, Jack. Of course it is. As real as anything. Be good. Maybe I'll talk to you again. Here, I mean, of course."

"Can't you help me?"

"It's why I told you not to look for me, Jack. There's nothing I can do now. You know that. And I'm afraid there just aren't very many others you could give them to at this point. I've tried finding Griffin and Ben, but I can't do it. Be good. You know what to do. I'm confident of that."

Then he hung up.

I walked to the bathroom and climbed back into the shower, under the warm water.

Nickie met me in the lobby. She'd brought a basket of things and we spread out a blanket where we had tea on the grass in the park. It was a perfect day.

And as much as I'd tried, I couldn't overcome my awkwardness with her. So after my first series of stumbling attempts at conversation — asking her about church, how she'd slept after our late dinner — she knew something was bothering me.

"Are you all right, Jack?"

I lay back on the blanket and looked up at the blueness of the sky, wondering if it really was blue.

"I like you, Nickie."

She touched my shoulder. It felt so nice, like nothing I'd ever felt before. "I like you, too. I mean, for an American and all." She laughed. "And you're mysterious. And clever, I think."

I sighed. "Really bad things have happened to me."

She leaned over me, inches from my face. Her hair fell, and shaded my eyes.

"What sorts of things?"

"Someone did something. Terrible. I don't know if I can tell you yet. But I feel like I need to say something. I think there's something wrong with me because of it, and I don't want it to affect you." I looked away from her, watched her hair. I wished it could cover me entirely. "I hope you can be patient with me."

"I can be patient, Jack," she said, "to a point, that is."

"I'm sorry."

She put her hand on mine and turned so she sat facing out onto the small lake.

"When you can tell me, I'll listen."

"Okay."

She tried to change the subject. I sensed she felt bad for me, maybe sorry.

"You must be excited to be seeing your friend tomorrow."

I thought about it. I felt so guilty for what we'd done, but now I didn't really know what I would tell Conner about Henry and those glasses. If I'd tell him anything at all.

I said, "Yes."

"You know," she said, "I'm going to Blackpool on holiday tomorrow with Rachel. I think I shall desperately miss you, Jack, until I come back to London next weekend."

"Oh, great," I said. "Now Conner will probably think I just made the whole thing up about meeting you."

"If you get lonely, you and he might come up to Blackpool. It's quite lovely. We can introduce him to Rachel."

"Not if you want to stay friends with her."

She laughed again. It sounded like a bird singing.

I sat up so our shoulders touched, and I wasn't scared anymore. There was no reason to be. Not after what I'd seen. So I decided to say it.

"Nickie, I've never kissed a girl in my entire life. Do you think there's something wrong with me?"

And she said, "I don't know. Let's see."

And in that moment, I forgot about everything. It was like nowhere else existed except the space between Nickie and me.

Nickie said, "No. There's nothing wrong."

twenty-four

I didn't want to say good-bye to her that evening.

We kissed again before she passed through the gate to the Underground. And we'd stopped an older couple coming in, handed them my camera, and asked if they'd take a picture of us together. I wanted to ride with her, but she told me to stay; and said if I really couldn't stand it in London without her, then I should give her a call and catch a train north for the coast.

I wished I could be more like Conner, and immodestly persuade her to come to my bed with me, even if the reason I wanted her with me was that the thought of going back to the room all by myself terrified me.

Because I knew what I would do.

I didn't eat dinner, didn't want to throw up again.

As soon as I'd gotten inside my room, I began the routine: taped notes to the door. Conner is coming. Six fifteen. I left the train tickets on the desk next to the phone. I rushed, my hands shook, like I was a junkie scrambling for another dirty fix.

And I was pissed off at myself, too. I took the glasses out from where I'd hidden them, then I picked up my pack and hurled it, crashing against the door.

"Fuck!" I screamed. "Fuck this, *Jack!*"

I couldn't stop it, even if I wanted to.

I kicked my clothes across the floor where they'd spilled out.

There were zip ties at the bottom of the pack. I remembered putting them there. The ones from Freddie's car.

"Fuck yourself, Jack!"

Shaking in my rage, I kicked the pack.

"Fuck you, Freddie!"

Then I tore my clothes off and bound my ankle tightly to the bottom rail of the bed frame.

It hurt.

I put the glasses on.

As far as we knew, we could have been the only living humans in the world. Who was there to argue differently?

On the morning of the second day, before we rode across the parched and salty flat of the desert, we drank our own piss that we distilled in the heat using a sheet of plastic and Griffin's empty water bottle, just to keep ourselves alive.

If we didn't find water, we knew it would be our last day.

The horses were failing, too.

My side oozed snot-colored pus that ran down my skin and glued the waist of my pants against my hip. We cut a hole in one of our blankets, and I wore it over my bare chest like a poncho to slow down my dehydration, but I don't think it worked.

We stopped talking to each other.

Griffin and Ben followed. I pointed our horses in the direction of the black spires of mountain peaks north of us, and I promised them there'd be water in the mountains if we could make it. So they believed me, and I wondered who among us would be the first to drop.

I hadn't seen Seth since we left the cave, but I could feel what he was doing for me, and I knew everything about him — how he was a foundling, and he'd killed a man. And I believed I knew why he'd been waiting for me, too. One day, I'd tell Seth's story to the other boys, just so they'd know he wasn't a bad kid.

Just unlucky.

Like me.

When we left on the first day, I looked across the flat of the desert and could see a shining black river spilling toward us like a flood. It was the harvesters, seeking out the cave where we'd been hiding; and behind the quivering insect sea rose the updrifts of dust from the mounted riders who were hunting us.

The Followers. Devils, we called them. Hunters. What else could they be? It would always be this way, and now there were almost none of us left. That's why we rode, looking for someone. Anyone.

When we left with Henry, trying to find anyone else, there were twenty of us.

The boys didn't remember anything other than this life — the war, and I wondered if my own memories were from here or some other place. But being in Marbury was in some ways like being imprisoned by Freddie Horvath: I didn't have the time or energy to worry about what was real. It made me wonder if anything was: Marbury, London, Conner, Nickie.

Griffin leaned forward on his horse, arms grabbing the animal's neck. Every one of the horses was bareback, guided only by crude rope halters. It was agony to ride them like this.

"Are you okay?" I asked. I moved my horse up beside him, close enough that I could touch him.

"No." His voice was a constricted rasp.

Ben rode in front. He stopped his horse and looked back at us.

"Do you have any idea what that is, Jack?"

He pointed forward, and I followed his arm.

"I don't know."

We saw what looked like a wall of black boxes stretched across the salt ahead of us, maybe a mile distant.

"Do we keep heading for it?" Ben asked.

I looked at Griffin.

He was going to be the first of us to die, I thought.

I said, "Yeah."

"What the fuck is that?" Ben said.

Griffin lifted his head. His eyes were black gashes.

I knew what it was. Remembered.

Stretching across our path ahead, buried in salt up to the bottoms of its doors, was a passenger train: seven cars and a locomotive. It looked like some kind of perfectly placed decoration that had been dropped there in the middle of nowhere, for there were no tracks visible in either direction.

I nudged my horse forward. He twitched and shook his head. I thought he could smell water.

"It's a train," I said. "Come on."

"Is it good?" Griffin said. He'd gone back to resting his head against the horse's neck. "Is it a good thing, Jack?"

"It's good," I said. "I promise."

We led the horses down one side of the train, around the locomotive, and behind it, where the dry wind was blocked by the height of the cars. Even on horseback, the windows were too high to see inside.

I got down first, then Ben and I helped Griffin from his horse.

I pulled my pants out from where they'd stuck to my hip.

Ben said, "Is that okay?"

"I'm holding up."

I unsheathed my knife.

Ben had a spear he'd made from sharpened rebar. That's all we had; all we ever had. It's why we decided to ride along with Henry Hewitt to the settlement in the first place, thinking we'd find something better than we'd been left with.

Barefoot, Griffin Goodrich didn't have anything. Just his hands and his meanness, Ben said of him. The younger boy had never known anything but the war, couldn't remember his parents. It was only riding and running, fighting and watching people die since Ben had begged Henry Hewitt to take them along with his riders. They'd both have been food for the Hunters years before if Henry didn't tell them yes.

Most of the time Griffin refused wearing clothes at all, saying there was no use for them that he could see. I took my poncho off and threw it over my horse's back. Then I put my hand on Griffin's shoulder and said, "We're going to find a way inside this thing. But we have to be careful. And we have to stay together. So you gotta try, okay, Griff? I'll find you some water."

"Okay."

Ben said, "Jack, if we open this thing up and there's something dead in there. Well. You know."

"It doesn't matter," I said. "They're following us, anyway."

"Maybe," Ben argued.

The boys followed me to the back of the last car. There was a rectangular sliding door with a window so people could stand there and watch what they were leaving behind, I thought.

And the door was surrounded by a thick black gasket, rubber that had gone scaly and gray. I stuck the blade of my knife into the gasket, testing its resistance.

Then I pushed it all the way through and levered the door until it slid open enough for Ben and me to wedge our fingers through the gap so we could push.

It was easy.

We went inside, and then I closed the door behind us.

twenty-five

The only sign that there had ever been people in that last car were the suitcases. More than a dozen of them had been left behind, carefully lined along shelves above the rows of windows on either side of the compartment. At the very least, I knew that the boys and I would be able to get some new clothes for us to die in, and maybe some shoes for Griffin.

I led the way. Ben and Griffin followed as we walked slowly down the dim aisle. Sometimes, the boys would stop just to run their hands over the cool smoothness of the leather seats and Formica tabletops in the car. One of the tables had crumbs of something on it.

"You think there's food in any of them bags, Jack?" Ben asked.

"We'll find something, that's for sure," I said. "We'll be better off if we walk the whole thing before we take stock of what we can get."

Ben said, "Okay, then."

I pushed open the door that connected us to the next car.

There was a whoosh of dry air, as if the car inhaled when the door swung open.

We smelled the death right away.

It wasn't the horrid, gagging smell of rotten death, but we all knew instantly that there would be dead passengers inside the car; and I could tell by the dryness of the odor they'd been there for years, at the least.

Six of them.

Mummified.

A man and woman sat, tilted against the window like they'd

fallen to sleep a thousand years ago and were still dreaming. Their skin had vacuumed in, brown, like overdone piecrusts against the sunken contours of their skulls. He was nicely dressed: new jeans with a leather belt and a striped blue shirt that still had pressed creases down the sleeves.

I hoped I wouldn't have to undress him just so we could have something better to wear. I caught Ben looking at him, too, sizing him up; and I knew he was thinking the same thing.

All three of us bent forward to look under the table so we could see his shoes. They were new. White tennis shoes.

Between his hip and the armrest beneath the window sat a liter-size clear bottle, capped, and three-fourths full of water. I pulled it out, opened, smelled. It was good, but I didn't drink it.

I handed it to Griffin.

The three of us took turns, carefully sharing, until the bottle was empty. I put it on the table in front of the dead couple.

In the next row of seats, three children had stretched out across the benches, lying on their sides, hands folded beneath their heads like pillows. Two girls and a boy, and not one of them could have been more than eight years old. They were hard to look at, even if the three of us had seen something enough like it plenty of times before.

"Looks like they were sleeping," I said. "Looks like they all just went to sleep."

I glanced at Griffin. I could tell he was bothered by it.

"It can't be a bad way to go," I said.

We found the old man at the end of the car. He had some kind of uniform on, with an oval brass name tag pinned to the chest of his navy-blue jacket, and he was sitting underneath a table with his knees bent up. His mouth and eyes were open.

Blackened scabs.

I decided I wasn't going to touch that one, no matter what.

The next car was the dining car. We trembled as we walked through it. None of us had to say it; we knew we'd find something to eat and drink there. The tables were all set: white tablecloths, place settings and silverware that still shined, folded cloth napkins, triangular crystal vases with orbital rings around their bases — the dried peppering from the ashes of flowers they once contained.

Three more bodies there, seated on the floor against the far door. Men. The workers at the last supper.

"If you want, you two can stay in here and see what you can find while I check out the rest of the cars up ahead," I said.

I held my knife out in front of me.

Ben looked at Griffin. His eyes were clear now, just from that small bit of water we'd shared. "We're staying together, Jack," he said.

There was not even a hint of resistance on Griffin's gaunt face.

"We need to move these three out of the way, then," I said.

Ben pulled at one of the corpse's legs, and fell back into us when it came detached inside the man's uniform trousers.

"Pull them by the clothes," I said.

None of them weighed more than a few pounds, and after Ben's grisly mistake, we easily pushed the three bodies behind the last table. I took the white tablecloth from it and blanketed it over their heads. I felt sorry for them, for our having to move them as we did.

Then, more cars of the same. Parched and desiccated bodies, suitcases, conductors, and none of them looked as though anything even remotely out of the ordinary had happened. Just another ride on a train.

The next-to-last car was a sleeper, with a narrow paneled hallway alongside the only row of windows.

Ben slid open the first compartment's curtained door and poked his head inside.

He threw himself back, collapsing against Griffin and me, screaming, "Fuck! Fuck!"

The three of us fell down in a heap on the dry carpet. I dropped my knife.

Something moved inside. I saw a flash, a shadow across the doorway, and then an old woman stepped out into the hallway and looked down at us, shaking her head. She raised her hand as though to touch Ben's face, and as he launched himself back to his feet, the woman spun around and faded down the corridor.

Ben sailed after the image, swinging his metal spear back and forth, hammering, pounding it into doors and glass, shouting, "Fuck you, ghost! I fucking hate ghosts!"

"Ben! Ben!" I stood, pulling Griffin up next to me, but Ben wouldn't listen. He ran the length of the car, smashing everything he could, cursing until the woman faded and vanished through the jagged cracks of one of the windows he'd shattered.

Ben dropped his weapon and fell to his knees, panting at the opposite end of the hallway.

"It's okay," I said. I put my hand on the back of Ben's neck. He just stared at the carpet between his knees, and I said, again, "It's okay, Ben."

Ben inhaled deeply. "Sorry, Jack. She just scared the shit out of me."

I heard Griffin making his way down the aisle toward us, opening compartment doors one by one.

People, bodies, in beds in most of the compartments, but we'd found one that was unoccupied and arranged as perfectly as it would have been at the moment the train left its last station.

I said, "We can sleep in here later."

The last car before the locomotive had the most people in it. There were twenty-two of them — we counted them. They were all soldiers, dressed in uniforms, their canvas duffel bags with stenciled names lined perfectly beside one another atop the luggage racks.

Ben dropped his spear. It clattered on the stained linoleum.

"They have guns!" Ben rushed past me.

I saw them, too.

In Marbury, guns made gods of boys like us.

Every one of them, save one, had been shot through the side of his head. Brown fireworks of blood were sprayed everywhere, in every direction imaginable. Some of the men still clutched their pistols in their leathered grips. A few of the guns rested in the place where the final spasms of death delivered them.

Suicide.

Every one of them. Griffin didn't know; I was sure of that.

Ben froze in his tracks. "Jack, these guys are . . ."

"I know," I said.

Ben swallowed and looked at me.

There was one rifle. It had a folding stock that had been collapsed, held upright between the thighs of a soldier who was seated on the floor, his thumb still curled around the trigger, his mouth hanging open at the end of the barrel, a whale spout of brown blood and crystallized bits of his head splashing upward along the fading rose patterns on the wallpaper of the car.

I watched as Ben scanned around the room from one body to another. I thought he was trying to read the names on the soldiers' uniforms.

"What do we do?" Griffin said.

111

"We take guns now," I said. "That's a good thing, Griff. We take guns, then we close this place up. And let's get us some clothes from these soldiers' bags. Then we'll see if we can't find something for us to eat and drink. It's a good thing, Griff."

twenty-six

It was a good thing.

The three of us stripped, naked and dirty. Ben began opening the soldiers' bags. I stood, twisting my head back so I could see the stitches Griffin had put into my skin. It was time to take them out.

Hanging on the wall beside a fire extinguisher was a metal case with a red cross painted on it. I pried it open and fingered through the contents: bandages, silver tubes with antibiotic ointment — they looked like the same stuff Freddie Horvath put on my ankle one night in that other hell — latex gloves, tape, tweezers, scissors.

And it was all the same, I thought — here, Freddie's house — all connected. Maybe none of it mattered. Maybe none of it was real.

"Hey, Griff. Come help me get these stitches out."

Ben continued digging through the bags, laying garments out, sometimes holding them up, squinting to read the tags that told the size of the men who'd never wear such things again.

Griffin, a moving skeleton of a boy, looking even smaller and more fragile without any clothes to cover him, took the scissors I held and began snipping away at his lacework. When he finished, he rubbed antiseptic over the places where the arrow had gone through me and we taped the wounds over with gauze and medical wrapping that still smelled like candy.

"I think you're going to be okay," Griffin said.

"I don't have a choice."

A tapping sound. A cylinder of white tape rolled down the aisle toward our feet, and we looked back and saw Seth, standing at the end of the car, watching us.

"Okay. You can get the fuck out of here now," Griffin said.

The ghost faded, just slightly, and hunched down on his calves between two dead soldiers. Seth watched me.

I felt lighter, somehow. I tried looking at Seth's eyes, but he turned his face down.

Ben began passing out clothes to us. We dressed. The boys couldn't remember wearing socks or underclothes before, it had been too long since the start of the war, since they'd been left alone. They wondered how it was that I even knew what to do with the things. I had to show them how to dress.

Griffin didn't like the way the underwear felt.

"It's too much," he said. He started taking them off.

"Keep them on," I said. "You'll get used to it. It's better for you. Trust me. Clothes are a good thing, okay?"

Griffin didn't say anything. Ben didn't like the way they felt, either. I could tell.

The pants we took were lightweight fatigues, camouflaged, with lots of deep pockets, button flies, and cinches inside the waists that held them up snug on our hips. We tied the pant legs tight to our ankles and fed thick webbed belts through the hoops. We tucked our shirts in, too, and each one of them had name tags sewn across the left side of the chest.

Ben's and Griffin's shirts came from the same bag. They said STRANGE across the pockets. Mine said RAMIREZ.

"That's a good name for you guys," I said. "Probably the best name you could have in a place like this."

113

Ben smiled. I hadn't seen the boys smile. "You want to trade shirts, Jack?"

I picked up the scissors Griffin used to snip out my stitches and began cutting the threads that held my name tag over the pocket.

"I'll be the guy with no name," I answered.

The boots we found were canvas with heavy treads. They'd never even been worn. They laced halfway up our shins.

Griffin didn't know how to tie shoes, but he learned after just one try at it.

"It feels good, doesn't it?" I said. I stood there, looking at Griffin and Ben in those clean clothes, the first time I'd ever seen them fully dressed.

Griffin shook his head.

Next thing: the guns.

We took as much as we could carry. We went through every soldier's bags and clothing and then carefully sorted and stacked every container of ammunition and metallic pouch of food we found on two of the tables.

I took the rifle. I slung the strap across my collar so it hung diagonally behind my wounded hip. Each of us fastened two semiautomatic handguns — 9 millimeters and .45s — to our belts. It was all so heavy, but I could sense how much stronger we'd become just by touching those things.

Seth stayed at the far end of the car, drifting back and forth like some sort of fading pendulum from one row of windows to the opposite. Sometimes he'd disappear entirely, especially if I caught him looking at me, and when he did, there would always soon come the impatient sound of his rolling and tapping noises.

For some reason, I just didn't feel sorry for those soldiers the way I'd felt for some of the other people in that train. The car was a gruesome mess when we opened it, and it was that much worse when we left it and pushed the door shut behind us. The bodies were scattered everywhere, mostly stripped of their guns, pockets out turned or torn completely open.

We went back through the sleeping car with its shattered windows and cracked paneling.

Ben shrugged apologetically. "I'm sorry about this, Jack. I got scared."

Griffin said, "Shit, Ben. No one cares."

I put my hand on Ben's shoulder and pushed him along, past the compartment where we'd sleep, to the buffet.

Ben broke into the car's water lines and fashioned a siphon pump from a hose and mop bucket. We'd be able to save the horses now, I thought.

"Don't drink too much," I warned. "It'll get us all sick."

There were so many treasures in that dining car we didn't know where to begin.

Griffin went behind the bar and placed a few bottles of liquor on the countertop. He opened an amber bottle of whiskey and sniffed at it, grimacing.

"Let me see that," Ben said.

I watched him with a look he understood to mean *no*.

"Don't be stupid, Ben."

"Just a little."

I watched him tip the bottle back, counted the gulps he took. Five. Despite the fact that Ben Miller didn't have the guts to watch little Griffin pull an arrow from my side and sew me shut with the rags of my own useless shirt, he was a survivor; and in my reckoning, both those STRANGE boys were monstrously tougher than I could ever be.

"You too," Ben said. "Just a little."

I shook my head. Griffin held up a football-size can that contained a whole chicken. And Ben argued, "We're never going to have a day like this again, Jack. Never. So have a little bit, too."

I looked at Griffin. "See if you can find a way to open that, Griff." Then I took the bottle from Ben and said, "But you're not going to have any, right? It's not good for you, Griff."

"Fuck no I don't want any of that shit." Griffin wiped his nose along the sleeve of his shirt. "And what do you know what's good for me? You told me to put all these clothes on — that they're good for me, too — and my nuts feel half-strangled. As soon as you two pass out, I'm taking this shit off again."

Ben laughed.

I drank.

It felt real good.

I sat down at a table and smiled, alternating my glances from the stacks of food Griffin had been arranging, to the crooked feet of the three dead train workers we'd hidden in a corner, and the lonely half-shadow of Seth, who sat across the aisle from me, watching.

Before I'd eat, I took a bucket of water and another with some dried fruit and old pieces of candy and bread outside for our horses. I made sure they were securely tied to the train; and I walked around the entire length of it one more time. I needed to be certain the harvesters hadn't followed us, and their chasers behind them, too. When I passed the dining car, Griffin and Ben stood up on their seats and pounded on the window and waved at me.

Ben was drunk.

Even if it would only be a few hours, I knew Ben was right: that we'd never have a day like this again, and it felt like we all were getting more than we'd ever deserve.

You're just drunk, Jack.

You haven't gotten away from anything.

The same voice came back. And I tried to think about Conner and Nickie; about Wynn and Stella, but they were difficult to picture, like they were images from a book that I'd read too many years ago to remember how the story came together.

Fuck you, Jack.

It was easy, somehow, to remember Freddie Horvath.

"You ever going to talk to me?"

Seth stood back, a dim shadow at the end of the train, watching me. He dropped his chin and began to fade, but I said, "Goddamnit, Seth, don't go."

He held his hand on the side of the train, like he was keeping it in place.

"You were in that room, weren't you? When Freddie . . ."

"Yes," Seth said.

"Thank you for helping me," I said. "You didn't have to do it."

"You remind me of someone." His voice was just above a whisper.

Then he was gone.

Nighttime in Marbury never turned entirely dark. The horizon stayed white, and the sky overhead became a starless, chalky, ash color; if color's even a word that could fairly be used to describe anything in this world.

We were full.

Ben and I could hardly stand.

We drank too much.

We followed Griffin through the hallways of death, found our sleeping compartment, and went to bed.

I woke first.

The compartment we'd slept in had four beds, two stacked

against either wall. I lay on the bottom, across from Ben. Griffin slept in the berth above me. And every last article of his clothing had been taken off and thrown down into the small space on the floor between the bunk beds. He lay there on his belly, naked on the sheets, barely breathing, with his hand resting on the guns in their canvas holsters beside his pillow. I picked up his scattered clothes and put them on the bed next to him.

I stepped into my pants and laced up my boots. I slipped the sling of my rifle over a bare shoulder. Then I shook Ben's arm.

"Hey. I'm going out to give the horses some water, okay?"

Ben half-opened his groggy, yellow-crusted eyes.

"What? Oh. Okay, Jack."

I patted his arm. "That was good shit last night, huh?"

"Heck yeah."

I went back and forth twice, filling the mop bucket for the horses, bringing them the bits of food we'd scrounged that seemed acceptable to feed them. The day before, I had been certain the horses were going to die, but now they seemed stubbornly restored.

The sky became pale white, the ground was already steaming again before the day fully broke across the Marbury desert.

I'd left my shirt in the room with the boys, and I looked at the pads where Griffin had taped medicine over my wounds. A little pus, some blood. It itched. I'd have our young doctor look at it again, before we'd leave the train for good.

I can't stay here much longer.

But it was already too late.

I saw the still form of one of the Hunters at the edge of the horizon, silhouetted against the blank sky: tall, lanky, spider arms, he stood perfectly still. And I could see the red mark on his chest, molten, burning like an eye, even at so great a distance.

They all had different marks somewhere on their bodies. They couldn't be covered, would burn through anything. Beacons. It made them easy to see.

It made it impossible for us to hide.

I was certain he was watching me — they could see better than we could. At the very least, he'd seen the horses, or smelled them.

I crouched against the train, watched him kick up bits of salt dust as he strode, unafraid, coming closer.

Tap. Tap. Tap.

The window behind me.

I turned, looked. Nothing.

Tap.

Seth.

Then came the banging, pounding against the glass. I heard things flying around inside the train, crashing against the walls.

He was getting too close.

He carried a hatchet, swinging it casually, pointed downward at the side of his knee. No bow. He would have already shot an arrow at me if he'd had one.

Seth, pounding inside.

"Quit it, Seth!"

I weighed my options: Would I wake Ben and Griffin, or deal with this scout on my own? I dropped to a knee. He was close enough now that I could clearly see him.

He was tall and arrow-thin, naked except for a loose codpiece of braided feathers and blackened, hairy skin tied around his waist on a narrow twine of dried sinew. It was made from a human scalp. They did that. His hair fell past his shoulders in twisted clumps, and oval purple splotches the size of grapefruits painted his sides from the tops of his thighs to his armpits.

119

Some of them got those spots, too.

The only other thing he wore was a necklace, draped over his shoulders. It had been made from old DVDs.

The mark on his chest burned like a red *W*, whose twin arrows pointed down to his rippled midsection from each of his nipples. The hand that held the hatchet was a three-fingered claw with long, shining spikes.

Some of them got that, too.

He stared intently at me, had to be wondering why I waited there in the obvious open. He twisted his neck, just a bit, raised his nose, and sniffed the air.

One eye was entirely white. The other was entirely black.

Every one of them had eyes like that.

He crouched, raised the hatchet.

I looked both ways along the length of the train. Things were still bashing against the walls on the inside. Ben and Griffin had to be awake now, I thought.

I unfolded the stock on my rifle and braced it against my shoulder.

The thing came running toward me at a full sprint.

I shot him twice in the neck, and as he spun around, he made a perfectly spiraled pinwheel of blood around the white ground where he fell silently dead.

I lowered the rifle, stood. Three more waning sprays of blood fountained from the side of his neck. I could hear the thick warm drops pelting his skin. I kept the barrel trained on his head and walked over to the spattered circle of ground where he'd fallen, legs twisted in a ridiculous ballet.

No more breath.

No more blood.

I looked at his face.

I knew him.

Brian Fields, my friend from the Glenbrook cross-country team, lay staring up at the white sky behind me with dead eyes, a hole as big as my hand lay open the side of his neck just below the crease of his young jaw.

"Brian?"

This isn't fucking happening.

"Brian!"

I spun around, and just then another of the things leapt down from the top of a train car and took me into the ground. His mouth was open, dripping his slobber over my face. I twisted my head to the side and the thing licked my mouth. I saw the teeth, sharp and long; and he squealed and put them right against my chest and bit into me.

I howled, tried to roll over on top of him. I tried pulling my gun around, but the stock was pinned beneath my leg. He clawed at my belly, brought his hand right up into my balls and twisted; and I screamed and let go of my rifle. I fought against his hand and he pulled his face back, mouth open. He was smeared with my blood, but I couldn't feel where he'd bitten me, only the pain in my crotch, where it seemed my guts were being pulled out from my body.

It was my best friend, Conner Kirk, who was attacking me.

"Conner! What the fuck!"

He tried biting again, aimed for my throat, but I palmed his forehead back. I heard the licking, smacking of his lips.

"Conner!"

Then there came the crack of a gunshot. Conner ducked and rolled off me. He ran away on all fours, scampering like a frightened dog, toward the front end of the train. I looked back and saw Griffin, wearing nothing, trying to steady his .45. Shaking, he took another shot at Conner, hit the locomotive, and Conner disappeared around the front.

I stood up, saw the blood running down my chest, the double moon-arcs of blackened teeth marks above my right nipple. My guts hurt so bad, I bent forward and threw up.

Conner bit me.

I fell down onto my face in the salt and passed out.

Then I felt Seth lying on top of me, melting again.

twenty-seven

What the fuck is happening to me?

Griffin's hand between my shoulders, rubbing, trying to bring me back.

It hurt so bad, like I was torn inside out.

"Get up, Jack. We don't have much time."

I could hear him, but I couldn't open my eyes.

"Jack."

I heard Ben coming up. "What the fuck?"

Griffin said, "Two scouts. Jack got one of them. But the other got away."

Ben grabbed under my arm.

"Come on. Let's get him inside. Then we gotta get the fuck out of here."

"I'll be okay." I raised myself onto my hands and knees. The boys steadied me when I stood; and they walked me back to the last car.

We had to hurry now. They'd be back soon.

While Griffin patched me up again, Ben started putting together some makeshift saddlebags by using pieces of luggage that he strapped to one another with belts from the men passengers. He'd made one for each of us, and began filling them with anything we might be able to use: clothes, food, ammunition.

"This looks nasty, Jack. As bad as what that arrow did, maybe worse." Griffin smeared ointment into the bites with his thumb. His face was so close to me, I could feel his breath. "I can't stitch it, though."

"I don't want you to."

He looked at me. "You said something to 'em both. I heard you."

"I know who they were."

"How could you know that?"

"I just do."

"Doesn't matter. That one's going to keep coming back till he fucking kills us now."

"Here." Ben dropped Griffin's clothes at his feet. "Jack wants you to wear them, so you're wearing them. We're not going to get chased across this desert with you running around naked like that."

"I'm not done yet."

"And here's your shirts, Jack. I got just about everything I could think of, so when he's done and dressed, we better get moving. It's not going to take that scout too long to get them all coming this way."

Conner.

Griffin Goodrich stuck his tongue out the side of his mouth, concentrating, as he smoothed out the white medical tape on my chest. "There."

"Now get dressed," Ben said.

Griffin tossed the underwear and socks aside. "Not these. I can't stand them."

I could tell Ben was about to get mad.

"It's okay, Ben. Let him go." I slipped my T-shirt over my head. It hurt. My chest was stiff. I began buttoning the outer shirt, tucking it in.

"One last thing," I said. "We need to take care of all those guns back there."

"I thought about that," Ben said. "I don't think we can carry them all."

Griffin laced up his boots.

"We don't need to. Come on."

I led the boys back to the car where the soldiers had killed themselves. I showed them how to break down the guns. With what we'd taken, there were only a few more than a dozen of them left, anyway. We took the barrel from each of them, then I used my knife to pry open the flap valve in the toilet at the end of the car, and we dropped every one of the barrels down into the blackness of the tank.

I slid the black valve, a big eyelid, back across the bottom of the toilet bowl.

"They'll give up looking before they figure that out," I said.

When we went outside, I saw the shining black forms of the harvesters moving onto Brian Fields's body. I could hear the clicking sound of their jaws cutting into his flesh. It made me sick.

We rode away from the train.

Griffin looked back every few minutes. We all did.

If there was any haze being kicked up by the Followers as they made their way across the desert toward us, it blended right into the white of the sky. At times, I began remembering about this ruined world, how it had been before the disease, before the war. It was a long time; so long, kids like Griffin couldn't remember anything else.

And Griffin said, "With tracks like we're leaving, we might as well pave them a road to follow."

"I know," I said. "That's why we got to get into the mountains."

"With the guns and bullets we got, I bet we could kill a thousand of them," Ben said.

"We might have to."

"That would be fun," Griffin said.

Fun game.

I kill Conner or he kills me.

So I didn't get away from anything. Not here, not there. I knew there was nothing real that could save me.

We rode.

twenty-eight

I knew where I was.

Somehow I'd gotten myself twisted around on the floor and woke up — if I can call it that — entirely under the bed. My foot was numb, still locked by that nylon strap to the metal frame where it was welded to the crossbar. I looked out toward the narrow slash of light.

I saw the glasses lying on the floor.

The sun was up.

What the fuck is wrong with you, Jack?

Freddie Horvath did something to my brain.

The phone was ringing. How many times?

How long was I there for this time?

I slid out from under the bed. The ringing of the telephone stopped.

I'd left scissors on the nightstand. I cut myself free and then crawled to the toilet so I could throw up, but my stomach was empty. I only managed to retch up a burning yellow mucus that stuck in my throat and nose. I curled up on my side on the cool floor and stayed like that until I felt like I could move again.

Get up, Jack.

You fucked up.

No more.

No more.

No more.

You fucked up again. Just like you did the night of the party, and it's all your fault.

You deserve this, asshole.

I got onto my knees, ran the water in the shower, and put my head over the edge of the tub.

I went back into the room. My hair dripped cool water onto my body. It rained a trail on the floor. The place was such a mess. I'd thrown my stuff everywhere. I twisted the clock around on the nightstand so I could see it. Six in the morning. I had to leave. Conner was coming.

I stripped off my underwear and stumbled along the wall, got into the shower, and turned it on full cold. I strained as my lungs imprisoned a scream that wasn't only from the shock of the water.

How would I even be able to look at Conner?

I fooled myself into thinking that I could get away from all that shit back home by coming over to England, but like the voice in my head kept telling me: I hadn't gotten away from anything.

And now I believed I killed Brian Fields, too.

I was sick and pale, shaking, as I sat on the train and stared out the window, seeing nothing, on the way out to Heathrow.

There are dead people on this train.

Quit it, Jack.

On Monday mornings, the trains to Heathrow got crowded, even in first class.

I must have looked like a smuggler or something; and I was certain that everyone in the car had been watching me, were whispering about the sick-looking kid who stared blankly and leaned his wet hair against the window.

Then the conductor came through, punching tickets.

And it was the same man that Ben, Griffin, and I had found curled up beneath that table in the first car with the dead bodies. The guy who died with his eyes open, hiding from something. He smiled at me, and my hand shook so badly I couldn't get it down inside my pocket to grab my ticket.

I had to stand up to do it, felt like my knees would give out beneath me.

The conductor's smile faded to a look of concern, maybe irritation.

He must have thought I was on drugs or something.

I saw you dead.

And, when I stood, I looked back down the length of the aisle. A woman and a man sat together at the back of the car. He wore a pressed, striped blue shirt, and there was a water bottle on the seat next to his hip. They both smiled at me. Three kids played on the bench seats across from them: two girls and a boy, laughing, dressed nicely.

I'd seen them before, too.

I handed my ticket to the conductor, my eyes fixed on the same oval brass name tag on his uniform I'd seen under a table in Marbury. As soon as he punched it, I collapsed back into my seat.

Fuck this place.

I stood right in front, waiting for Conner to come out from the customs hall. I tried to look as normal as I could, but I was certain everyone there was staring at me. I kept my eyes on the feet of the people coming out through the automatic doors. I'd know Conner's shoes. But he probably wouldn't know my eyes; at least I convinced myself that he'd see something in them. He had to. We knew each other too well to cover up shit like this. So when Conner passed through the doorway, I waited there on the other side of the blue ropes and he dropped his backpack, then ran around the end and hugged me.

I didn't want him to touch me, forced myself to put my arms around him, anyway.

It seemed like years since I'd seen him.

Years and worlds.

I held him at arm's length so I could look straight at his eyes. They were clear and gray, like they'd always been. Just Conner. None of that white-eye, black-eye bullshit that I must have been hallucinating.

Crazy Jack.

This is real.

"Dude," Conner said. "Are we getting ready to kiss or something?"

I forced a smile. "Asshole. I guess I just missed you, Con."

"It's only been three days."

I thought about it. Conner stood there looking at me like he was expecting me to confess to something.

"You look different. Did something happen to you?" he said.

"I don't think so." I cleared my throat. "Let's get on the train. You're going to like it, Con."

"I want to hear about that imaginary girl you met."

"Imaginary girls don't talk on phones or show up in pictures," I said. "And please tell me you brought my charger."

While we waited on the platform, Conner dug through his pack to prove he hadn't forgotten it.

"Stella bugged me about it every day," he said. "She actually bought an extra one so I could bring two in case you lost it again."

"I guess I have been kind of losing it."

Conner laughed.

"Hey, let me see your phone," I said.

Conner handed me his cell. "You gonna call that girl? Nickie?"

"No. Later." I thumbed through his contacts list, found what I was looking for, hit the send button, and put the phone up to my ear. Then I turned my back to Conner and took a few steps away from him. He understood. I didn't have to say anything to him about my not wanting to be heard right then.

I came back and gave him his phone as the train entered the station.

There were dozens of people waiting for it, all of them spaced at careful distances from one another.

Conner opened his phone as he hefted his pack over one shoulder. I took his day bag in my hand.

"Why'd you call Brian?"

"Oh. Nothing. I remembered I promised I'd call him when we were both in London together."

"Oh." Conner shrugged. "What did he say?"

"He was pissed. I forgot. It's the middle of the night."

Conner laughed. "You really are losing it, Jack."

We got on the train.

I tried to stay focused. But I couldn't. Finally, Conner'd had enough and he punched me in the chest.

"What the fuck, Con?"

"You have to quit it, Jack."

He didn't know how right he was.

"I know. Sorry." I shifted in my seat and rubbed the spot where he hit me.

"'Cause there's nothing that can be done about it, anyway. So stop beating yourself up and just settle things in your stupid head."

"You're right," I said. "I am so glad you're here, Con. Are you tired or anything?"

"No. I want to go out."

"You bring stuff to run?"

"Yeah."

I kept telling myself on the ride in to London that it was finally over, that I wasn't going back to Marbury ever again. Then the Jack and Conner from Marbury could settle what they had to one way or another, and it wouldn't matter to me because this is where I was going to stay.

I kept telling myself I'd have to find a way to get rid of those goddamned glasses.

I kept telling myself.

"Let's do a few miles when we get back. It'll make you feel better," I said.

"That sounds good. Then can we go out and get a couple beers after?"

"Sure."

"You been drinking?"

"Nickie doesn't drink. I did once. Beer."

I thought about the whiskey I drank with Ben Miller — and when was that, anyway?

Quit it, Jack.

Get rid of those goddamned things.

I only hoped Ben and Griffin would be okay.

"Don't tell me you haven't been partying, Jack."

I forgot about how messy I'd left the place.

"And don't tell me you didn't bring that Nickie around and nail her. This place says 'Jack's been having crazy rough sex' all over it."

I felt myself turning red. I began crumpling up the notes I'd scattered around, kicking my stuff into a pile so I could stuff it all back into the pack.

"Not like that. She's not like that, Con," I said. "I got pissed off last night, I guess."

I could almost feel Conner's shoulders slump when I said it.

Subject change: "Check out the trapdoor shower," I said.

Conner went into the bathroom. I heard him peeing, and I got everything wadded up, back inside my pack. I plugged my phone into the charger, and the voltage adapter that I did remember to bring. Missed calls and text messages. I didn't want to look at them.

The glasses — somehow I'd kicked them under the bed. I got down onto my hands and knees and pulled them out. The cut zip tie was under there, too.

Roll. Tap. Tap. Tap.

I panicked. I folded the glasses and shoved them as far down into my pack as I could get them.

Roll.

"Shhhh . . . ," I said, whispering, pleading. "Don't."

Tap. Tap.

Conner came out from the bathroom.

"Yeah," he said, "this place is kind of odd. What side of the bed do you want?"

"Whatever one you're not on."

Conner smiled. "You never know."

I pointed out the window to Regent's Park. "That's a great place to run. You ever see a cricket match?"

We changed into our running clothes. I was tense, kept turning my head, cocking my ear to listen for the sound of Seth making his little signs, but it didn't come.

Take a deep breath, Jack.

Calm down.

This is real.

"Before we go, you gotta see this," I said. I took my camera out and turned it on, scanning through the images — the ones I'd taken that first day, that I couldn't remember, ones of Nickie in the park, the picture of the two of us together when we'd said good-bye at the Underground.

"This is me and Nickie." I handed the camera to Conner.

"Okay," he said. "I guess she is real. And hot."

He studied the picture for a while. He messed around with the zoom. Then he smiled and handed the camera back to me and said, "That guy in the background looks a little creepy, though. Stalker ex-boyfriend, maybe?"

I didn't even notice it. Standing half in the shadows behind the turnstile at the Tube station, Henry Hewitt had been watching us.

He was still following me.

I looked at Conner and shrugged. "I don't know who that guy is."

But I'm a terrible liar. Conner had to know there was something wrong with me.

How could he not see it?

"Hey, Con," I said. "Come here. Let's take a picture together."

We put our arms around each other's shoulders and smiled. We stood in front of the open window while we both steadied the camera at arm's length. My thumb found the shutter button.

Tap.

Then I tossed the camera onto the bed and said, "Let's get out of this place."

The run was good. I pushed him hard, and he started to complain a couple times about being tired from the plane, but I wasn't really listening. We stopped and drank at a fountain, then stretched for a while in the shade beside the lake.

I started running again, and Conner was right behind me.

"You got somewhere to go, or something?" he said.

"Oh, sorry," I said. "I've been thinking about some crazy stuff."

"Oh." There was disappointment in Conner's voice.

"Not like that," I said. "You know how you just think about stuff when you run? How it just kind of pops into your head?"

"Sorry, Jack," Conner said. "If I do think when I run, it's usually about having sex."

"Oh. Yeah."

"And, of course, you never do that, do you? Okay, Einstein, so what were you thinking about?"

So I told him.

I said, "You know those weird nesting dolls that Stella collects? The ones that open up and have all kinds of different things inside them?"

"Yeah. So. You think about *dolls* when you run?"

I had to laugh at that. And I thought that no matter what crazy shit I was dreaming up, that I'd always have Conner Kirk here as my best friend; that he could always manage to get a smile out of me, and I loved him for it, and it was real.

"I was thinking, What if the world was like that? What if we only saw one surface of it, the outside, but there was all kinds of other stuff going on, too? All the time. Underneath. But we just don't see it, even if we're part of it? Even if we're in it? And what if you had a chance to see a different layer, like flipping a channel or something? Would you want to look? Even if what you saw looked like hell? Or worse?"

Conner stopped running. I didn't expect him to do that. I'd gotten a few paces in front of him, so I had to double back to where he stood.

"Have you been smoking pot, Jack?"

I shoved him. "Asshole."

"You sound like you've been seriously hitting the weed, dude."

I laughed. "I was just thinking."

"I recommend next time you start wondering about shit like that, tell me about it so I can convince you to start thinking about sex," Conner said. "You know, like a normal kid does. Someone needs to seriously straighten you out."

"I'll remember that," I said, and smiled at my friend. "But you know, Conner. You're like the only person I can talk to about shit."

Conner shrugged and slapped my shoulder. "I'm thirsty, Jack. Don't you think we've gone far enough for jet-lag boy today?"

"Okay. Let's go back."

And Conner just shook his head and laughed as we turned back toward Marylebone Road, saying, "Seriously, dude. Seriously. Maybe I should give you a play-by-play of the porno I'm visualizing right now."

"I'll get back to you on that, Con."

twenty-nine

That night, we got drunk at The Prince of Wales.

It wasn't like we hadn't planned it: It was the one thing that Conner and I had talked about since deciding to take this trip in the first place.

Conner had me laughing so hard, I thought I would pee in my pants.

It felt good. Finally, good.

There were only a few other people in the pub; even the bartender sat down with us and had a beer. He wanted to talk about basketball, and assumed we did, too, since we were from California. He said he was a Lakers fan, but neither of us cared about basketball much at all.

And he said, "That gent who bought the beer for you the other night, he did come back yesterday. I told him that you had his glasses, but he said they weren't his. He said they belonged to you."

Conner looked at me. I just hoped he was so drunk that none of this would matter.

I wasn't really scared that Henry was looking for me. He had to be hurting so bad, wanting to return to Marbury, but he was dead there. Game over. And, sitting in the pub in that weak state, I couldn't help but think about Ben and Griffin, even if I hated myself for it, too.

"Well, it was just a mistake," I said. I emptied my beer, even though I was full. I only wished the bartender would get the idea to shut the hell up and go pour some more for us.

"But the girl," he continued, "I haven't seen her since the night you left here with her. Very pretty."

"She's in Blackpool," I said. "And, yeah, she's beautiful."

"Hey," Conner said. "You should call her, Jack!"

"Dude. I am not going to call her when I'm drunk."

"Then let me."

"Not going to happen."

The bartender scooped up our glasses and walked back to the bar.

Conner grabbed at my pocket. "Let me see your phone."

I laughed. "Get off me. I think I'm done for tonight."

"Have one more," Conner pleaded.

"Okay. But that's it." I waved an order to the bartender and got up. "Be right back. Gotta pee."

I lied again. I just wanted to get away from Conner. I really did want to call Nickie, I just didn't want to do it around him. So as soon as I'd closed the door to the toilet behind me, I had my phone out of my pocket.

"I'm sorry for calling so late, but Conner's here and I just wanted to say hello. I needed to hear your voice."

I could hear the smile in her tone. "Why?"

"To prove you're real," I whispered. I tried to make it sound like a compliment, a line, even if it meant something entirely different to me.

Nickie said, "You don't strike me as being that needy, Jack."

"I try to manage, I guess."

Nickie laughed. "Is your friend enjoying himself?"

"I think he's finally tired enough to go to sleep."

We talked for a few minutes, and eventually I promised Nickie that I'd come up to Blackpool before the end of the week, and she sounded happy about that.

"There's something about you that's different, Jack," she'd said.

"I know. Try and not let it get in the way of your starting to like me."

When I came out to the bar, I saw Conner was already halfway through the beer I'd ordered. There was a full glass waiting for me. Conner leaned slightly to one side, looking relaxed enough that he could fall to sleep right there in that pub.

I'd had enough. My legs were rubber.

Then I looked over at the bar.

Henry Hewitt was leaning against it, wearing the same sweater and long coat, unshaven and scruffy-looking. And he just kept glancing back and forth, from me to Conner, with an expression on his face like he was watching something horrifying, like an execution.

You haven't gotten away from anything, Jack.

But Conner didn't notice him.

I half-stumbled toward our table, leaned over my friend, and said, "I'm going to pay the tab, Con. I think it's time to get to sleep."

Conner nodded and finished his beer.

And when I got up to the bar next to Henry, I pulled some money from my pocket and whispered. I kept my head turned straight so that it didn't look like I was talking to him. "Wait here for me. I need to talk to you. I'll be back as soon as I can. Just, don't leave."

Henry Hewitt didn't answer.

I said, "Please?"

And then I turned around, grabbed Conner to help him to his feet, and we left.

I think we must have looked like caricatures of inebriates, Conner and I, as we walked crookedly, arms locked around one another's shoulders, trying to make our way back to the hotel. I'll admit that

I kind of exaggerated it, though, because I wasn't nearly as drunk as he was. In fact, although Conner babbled on in a singsong voice about every kind of nonsense, I hardly paid any attention to him at all as I ran through the dozens of things I wanted to say — and do — to Henry Hewitt.

By the time we'd gotten up to the room, Conner could hardly manage to stand without leaning on me, so I guided him over to the bed and dropped him down at the nearest edge.

"Looks like this side, Con," I said.

"This side what?"

"Where you sleep."

"Oh. Okay. Take my clothes off, Jack."

"You are gay," I said. Then added, "Here." I slipped his shoes off.

"Now you're on your own. Good night." I threw his shoes onto the floor next to my pack.

"Night," Conner said. "I'm glad we did this, Jack. We're going to have a great summer."

"Maybe." I opened the pack, began snaking my hand down through all the things I'd balled up earlier. "I'm going outside for a minute so I can talk to Nickie. I'll be right back."

"You don't need to go outside. Talk to her here, so I can listen."

"Go to sleep."

My hand closed around the familiar wire frames of the glasses Henry left for me.

Roll. Tap. Tap. Tap.

"What are you doing?"

"Nothing," I said.

Roll.

"What's that noise?"

I pulled the glasses out. In the dark of the room, I immediately saw through the lenses: windless white sky, the blackened peaks of mountains, a flash of Griffin Goodrich looking at me from on top of his horse.

I shut my eyes tight, felt like I was standing halfway between the panic that Conner would pay too much attention to Seth's stubborn tapping and the pull of needing to look one time — just a peek — to see if Griffin was okay.

"Nothing. It's coming from the street. Go to sleep."

Conner rolled over onto his side. He was trying to get his pants off, but gave up.

I found one of my socks that I'd stuffed into a running shoe earlier; then I blindly felt down inside the pack as I fed the glasses into it. I didn't want to look at them.

But I was lying to myself. I wanted to look through them so bad that I began shaking and went completely sober, sweating as though I'd just eaten a bottle of caffeine pills.

I tucked the glasses into the waist of my jeans.

Conner began breathing heavily. He was asleep.

And for just a minute, I stood at the side of the bed watching him. He looked so relaxed and happy. I envied him. And I thought, *No matter what goes on anywhere else, Con, you will always be my best friend.*

I promise.

I turned the lights off and hurried back to The Prince of Wales.

The whole way there, dripping with sweat, and once stumbling out into the street, stupidly looking in the wrong direction and nearly being run down by a car, I kept wanting to pull the glasses out and slip them onto my face.

It'll only be a second, Jack.

Just a peek.

Ben.

Griffin.

I wanted to howl, to hit someone, to hit myself.

I'm sick of this shit.

I'm sick of me.

I had to stop. I bent over a trash barrel near Warren Street and forced myself to hold in the urge to vomit.

My guts ached.

Roll. Tap. Tap. Tap.

Something moved along the ground, a quiet vibration against the steel can beside my foot.

I felt it.

Tap.

Tap.

My hands shook so badly. I couldn't control it. I grabbed the sock with the glasses, pulled it out like a junkie opening his kit. Sweat poured from my scalp. I put my fingers into the sock.

"It's a difficult thing to control once you step foot over the edge, Jack."

I gasped, straightened. My stomach caved in again.

Henry stood in the darkness by the edge of the street, watching me.

I dropped the glasses into the trash can.

Roll. Tap.

"Fuck you!" I screamed, "Fuck you, you goddamned sonofabitch!"

I ran at Henry, both fists balled tight, and began punching him as hard as I could. Everywhere, until he fell to the sidewalk, trying to cover up, but I kept hitting him until my hands ached and I dropped down beside him and sat there on the ground next to him.

I didn't cry.

Jack doesn't cry.

"Fuck you, Henry."

Fuck you, Freddie.

thirty

Henry moaned and rolled away from me.

He spit blood; there was a small puddle of it on the pavement stone beneath his face.

Then he wiped his mouth and said, "Unfortunate to have waited around for that, I should think."

I pulled my knees in to my chest and just sat there, out of breath. I watched the street.

"Well." Henry pushed himself to his feet. I could tell he was looking at me, but I didn't move. "If it means anything, I felt the same way about it, Jack. And now look what's happened to us. I apologize."

"Why are you still following me?"

"You know. How can you stop? Part of me is grateful to be free of that place, but most of me wants to go back more desperately than I can say."

"Then take them back."

"I can't go back. And you wouldn't want to give them up, now." Henry took a step closer to me. I tensed, still wanted to hit him. "I would give anything to go back. The glasses show me nothing. Only black. Did you see what happened to me? You saw it, didn't you, Jack? In Marbury?"

I saw your head nailed to a fucking wall.

141

"Yes."

"Not a very pretty world, is it?"

"Which one?"

Henry laughed. "I like you, Jack. I always have. And those boys love you. You're all Ben and Griffin have now."

"Are there any others?"

"I don't know." Then Henry kneeled down behind me, almost whispering, "I didn't realize about your friend. The one I saw you with tonight. I swear, I didn't know."

"You've seen him before? In Marbury?"

"Yes." He put his hand on my shoulder, but I pushed it away. "I didn't know. If I did, I wouldn't have looked for you, Jack. I would have looked for Ben. You have to believe me. His name is Conner."

"What am I supposed to do?"

"I don't know. It's why I told you to be careful. About who you look for, about looking for your friends. I don't know. I'm afraid there's almost nothing alive there now. And fewer of us than them. But I know our connections in this world connect us in Marbury. That's why I never lost hope that I would find you. I swear I thought I would find Ben and Griffin, too." Henry stood up and took a step away from me. "It's how all worlds begin, Jack. How they all end. War. I haven't been able to tell if it's the beginning or the end in Marbury."

I didn't want to hear him. "Because you're full of shit."

"Look, I'm going to leave now. I'm going to make myself leave you alone now, I promise, Jack. Only one thing: Can you tell me, please, what's happened since you've gone there, to you, and Griffin, and Ben? Tell me that, and I'll try and forget all about it and leave you alone. Can you tell me?"

"Fuck off."

I wouldn't look at him, didn't want to. He was just another

142

monster out to take something from me. I was through with him, with Marbury, with everything.

I sat there and stared at the road. I listened to the sound of Henry Hewitt walking away from me.

Tap. Tap. Tap.

Leaning over the garbage can, I pushed my arm down into the darkness until I found the sock with the glasses wrapped up inside. I looked back once and saw that Henry had watched me do it.

"It's a difficult thing to control, Jack, once you step over the edge."

I pushed the glasses down inside my pants and walked out into the street, away from him.

And Henry called out after me, "Take care, Jack. I'll be around."

"Fuck you, Henry," I whispered.

One in the morning.

I shook.

I sat at the desk with my elbows propping me up, looking at the little white bundle that lay on the polished wood in front of me.

Like being born.

One in the morning.

I watched Conner as he slept, wished I was asleep.

I wrote it on the paper and my hand shook doing it: *One in the morning.*

Roll.

Tap.

Tap.

Tap.

"Shhhhh . . ."

And he said, "Seth."

143

"My name is Jack," I whispered.

"I know."

"Why can't I see you here?"

"I'm scared."

"Of me?"

Then I realized he was standing right there between the empty side of the bed and the wall: the faint image of the boy I'd seen in the cave and, later, on the train in Marbury, standing, not moving, his dark eyes fixed on me, with the steadiest, most relaxed expression on his face. It was Seth, barefoot and shirtless, wearing thin, ragged pants tied around his bony hips on a strand of twine. And almost as soon as I could focus on him, he vanished again, and his little song began from somewhere beneath the bed — the rolling, tapping, rolling, tapping.

"Shhhhh . . . ," I said. I swallowed. "I'm supposed to go, aren't I? You want me to go?"

I slipped the glasses out of the sock.

I could already see the Marbury sky on the other side of the lens.

A world between my fingers.

I can't get away, don't want to get away.

I deserve this.

Fuck you, Jack.

My hand quaked as I unfolded the glasses.

One in the morning.

It'll just be for a second.

part three

BLACKPOOL

thirty-one

In the foothills, we rode through a forest of crucifixions.

At first, in the washed-out haze of the distance, I'd thought they actually were trees. Trees would be nice. Maybe we'd see some up in the mountains, I thought.

But they weren't trees. They were the broken-off fragments of utility poles and other structures, lashed together with impotent black cables like childhood jacks, X's with prop-braces, the skeleton frames of squat, naked tepees, tumbled and strewn among the rocks and ravines where it appeared there once had been a small community of houses, a stream. And every one of them was decorated with three or more bodies.

This happened a week ago.

Maybe just a few days.

There are others somewhere.

We can't be the only ones left.

We rode in single file, Ben at the lead. I followed Griffin, watched as the horses swayed before me, weighed down by the bulging packs we'd invented from the belongings of dead people. Somehow, Griffin had managed to make a seat between his saddlebags, stuffed and rounded with the filthy blanket I'd used as a poncho. He looked back at me one time as the horses took us up through that savage maze.

Harvesters still moved among the sunken and hollowed remains of the bodies, in and out of sleeves and collars, waist bands, the bulges of their thick shells occasionally animating a trouser leg or crotch from the underside, constant as the sound of their feast.

There had been women here. We didn't say anything, didn't need to. Each of us knew what the others thought about.

Most of the bodies hung upside down, those with heads arched their necks backward, chins petulantly angled like hell-trained magnets at the ground. Men and children, adorned, every one of them, with stained stakes or arrow shafts. Every one of them had been stripped of their clothing, rendered hairless and neutered, bellies laid open, the red-black domes of their naked skulls congealing in the dry heat. One of the structures held the remains of two boys and the carcass of a dog that had been skinned from ears to paw.

We rode.

"There might be something we could maybe use here," Griffin said.

Griffin nodded at a sloping shelter fashioned out of the rubble and shards of a liquor store.

"We don't need anything that bad," I said.

There was an old paved road that carried other movement through the community at one time. The horses walked easily on it where it rose level and dark from the ashy ground. It led away from the graveyard of stilts and climbed, line straight, up to the blackness of the craggy mountains north of us.

"Who knows what's up there?" Ben said. He stopped his horse and turned around to face us. "Anyone want to guess?"

Griffin played along. "A miracle."

Ben squinted. He saw something behind us, I could tell from the look on his face.

I turned around. A spotted white and black dog came following our horses from out of the ruin we'd left behind, hunching low as though it somehow made him invisible.

The dog came up, stopped ten feet behind us, and sat in the road, ears down, head lowered. He was a small thing, shin-high, maybe. He shivered, but not from any cold he could ever have known. Not here.

Griffin got down from his horse, pulled his pants away from his butt. When he moved closer to the dog, he curled up and slunk away down the road, nervously glancing back at the boy.

"We don't need a stupid dog hanging around us," Ben said.

Griffin's face showed his disappointment. "I never had a dog, I don't think."

He got back up onto his horse and we started off toward the mountains again. Griffin looked back and smiled. The dog followed along.

"I'm going to name him Spot," Griffin said.

Ben turned back and shook his head disapprovingly. "How're you feeling back there, Jack?"

"Okay," I said. "The little guy makes me feel good. It really works."

Ben said, "I don't know what we need with a dog and a ghost both, tagging along."

"I wasn't talking about the ghost." I grinned. "I was talking about Griffin."

"Shut up." Griffin laughed. Then he turned back and held his fingers out and said in a high and songlike voice, "Come on, boy."

"Stupid dog," Ben said.

"I wasn't talking to the dog, I was talking to Jack."

We laughed about that, all of us.

In the evening, seated high on our horses at the first ridge of mountains, we could see the flat of the desert clearly. But it was still impossible to tell who, if anyone, was following the trail we'd left.

Things grew here. It was cooler. The horses poked their sagging, leathery faces into the brush and ate. We hobbled them before nightfall when we found a small circle of clearing inside a rounded blind of something that looked like manzanita, and here we spread out our belongings and our weapons.

We sat facing one another. Ben and I took our boots off, moaning quietly. Griffin was barefoot, as usual. He'd been like that all day. Ben passed a water bottle around and began sorting out bits of the food we'd salvaged: a small can of sausages and a bag of peanuts. The dog hid behind Griffin, and every time the boy would go to pet him, the dog would expertly dodge his touch and move a few feet away, waiting.

Ben watched this, and just shook his head.

"I'll give him some of my food," Griffin said.

"You don't have to do that," Ben said. "I vote that we all feed the dog."

Then Ben looked at me.

I raised my hand. "Passed. We feed the dog."

I took my shirt off and folded it on the ground between my legs. I pressed a palm down over the bandage on my chest. It ached, but not just from the bite. I still couldn't get over the image of Conner, how he looked here in Marbury.

"Do you want me to change the medicine on that?" Griffin said.

"In the morning."

Ben gave a sausage to Griffin. "Here. See if he'll take it from you."

The dog wouldn't come close enough to take any food from Griffin. Eventually, Griffin left the scrap of meat on the ground next to his hand and said, "Good boy, Spot," when the dog finally came for it.

"At least *that thing* doesn't eat," Ben said.

I didn't realize Seth had been sitting beside me. He faded away into the brambles at Ben's dismissive words.

"He has helped me, you know," I said. "A few times."

"We helped him, too," Ben said. "We got him out of that cave. You ever seen what harvesters do to ghosts?"

I thought, tried to remember if I had or not. It was there, I knew it. Somewhere.

"I've been having a hard time remembering some things since I took that arrow."

I tried picturing Conner, the way I knew him. But I kept seeing the image of the devils that tried to kill me earlier that morning when I stood with the horses outside the train.

It couldn't be Conner.

"He told us you'd forget stuff. Henry did," Griffin said. "You think we don't know what's going on, Jack? You think he didn't tell us this would happen?"

Shaking in the brush. One of the amber-colored nuts fell from the spiny branches and rolled across the ground, coming to rest against my foot. Then it rolled back into the darkness, pushed along by an invisible hand.

Tap.

"Quit it, Seth," I said. "What did Henry tell you two?"

"He said you'd be different." Ben leaned forward where he sat, looking across at me. "He said he knew you from somewhere else, and he said that things were going to change about you."

"Is there any more food?" Griffin asked.

Ben fumbled around in one of his bags. "Hang on. There's candy."

"Candy?"

"Well?" I said. "Am I different?"

Twigs snapped in the brush. Three small sticks dropped onto my foot.

"Shhhhh . . . ," I said.

151

"What's he want?" Griffin said.

I shifted, tried to look for Seth in the dimness around us. "I don't know. Am I different?"

Ben tore open a small blue sack of candy. Skittles. "Here," he said, "hold out your hands."

And he poured the little colorful beads into our palms.

Griffin closed his eyes. "These are the best things I've ever tasted in my life."

I tapped his shoulder. "Have mine." And I put my candy into our little doctor's hand.

"See?" Ben said. "It's like that. You wouldn't have done that a week ago, Jack."

"Are there girls?" Griffin said.

I looked at him, didn't understand.

"Are there girls in the other place?"

"Yes."

"Are Ben and me there?"

"I don't know. I really hope you are. Henry told me you would be."

"Is it a nice place?"

I looked from Griffin to Ben. "No. It's the same as here."

"Can you tell us about it?" Ben asked.

I thought about Conner. Nickie. Freddie Horvath.

"I don't think I can, Ben. It doesn't matter, anyway."

Roll. Tap. Tap. Tap.

"Seth," I said.

"Shut the fuck up, goddamned ghost," Ben said.

More snapping of twigs. Then bits of stems fell from the sky, scattered onto my legs.

"I can tell you about him. The ghost," I said. I could see Seth's face, watching me from inside the brush behind Ben.

"Here," Ben said. He poured some more candy into Griffin's hand. "That's the last of it."

The dog inched in and sat beside Griffin. The boy gave him a little red piece of candy and stroked his hand one time along the dog's spine. I could see the little thing tensing up.

"Tell us about him," Griffin said.

"Okay," I said. "This is the first thing I learned about him. When I was in the cave. But it's not the beginning of his story, it's the middle. Somehow, it seems like it's the part he wants me to tell you."

"How do you know?" Ben asked.

I thought about Ben's question, but I wasn't certain I could explain the answer. There was something deep that connected me to Seth, but I couldn't quite understand it, or see the entire picture yet. And it wasn't how I imagined that being haunted by a ghost would be, like I'd seen in movies or read about in scary stories. To me, there was nothing scary about it at all, not in the way I was haunted by the echoes of what Freddie Horvath did.

And the first really vivid image I saw of Seth's life was of him and his father carrying a dead man's body out into a field. It was the turning point for Seth, the one that set his course along a path he could not escape.

Like me, putting on the glasses Henry had left behind that night at The Prince of Wales.

"It's . . . ," I began, and I had to think about it, how it felt. "When he helped me those times, it was like I could see everything about him. It's almost like I *am* him. There's no difference, and I can talk for him."

I helped Pa drag Uncle Teddy's body down from the floor of our wagon, the buckboard we used to haul firewood, and sometimes animals, in. He was really heavy, but I never had to carry a dead man before. I never even saw a dead person before Uncle Teddy. He hardly moved, too, he had stiffened up so much in the cool before morning; and half his blood must have been pooled out there all over the splintered wagon bed that just couldn't absorb it all.

Pa smoked a cigarette. It was impressive to me how he could smoke with no hands while we got Uncle Teddy over the side of the small ditch that ran along the road.

Uncle Teddy's shoe came off in my hand, and I just threw it down and tried my hardest to drag him by the cuffs on his jeans. I didn't want Pa to think I was weak.

Pa and I tried to get him into a culvert after Pa peeled back the wire grate that covered its end, but we found out that pushing a dead body was impossible, so we had to leave him with just the top of his head inside the pipe. Pa went back to the wagon to fetch the stuff he'd use to burn him.

Uncle Teddy wasn't my uncle. He wasn't related to either one of us at all, we just called him that ever since I knew him. But Pa wasn't my father, either. He's just the man who found me nine summers before, when I was seven years old and sleeping in the dirt along the side of the road one morning. So Pa took me home to live with him and Ma, and Davey and Hannah, who were like brother and sister to me, only a lot different, too. Especially Hannah.

"Are we going to be in trouble for this, Pa?"

"No, Seth. The only people who ever get in trouble have to get caught, first. And we ain't getting caught."

It was beginning to get light. I tried to stand where the smoke wouldn't blow on me, but it seemed like every way I went, that smoke would just circle around and get in my face like Uncle Teddy was trying to follow me.

Pa threw stove wood on top.

And Pa was wrong about things.

We did get caught.

Tap. Tap. Tap.

I stopped telling the story.

Griffin was asleep on his back, barefoot, his shirt pulled up out of his pants and twisted around him so it made him look just that much smaller. His dog was stretched out right alongside the boy's leg, but he kept his eyes open, watching me, watching Ben.

"What did they do to him?" Ben asked.

"The boy? Seth?" I said. "He got hanged."

"Oh." Ben had a softened look in his eyes. Maybe what I said meant something to him.

Then the bushes behind Ben shook violently, and we heard a kind of pained cry that made the dog sit up and growl.

"I won't say anymore," I said. Seth's dim ghost appeared, standing in the middle of the twisted branches, staring at me, his narrow hands, just faint breaths of fog, twisted around the spiny antlers of brush. "It's okay. I said enough."

Ben stretched his legs out. "Do you think we should take turns sleeping?"

"I think that would be a good idea," I said. "You go ahead, Ben. I'll be okay."

He didn't argue with that, put his head down on one of his bags, and rolled onto his side so he was facing toward Griffin.

It was easy enough to see them coming at night, anyway.

I got up from the ground. Seth was standing right next to me, so close I could feel a kind of warmth coming from him. I went to the edge of the clearing and looked out across the desert floor.

"Who are you?" I whispered.

And Seth said, "Nobody."

thirty-two

It always looked the same, always looked like death itself, the most terrifying part of the dream that wakes you up.

I saw them coming for us an hour later, a small sea of fiery red brands burning across the desert in the distance.

"Ben." I shook his shoulder, whispered, "Ben. They're coming."

Ben shot up, eyes wide, looking around. I could see he was trying to figure out where we were, what was going on.

"We have time," I said. "Get your shoes on. I'll wake up the kid."

Ben rubbed his eyes and walked across the dirt in his socks to the edge of our camp.

"There's not that many of 'em," he said.

"That's what I was thinking." I kneeled down beside Griffin. His dog ran off under the bushes to hide.

"Hey, Griff." I leaned into him and put my hand on his chest. "Griff. We gotta get up now."

Griffin slowly opened his eyes. He lay there motionless, on his back, all twisted up in those ill-fitting clothes, brow creased, con-fused, looking at me.

"Where's Ben?"

"He's right here," I said. "It's okay. We gotta get going, is all."

Higher up, before the white dawn spread over us, we found the place where we would make a stand against them. Griffin took the horses up a mile past the spot; and, afterwards, came running back, barefoot, no shirt, his guns flapping and tugging down the waist of his pants, the little dog trotting two steps behind him.

We stacked boxes of ammunition by the dozens, and had pre-loaded magazines for the handguns, all ready to go. I had two extra clips for the rifle attached to the sling, too. All we had to do was wait, but that was a painfully difficult thing.

Ben kept his eyes focused sharp on the rising wave of dust kicked up below us by the horses and wagons they inevitably pulled. They'd have to leave the wagons below; the mountain was too rocky for them to make it up to the height of our post.

"If we don't miss any of 'em, we probably won't even have to re-load a single clip. It looks like it's no bigger than a platoon," Ben said. "Fewer than the number we met the day we lost Henry and the rest of 'em. Maybe the same ones. Today'll be a different turn, though."

"There's a possibility they won't even find us, anyway," I said.

"Not with him here." Ben nodded at Seth, barely visible, crouching against the ground.

Harvesters followed ghosts. Even though they were slow, the bugs followed ghosts; and the devils followed the bugs.

Griffin peered out at the desert floor from behind a crooked ridge-line of broken granite, holding his gun pointed upward.

"They're still far away," he said. "Maybe that thing can get back inside you now, Jack."

"I don't know."

"Take your shirt off so I can fix that bandage, anyway," Griffin said.

"No. It's okay," I said.

"Don't fucking argue with me, Jack!" Griffin glared at me.

I sighed, put my rifle down, and slipped out of my shirt. Then I sat down on the ground in front of Griffin. We all had our jobs. I had to listen to the kid.

Ben kept watch.

"Lay down." Griffin opened the white first aid kit and squeezed some of that cold goo out onto the wounds above both sides of my hip. It hurt when he rubbed on them, and I thought that he was just trying to be a hard-ass to show me he could handle the job we'd given him. I was still bruised from front to back where that arrow had gone through my hide.

"This doesn't look good, Jack," he said.

"It's from all the riding. I'm okay. Really."

Then Griffin pulled the tape away from my chest. The gauze pad had stuck inside the wound, and I gasped in pain when he jerked it free. It smelled bad, was stained yellow. The dog sniffed at the bandage, and carried it off in his mouth when Griffin tossed it away from us.

He took another piece of gauze from the kit and lay it on my belly, then leaned over me and squeezed around the bite mark with his fingers.

"Fuck!" I instinctively pushed him away.

"It's full of pus, Jack."

Griffin wiped, squeezed again, wiped.

My eyes watered.

He turned his chin over his shoulder and said to Ben, "You ever hear of anyone getting bit by one of those pieces of shit?"

Conner is my best friend.

Ben just looked at us both and shook his head. "Is it bad?"

Griffin shrugged. Then he put some more antibiotic over the marks and used his thumb to smear it around. He looked right into my eyes, and I could tell he was sorry for pushing things a little too far with me, but he didn't need to say anything. "You gonna be all right, Jack?"

"It's okay, Griff."

Then I noticed that Seth had been watching me, hovering beyond Griffin's shoulder, and the boy just dissolved into a soft fog that swirled above my chest. Soon, I could feel every bit of him like warm jelly as he poured into me through each one of those toothmarks. It made me dizzy, like there was too much oxygen in my head, so I closed my eyes and lay there while Griffin finished taping a clean bandage in place.

And for just a half of a second, maybe less, I could see it all: the man Seth called Pa, Uncle Teddy, Hannah, and I could hear Conner's voice, too, saying something to me like he was far away, at the end of a dark tunnel.

I fell out of Marbury.

"Hey, numbnuts."

When I opened my eyes, I was standing under the shower. The light coming from beyond the doorway was the color of late afternoon. Conner stood, wearing a white shirt, slacks, an unknotted tie hanging from both sides of his collar, bouncing from foot to foot with wet socks in the middle of a puddle of water that pooled on the floor through the open glass shower door, saying something to me, holding my phone in one hand.

thirty-three

"Dude, are you fucking *high* or something? I said *Nickie's on the phone.*" Conner pulled the shower door wider, swinging it back through the bathroom's doorway. He put the phone back to his ear. "Nickie? Yeah. He's standing here naked, in the shower. Hang on just a second."

He waved the phone in front of me, teasingly, the look on his face an obvious confession that he'd been flirting with Nickie.

What else would I expect from Conner, anyway?

Then he flipped the phone around and snapped a picture of me.

That's what I'd expect.

"I'm going to hang up and send you something, Nickie. Give me ten seconds, babe." And he ran out of the bathroom.

"You're a fucking asshole, Conner."

Under the running water, I could hear my friend as he fell down and began laughing hysterically.

"Oh yeah, baby. And . . . send!" He laughed.

I shut the water off, closed my eyes. I stood there in the tub, dripping, rubbing my face with my palms.

Seth, take me back.

Fuck this place.

I have to go back. Ben and Griffin need me.

And in a flash of clarity, I came to the realization that it was Henry's glasses that opened my eyes onto Marbury, but that it was Seth who'd brought me back each time.

Think, Jack, think.

How long was I gone for this time?

The glasses.

Fuck! The glasses.

Seth!

"Fucking Seth," I said.

"What'd you say?" Conner called from the bedroom.

I wound a towel around my waist and stepped out of the bathroom.

Conner was flat on his back, on top of the bed, still laughing, mesmerized by the screen on my cell phone.

"She's gonna like that, Jack." And then he giggled, and added, "My bad, dude. I think I accidentally sent it to Stella, too."

"You are such an asshole."

"Just kidding, Jack." He wiped the wetness from his eyes. "But I did send it to Nickie."

I didn't care at the moment. The only thing I needed to do was find those goddamned glasses.

"Fuck!" I threw my backpack against the wall, scattering the contents in a debris field from the bed to the window.

"Hey," Conner said, his voice dropped to a soothing tone. "Dude. Take it easy. You know I'm just messing around."

I kicked my wet feet through my belongings, looking.

"Hey. Jack. I'm sorry."

"Fuck!" I bent over and felt around inside the pack. "It's not you, Con. I don't give a shit about the fucking picture."

The sock. At the bottom of the pack. I felt the glasses folded up inside my sock. Somehow I'd managed to put them back, to hide them from Conner. I exhaled in relief, wouldn't let go of them.

My towel fell off. I was standing in front of our open window completely naked. I picked up the towel and screened it in front of me, turning around. The clock showed that it was past six in the evening. On top of the bed, Conner was sitting on the shirt and tie that I must have been wearing earlier. He looked concerned, scared almost.

Why were we dressed up?

"What day is it?"

Conner sat up, scooted back on the bed slightly. He shut off my phone, and put it down on top of my dark blue dress pants.

"Dude. Are you okay, Jack?"

I saw the look on his face.

I'm scaring Conner.

Fuck you, Jack.

I deflated, sat down on the chair at the desk, put the glasses in my lap, and dropped my face into my hands.

"Fuck this shit," I said.

Conner got up, moved to the corner of the bed, and sat down right across from me.

"Jack. What's going on?"

"What day is it, Con?"

"Are you kidding me, Jack?"

"I wish I was."

"It's Thursday, Jack. We just got back from St. Atticus School. Thursday." He held the end of his tie up between two fingers. I remembered Wynn insisting we wear ties when we visited his old school. "We were going to change out of these things and go out."

Three days.

I didn't look up.

What the fuck happened to three days?

"Something's wrong with me, Con."

The nausea. I stood up, ran past Conner. I dropped to my knees at the toilet and began puking my guts out.

Freddie Horvath did something to my brain.

There's nothing I can do about it.

I don't want to do anything about it.

Fuck you, Jack.

"Jack? Jack!" Conner stood behind me. My knees, in a puddle of warm water on the slick floor, slipping out from under me.

Just like being born.

The trip of a lifetime.

"Jack? You're scaring the shit out of me, dude."

I must have looked ridiculous. Conner stepped away and came back carrying my towel. He draped it over me as I spit acid down into the bowl.

"Just get the fuck away from me, Conner. There's something wrong with me. I'm all fucked up. Just get the fuck away!"

I rested my forehead on the bridge of my arms. Shaking, I still held on to that sock and those goddamned glasses that were inside of it. I could hear Conner backing away from me.

"I'm sorry, Jack."

"I'm sorry, too, Con. I'm sorry, too."

I squeezed my eyes shut. I wanted to cry so bad at that instant. I could feel my eyes swelling up. But I'd never cried, and I didn't let myself do it then, either.

Breathe, Jack. Breathe.

"Is it really Thursday?"

"You're not fucking with me, are you?"

"No."

"Dude. You need to talk to me, Jack."

I nodded my head, but I didn't look at him.

And I didn't cry.

"I need to lay down."

Conner stepped out of my way as I passed him. He had this uncertain and terrified look on his face, like he was watching me do something really bad and couldn't stop me.

You've been doing something really bad, Jack, and nobody can stop it.

I got into the bed and pulled the sheet over me. I lay there on my side, facing the wall, just staring at it, my hand wrapped tightly around the glasses that I tucked under the wet pillow beneath my head.

The toilet flushed.

I heard the chair scooting across the wood floor. For a moment, I thought it was Seth again, but when I glanced down to the foot of the bed I saw that Conner was sitting there beside the wall with his hands on his knees, staring at me, like he was waiting for something.

"I can't remember anything, Con."

"Okay," he said. "But you remember who I am, right?"

"The last thing I remember is Monday. When we went out. I don't remember anything that happened after the fight."

"We didn't get in any fight."

"I did," I said. "After you went to sleep, I went back out. I got in a fight. I beat the crap out of this guy who's been following me around ever since I got here."

Conner said, "Is he a cop or a perv?"

"Neither. He's just fucking with me."

"You sure, Jack?"

"I'm not lying to you, Con." I cleared my throat. "Tell me what happened since Monday."

He scooted his chair closer to me, and almost whispered, "Really?"

I looked right at Conner. "Yeah."

He sighed. "I'll be honest, Jack. I don't remember going to bed on Monday night, either. I hope it was good for you, too, Jack."

He tried smiling. Conner was always trying to make a joke out of everything.

Then he said, "Do you think you need help, bro?"

I knew what he meant. He thought I was going crazy. It didn't matter. I thought so, too. "I don't know."

Conner leaned forward.

"We woke up late on Tuesday. After noon. We ate. Went for a

164

run. Then we went all over the place by the Underground. Drank a couple beers. Pretty much the same as yesterday, only you and Nickie have been calling each other, like, every five minutes. And you told her we were coming out to Blackpool tomorrow, to hang out with her and her friend, so we'd all come back to London together this weekend. We already got bus tickets to do that. And we went to St. Atticus this morning. Do you remember that?"

I tried to remember.

"Did we take any pictures?"

"You mean besides the one I just sent to Nickie's phone?" Conner shoved my foot, smiled. When I didn't react at all, he said, "Dude, you really are fucking scaring me."

"It's not the first time this happened, Con, where I just kind of drop out and then come back and it's, like, later. But I've never been out of it for three days before."

I heard him inhale, deep, slowly.

"Where do you go when that happens to you?"

"You tell me."

"I'll get your camera," he said.

My phone buzzed on the bed next to me. I rolled over and grabbed it, looked at the screen.

Nickie.

thirty-four

"Now I can see why you warned me about your friend Conner." She laughed.

"Nickie. I am so embarrassed." I flipped Conner off, but he didn't notice. He was too busy trying to find my camera, digging around through the stuff I'd kicked all over the floor. Then I realized that I still didn't have any clothes on, and that made me feel really stupid.

"Actually, it's not at all an unflattering picture," Nickie said, and I could almost hear the smile in her voice. "Rachel thinks so, too."

"Oh God." I picked a towel up from the floor and wrapped it around my hips as I brushed past Conner. I went back into the bathroom. "What would you do if Rachel ever did something like that to you?"

"If she did that to me, I should think I'd get even with her by introducing her to Conner."

I fumbled through the folded and clean clothes on the bathroom's marble counter. I must have put them there, but couldn't remember doing it. I pulled a gray T-shirt down over my head and caught a glimpse of myself in the mirror.

Nickie made me smile.

Conner insisted I get dressed, said he was starving to death, and that he wasn't about to let me stay by myself in the hotel room, even though I pleaded with him to leave me alone. We found an Italian place that made plate-sized pizzas. Conner drank beer, and tried to talk me into having some, too, but I didn't want anything to do with that.

While we ate, he sat beside me and thumbed through the images we'd taken since Monday on my camera.

Some of the pictures seemed familiar to me as Conner narrated what we'd been doing — just like it did when I talked to Nickie on that first night — but three days was a big hole to fill up.

The last picture showed Conner and me, wearing white shirts and ties, leaning our shoulders together in front of the brilliant green of a school's soccer field.

We were smiling.

"Is any of this coming back to you, Jack?"

I sighed. "Kind of. Not really, though."

"Do you think the shit that Freddie guy gave you messed up your brain?"

Freddie Horvath did something to my brain and I need to get help.

"I don't know, Con. I think it did. Maybe."

I was nervous. I kept thinking about how I'd left those glasses wadded up under my pillow. I needed to get back to them, to keep them safe. I felt ashamed about it. And I kept looking around to see if Henry was still following me. I think Conner picked up on it, so I tried to relax and took an awkward drink of water. It made me cough.

I asked, "Well, did we like St. Atticus enough to want to spend a semester or two here this year?"

Conner shook his head. "I keep waiting for you to start laughing and tell me you're just shitting me, Jack."

I poked a finger at my food.

Not hungry.

"I think you seemed to like it a lot, but that's just 'cause you're, well, you know, so *Jack*. But, for me, well . . . I'm a tough sell on that whole boys-only thing."

That made me laugh. "You are so fucking weird and hung up on that shit, Conner."

Then Conner got serious. "I wish I could help you, Jack."

"Me too, Con."

"When we get back. You know, back to California. I'll go with you. We don't need to tell anyone else. So you can get this sorted out. Okay?"

He didn't know.

Nobody was going to help Jack.

167

At least not here.

So I said, "Okay."

"Sure you don't want a beer?"

"No thanks, Con. Go ahead and have another if you want. I'll get you home."

I waited.

I lay there in the dark. Occasionally, I'd turn my eyes toward the window, trying to be as quiet as I could, so I could listen to Conner — to see if he'd fallen asleep. It was making me crazy. I thought he was listening to me, too.

And those glasses felt like they were burning a hole through my pillow and straight into my head.

Sweating, I threw the covers off, looked out the window again.

"You okay, Jack?" Conner said.

"Fucked."

"Go to sleep."

"Sure."

I could feel him rolling over in the bed. I knew he was looking right at me, and I wished he would quit it and go to sleep.

Conner whispered, "I don't feel bad, or guilty, at all. I mean, about what happened to that guy."

I rolled away from him. I stared at the wall. "I don't want to talk about this, Con."

"Just think what he would have done to you. If you didn't get away, you wouldn't even be alive right now."

"So fucking what?"

"And what happened to him was an accident. No. It was his fault, and he would have done that same shit again to another kid as soon as he got the chance to. You know what they said about him — what they found — on the news. So, fuck you, Freddie."

"Okay."

"Say it."

"What?"

"Say, *Fuck you, Freddie.*"

It was hard to get the words out. I sounded weak. "Fuck you, Freddie."

"Louder."

"No. That's enough."

"I'm not going to let you do it, Jack."

"Do what?"

"Whatever fucked-up thing you're doing to hurt yourself."

"I'm not the one who's doing it."

"Then who is, bud?"

"Okay, Con. Good night."

I waited, and it finally came: the sound of a metal edge, each individual groove cut around the circumference, tumbling, turning one over the next, so faintly, near the wall, in the triangle of space between my leaning backpack and the windowsill. A coin.

Roll.

I held my breath, lifted my head from the pillow so I could look over at Conner. He slept.

Tap.

I slid my hand beneath the pillow. I felt relief like cool waves pouring over my body when my hand closed around the glasses that lay twisted inside that sock of mine. And I felt guilt, too.

We'll only just take one peek.

Tap.

Just one short second, Jack.

A second.

Tap.

I took them out, unfolded them.

But he'd been watching me.

"What the fuck is that?" Conner shot straight up in bed, like he'd been frightened awake from a nightmare.

My hands jerked. I nearly dropped the glasses, then I twisted in the covers and tried jamming my hand down under the bedsheet. But in that brief instant, I saw through them. Just a flash. I could see Griffin's face, how he looked, concerned and angry, as he kneeled over me and fixed that bandage to my chest. And all through the room there glowed a dim purple light, muted like the radiation from a television screen that had a blanket over it.

Tap. Tap. Tap.

The noise from behind the backpack came sharp, insistent.

Conner caught my wrist in his hand, squeezed tight.

"What the fuck *is* that?" he repeated.

I fumbled, wanted Conner to stop looking at me. "A mouse, I think."

"Not that. What's in your hand?"

Conner tried pulling my arm out from the covers.

"Let go, Con!"

"Did you see that shit? Let me see what that is."

I let the glasses go.

Tap. Tap.

I scooted over and covered them beneath my leg.

"What the fuck, Con? Let go of me."

When my hand came up, I pushed Conner away. I started to make a fist. We both sat there looking at each other. I knew I looked sick, was out of breath.

Tap.

"What's going on, Jack?"

"Shhhh . . ."

I took a deep breath.

Calm down, Jack.

"Did you see that shit?" Conner said. He turned toward me in the bed, crossing his legs and leaning into me. He was practically touching me. I could feel his warmth. He panted. "Show it to me."

"I can't."

"Did you see that shit? Let me see it."

Conner knew I was hiding something under my leg. He pushed me back, but I slipped my hand under myself and shoved the glasses behind me.

"Quit it, Con. Please."

"What is that thing?"

"It's . . ." What could I tell him? "Forget about it. It's not good."

"Let me see it. I want to see that shit again."

I squeezed the glasses tightly in my hand. Part of me wished I could crush them. Most of me didn't.

I pulled my knees up. "What did you see, Con?"

"Are you going to show whatever that thing is you got in your hand to me, or what?"

"Tell me what you saw, first."

Conner looked at me. The colorless rectangle of the window reflected in his eyes. He didn't blink. "It was a flash of something. Like a whole movie condensed into half a second, burning through two holes. Like eyes. It was white. I could see a bunch of people who looked like cavemen running around. And me. We were all practically naked. And we were eating by a fire, and it was like I was right there. I could taste it and feel it. It felt like being totally wild. And

171

the next thing I saw were all these nasty-looking bugs. It was fucking intense. Did you see it, Jack? Did you see that same shit? Was that some kind of a fucking dream?"

"No."

"What is it?"

I was terrified.

Please stay away from there, Con.

Don't do it.

"It's a mistake." I sighed. "Look. I'm going to ask you to do something for me, and I want you to make a promise you'll do it because we're friends. And we're not going to fight about it, okay? Will you promise?"

"I promise, Jack. You know I'd do anything for you. You don't have to ask. I'd never fight with you. You know that."

"Promise not to ever look at this again."

Then I pulled the glasses out from under the cover and I folded them shut. I held them in my palm and Conner just stared down at them. Into them. I knew he could see something. I watched him. I had my eyes right on his.

Neither one of us blinked.

"Look at me, Con."

He raised his eyes.

"What is that shit, Jack?"

"I don't know. But it's bad, and I'm going to get rid of it."

I slipped the glasses back inside my sock.

"Remember what you promised me, Conner."

Then I put my hand out to shake, and Conner took it, but he had an unsure look in his eyes. I'd known him too long for him to fool me about it.

I slid my hand back under the damp pillow and left the glasses there. I watched Conner while I did it. I saw his eyes follow the movement of my hand.

"Is this for real?" he asked. He just stared at the pillow.

"If you saw it, then that makes it real." I lay down and stared up at the ceiling. I folded my hands behind my head. "I thought I was crazy, but you saw it."

"What are you going to do?"

"I need to get rid of them," I said. "You don't understand. I need to get rid of them. I think I know what I need to do."

"Let me look at them again, Jack," he said. "Just for a second. Come on."

He tried to slide his hand under my pillow. I grabbed his shoulders and started to push him away, but I held him there and said, "You promised, Conner. You have to trust me. I don't want to fight you."

I loosened my grip on his shoulders. I don't know what I was thinking, because if he and I ever really fought, Conner would kill me. But he loosened up, too, and slid back over to the far side of the bed.

"I'm sorry, Jack," he said. "I'm sorry."

"Me too."

"What is that shit?"

"I think it might be hell. It fucks with you, Con."

"Is that what's wrong with you, Jack?"

"I think so," I said.

"You don't think it's going to fuck with me, do you?"

I thought, maybe, Conner sounded scared.

"No."

"Where'd they come from?"

"I don't know. The guy I beat up the other night. He left them for

173

me." I was burning up. Sweat beaded on my chest. "I need to get rid of them."

"Could I take one look?"

"You have to trust me."

"Can I?"

"No."

And when Conner went to sleep, I lost control.

Fuck you, Jack.

I eased out of bed so slowly, carefully, not making the slightest sound, the faintest ripple of movement. I carried the glasses into the bathroom.

My stomach was shaking, giddy, like being five years old and waking up in the dark before Christmas when you still believe that there is nothing anywhere that isn't good, and you need it all.

I was soaked in my own sweat. I folded the seat of the toilet down and sat there, trembling — and I was getting shocked again by Freddie Horvath, pale, damp in my underwear like some sick and palsied addict.

"Bring me back, Seth. Soon. Before he wakes up."

Tap. Tap. Tap.

Just for one second.

Just a peek.

I put them on.

Somewhere, I heard Conner, faintly knocking.

"Jack! Open the fucking door!"

Tap.

"Jack!"

Tap.

thirty-five

Tap.

The only captives they'd ever take were kept for food, or for worse things than that.

They were coming, close enough that I could hear the hooves when they slipped on fragments of rock, the grunts of riders, a cough. Griffin's dog cowered, shaking beneath a broken catalpa bough. We had picked our spots, stocked them with ammunition. It was time to separate.

"Let's be good, boys," I said. I stood between Griffin and Ben, and we put our arms around each other's shoulders and leaned in until our heads touched.

"Let's fuck them up," Griffin said.

And Ben squeezed hard and said, "They won't even know what hit 'em. And when we're finished, we'll have some more candy."

The kid flashed a smile.

"And whiskey," I said.

"What makes you think I took the whiskey?" Ben asked.

"I'll ride back if you didn't." And when Ben smiled, I said, "Shit, I'd walk back to that train for some whiskey if we make it out of this one."

And Ben said, "We're getting out, and you're not walking nowhere."

Griffin's position was at the point of our ambush line, perched on a granite ledge where he could belly out and see almost all the way down to the field of crosses below us. Ben and I flanked him, higher up but more exposed, about thirty yards off to each side of the boy.

"Make sure you just don't fucking shoot me," he'd told us before we left him.

The platoon came up through steep ravines, natural pathways between fractured rocks and patches of scrub brush, riding or walking two across. Maybe forty of them, I estimated, with crude and gore-stained weapons made from wood, hide, stone, jagged pieces of metal, glass, and bone. No women or children among them. The world was like this.

Just below the cocking mechanism on my rifle was the switch that set it to automatic. I clicked it over.

You haven't gotten away from anything.

Nearly every one of the men wore a codpiece of human hair, some were golden or white. A few of them were completely naked except for their own trophies and decorations: dried hands strung around their waists on cords of braided gut strand, useless car or house keys dangling from holes in their ears, anklets of teeth. Some grew spots along their sides, the older ones had hornlike spines of piss-colored bone jutting through calloused skin from their vertebrae and elbows, some tusklike, curled. And each of them had his own red brand that burned hot searing images into our eyes, even in the daytime, all different. I remembered seeing it on the morning of the day before: Conner's, small, shaped like a fish or an incomplete side-tilted figure 8, four inches below his belly, among the first pale strands of his pubic hair. I looked for him among the Hunters, but couldn't find him anywhere. I didn't want to.

I worried about it; so I scanned each of them, knowing that even at a distance I would recognize the way Conner Kirk carried himself. And they came, all black and white eyes, nearly close enough for me to see reflections of what they were looking at, looking for; so near to us that we all squeezed sweating fingers on the triggers of our guns, one in each of the boys' hands, and me with the rifle, waiting.

Waiting.

I watched as Griffin rolled away from his promontory; they were that close. He would let them pass, and our plan was that when Ben and I began firing at them, Griffin Goodrich would not let the first one of them back down from the mountain.

This was our mountain, we'd said.

As they ignorantly passed him, I thought that if that dog came running out, I'd have to start shooting. So I held steady, kept the apex of the rifle's pointed sight centered directly on the sternum of the rider at the front of the line.

I looked over at Ben. He was watching me, and nodded.

I shifted my eyes back onto the rifle sight.

The last of them, at the rear of the foot soldiers, a lone horseman who was missing an arm from just below his left elbow, passed Griffin's position.

At that moment, I suddenly became dizzy and cold. I ached everywhere, and realized my last sleep was two nights before, when we were on the train filled with mummified corpses. It was suddenly almost as though I didn't even have enough strength to hold up the weight of my rifle.

I turned my head, saw Ben waving at me. He motioned it was time.

I lowered my gun and Ben's signaling became more frantic. I knew he was wondering what I was waiting for. I saw Seth squatting against the rocky face of the ledge behind me. He was leaving.

"Seth," I whispered.

His voice was just a breath, out of sync with his mouth. "No, Jack. No. I have to leave."

It was because of the harvesters, I knew that.

And he disappeared.

Our pursuers were almost even with me and Ben. I sighted the first three of them down the barrel of my rifle. The one at the point rode a spotted white horse that wore a collar of human jawbones. It looked like he had black chaps covering his legs, but it was dozens of harvesters, just clinging to his naked skin in anticipation of some kind of reward, clicking their shells, buzzing their pale wings. Licking their chops. He was so close, I could smell him, shaved bald, his scalp patterned with zigzagging scars, each cheek pierced with black barbs that looked like cat whiskers. He was relaxed, balancing a crossbow with black-feathered arrows against his forearm, pointing upward from his crotch.

I could see his face clearly, and couldn't help but wonder if I knew him, had passed him, maybe, one day on a run in the park or eating breakfast at the pancake place Conner and I considered our hangout in Glenbrook.

When I pulled the trigger, the spray of bullets nearly cut him in two. It splashed warm crimson bits of him like pudding across the bare bellies of the next two riders in line. They didn't even have time to express shock. I shot them both in their faces, continued firing until the rifle's magazine clicked empty, and the horses at the front collapsed in wheezing and agonized cries, blocking the advance, rolling their eyes back and spouting mists of blood from their enraged nostrils as the column of unsuspecting demons froze in their tracks and stared, gape-jawed in terror as line after line of those in front fell in flailing and shocked heaps of gore.

Then I heard the heavier, more solid concussion of Ben's handguns firing while he carefully picked away at the ranks of Followers from the opposite side.

Panic.

Screams.

They'd never seen shit like this.

We were gods.

I ejected the magazine, reloaded.

Arrows came hissing their wind wakes over my head. A thrown hammer of some kind smashed into the granite rock face with enough force that I saw sparks fly at its impact. I stayed down, below the ridge, looked over at Ben as he calmly fired into the platoon. Already, one of the devils had scrambled up around Ben's position. He was smeared wet, had a loop of one of his comrade's intestines wrapped around his neck and armpits. It trailed away behind him to some indistinguishable spot lower on the mountain. He grasped a narrow pike with a barbed blade lashed to the end, and calmly raised it, pointing it down at Ben.

More arrows.

I heard another gun being fired: Griffin's. The survivors were trying to double back.

Without aiming, I shot across the lancer standing above Ben, taking his legs out from under him. He tumbled down the jagged rocks, absurdly waving his scarf of entrails behind him and dropping his spear on the way. He landed beside Ben, spraying blood from his shattered legs. He rolled himself on top of the boy, clawed at Ben's hair and back, slobbering with open mouth, trying to bite.

Ben grunted and rolled around beneath his attacker. He brought his .45 up into the thing's armpit and fired twice. I could see the wheezing mist that spouted from the opposite side of him. Ben pushed the corpse away and turned back over onto his belly, shooting, as though nothing had so much as distracted him, into the panicked and decimated platoon.

I raised myself up and fired again, making wide sweeping paths across the soldiers as they attempted to turn back. Following a trail of retreat that gravity painted for them in flowing red, they ran headlong into Griffin's ambush.

Standing now, Ben and I chased after the remaining devils.

Ben shot the last one in the back of the head, not ten feet from where the entire platoon had passed Griffin's position just a few minutes before.

It fell, facedown.

Then silence.

We were completely unmarked, but Ben's clothes were splattered all over with blood.

"They never seen shit like us," Ben said. "Never."

Griffin stood up, shoeless, his bare chest heaving in excitement, straining the fingers of his small ribs beneath his dusty skin, still holding guns in each of his hands, raised up above his head, and said, "Fuck yeah."

A ribbon of glossy black began winding up the face of the mountains toward us from below.

The harvesters were already coming.

"We need to check them all," I said. "There's one I need to find."

Conner.

Griffin and Ben holstered their guns.

"He has a mark on him like this."

I crossed extended index fingers and overlapped my hooked thumbs.

"Small, almost looks like the shape of a fish. Right here." I traced the mark just above my own crotch. "He's the one that bit me yesterday. I need to find him if he's here."

Griffin eyed me skeptically. "He's the one that you know his name."

I bent forward and turned the last one Ben killed face up. "Yeah."

"Okay, Jack. Okay," Ben said, but I could hear his heavy sigh as I stepped away from them and began looking over the next of the dead. And he said, "Come on, Griffin. This won't take more than a few minutes."

Griffin sighed. "Fuck 'em." Then he unbuttoned his fly, and started peeing on one of the bodies. Ben looked at the kid and shook his head, but Griffin argued, "Fuck 'em, Ben. This is for what they did to Henry, and all of us, too. Fuck 'em." And his little dog came out from beneath the brush where he'd been hiding, sniffed at Griffin's piss, and lifted a leg to celebrate on the same place.

"Good boy, Spot," he said.

A gunshot.

I spun around and saw Griffin, his pants still hanging open, standing over one of the soldiers with his gun pointed down.

"This one was still alive," he said. "And he's not your boy, Jack."

thirty-six

There were forty-two dead in all.

My friend was not among them.

Conner.

We checked every one of the corpses. Griffin's dog sniffed them all, one by one, as we moved together through the field of slaughter. It was disgusting, a waste.

"Let's get the horses, Jack," Ben said.

"Yeah."

Griffin finally holstered the gun he'd been carrying. He seemed to be hoping he'd get a chance to shoot another one. "I'm sore from riding," he said. "How much farther do we have to go?"

"Till we find someone else, Griff," I said. "Let's just try to get to the top of these mountains today, so we can see which way we want to go."

Every few minutes as we trudged up the slope to where Griffin had tied the horses, I'd stop and look back, trying to focus my eyes on anything that might show a sign that we were still being followed. It was stupid, though.

Of course they were still following us.

I could only hope that once the others came upon the massacre we'd left behind, they might decide to just leave these three boys alone.

The higher we climbed, the more the white air of Marbury cooled our skin. We even found a few large pools that had accumulated in the swayback basins of some large granite boulders. We let the horses drink from these, and Griffin laughed when the dog waded right out into the middle of them and tried to bite at his own reflection on the surface.

Ben and I went off to a clearing in the brush, where we stood and looked down along the path we'd followed. It was night, but there was still no sign that we were being hunted.

"You think we got some time?" Ben said.

"With these rocks like they are, I think maybe they won't be able to track us up here."

"You want to get going then?"

"Yeah. Let's get the kid and get back on it, Ben."

But when we got back to where the horses had been drinking, Griffin and his dog were gone.

I looked at Ben, then called out softly, "Griff? Griff?"

Ben said, "Maybe he's just taking a piss or something." He jerked. His hand went to his gun, and I saw something move beside me. I spun around and saw a tall man who looked back at us quickly and vanished into a haze.

A ghost.

"Fucking hate those things," Ben said.

"Just don't shoot me by mistake."

"Where's that skinny one of yours?"

"I don't know. He's gone," I said.

"Griff?" Ben was nervous. He kept his hand on the top of his holster.

I walked around to the other side of the water, and I could see Griffin's bare footprints, wet, heading away from us, along the ridge toward the east. There was a thin natural trail there, formed between the crooked spines of ponderosa trunks and branches, and I waved back at Ben. "I think he's gone this way."

Ben took a breath and followed me out through the trees.

And not more than thirty feet ahead of us, the dog began yelping; and Griffin called out, "Spot! Get back here! Let go! That's my dog!"

I cocked my rifle and ran in the direction of Griffin's cries.

"Griff!"

Ben followed, chasing behind me.

"Give him back!" Griffin howled angrily.

And when we'd caught up to where he was, we found the half-naked boy pulling on the skirt of a woman who had the dog wrapped

up in her arms, her fingers tightly clasped around the animal's struggling snout.

There were people here.

"Griff! Get back!" I yelled at him and pointed my gun at the
woman.

I can't say it was a strange sight, because nothing was stranger
than anything else in Marbury. But the woman was big, strong-
looking, with wild white-gray hair that flung away from her head as
she tried to shake free from Griffin. And she was dressed in a nun's
habit, her eyes crazed and desperate.

"Pierre!" she called out. "Pierre!"

"Mary!" A man came running toward us from farther off in the
brush.

Ben already had both his guns drawn, one pointed at the woman
with the dog, and the other aimed at the sound that came crashing
through the trees in the dark.

"Let go!" she said, tried kicking at Griffin.

"That dog is mine!"

"Hey!" I said. I wanted her to look at me, to see I held a gun. But
I wondered if she even knew what guns did. "Hey! Give the boy his
dog back!"

"We can share. Please. We can share," she said.

"You're not fucking eating my dog!" Griffin held on to her sleeve
and kicked her legs.

"Mary!" A man appeared behind them, holding a large, gnarled
club that had sharpened branch-spikes sticking from its end. He
raised it, but Griffin spun the woman between them, kicking her
again.

"Let go of my fucking dog!"

Ben raised his gun, pointed directly at the old man's chest.

184

"Don't shoot him, Ben!" I said.

I could tell Ben didn't know what to do. These were people. How long had it been since the boys had seen any people?

The man swiped his club at Griffin's back, but the boy was too quick. Still holding on to the woman's clothes, he dropped, attempting to use his weight to pull her down. He looked like a bug trying to tip a tree.

Then Ben raised both of his guns and fired them into the air above the man's head. Pierre, shocked and dumbfounded, dropped his club immediately and covered his eyes with his palms as the deafening report and white-yellow flame balls exploded from the barrels.

Everything froze in stillness.

Griffin let go of the woman, and looked around at the ground to see if anyone had fallen dead.

I gave Ben a disappointed look. We didn't need that noise, and he knew it.

"Shit," I said.

"There was nothing else I could do, Jack. That sonofabitch wouldda killed Griff."

The woman shuddered, still smothering the dog inside her arms. She sniffed at him hungrily. "Have mercy on us, please. I can cook. I can cook. Mercy! We can share, can't we? Surely you are men of God. And I can cook for you."

"You're not going to cook my fucking dog," Griffin insisted.

"Griff," I said, trying to calm him down. Griffin looked like he was ready to fight again. "Lady, put down the boy's dog."

Ben kept his guns pointed at the man, who still hid his face in his hands.

"They must be gods," he said, quivering.

185

"Devils. Devils," Mary said. Muddy tears streaked from the nun's eyes, but she glared at me defiantly and bent forward, dropping the dog at her feet. He took one failed snap at her dirty hand, then ran behind Griffin and hid, the hair on the back of his neck bristled like quills.

Griffin patted the dog and looked at the woman. "That's an old woman, isn't it, Jack."

"You are unkind heathens," Mary said, wiping her face. She sat on the ground and shook her head. "Cruel little devils with hidden brands. Pierre!"

The man lowered his hands and looked at us.

She snapped at the bent man. "Tell them! Tell them the truth!"

The man, stoop-backed and ancient, shrugged like he didn't understand what the woman was asking him to do.

Griffin stepped cautiously toward the seated woman. Carefully, he reached his fingers out and touched her cheek. "This is a woman," he said. Then he lowered his hand so he could cup the softness of her breast. And Mary slapped him across his face so hard it sounded like the crack of another gunshot. The swipe of her palm sent Griffin to the ground, and nearly knocked the skinny kid right out of his pants, his guns clattering noisily against the granite. Griffin launched himself back onto his feet and rushed at the woman, fist balled. He punched her squarely in the nose, and the nun flattened, face to the sky, on the rocky ground behind her.

The old woman began sobbing; and Pierre came rushing to her, stroking her crazed hair, moaning, "Mary, Mary! Look what the filthy and wicked will do to us!"

It looked like Griffin was getting ready to kick Pierre, too, so I swung my rifle behind me and grabbed the boy by his shoulder.

"That's enough, Griffin," I said. "You had it coming. I'll talk to you about it later."

And Griffin just stood there, staring at the pathetic couple, dazed and rubbing his cheek. I could tell he was genuinely mad about getting slapped like that, and I know he would have continued fighting both of them if I didn't hold him back.

And I believe that Griffin Goodrich had never cried about anything one time in his life.

"Please show some mercy," Pierre begged, his shaking hand patting the frantic woman's head. "We are hungry. She was only helping me look for food. Please let us go on."

The nun pinched her nostrils shut between bloodstained fingers.

Ben put his guns back in their holsters. "Are there any more of you up here?"

Pierre looked at me to answer. I thought he was most likely terrified of Ben's guns. "There are a few. It is an inconsiderable community."

"Fie!" Mary whined. "Fie! They are devils, Pierre. That dirty one raped me! Did you not see him? He raped me!"

The nun sat forward, her head hidden in the draping hammock of black between her knees. She clasped her hands above her and, rocking forward and back, began muttering a prayer in Latin.

"Where are the others?" I said.

"We see them," Pierre answered. "We see them here, there, sometimes. They hide well; we all must. Mary and Pierre, we hide always in the days. And with the ghosts. But we are good. We share our food, our kindness. It is all we have, if it is nothing but that."

"You're not eating my fucking dog," Griffin growled.

"Shhh . . . ," I said. "I vote we give them something to eat."

I raised my hand.

"They're crazy," Ben said.

Griffin stopped rubbing his face and raised his hand. "Let's feed them."

Ben showed his palm. "Well, okay, then."

"Listen to me," I said to the old man. "We are good, too. We have some food and will share it with you."

"Devils!" Mary said, her head still buried in her tunic.

"I'm sorry," Griffin said to her. "I didn't rape you. I don't think I ever saw a woman. At least, I don't remember it. I'm sorry."

"It's okay, Griff," I said. I turned to the man. "We're going to get you something to eat. We'll bring it back in just a minute. Trust me."

"Please," Pierre said. "Please."

With the dog leading the way, the three of us went back to the horses to get a few bits of food for the old couple. I took out two foil pouches of something that we'd taken from the soldiers on the train and slipped them into one of the pockets of my fatigues.

For just an instant I saw Seth, standing across the water puddles from us. He was so faint, it was like a blur on my eye. Then he was gone again, with his whispering sound, "Seth."

"We need to get ready to ride hard," I said. "I don't want to feel like we've led those Hunters up here, in case there are any more people around. We're going to need to go back on our own track and pick a different way over the top."

Ben said, "How much longer are we gonna keep this up?"

"As long as it takes, Ben. What do you want me to say?" I shook my head. Ben looked guilty, got up onto his horse. "You guys get ready. I'm going to give those two lunatics this stuff and I'll be right back."

"Jack," Griffin called out after me, his voice urgent and edgy. "Jack! One of my guns is gone."

Not more than five seconds later, as I was walking back to see if

Griffin had dropped it around the horses, we heard the sound of two shots coming from the direction where we'd left the old nun and the man.

I ran.

I looked back once, saw Griffin starting to dismount, and I yelled, "Do *not* follow me unless I call you!"

I stopped running when I came to the last few trees beside the clearing where Mary had caught Griffin's dog. I tried to control my breathing, to listen for any sounds.

Nothing.

I got down flat, onto my belly, pointing the rifle out in front of me, and slowly crawled forward.

Feet.

I saw their feet. Paired beside each other and pointed upward as though they were both lying together, watching in delusional awe the unremarkable Marbury sky.

I stood.

The nun still clutched Griffin's pistol. Pierre wheezed a bit of blood through his nose. His eyes were open, and there was a black, fizzing hole just above the tip of his right ear. The nun had shot herself in the chest, perhaps her own way of branding the part of her body the boy had touched in curiosity. Her teeth were showing, her mouth screwed back in an angry grimace.

I took the gun from her hand and walked back to the horses.

I held the barrel of the gun and handed it up to Griffin.

"Here. Be careful," I said. "The old man just about gave himself a heart attack when that gun went off in his hand."

"Are they okay?" Griffin asked.

"Yeah. I think they never had food as good as that we left for them. They said we were good, Griff."

We backtracked for two miles before choosing another path toward the summit. Griffin and Ben both seemed to be on the verge of falling asleep atop their horses, but they followed me anyway. And just before I turned my horse up between two thick stands of creosote, I looked down the dim face of the mountain and saw two winking red brands — just a flash, but they were there.

Two of them. Coming.

Then they were gone.

Maybe I was tired, too. Maybe I wasn't thinking clearly, or had started dreaming with my eyes open. No matter what it was, though, dream or real, I knew that one of the things coming up the mountain after us was Conner.

thirty-seven

"Open the fucking door, Jack!"

My hands jerk out, palms forward, ready to hit something.

A dream where I'm falling, trying to catch myself.

Fuck you, Jack.

My eyes focus. I'm sitting on the toilet.

Sweating. Everything is wet.

Oh yeah.

The door. I open it.

I'm sick as shit. I need to throw up.

Conner is standing above me. He's saying something.

"What the fuck are you doing, Jack?"

I say, "Huh?"

He's in his underwear.

Remember.

It's because we were asleep.

He's in his underwear and he's holding those purple glasses in his hands.

He's putting them on. I try to get my head down, twist around onto my knees so I can puke into the toilet.

I'm puking but I'm watching Conner's bare feet on the floor beside me.

He's just standing there.

I'm sorry. I'm sorry.

Don't leave, Con.

Please don't do it.

The bathroom door is open.

I picture that devil, slick with the bile and blood of his friend, a rope of guts twisted around his neck.

The nun and the man, staring up at nothing with relaxed, blank eyes.

I had to lie to the kid.

I had to.

I look up.

Conner has the fucking glasses on.

Fuck you, Jack.

"Con?" I raised myself up from the toilet and nearly fell into him.

"Con? Don't do this, man. Please."

Conner stood, motionless, his arms down at his sides, breathing so hard, like he was about to explode, or he'd been drowning. My hands shook when I reached out and pulled the glasses away from him. I didn't look at them, folded them blindly, and dumbly groped around the floor with my foot to find where I'd dropped the sock I used to hide them.

Conner had his eyes open, but I could tell that he wasn't really seeing me. He gripped the edge of the counter when he began tipping toward the sink. I pushed past him and wedged the glasses down inside the sleeve of my pack's frame. Conner wouldn't find them again, I thought.

I wouldn't let him.

"Con? Con?" I went back to the bathroom.

The water was running. Conner was bent over the sink with his head under the faucet.

"Conner!"

He raised his head up, dripping cold water everywhere. His eyes looked like ground hamburger meat.

"Jack?"

I could see he wasn't all there yet. Then he said, "What the —" and fell to his knees, catching himself on the toilet.

"I need to sit down, Jack. I need to sit down."

Then Conner threw up, too.

I was terrified, imagining the worst of what my friend might have seen; what he might know.

Okay, think, Jack. Think.

This time it wasn't Seth who brought you back here, it was Conner. And I must have done the same thing to Conner, too. How long was he in Marbury? A day? A month? Maybe just a flash.

Fuck!

Think!

He couldn't have been among those devils in the mountain ambush. If he was, he wouldn't be able to see anything. That's why Henry can't use the glasses anymore. You could be dead there, and not dead here. That's why I saw those people on the train to Heathrow.

That's why I saw Henry Hewitt's head nailed to a fucking wall, but I drank beer with him the other night.

I've got to get rid of those fucking glasses.

You can't.

Fuck you, Jack.

He finally started to calm down.

Conner sat with his back resting against the bathtub, elbow propped on the toilet, his legs straight out in a **V** on the wet floor.

Just like being born, Con.

How's it feel?

"You okay?"

"That was fucking insane, Jack."

"You're not insane, Conner."

"This is real, right?"

I could see how he pressed his fingers down onto the slick floor.

"Yeah."

"What about that other shit?"

"I don't know. You want to talk about it?"

"Fuck that shit, Jack. I don't ever want to see that shit again."

"Okay."

"You told me. I didn't listen."

"It's okay."

Conner bent his arm back and pushed himself up to his feet. He looked like he'd been beaten up or something. He looked small and weak, defeated, not like Conner Kirk at all.

"Will you have a beer with me, Jack?"

"Sure. Let's have a beer, Con."

thirty-eight

We caught the bus to Blackpool outside Victoria Station before eight in the morning. Neither of us slept much after the way we both fucked up the night before. We'd emptied the refrigerator bar of everything that had the least bit of alcohol in it, but it didn't help. I'm sure we both just lay there all night, wondering what the other saw, what he knew. We hardly spoke at all after Conner picked himself up from the floor in front of the toilet.

It would be a six-hour ride.

I called Nickie once the bus got out of the city. It was almost like I had to hear her voice just to prove that *this* was what was really happening, to know there was such a place called Blackpool, to be able to count on her meeting us there when our bus arrived in the afternoon.

I'd taken a picture of Conner on the bus with my cell phone and sent it to her with the text message: *this is a pic of conner. dont worry, he isnt naked for once in his life. its so rachel can see how ugly he is lol.* He leaned against the window, sleepy-eyed, wearing a black beanie that was pulled back at an angle on his head. His stringy, dishwater blond hair hung down over one eye, and he smiled a closemouthed grin that looked too much like he knew something. But it was a great picture of Conner because it really looked like him. The Conner from here.

Quit it, Jack.

You know you're not going to leave Griffin and Ben by themselves.

How long do you think you'll last before you have those goddamned glasses back in your hand?

194

How long till Conner asks where you're hiding them?

Conner cleared his throat and shifted in his seat. His knee bumped mine.

"Oh. Sorry," he said.

Conner would never say that to me.

Fuck this place.

I sighed. "Yeah. Whatever. I'm sorry, too, Con."

"What's that supposed to mean?"

"Are we just not gonna talk to each other anymore?"

A gray-haired woman sitting in front of us turned around and looked through the gap in the high seat-backs.

"Bullshit," Conner whispered.

"Yeah. Just like *Gary* in the airport toilet."

"You knew that guy's name?"

"He fucking sat next to me in business class," I said. "He tried hitting on me the whole time, invited me to come clubbing with him in London. Then the flight attendant felt sorry for me and upgraded me to first class after he tried to grab my nuts."

"Dude, why are you such a fag magnet?" Conner laughed.

"You tell me."

"So," he said, "which one of us is going to talk about it first?"

I felt myself going tense. I looked between the seats in front of us. The woman up there seemed to be ignoring us, but I kept my voice low and leaned over to my friend's side of the armrest. "You. Tell me about it."

Conner looked around, had a strange and guilty look on his face. It was weird and scary for me. I mean, here was this guy — my best friend, who I'd grown up with — and we both knew every minute detail about one another's lives. There were no secrets or embarrassed frailties between us. Conner Kirk wouldn't even bat an eye about me walking in on him having sex with his girlfriend — and then ask me to join them like it was no big deal at all, like I was strolling by and caught him in a pickup game of basketball or something.

But in that moment on the bus to Blackpool, while he began forming the words he'd use to tell me what he saw on the other side of the Marbury lens, my best friend looked frightened, embarrassed, and unsure of himself.

And I'd never seen Conner Kirk that way in my life, before that day.

"I keep thinking I'm nuts or something," he began. "Like it didn't happen."

"I know."

"How many times have you done it?"

I wasn't sure. I shrugged and shook my head.

Conner looked down at his knees. His fingers were twisted together, and he was gripping his hands so tightly that his nails turned white. "The longer I was there, I started remembering things about that place, and who I was. It was like filling in all these holes, like I knew this entire story that I never even saw before last night."

"How long were you there?"

"Two days."

"It wasn't even five seconds in the bathroom, Con."

"I don't get it, Jack. I was there for two days." He glanced out the window. "At first, it was like we were in a desert. It was night, but the sky wasn't completely dark, just a whitish gray. No stars. It was like some kind of foggy ceiling overhead, the way the sky looked. We made a big fire."

"Was I there?"

"You? No. You weren't there. But there were people that I knew. I knew their names and everything, but I'd never seen them before in my life." Conner released the grip on his hands and flattened his palms on his thighs. "It was like I said, like we were cavemen or something. Seemed like there were a hundred of us there, at least. A big wild party or something. Most of us didn't hardly have anything on at all. The girls were all totally naked, and the guys were, like, running around wearing just cups and nothing else."

He looked at me apologetically. "They were made out of scalps, Jack. I remembered that. Is that fucking crazy or what? Everyone was eating. We fucking killed a horse with a hammer and threw it on the fire to cook it. And we were eating a goddamned person, too, cooking him, pulling him apart. I ate it. Everyone did."

I could see he was scared when he told me. "It isn't here, Conner. It's something else. Something like hell."

"And we're different," Conner said. "Not really people. Our eyes are all messed up, solid black and white. Some of the guys have spots on their skin, and spikes growing out of their bodies. There's some fucking disease that's doing that to us, and everyone's got it."

Not everyone, Con.

"I remembered something about that," I said.

"And everyone's got these fiery designs from it, like tattoos or something, but they glow. I don't know what else to call them."

"Yours is right here." I pointed to the spot on my body where I'd seen Conner's mark. "Shaped kind of like this."

I drew the outline.

"You saw me?"

"Yes."

"When?"

"You can't remember?"

Conner just stared straight ahead. He shook his head.

"Where's yours at?"

"I don't know."

"I'm not going to lie, Jack," Conner said. "But I keep checking myself for that mark. I keep looking to see if it's there because that shit seemed so real."

"I got shot by an arrow," I said. "Right here."

I lifted up my T-shirt and pointed with my finger to the place on my skin where the arrow had gone through.

I twisted around. "In here, and out here. I almost died. I can't tell you how many times I keep looking at myself to see if that wound is there."

He leaned over and looked at my side, like he was trying to see some trace that I may have missed.

Conner shifted in his seat, his hands fidgeting. "And then that night, after we ate, there was this completely insane orgy, Jack. Everyone was just, like, having sex with everyone all over the place. It was wild. It went on all night, until we all just passed out in the dirt and slept like that. And I remembered thinking how fucking cool it was to live like this, and how I never wanted to come back because being there was so wild and fun. But I thought about you, and I remembered about being in London, too, but being there was so intense, and I wanted to stay there, like that, and make it last forever."

I remembered how Henry Hewitt asked what Marbury looked like to me. And I thought that for as long as Henry had owned the glasses, he'd probably had doubts about his own sanity, too. But I can't say, even now, if hearing Conner's description of Marbury made me feel any better about things, even if I was certain that we had both been in the same place, at the same time.

Conner rubbed his eyes. "It's like there's a war going on or something, isn't it?"

I nodded.

"In the morning, everything was white," Conner said. "Like being snow-blind, but it's a desert, and it was so fucking hot there. We were all following a group of our soldiers who had taken off ahead of us, but we were way behind because most of us were walking, and we had pregnant girls and little kids with us, too. But we were following them up into the mountains, these black, jagged mountains. And I was, like, one of the guys in charge. I remember that. I was important. After a few hours, we came to this place where there were all these bodies that had been nailed up to posts, and they were upside down. Most of them didn't have heads, or they'd been scalped, and the guys had their dicks and their balls cut out. And there were all these huge fucking black bugs eating the bodies. I could hear them chewing."

"Harvesters," I said.

Conner looked at me, his eyes wide. "Yeah. That's what we called them. You seen that shit, too, Jack?"

"Same shit, Con."

"We kept on going into the mountains. Just before the second night, we found the soldiers we'd been following. Every one of them had been killed, torn apart in some kind of attack. Forty-two of them, just massacred. There was blood and guts everywhere, and those bugs so thick on them we couldn't hardly tell what was left of any of them. Their horses, too. It was the worst thing I think I've ever seen, only I'm not sure that I really saw it. Then, next thing I knew, I was in the bathroom with my head under the sink and you were standing there trying to talk to me. And it was, like, two fucking days, but the last thing I remember was being in bed, and how we kind of had a fight, and then . . ."

"That's how it's been for me, too," I said. "Just like that."

199

"What about you? What did you see?"

I didn't know what to tell him.

Oh yeah, Con. We're, like, trying to kill each other, dude. You bit me, tried to chew a hole into my chest. And, by the way, I was one of the guys who slaughtered your buddies on the mountain. Yeah, Con. Same shit as you.

Oh. And that disease you have? Bad news about that, Con.

Fun game, isn't it?

So I lied. Again. How could I tell my only real friend the truth? "Same place. But there are only two other guys with me. Kids, basically. One's twelve and one's fourteen. Everyone else was killed."

"I don't want to see it again," Conner said.

That's what Jack said, too.

"You won't." I looked at his face. I knew he'd been telling me the truth — whatever that is. "And you don't remember seeing me at all when you were there?"

Conner shook his head. "What'd you do with those glasses?"

"Nothing."

"We should destroy them."

I can't.

I didn't answer him.

"You want me to tell you something, Con?"

"What?"

"There are ghosts there, too. One of them's been following me around. His name is Seth, and he's just a kid. But he's even been in our room at the hotel a couple times, so I know that place is real. And you heard him, too. I know it. He makes a kind of tapping noise on the floor when he comes."

Conner swallowed. I watched his Adam's apple jerk and relax. "Seems like I knew something about ghosts from there, but I can't remember."

"It's hard to remember things sometimes," I said. "But I know a lot about this boy."

"Like what?"

"I'll tell you something."

thirty-nine

Seth's Story [2]

Blake Mansfield found me sleeping in the ditch at the side of the road when I was seven years old. Well, we guessed I was seven. That May morning, he was hauling some calves and a pig he'd sold into Necker's Mill when he noticed me there and thought I'd been killed, so he stopped.

I was so small, he told me, he didn't even think I was a boy at all until he got down from the wagon and touched me. But for a pair of torn britches, I was naked and probably dirtier than the pig he was selling.

And I don't remember at all where I came from or how I got there on the side of the road that morning. It was too long ago, and I was too little. Ma used to make jokes about it; and said I was a monkey who fell out of the tree after my tail got plucked off by an owl, but Pa — that's what I came to call Mr. Mansfield — said I was too dirty to come from a tree, that I must have got dug up from the ground by a coyote, and it was only my luck, he said, that the coyote wouldn't eat me on account of how bad I smelled.

No matter, because Pa just took me up in that wagon and drove me in to Necker's Mill with him that day and introduced me as his son; and gave me the only name I ever knew, Seth.

So that was that.

I guess you could say that he saved my life, maybe, but I also know that I was cursed from that moment on, too. It doesn't matter. It was all worth it, in the long run. There's nothing that ever was better in my life, because I never loved anyone in this world before or after I fell in love with Blake's daughter, Hannah.

She was a year older than me, and her brother, Davey, was eleven when they took me in. And neither one of them ever so much as questioned or complained one time about my right to be a part of the family. That's just how the Mansfields were.

So whether I dropped out of a tree or got dug up from the mouth of hell itself, all I can remember of my life was that it started one perfectly blue day in spring, in the year 1878, on a farm in a place called Pope Valley, California.

The first thing Ma did when she saw me that day was hug me and kiss my dirty head like I was her own son who'd been away for some time. Then, with all of them standing by and asking questions, which I didn't answer because it took me some months before I even started talking at all, she took me out to the well house, stripped me naked, and threw my tattered pants to the dirt, saying they smelled so bad she didn't think fire would hold on to them. Then she gave me a bath in the coldest water I'd ever touched. Hannah and Davey laughed at that, but Ma scolded them that they'd be next in the tub if they didn't act respectable and kind around their new brother.

That hushed them both up, but Ma left me there, sitting naked in a leaky steel basin that I could tell was more of a horse trough than a bathtub, and went off into the farmhouse to fetch some of Davey's clothes for me to wear. But before she left me in their care, she warned Davey that if he teased me about anything and made me cry, she was fixing to give me the only britches he had, and he could get used to wearing a dress till she could make him some new ones.

That's how she was, always teasing us and making us laugh and worry at the same time, because being as tall as he was, and growing a foot a week, according to Pa, Davey had plenty of clothes that he'd managed to grow his way out of.

"Don't mind her, Seth," Davey said. "She never tells us nothing what ain't twisted around to keep us thinking and fretting."

I sat there shivering, not understanding at all what he was talking about.

"Poor boy. He's so cold, Davey," Hannah said. And then she came right over to me and started rubbing my back with her hands, up and down, from right between my shoulder blades up my neck and into my hair. At first, I was terrified of her, but the touch of that girl's hands on my bare skin soon made me feel so good I thought I'd never want to get out of that spot and put on clothes ever again.

At least, not until I saw the things Ma brought out of the house for me. Because after she dressed me from head to foot, and even with drawers and a pair of shoes that I promptly took off not more than five minutes later, I felt like I was a prince in a palace.

Pa rolled a cigarette and lit it while he judged my appearance.

"He looks like a regular Mansfield now," he said.

"Seth Mansfield. I guess that's a decent name," Davey confirmed.

Hannah helped me roll one of the cuffs on my new shirt. "He don't say nothing, Ma. Do you think he's a Russian?"

Ma waved her hand at Hannah. "He's just shy, I reckon. I'm sure he's got plenty of thoughts going on inside that little head of his."

Then she looked at Davey and said, "Why don't you take Seth out to the river and see if he ain't good at fishing, Davey?"

"Fishing or being the bait?" He laughed.

Then she gave me another kiss on the top of my head and a swat on my butt and shooed me along to follow the boy off. I glanced back at Hannah, and she kind of looked hurt and said, "Ma, I want to go, too."

"Let the boys be, Hannah."

Then Davey took off, running into the woods as fast as he could, and I was right behind, chasing him.

"How do you know all that stuff about him?"

"I don't know. I just do. But the weird thing about it was Wynn told me how the Whitmores came from Pope Valley, too. So when we get back to California, I'm going to look up and see if there ever was a family living there in 1878 named Mansfield."

I didn't tell Conner about how Seth could disappear inside me, and I could feel it when he did, how that had helped me heal when I'd been hurt in Marbury. And I didn't tell him that I was worried that Seth would be going away, too, and that I might not see him again. I knew that what he was doing for me was making him weaker, fainter, like he'd disappear.

"But I know a lot more stuff about him," I said. "Sometimes, I think he doesn't want me to tell it all. But sometimes, I feel like I have to."

forty

After we'd stopped for lunch, Conner leaned his head against the window and went to sleep for an hour. My phone buzzed in my pocket. Nickie sent a text message: *r says c is very handsome and thx vry for bringing him. heres a pic for him.*

Rachel, smiling on the beach, a pier and Ferris wheel in the background. She was barefoot, walking on wet sand with her shirt unbuttoned, so I could see the piercing at the top of her navel, and the cups of her heavy breasts in the bikini top she wore. Her skin was olive-colored, her hair hanging straight and spilling, slick, adhesive, like black oil over her shoulders.

I nudged Conner. "Hey. Look at this."

I held my phone in front of him and said, "That's Rachel."

Conner sat up like hot water had been poured on his lap. "I just totally got a boner, dude. Let me take your phone for a minute. I need to go to the bathroom."

My phone buzzed again.

hi jack

A picture of Nickie, laughing, the expanse of the beach spreading behind her, an enormous flat plain that seemed to stretch out to an ocean that was miles in the distance.

I texted her back: *call me.*

Within a minute, my phone was vibrating again. I looked at the screen. It wasn't Nickie.

"Hello?"

"Hello, Jack."

Henry.

"There's trouble, isn't there? I'm worried about you and the boys."

"No."

Quit it, Jack.

Silence.

He said, "I can help you, if you need me."

"No."

I looked at Conner, swallowed, and hung up.

"What was that?" Conner asked.

"Nothing."

The phone buzzed again.

"Yeah, right," Conner said. "Nothing."

I showed Conner the number on my phone. "It's that guy who left the glasses with me. I don't want to talk to him."

Still vibrating.

"Then give it to me." Conner snatched the phone from my hand and flipped it open. He said, "Hello?"

He waited. "There's no one there, Jack. Hello?"

There had to be someone there. I saw the number. This was real.

"Don't fucking call again, okay. Leave us alone, asshole."

I felt sick. Conner handed the phone to me.

"There wasn't anyone there," Conner said. He kept his eyes on me. I could tell he thought I was lying. Or crazy.

"It was him, Con."

"Maybe he's some kind of fucked-up cop or something. Maybe he knows what we did, Jack."

"He's not a cop. He can't be," I said.

"Well, he didn't say anything at all. I couldn't even hear breathing. I don't know what's wrong with you, Jack. There was no one on the fucking phone."

"Call it back," I said.

"What?"

"Call the fucking number back and see who it is."

Conner took the phone again, fumbled with the screen.

He listened.

"Okay. Here. Go ahead and tell me what you hear, Jack."

He handed the phone back to me. I looked at the display. The same number that showed when Henry called me.

There was nothing. No connection at all.

Nothing.

206

I closed the phone.

This is real.

Isn't it?

My voice was just above a whisper. "Sorry, Con."

I sank into my seat, shoved the phone into my pocket.

"Okay, so first, we really need to do something about those fucking glasses, Jack. I thought about it for a long time and I know that shit isn't real. If that guy's really doing this, then maybe he's trying to do some kind of fucking experiment on us to see how those things just fuck with people's brains. It's gotta be some kind of secret research or shit like that, but it is not real. So let's fucking throw that shit away."

It was amazing how simple Conner could make things sound sometimes, and how, once he made up his mind about solving a problem, that was it, and he wasn't going to consider anything else. I suppose those were some of the things I liked, and counted on, most about Conner Kirk, even if I couldn't ever be like that.

Fuck you, Jack.

"Yeah. You're right, Con. That shit can't be real."

The phone went off again.

I sighed, relieved.

Nickie.

The girls stood on the sidewalk, their bare feet showing in painted sandals, waiting for us as we stepped down from the bus, carrying our packs. Conner smiled and whispered, "That's what I'm talking about, Jack," when he saw them, and Nickie came right up and gave me a kiss on my mouth.

I saw Rachel give Conner a hug out of the corner of my eye, then she hugged me, too.

"Thanks so much for coming up to visit us. I think we're going to have a very fun time together," Nickie said.

"Do you think we'll be able to get a room at the same place you're staying?" I asked.

Nickie held my hand. "Come on, it's this way. And our room is big enough for the four of us. You and Conner have to stay with us."

Conner elbowed me. I dreaded that he was going to say something totally embarrassing, which he did. Thankfully, it was just a whisper in my ear.

"Massive hard-on, dude."

But there were only two beds in the room, and double beds, at that, much smaller than the king-size one Conner and I were stuck sharing in London. And Nickie made it clear which one of them was going to be the "boys' bed." Then she and Rachel stepped out into the hallway so Conner and I could change out of our clothes and into stuff for the beach.

And I already knew what Conner was thinking, so I said, "They're nice girls, Con. Don't screw this up."

All his clothes were off him and scattered at his feet, and Conner began digging through his pack for some shorts. "Yeah, we'll see how nice they are after we get them back here tonight. Besides, this bed is way too small for me and you both. I don't know if I can trust myself with you snuggled up against me in that micro sleeping bag."

"Well, you're going to have to try some self-control for once, Con." I pulled on some shorts and slipped my feet out of my socks and into my running shoes. "Maybe we could go run a few miles on the beach before dinner."

"And leave Rachel and Nickie alone? Just so we can go running? Dude, you *are* a homo."

I put on a fresh T-shirt. I was ready to go, and I noticed that Conner had his running flats on, too.

"Homo," I said, pointing at his shoes.

"Whatever. Anyway, I think we should activate Plan J as soon as the lights go out tonight."

"Okay," I said, knowing it was going to be something entirely ridiculous. "What's Plan J?"

Conner smiled wickedly. "About five minutes after we say good night to them and it's all dark and quiet, I'll yell at you, 'Jesus Christ, Jack! It is totally inappropriate for you to be jerking off right now with these girls in the room!' And so the girls will, like, feel sorry for the pathetic and horny American virgin I have to sleep with, and they'll offer to switch bedmates so they can give us both some righteously hot sympathy sex."

Conner started laughing.

I knew he wasn't serious, but I also knew that if I didn't say something, he'd probably actually try it.

"Con, you're my best friend, and you always will be my best friend, but if you pull anything that's even close to that, I will punch you in the fucking face without even thinking twice about it."

Then he laughed again.

Knocking on the door. I heard it creak open just a few inches, and then Rachel asked, "What's taking you guys so long?"

Conner started, "Jack's —"

I made a fist at chest level, and Conner finished his answer, "Jack's giving me a lecture about proper manners. Jeez!"

"You can come in, girls," I said. "We're ready to go."

forty-one

I took off my shoes and shirt and sat in the cool sand beside Nickie, facing out at the ocean, our knees bent up so our legs crossed over each other's and the brace of my left arm rested against her waist.

It was nice.

We could see Conner and Rachel walking nearer the water, toward the pier. They were laughing about something.

"They look as if they like each other," I said.

"What are you going to do? I mean, after the summer, Jack?" Nickie asked.

"I don't know. Go to school, I guess."

"Are you going to come back? To Kent?"

"Oh, I'll definitely come back. I don't know if I'll go to that school, though. I wouldn't want to go alone, and I don't know if Conner wants to do it. But I'm coming back."

"You like being in England?" she said.

I gulped. "I like hanging out with you."

"Kent isn't very far from London," she said. "I'd imagine if you were at St. Atticus, we'd see each other every weekend. I mean, if you wanted to. You'd always have friends."

"Will I?" I looked out at the water. "What do you see in me, Nickie?"

"Oh," she said, "I see someone, I think, who is very genuine and honest. And I believe that you are a young man who values his friendships more than anything. I can see that."

I felt myself turning red, so I lay back in the sand, and my head came down to rest on Conner's cast-off shoes. I pushed them away.

"I am so tired," I said. "I haven't really slept in two nights."

Nickie stretched out next to me. She lay on her side with her head propped in her hand so she was looking down at my face. Her breast was touching my left arm, and I thought she had to be aware of it. I froze, keeping perfectly still, hardly breathing. I think she sensed my tension.

"Have you and Conner been staying out all hours?"

When she said it, I couldn't help but think about the real reasons: Marbury, about Ben and Griffin, but there was something powerful, magnetic, in feeling her warmth beside me, and it kept me from drifting too far from that spot on the beach.

"I guess. Yeah."

"Well, we'll have you in early tonight, in that case. I promise."

"No. I'm okay." My voice cracked saying it, and I noticed that it made her smile.

Nickie was seventeen. She was smart, so must have known how nervous she made me. After all, I already confessed to her that I'd never even kissed a girl until that day we sat together in Regent's Park. She couldn't possibly be wondering, I thought, about whether or not I'd ever slept with a girl.

I hated being sixteen. It was worse than anything. For all the crap I'd ever read in "teen issue books" about the clumsy awkwardness of my age, how a guy's voice changes, how goofy we act, and how we are enslaved by embarrassing and involuntary bodily functions like wet dreams and unmanageable boners at the least convenient times, being sixteen was never comfortable, cool, or even remotely humorous for me. I couldn't stand having to deal with all this shit — guys who hit on me; guys who actually tried to rape me; my over-confident best friend who could have sex whenever he wanted it.

And now, here I was with this most incredible and brilliant girl, lying next to me, touching my skin, and at the same time, I was feeling like such a monumental failure.

I hated every imaginable thing there was about being a sixteen-year-old boy.

Fuck you, Jack.

Fuck you, Freddie. I killed you.

She moved, so that her eyes were straight above mine and her hair fell down on either side of my face. "Look at you," she said. "You look as though you're in another world, Jack. What are you thinking about?"

She put her arm across my body. Both of her breasts pressed into my bare chest.

I stared into her eyes, didn't blink.

"Sometimes I don't like being me, Nickie."

She sighed and rolled onto her back, lying beside me in the sand, staring up at the gray-bellied clouds above us. She held my hand.

"If you could be anyone else, who would you be?" she asked.

I thought about it for a few silent seconds.

"Griffin Goodrich," I said.

"Who's Griffin Goodrich?"

"He's just a kid I know."

"What is it about him that you admire?"

I squeezed her hand. "He's tough. He doesn't take shit from anyone. And he's not uptight or self-conscious about anything."

She turned back onto her side and put her hand flat on my belly, gently sweeping bits of sand away from my skin with her fingers. It felt better than anything.

"I believe you're all those things, too, Jack."

I wanted to kiss her so much, but I didn't.

"I think it's going to be quite a project for me to prove you're right," I said. "I want you to be right, Nickie."

"You two definitely should get a room." Conner appeared at my feet, smiling. He was holding Rachel's hand. "Oh, wait. We *do* have a room. Hey, I just got a daring idea concerning that particular room and the four of us."

I sat up and threw one of his shoes at him. "I got an idea, too. Time for our run." Then I looked at Nickie and said, "We'll meet you at the room in an hour or so. You can both get ready for dinner without Conner drooling all over the place."

I slipped my shoes onto my feet and began pushing Conner toward the packed wet sand. "Let's go."

The tide was out so far from shore, it was easy for me and Conner to run on the flat of the gray beach that seemed to stretch endlessly before us.

"What do you think?" I said.

Conner slapped my shoulder. "I can't believe that Jack actually scored this setup on his own. I have to say I have totally reconsidered my assessment of Jack Whitmore's sexual orientation."

"Asshole."

"Rachel is incredible," Conner said. "It's kind of scary, Jack, to be honest, because I've never really hung out with a girl who wasn't, well —" He trailed off.

"A slut?" I said.

"Basically. Yeah."

"What are you going to do about Dana?"

"There's a reason why my phone hasn't been ringing since I got here," Conner said. "I broke up with her the day before I left."

"Lucky you," I said.

Conner smiled. "My thoughts, exactly. I owe you. Big time."

"I'll remember that," I said. "I'm really thinking about coming back to do that semester here, Con. Maybe the whole year."

He reached his hand out to shake mine and said, "If you do, I'm in, too. I could put up with the boys-only and neckties-at-school bullshit as long as there's non-boys like Rachel to hang with afterwards."

"I'll give Wynn a call this weekend. Let's see how things go the next couple days."

"And get rid of those fucking glasses."

"Yeah. Done."

"I'm not kidding, Jack."

"Okay, Con."

I just kept lying to him. It was getting easier.

I sat with the girls and watched television while Conner took his shower. Predictably enough, he came out wrapped in nothing but a thin, sodden towel, dripping water all over the place. He opened his backpack.

"Sorry," he said, "I forgot to bring my clothes in there with me."

Then he lifted a pair of boxer briefs from his bag, shook them out, slid them onto his legs, and, just before pulling them up, he let the towel drop onto the floor around his feet. And he stood there like that in his underwear, after flashing everyone in the room, non-chalantly digging through socks and T-shirts, trying to choose what he'd wear for our date with the girls. I watched Nickie and Rachel, but they didn't react to the Conner show at all.

I didn't get it, how he could do stuff like that, because I was already feeling a little nervous and scared just thinking about bedtime and undressing in front of Nickie and Rachel, since, among all the things I'd never done, stripping down to nothing but my underwear in front of a girl was somewhere near the top of the list.

I rolled my eyes at Conner, picked up my pack, and went into the steamy bathroom.

I closed the door behind me.

The silence, the isolation, was sudden and overwhelming.

I knew it was starting to happen again.

You're a fucking liar, Jack.

You'd lie to your best friend, wouldn't you?

Something rolled around in the bottom of the tub.

I looked. A shampoo cap, spinning in a small circle like it was on some kind of track.

Not now. Please.

Roll. Tap. Tap. Tap.

Freddie Horvath did something to my brain and there's nothing I can do about it.

Fuck you, Jack.

You have to control yourself.

I sat down on the toilet. My body shook. Seth was signaling from somewhere I wanted to be so bad that I started feeling sick again.

What the fuck is wrong with me?

"No!" I whispered it aloud, urgent, pleading.

Maybe Jack should fill the tub.

Maybe he should fill it up and stick his head in it so he can end this shit.

I opened my backpack, tried to concentrate on picking out the clothes I'd change into, but my sick hands went straight for the glasses. I had to feel them, know that they were still there, tucked safely away along the metal framing inside the pack. Maybe I could just put my finger on the lens. Just a touch. I had to know they were still there.

Quit it, Jack.

I begged myself, Seth, whoever. "No!"

I hammered my fists down into my thighs. I stripped naked, shaking, stood in the tub, turned the shower on full cold.

Cold, like Ma giving me a bath in the well water.

Quit it, Seth.

Roll. Tap. Tap. Tap.

Come on, Jack. It's only going to be for a second.

Come on.

"No! Please!"

It's too easy.

Sitting in the bottom of the tub.

Shivering.

The water rains loudly down, spatters against the tiles on the wall, the white porcelain of the tub, my cold skin.

My hand touches the glasses.

I slip them on.

Just for a second, Seth.

Please.

forty-two

Once our horses made it to the top of the mountain range, the air became damp, and fanned us with a constant breeze from the west. It felt like there was an ocean out there, I thought, even though all we could see was the constant white haze that made the horizon vanish as though we were riding toward the end of the world.

And the end of the world was constantly receding away from us, tempting us: *You'll have to try harder if you want out of Marbury.*

On the other side of the divide we found more water. Things grew here.

It had been two days since the ambush of the soldiers in the pass, and we all shared a tenuous confidence that, maybe, we were no longer being pursued. All three of us were weary and sore from the riding, so when we found a suitable place in the basin of a flat canyon, we agreed to settle in and camp for at least a day, so we could rest the horses and think about our next steps.

The shape of the canyon followed the bending path of a wide stream. There were thick stands of cottonwood and willow along the banks, and signs that game lived here, too. It was the most decent place any of us could remember seeing, but we also knew that we couldn't stay here by ourselves for too long.

We had to keep moving.

There would always be more Hunters.

We kept the horses on lines that were long enough to allow them to eat and drink. Ben unloaded the bags, still full of what we'd taken from the train. We hadn't stopped for rest or food for more than a few hours at a time since the ambush. Griffin, barefoot as always, scrambled to the riverbank, stripped off his guns and pants, and jumped into the water while the dog, eyeing him, stuck trembling forepaws into the stream and yipped confused and pleading cries at the boy.

Ben unhooked his gun belt and sat next to me. We leaned our backs against a smooth and split-trunked cottonwood, facing out toward the river so we could watch Griffin while he swam and thrashed in the water.

"I could fall asleep right here," I said.

"I'm not going to lie, Jack, this is about the nicest place I ever seen in my life, I think."

"Yeah."

Beyond those tall mountains, in the colorless world of Marbury, we had stumbled into something green and alive, if only pale and temporary.

I watched as Griffin's head disappeared beneath the slate surface of the river, counted silently to myself, and saw him pop up again, fifty feet downstream. The anguished dog howled at him, but Griffin laughed and slapped rooster tails from the water. He spit a mouthful into the air and waved a scrawny arm at us. "Hey! Come on! You two stink like shit, anyhow! I never seen water like this. Ever!"

"Give us a minute, Griff," I said.

I unlaced my boots and pulled my socks off.

"You know, I really did bring that bottle of whiskey along," Ben said. "You think we should have some?"

"I don't know."

"We came a long way. Henry would be proud of what you did."

"Would he?"

"It's like he said. I don't know why, but he did say it. You really don't remember, do you?"

"Not too good," I said.

"Well, you were like his son, Jack. His favorite. He trusted you more than anyone in the world."

"I wish he never did."

"He always said that you were the same as him. That you both came from the same sorry place. Don't you remember that?"

And I said, "What could possibly be sorrier than this?"

Suddenly Griffin began jumping and screaming. "A fish! I saw a fucking fish! Get a fucking gun, Ben, there's fucking fish in here!"

Ben and I laughed.

Ben took off his boots and socks, began emptying the pockets of his fatigues. "I guess we can wash our clothes out if we get in there with him. You know he's not gonna let us rest till we do, anyway." Then he gave me a confused look and said, "Do you shoot at fish?"

"You don't shoot fish," I said. "I can figure out a way to catch one, though. And maybe I'll have just a little bit of that whiskey, too."

Ben stood up and went over to the suitcase he'd tied into a saddle-bag, opened it, and looked across the shore at Griffin, who had his eyes pinned down on the surface of the water like a cat that had cornered the prey he'd been stalking.

"Don't shoot nothing, Griffin," he said. "We're coming in with you in just a minute. And get over there and empty your pockets out, too, so you can wash your pants!"

There were some bullets in my pockets. I took off my gun belt and lay my knife down beside it. Then I pulled out the foil pouches of food that I'd intended to give the nun and that crazy man two nights before. Ben saw them.

"You didn't give them the food," he said. It wasn't a question.

"No."

"It's good you didn't say nothing to the kid."

The water was good, the only pure and refreshing thing I'd run across since that first day in this place when I found Henry Hewitt's head staked to a wall. From where I stood, waist-deep in the middle of the stream, I could see Seth, waiting in the spot where Ben and I left the half-filled whiskey bottle, just watching us as we swam or chased each other. But when I looked at him again, he flattened out and disappeared beneath the trees.

And I felt so certain then that Seth was going away.

So we washed all our clothes, but the bloodstains on Ben's pants left permanent black splotches; and when we were all tired in the water, I promised to show the boys how to fish.

Using a hook I'd made out of a safety pin that I tied to thread from Griffin's first aid kit, and with nothing more than a piece of a white medical cotton ball as our bait, we caught two fish. I cut them up with my knife and we sat naked on the shore and ate the meat raw while our clothes hung on willow limbs, drying in the heat of the afternoon.

Neither of the boys had ever tasted fish before, and Griffin said he preferred it to candy.

"Could we live here?" he asked.

"I think we haven't come far enough, Griff," I said. "We could stay here maybe a couple days and see how things go."

Ben threw a scrap over to Griffin's dog. "How far do we need to go?"

"I don't know. I think we're heading the right way, though. The air feels like there's an ocean if we keep going down country. We'll find people there. I have a feeling."

"Regular people," Ben said.

"Okay," Griffin said. "You been right so far, Jack. If we find people, maybe they'll be all kinds of 'em. Maybe they'll be some girls, too." Then he leaned over to look at the place on my chest where I'd been bitten. "That looks better now. Does it hurt anymore?"

"Itches."

"That's good."

The dog let out a bark. We all tensed, listening, watching, trying to get a sense of what was out there. He moaned a threatening growl and his ears shot up in twinned points.

Something was moving toward us from behind the trees.

Then I saw them.

There were two of the things out there.

They froze when the dog barked a second time, but I could clearly see the red blaze that showed through from one of their marks.

It was Conner.

Knocking.

The sound of the door latch turning.

"Dude, are you fucking sleeping in the tub?"

I opened my eyes, had to think about where I was.

Conner stood over me.

He reached into the stall and shut the water off.

"It's freezing cold, Jack. Were you doing that shit again?"

I touched my face. No glasses.

It was like I'd just bounced there. That's the only way to explain it: Marbury was getting more and more just like here. As easy as walking into another room. Changing a channel on the TV.

This is real.

You fucked up again, Jack.

I need to get back there.

"No, I . . . I . . ."

"Jack? Conner, is everything all right?" Nickie's voice from the other side of the door.

"He's okay," Conner said. "I think he fell asleep in the tub."

He looked pissed off.

I rubbed my face. It was coming again, the nausea, but I couldn't make my legs move.

Conner bent down, grabbed a hand tightly around my arm. It didn't feel helpful at all, not like Conner. It hurt me. He put his face right next to mine and whispered, "You were doing that shit again, weren't you?"

He tried pulling me up.

"No, Con. I swear, I . . . I fell asleep."

"Look at you. Your lips are fucking blue, Jack. Get up."

As soon as I straightened up, I leaned over the side of the tub and vomited into the toilet.

"You did it, didn't you?"

"No."

Where did I put those goddamned glasses?

Conner just looked at me and shook his head.

He knew I was lying to him.

You're a fucking liar, Jack.

"Get dressed, asshole," he said. "The girls are ready to leave."

Conner never sounded like that to me. It felt like I'd been punched in the face.

I deserved it, though.

Fuck you, Jack.

He threw a towel down over my head, and exhaled a disgusted sigh.

"You told me you'd get rid of those fucking things, Jack. Look what it's doing to you. Look at your fucking self!"

Then Conner left. He shut the door, but I could hear him on the other side as he told Nickie, "I don't know what's wrong with him. He fell asleep in the tub. He swears he's okay, and he'll be out in a minute."

I felt terrible, mostly for how I'd let Conner down, how he knew I was lying to him. He had to think that Jack didn't give a shit about him, that all I cared about was screwing my head up with those glasses.

I wiped my face with the towel. I looked so pale standing there, my muscles locked and quivering from the cold.

Tap. Tap. Tap.

No.

"Jack?"

It was Nickie, her hand rapping on the door.

I exhaled.

Fuck you, Jack.

It cracked open, and she peeked an eye in at me.

Nervously, I held the towel up in front of my belly. It hung loosely, a narrow drape between my knees.

"I'm sorry," she said. She ducked back behind the door like I'd scared her.

"It's okay." I twisted the towel's ends into a skirt around my waist.

"If you aren't feeling well, we can stay in," she said.

I felt like such an idiot. I looked down at my clothes, erupting from the top of my open pack. The door. My clothes. I didn't know what to do. I pulled the door open so she could see me.

"I'm okay. Really." I tried to smile. "Remember, I told you how tired I was. I just kind of dozed off, I think."

Nickie gazed straight into my eyes, her face showing a confident smile. Her eyes lowered, tracking down the length of my body, and she made no attempt to conceal her stare.

I was so embarrassed. My hand nervously clawed the knot at my hip as though I were somehow certain my cover was about to fall away. The look on her face made me feel so weak and out of control, and I was suddenly aware of something beginning to strain against the flimsy towel that hung doubtfully around my waist. I tried putting my left hand over the conspicuous bulge.

If I could have killed myself on the spot, I wouldn't have thought twice about doing it.

"Oh," she said, and there was a slight surprise to her tone. "Are these yours?"

Then she bent forward, her head so near my waist that I could feel the cool air that moved from her swinging hair onto the hand I kept pressed against my dick. Nickie reached down and picked up the glasses that were peeking out from beneath my discarded shorts on the bathroom floor.

"Groovy, Jack." She laughed. "Purple."

I nearly collapsed from the rush and confusion.

"No, Nickie —"

And I helplessly stood there, in sickened paralysis, one hand trying to hold down my irreconcilable penis, and the other keeping my towel in place, watching as she unfolded the glasses and slipped them onto her beautiful face.

"Nickie."

As she turned to look at me, I could see the lenses come to life, like they were blowing holes straight through Nickie's head, and lighting up another world.

The woods.

I can see Conner standing there.

And Griffin.

He's running from something. Fast, like he's afraid. He's naked and wet from swimming, his pants still hanging where we'd left our clothes on the quivering fingers of a willow tree.

Running.

Look away, Jack.

I reach up and put my hands on the frames.

"Come on, Nickie. Don't mess around."

As I pull them away, I see him.

Freddie Horvath.

He's there, too.

Freddie Horvath did something to my brain.

224

Help.

I could hear Griffin's voice, crying out.

He needs help.

Nickie smiled, a puzzled look creasing her eyebrows together. "Don't tell me you can actually see through those things, Jack."

"Um. Yeah." I brushed the towel down smooth over my crotch.

Nothing going on down there now after Jack saw that shit.

Then I folded the glasses up without looking at them again, wrapped them in a pair of underwear, stuffed them as far down into my pack as I could.

Freddie Horvath is there.

He saw me.

Griffin needs help.

I swallowed, straightened, made sure the towel would stay put. "Did you see through them?"

Nickie shrugged. "I couldn't see a thing. Pitch-black. Nothing."

I sighed. "Oh."

Relief.

Maybe.

"Now come on," she said, and rubbed her hand on my chest. "Rachel and I are starving. But you really should put on some trousers, or at the very least, something substantial enough to cover up . . . uh, your bumpy parts, Jack."

Then she smiled, winked at me, and whirled out of the bathroom.

part four

THE
MARBURY
LENS

forty-three

Let me tell you a few things about Jack.

My father's name is Mike Heath. Despite that, I was born John Wynn Whitmore IV, named for Amy's father, who goes by Wynn.

I've never seen Mike one time in my life. In fact, the only way I found out about him was by looking through one of Amy's old high school yearbooks. They didn't think to keep it from me.

Who'd have thought Little Jack would be so curious, anyway?

Mike Heath was in the same grade as Amy: eleventh in 1994, the year before Jack showed up on the floor between Amy's feet. He was a kid of few words, I guess. He wrote only *I love you, Ames* under his photograph. And when I saw that picture, it was like Jack was staring straight into a mirror. There could be no question at all as to paternity in the sad case of Jack Whitmore.

Mike was on the basketball team, tall and skinny — all kneecaps and elbows, just like his boy — and even though more than half the guys at Glenbrook High had short, perfectly groomed hair in 1994, Mike wore his the same way the son he carelessly sired would wear his own when he was in grade eleven, too: long enough to hang to his chin in a light brown wave that had just the slightest blond tips at the end. Mike even had the same crooked smile that Jack showed in his Glenbrook High School junior-class yearbook photo.

Gee, my dad.

Kind of chokes you up, doesn't it?

Fuck you, Jack.

And I found out that Mike moved to San Luis Obispo after he graduated. I looked him up regularly on the Internet. He still lived there. A couple times, I started to drive down there just so I could look at his face, maybe to get a glimpse at what Jack might look like in his thirties, but Conner always talked me out of it. I mean, why bother, anyway? It wasn't like I was going to bring the old glove and ball down and go throw a few with Dad at the park.

Yeah, and fuck you, too, Mike.

Amy never graduated from Glenbrook. Wynn and Stella sent her away as soon as Baby Jack splattered himself all over their nice kitchen floor. It didn't matter. They didn't need to tell me the story, anyway. Who couldn't guess that Mike dumped Amy's ass as soon as his lucky load of semen found a home that wasn't just another toilet — or some wadded tissue paper — in Amy's Jack Factory? And once my grandparents sent her away, they kept sending her, so Jack never saw his mommy, either.

By the time I was sixteen, Amy was living in Indonesia with an Australian artist who was a year older than Wynn.

Awww. Jack's mom.

Fuck you, Amy.

So, yeah, I hated them both: Mike and Amy. But I didn't hate Wynn and Stella. That was different. I didn't have any feelings for them at all. They might as well have been furniture or wallpaper, as far as Jack was concerned.

And saying it doesn't make me feel sorry for myself, either. It's just the way it was, and Jack had sixteen years to get used to it. In fact, to be honest, the only person I loved, in this world at least, was Conner. Griffin and Ben on that other side. And I believed I was starting to get those kinds of feelings for Nickie, too — and not just because she and I both noticed that she gave me a boner.

But Jack was fucking it up with Conner, and I could see myself easily letting it go that way with Nickie, too.

I didn't like that.

I didn't have any clue what I could do about it, either.

We ate Indonesian food that night in Blackpool, and went around the table telling our little autobiographies. I was not ashamed for talking about Mike Heath and Amy, and how much I hated them, especially because of how bad I felt about letting Conner down, how terrified I was for what was going on in Marbury, too. Of course, I'd left out the part about Griffin and Ben, and how Nickie made me get an erection just by looking at her, but I did stare Conner straight in the eye when I told him that he was the only person in the world I loved.

I know that mattered to him, too, because he didn't crack a Jack-is-gay joke about it, he only patted my hand on the table with his and looked kind of sorry when I'd said it. At least, I could tell without him saying it that he felt bad about calling me an asshole, even if I did deserve it.

"And then, something terrible happened to me about three weeks ago," I said. I looked down at all the little circles of food in front of us. "A man drugged me and kidnapped me and tried to rape me. He stripped me and tied me up for two days, and I guess you could say he tortured me, too. With a stun gun. But I got away from him. And sometimes, I still feel like all the drugs he shot into me have messed up my brain."

Freddie Horvath did something.

Conner bit his lip.

Nickie and Rachel alternately looked at each of us, trying to measure whether this was some kind of weird joke.

I took a drink of water. It felt like I was choking. "I'm sorry. I just wanted to see if I could say it. I never told anyone about it except Conner. And he saved my life. Look. This is where he tied me down."

I slid my chair back from the table and lifted my foot out of my shoe. I pulled my sock down so Nickie and Rachel could see the scar where Freddie had bound Jack to his bed. Nickie looked at me, and I could tell it hurt her to see that. Or maybe it was relief I saw on her face, like I had finally shown her something real about me, but I don't know. She put her fingers on the scar and stroked my ankle so softly. I could tell she knew that what I'd said was true. Then she kissed me on the side of my face and whispered, "You are very brave, Jack."

I cleared my throat. "There. Now it's Rachel's turn."

Rachel shifted uncomfortably, looked at each one of us. "I live near Harrogate with four younger brothers, my mother, and father, who is a doctor at a clinic in Leeds. I suppose my life is rather common. I enjoy visiting Nickie as often as possible. I have traveled to the States, but never to California and, until very recently, never cared much for American boys." Rachel laughed softly and covered Conner's hand.

Conner smiled. He always had this same expression when he was nervous. I never understood that about him: how being onstage made Conner self-conscious, but he was such a show-off around me. "I was born and grew up in Glenbrook. Jack was the first friend I ever had, and he's my best friend. I would do anything for him. And I love him."

Then he gave me a quick, serious glance and said, "We know everything there is to know about each other. Nothing is secret between me and Jack. We run cross-country together, drive the same kind of truck, pretty much we're like brothers, I think. My parents both work in real estate, and I love them, too."

He looked at me when he said that, but he had to know better than to worry for even a second that I'd take that as some kind of jab. I knew well enough how close Conner's family was.

"I have an older brother named Ryan who goes to Berkeley, so I'm the only kid at home," he said. "Oh, and I do not have a girlfriend, either, no matter what Jack says about me. And me and Jack talked it over, and we decided to come to school in Kent this year, too. Okay, Nickie's turn."

I already knew what she'd say. Her name was Nickie Stromberg, and her father worked for a shipping firm located in Stockholm, where the family kept a second home. "I have a younger brother, Ander. He's fifteen and plays football. He's very funny, and I know you would like him," she said. "I really hope you both come to England for your studies this year, as I believe I am really taken by one of you."

Nickie turned red when Conner asked, "Which one?"

Her hand brushed along my thigh and stayed there. It made me crazy. I'll admit it, I was positive that I wanted to have sex with her more than anything else on my mind at that exact moment. And when her hand moved toward my crotch, I figured something out, too, about Jack and sex: that I didn't want to be the same kind of asshole that Mike Heath was to Amy and me.

"There's one more biography I could tell," I said. Nickie's hand was curled under my leg, and I didn't want anyone to get any ideas about leaving the restaurant. My voice shook, and I tried to think of anything other than Nickie's hand. "It's a ghost story, about a kid who lived in California in the 1880s. His name was Seth Mansfield."

forty-four

SETH'S STORY [3]

In the summer of the year 1885, Uncle Teddy showed up one swel-
tering morning, walking past the farm like he knew where he was
going, heading in the direction of town. It was just past breakfast,
and I sat on the steps of the porch, watching while Hannah threw
scraps to the chickens, when I saw him standing there, holding a
bundle under his arm, like he was waiting for one of us to invite him
up to the house. Davey had been working at the mill, and Pa was already gone out to tend to our cows. And I must have been in a par-
ticularly guilt-ridden mood that day, because, at first, I swore my
eyes saw Uncle Teddy as the Devil himself, and I believed he was
on his way right up to the farmhouse to confront me and Hannah
about our wickedness.

He raised his hand and said, "Hello, children!"

Hannah set her bucket down at my feet. "I'll get Ma."

"I'll go down and just see if I can't make him keep walking."

"Seth," she scolded, and patted the top of my head when she
brushed past me and disappeared into the house.

By the time I was fourteen years of age, I only knew two things
that I believed were absolute and immutable truths: that Hannah
and I loved each other; and that one day we would live together as
husband and wife. She believed it, too, and we'd sneak away frequently and hide in the woods, or up in the haymow of Pa's barn, and
talk about it. And afterwards, we'd fondle each other and kiss with
our mouths open, slipping our hands inside one another's clothing

and getting dangerously close, at times, to doing the thing we both knew young folk our age shouldn't ever get caught doing.

I tried to make myself pure, to be good, and I knew it was wrong what me and Hannah did together, but every waking moment — and most of my dreams, too — were consumed by my fantasies concerning the next time we could be alone together.

Davey was eighteen then, and he knew well enough what his sister and I were doing, but he loved us both enough to keep a watchful eye out for Ma. All of us felt desperately guilty most of the time about that.

I tried reasoning about the consequences of what came to be an uncontrollable attraction between Hannah and me. There were times when I was convinced that Pa and Ma would welcome our union, but mostly — and especially on those occasions when Hannah and I would sit as brother and sister, ordered and neat in the pew of the church: Pa, Ma, Davey, Hannah, and me — I felt wicked and sinful for ever having such thoughts.

But then I felt even guiltier, in many ways, when the old minister fell ill and died at the end of winter, because it left Necker's Mill without a preacher, and it left me feeling relieved and unscrutinized by the Lord at least one day every week.

Uncle Teddy put his bag down next to his foot when he saw me coming down.

"What a fine-looking boy!" He smiled, and held out his hand for me to shake, but it was no proper handshake as I learned it. Uncle Teddy's was soft and wet, and I detected the sides of my mouth turning downward as I considered my degree of repulsion.

"I am the Reverend Theodore Markoe," he said. "Folks have always called me Uncle Teddy, though. Tell me, son, am I far from Necker's Mill?"

"Not far enough," I said, and thought I'd best reform my opinion of the man, since I could hear Hannah and Ma coming down the walk from the house.

And before I knew it, Ma was having me carry Uncle Teddy's bag up to the house so she could fix him breakfast, saying it would be an unkindness to allow a minister to walk all that distance in such heat without first giving him a proper meal. So she'd promised him that she'd see if Pa or Davey wouldn't be able to carry him the rest of his journey with our buckboard.

It wasn't difficult for the folks who lived around the mill to adjust to Uncle Teddy's Preterism. It was a popular version of Christianity in many communities across America at the time and, in many ways, added to a collective sense of relief in the minds of all us sinners that, as Uncle Teddy promised, "All things have been accomplished," and we were truly living in the glory days of heaven.

At least, I believed that was true every time I'd sneak off with Hannah.

The best I could do was put up with it, though, for there was no arguing with Ma and Pa about my intentions whenever Sundays came around. Davey set the best example of endurance when it came to sitting still in church, and instructed me at a young age how to concentrate on other distracting things, like hunting or fishing. But I will admit that I looked forward to the prayers most of all, because that's when we would all hold hands, which meant I got to touch Hannah's lovely fingers.

Hannah was every bit as wayward and corrupt in her thoughts as I. In the spring of that year, we'd celebrated my fourteenth birthday, as always, on the same day that Pa found me asleep in a muddy thicket of weeds. It was anyone's guess how old I truly was, but the Mansfields decided it was so that I should be one year younger than

Hannah on account of my scrawniness that day when Ma stripped me of the only garment I had on my body, sized me up, and gave me my first bath in the well. Still, by the time I was fourteen, I was half a head taller than Ma herself, and everything imaginable had begun changing about my outward features.

So it was on a day about a month after the preacher, Uncle Teddy, showed up at our front steps, that Davey and I had gone swimming in the river before supper, which was the only way we'd tolerate washing ourselves in summers due to the discomforting coolness of the water in the well house. Hannah had stolen away from the house and stayed hidden in the trees on the shore spying on us, which was daring and wicked of her since, naturally, neither Davey nor I had on the first stitch of clothing.

"David Ewan Mansfield!" she called out, sounding so commanding when she'd use our entire names. "Get your clothes on and get yourself up to the house. Ma's wanting you."

Davey stood next to me in the river, both of us up to our necks in the cool green water.

"What's she want me for?"

"I didn't ask her that!"

We started in for the shore and I hollered, "Hannah, turn your face."

"She didn't ask for you, only Davey."

Davey whispered under his breath, "Damn."

And that was a shocking thing for me to hear him say, so maybe, after all, it was a good thing in the long run that Uncle Teddy did show up to minister to us.

Once Davey had slipped into his britches, he dejectedly slung the rest of his clothes over one shoulder and disappeared among the reeds that lined our footpath from the shore.

I heard Hannah there, laughing.

"Davey's going to be ireful with me, Seth. Ma ain't even home at all."

"That's a wicked turn, Hannah. What'd you do that to Davey for?"

"'Cause I wanted to see you by myself." And she stepped out from behind the trees where she'd been hiding.

"Well," I said. "Do you want to come in the water?"

"No. You come out."

"Well, then turn your head."

"No."

"Then I ain't coming out," I said.

Hannah turned around and sat in the grass, and I watched her while she patiently waited for me to get my britches fastened.

"There," I said. "You can look at me."

Hannah held out her hand, and when I grabbed on to it, she pulled me down to sit beside her.

I sat there and just looked at her kind face, listening to the sleepy sounds of the water. I knew, unquestionably, that there was nobody in this world that I could ever feel closer to, or believe was more beautiful than Hannah as she sat there under the summer sky.

"What are you looking at?" she said.

I closed my eyes. "Do you think it's true, what Uncle Teddy says, that this is the final world? The world of all glory?"

"As long as you're here, Seth, I don't care to think about other days, not before nor after."

"Do you ever feel bad, Hannah?"

"Why? Do you?"

"Not about loving you. But I'm scared sometimes."

"I get lonesome for these times we can sit together, Seth."

I brushed her hair back from her face, and she blushed when I kissed her.

"I love you, Hannah."

She'd brought a book from the house, and she read to me as I lay on the grass and watched her, lulled by the beauty of her voice.

"Do you remember where we last read?"

"*The March*," I answered.

"*The March of Miles Standish*," she said, and found the passage inside her book.

After a long moment, Hannah stopped reading and looked at me. "We've already read this, Seth."

I smiled and touched her hand. "I like this part. The part with the Indians."

"I expect we'll never get to the wedding if we keep reading the passages regarding fighting and killing."

"Whose wedding?"

"Ours," she said. "Or might be mine and Brett Whitmore's if you don't beat him to it."

Like her Ma, Hannah enjoyed teasing Davey and me; and everyone knew how fond the Whitmore boy was of my Hannah.

"Brett Whitmore would make a fine husband," I teased back.

Hannah laughed and put her hand flat on my bare chest. At that instant, I was overcome by my frailty in her regard, and I pulled her onto me and, madly, found her mouth with my tongue.

That afternoon, there in the grass beside the river, Hannah and I did the thing we should never have done, the act we both recognized was inevitable. Afterwards, I stood behind her on the bank and watched while she squatted low at the water's edge with her skirt pulled up past her knees and washed between her legs.

"Did I hurt you?"

"A little bit."

"I'm sorry, Hannah."

"Don't be, Seth. I love you too much."

"I'm sorry."

And I was so consumed by my guilt and shame later that when we returned to the farmhouse I said nothing to her, but went directly to my room and prayed for both of us. I lied to Ma that I was feverish, and stayed in bed until the house was completely at rest. I bundled what clothes I could carry and stuffed them into a pillowcase, and I left the Mansfields' in the middle of that very night, convinced that if I stayed another day, I could only bring ruin to the family that loved me as one of their own.

I remember in the dark as I walked alone on the road, how I'd looked up and witnessed the fiercest display of the Perseids, and convinced myself that heaven itself wept tears of mourning for me and Hannah, and for my black soul.

In time, Ma and Hannah had become so distressed that Davey came looking for me.

A kid named Whitmore.

And I knew, remembered how Seth and I were connected.

"That's a lovely story, Jack," Rachel said. Her eyes gleamed in the dim candlelight.

"Very romantic," Nickie agreed. "Where is it from?"

"Do you believe in ghosts?"

Conner kicked my shin under the table. "He's joking around," he said. "It's just a common legend in the area where we grew up."

"Do they ever finally get to be together?" Nickie asked.

"Seth ran away to a city called Napa," I said. "Davey did find him there about four months later, in the wintertime."

"Come on, now," Conner said. "I think it's time for us to go dancing or something. Jack can save his bedtime stories for . . . well, bed-time."

Then he laughed.

I patted Nickie's hand. "I'll tell you more later."

"Promise?" she said.

"I do promise."

forty-five

We went dancing at a club after dinner, and by the time we got back into the hotel room, at two in the morning, we were all sweating and tired.

Nickie held my hand on the way home. We'd walked along the promenade and she rested her head on my shoulder and quietly asked me to tell her what was scaring me — why I was still afraid.

Well, it's like this, Nickie. He did something to my brain, and now I'm fucked up.

And I tried not to be ashamed, was glad for the quiet and the dark-ness, and I told her everything I could remember about those days up until I'd made it back to Conner's house. I even told her about how I believed I'd deserved it, and I'd even tried hurting myself afterwards, but I couldn't bring myself to tell her about how Freddie died.

Jack killed Freddie Horvath.

It wasn't about me, it was about Conner. I didn't need to drag him into this. Everything Conner had ever done, it seemed, he'd done for me; so the least I could do was just shut up about my best friend.

Nickie stopped walking. She sighed. The night was cool and I could just faintly hear the break of waves on the beach.

"What if I'm not the help you need?" she asked.

"It's not about that, Nickie."

"What happens if nobody can help you?"

She sounded frightened.

So I lied to her. "I'll get better."

Conner and Rachel were ahead of us. He stood, smiling, leaning against the open door of the hotel room as Nickie and I kissed one last time in the hallway.

And then everything kind of crashed into Jack all at once.

It was easy enough for me to keep my mind off things as long as we were out in the music and diversions of Blackpool, but as soon as the door shut us inside that quiet room, Jack felt panic setting in. I was scared about undressing in front of the girls, and that maybe I was driving Nickie away from me and there was nothing I could do about it. I knew Conner expected me to give the glasses to him. I worried, too, if Seth was going to start making noises. And I tried, unsuccessfully, to shut out those images that flashed from the other side of the Marbury lens: Griffin running in fear, crying for my help, and seeing Freddie Horvath was there, like he was waiting for me, hunting.

The distance, the gap, between here and there was narrowing into nothing.

Frustrated, I didn't say anything. I pulled a blanket and pillow from the "boys' bed" and threw them on the floor beneath the window.

"You can have the bed, Con. I'll sleep on the floor."

Shaking, terrified, keeping my eyes down like the act somehow made me invisible, I stripped down to my underwear as quickly as I could, before Conner even had a chance to say anything; then I wound myself up in my covers.

"Are you sure, Jack?"

"No worries, dude. I'm so tired, I could sleep in the tub again."

I shouldn't have said that.

I tried to pretend that I wasn't watching her, but I just couldn't take my eyes off Nickie as she slid her long slender legs out of her jeans and lifted her sweater over her head, standing there, right above me, wearing only a bra and panties.

Conner was completely unfazed by it, and casually tossed his clothes down onto the floor before swinging his legs up onto the bed. "Remember what we talked about, Jack. We can take care of it in the morning. Right?"

Of course I knew what he meant.

The glasses.

"Yeah. We will. Good night, Con. Good night, everyone. I had a great time tonight."

"Me too," Rachel said. "I especially liked your stories, Jack."

"Yes. You are beautiful." Nickie dropped down onto her knees beside me and told me good night. She put her mouth to mine, and it was the first time that Jack's tongue had ever tasted a girl's. And I knew that if she'd kissed me for about one second more that I would have completely lost control.

She flicked out the lights, but I silently watched the paleness of her legs, and Rachel's, too, as they climbed up into their bed. My heart was pounding so hard. Jack had never felt like this about another person. It was frightening. It was exciting.

I heard Conner's heavy breathing. He fell asleep as soon as the lights went out.

But as tired as I was, I still couldn't sleep. It was impossible for me to slow my mind down for one second from its back-and-forth bouncing: from Nickie to Conner to those goddamned glasses. And I wanted to get up from the floor so bad, so I could just dig them out of my pack and go back to Marbury, but I couldn't do that to

Conner, I decided. Or, maybe it was just that I was a coward, and knew he'd only find out and get pissed off at me again.

I rolled onto my side and stared out the window.

Fuck you, Jack.

Then I heard something moving, and thought, *Okay, it's going to happen again.*

Nickie.

She lifted the cover of my blanket up and slid her body along the floor and into my little bed.

I thought my heart would come out through my throat when she put her arm around me and pressed her warm lips against the back of my neck.

"Nickie," I whispered.

She didn't answer. Her hand rubbed my body. Down, she tracked along my belly and to my side.

I shook. "Nickie. I can't do this. I don't . . . know anything . . ."

Her hand tracked a circle over my heart, and as she pressed against me, I realized that she wasn't wearing anything. I could feel the points of her nipples rubbing against my back. She squeezed into me. I felt myself letting go, shaking everywhere, like there was an itch on every thrumming nerve ending in my body. But it felt so good. She hugged me tightly, her tongue lightly tasting my neck.

I never imagined this.

I couldn't want to be anywhere else.

"I never did anything like this," I whispered. It didn't sound like me. I was scared.

"I know." Her voice, just a warm breath in my ear.

Her hand slid across my belly again, fingers suddenly lifting up the waistband of my briefs, her warm hand slipping inside them and following the curve of my hip forward. And almost as soon as she grabbed me, Jack gave up trying to hold himself in; and everything, rushing, pouring out of me, so it felt like I was turning inside out, everywhere, inside my underwear, spilling all over Nickie's hand.

"Oh God, Nickie," I breathed. I was terrified and so embarrassed. "I'm sorry."

"Shhhh . . . ," she said, and kissed my ear, her fingertips smearing a trail of stickiness up over my belly.

I rolled onto my back and Nickie put her shoulder in my armpit so her hair fanned out over my chest. I was horrified at the mess I'd made all over us, in this bed on the floor, felt like someone had poured a quart of motor oil inside my boxer briefs, that were now drenched and plastered down to my skin. Nickie kissed me so softly.

I wished I could stay there forever.

In the dim light that fell on us through the uncovered window, Nickie and I made love two more times that night.

And finally, Jack slept.

forty-six

We woke just before noon.

Conner and Rachel had somehow ended up together in the "boys' bed."

So much for that assignation, I thought.

Nickie and I lay together, facing out at the gray sky on the other side of the window, twisted up in the one blanket I'd taken down onto the floor with me. I replayed in my mind what had happened to us there on the floor, felt embarrassed and foolish.

You're just like fucking Mike Heath, aren't you, Jack?

Like father, like son, asshole.

And Jack already felt the urgency, shaking, wondering if there was some way I could slip my hand inside my pack and just take the smallest peek through the glasses, just so I could see if Griffin was going to be okay, if Freddie Horvath really was there like I'd seen him in the bathroom before dinner.

I needed to.

And, in that need, I swear I heard something small rolling along the floor under the bed where Conner and Rachel lay together.

Something was wrong inside me. I felt sick, but in a way that scared me. It was getting worse.

Conner was the first of us alert enough to notice what had gone on in the room. He crawled over and looked down from the foot of the bed, and when he saw me and Nickie lying together, his face lit up and he said, "Holy shit! Do *not* fucking move!"

Then he jumped from the bed, pulled my cell phone out of its charger, opened it up, and, straddling the two of us with his long, hairy legs, began snapping pictures, announcing, "Jesus Christ! I am so proud of my Jack!"

I hid our faces behind the blanket, and Conner snapped one last picture of my extended middle finger, while, under the covers, Nickie kissed me and said, "Good morning."

"Well, now that we've got all this sorted out, I guess nobody's going to sleep on the floor tonight," Conner said.

Nickie peeked her head out, looked over at Rachel. "We've got to take Rachel back home to Harrogate today," she said. "Then, it's down to London for me, sorry to say."

Then Conner exhaled a deflated sigh and sat down on the bed. I grimaced and pulled my underwear on. Nickie wrapped our blanket under her arms, dragging the end along the floor as she made her way into the bathroom. I heard the shower running.

She called back, "Rachel, could you bring my things here, please?"

Rachel got out of bed. She wore Conner's T-shirt, and it hung down to the middle of her thighs.

"Good morning, Jack." She smiled at us, grabbed Nickie's bag, and shut the door to the bathroom behind her. We could hear them talking and laughing in there. I sat on the floor, my knees bent, still dizzy from the night before.

"Dude," Conner said, beaming. "You actually, finally, totally *did it.*"

He slapped my palm and I said, "Three times."

I felt myself turning red.

"God damn." Conner shook his head. "Me and Rachel only slept. That's it. We just fucking slept next to each other. How can that be? It's like I've reclaimed my virginity with one of the hottest girls on the planet. And now, she has to go home."

I smiled at him and shrugged my shoulders. "You want some pointers or something?"

"Shit." Conner collapsed backwards on the bed, moaning, his forearm across his eyes. "Three times? I must be sick."

I slapped his knee.

"Run on the beach while the girls get ready?" I asked.

And I wondered if he realized that I was just trying to distract him.

Conner grunted and pushed himself up. "Okay."

Once we'd gotten into our shorts, I sat beside him at the foot of the bed and we laced up our shoes. And even though I almost had convinced myself that we were going to avoid it, I also knew Conner. He never forgot things once he'd set his mind on them.

I felt like a thief, and I was trying to come up with some way of stealing from myself.

So my stomach knotted up when he cleared his throat and looked at me with a stern expression and said, "Okay. Let's take care of that shit now, Jack. Give me the glasses. I'm throwing them in the sea, dude."

Fuck you, Jack.

I rested my elbows on my knees, looked back once in the direction of the bathroom. The water was still running. The girls were in there, talking, laughing.

"I don't want you to do that yet, Con."

"Dude, you're going to fuck up your head. Your life."

Freddie Horvath.

Did something.

"You don't understand. Don't get sucked into it, Con. It's not what you think. You have to trust me. Leave it alone. Please."

Conner sighed. He pushed himself up from the bed and stood in front of the window, looking out at the flat of the beach.

"Fuck it," he said. Then he started emptying out the stuff from my pack. "You promised, Jack. You swore to me."

"Quit it, Conner."

Quit it, Jack.

Everything came out. He dropped it in a heap on the floor between us. I didn't know what to do: Here I was, watching my best friend as he tried to fuck with my life. I stood, thought about pushing him off my stuff when his hand came up, squeezing a balled-up pair of my underwear. And I could see the braided gold frames of the Marbury glasses that I'd twisted up inside of them.

I pleaded, "Conner, don't."

He's becoming my enemy here, too.

He's trying to kill me.

I tried grabbing his hand, and as I did, he pushed me away. It felt like a punch. I fell onto the bed and the glasses tumbled from Conner's grasp. And as they fell, spinning in the air, I saw flashes of

Marbury through them. The other side, shooting blazing white pictures at my eyes like spotlights in the night. Conner had to see it, too: Griffin running; me, chasing something through the woods. I could even hear the sounds of the brush snapping against my skin while I ran wildly, shouting, "Griffin! Griffin!"

And we saw Freddie Horvath there, too.

"Fuck that shit!" Conner kicked the glasses under the bed. "Don't look at that shit, Jack!"

I rolled over onto my stomach, tried reaching under the bed.

Just like you're back in bed at Freddie's house, isn't it, Jack?

All tucked in, Jack.

Conner slid beneath me, lying on his belly, his arm extended, sweeping across the floor.

"What are you two doing?" Rachel, smiling, had come out from the bathroom. "Are you wrestling?"

I tried grabbing at Conner's hair.

I wanted to fucking kill him.

I was mad enough to scream.

He straightened up onto his knees, gave Rachel an embarrassed grin, and said, "Nothing. Dropped something."

Then I saw him slip the glasses inside the brief liner in his running shorts.

He looked at me. There was almost a smile, a challenge, in his eyes, like he was saying, *Now what are you going to do, Jack? I won, it's over. Give up.*

You're dead.

Then he spun around, gave Rachel a kiss, and said, "We're going out for a quick run. We'll be back in twenty minutes, tops."

I chased after Conner as he pushed his way out the door.

He ran fast.

forty-seven

Let me tell you what Jack believes about friendship.

There was part of me — it sounded like a reasonable voice trying to talk while being smothered beneath a pillow, or maybe while drowning — and I knew deep down that what Conner did was out of love for me. The reasonable part of Jack knew this, but still, as I chased after him — across the street and onto the flat of the beach, running, running, all along the slithering reflection of the long North Pier toward the distant edge of black water beyond its end — a stiff middle finger that said, *Fuck you, Jack, this is the way to the end of the world, here you go, just keep running,* Jack's head was howling, *Fuck this shit.*

Conner didn't understand.

He was trying to save me, but it felt like he was killing me.

It felt like an arrow stabbing through my side.

How long ago did that happen?

"Conner! Wait a second!"

And he'd turn back and glance at me, without slowing his pace the least bit, holding those glasses tightly in his fist.

I needed them back. I had to go back to Marbury.

All I could feel was this unexplainable, desperate commitment to Griffin and Ben, two friends I'd never seen before but, somehow, I'd known forever; and, perhaps, a greater and more dreadful compulsion that drove me to need to reach some kind of final resolution between myself and my ghosts from the here and now — Conner, who I loved, and Freddie Horvath, who did something to my brain — and now I knew I was completely fucked.

If Conner got rid of them, I knew it would kill me. Here and there. *Fuck you, Jack.*

So, you have this ugly choice: Save yourself or save your friendship. It's why the shitheads who run things turn boys into soldiers: to us, the bond is more important — a flag, an officer, your teammate — the things that deserve our lives more than we deserve to hold on to them.

It's why Seth ran away from home.

It was why Conner was running away from me.

And it was why I needed to get back to Marbury, at least one more time. I needed to save them, and save Conner there, too. Even if it meant losing.

Run away from here.

Just once.

Just a peek.

"Conner!"

Fuck this place.

When Conner was nearly to the edge of the cold water, I caught him. I didn't want to fight, but I had to make him stop. So I leapt at him and wrapped my arms around his waist. He landed, face first in the salty mud with me on top of him.

And I don't believe Conner intended to hurt me, but he threw an elbow to get me off his back. It caught me in the mouth and split open my lip.

Groggy and out of breath, I raised myself onto my hands and knees, watching as my blood dripped, brilliantly, into the water. It painted a constellation in red on the sand between my spread fingers. The purple glasses had broken when we hit the ground. One lens lay flat atop the shallow slick of seawater, opening a coin-sized hole that showed downward into the white-hot hell of Marbury.

Conner got to his feet, soaked and covered in mud. He stared down into the lens, the twisted frames half-buried in the muck beside it.

"What the fuck, Jack?" he said.

It didn't sound like Conner.

I wiped across my mouth, swiping a red slash through the hairs on my forearm.

Then I saw Conner turn away from where he stood. With one hand, he scooped up the glasses and the dislodged lens and, no longer looking at them, threw the pieces out into the dark water.

A small wave came in and washed over his shoes and the tops of my hands.

The tide was coming.

At that moment, Jack gave up.

I dropped my head down into the mud. The water swept over my hair, into my eyes, and mouth.

It was over. I couldn't go back.

It was like the universe collapsed when Conner threw the glasses into the sea.

And now the tide was coming.

"Get up. Let me see you." Conner's hand rubbed my shoulder. "Get up, Jack."

I lifted my head from the water. I pulled the bottom of my T-shirt out of my shorts so I could wipe the last drops of blood from my face. A couple who'd been walking along the beach stood back, cautiously eyeing us, no doubt wondering if we were really fighting or just messing around like boys do, sometimes.

Neither one, I guess.

They turned away and kept walking after I stood up and gave them a dirty look.

Conner touched me, tried to get me to raise my face so he could look at what he'd done.

"I'm okay." I pushed his hand away.

"Who was that in there?"

I started walking back toward the beach. I wanted to go home, wherever that was. Jack was dead inside.

Conner followed, a step behind me. "Who was that, Jack?"

"I don't know what the fuck you're talking about."

"I saw you. It looked like you were running in some woods. And I saw that doctor guy, too. Freddie. I'm not lying. But the kid. He was screaming for you, Jack. I don't know who he was."

"Just a little kid. Griffin."

I kept walking, wouldn't look back at him.

"How do you know him?"

"I only know him from there. That's all."

"That kid was scared. He was scared and he was trying to run away from me, wasn't he?"

I kept walking. "It doesn't matter now."

We didn't talk to each other for the rest of the morning; and I felt like it, but I didn't cry.

Of course the girls knew that something had happened between us. My lip was busted open, and I wouldn't talk to, or even look at, my best friend. Conner and I just sat there, across from one another, sulking, facing out the train window on the three-hour ride into Harrogate. I pretended to sleep.

I tried to think of something else: about calling Wynn to tell him about St. Atticus; Nickie's touch on my skin; Freddie Horvath.

Freddie Horvath.

Fuck! Henry Hewitt; those fucking glasses; Nickie couldn't see anything in them; black; nothing.

She's dead there, that's why.

Like Henry.

Like everyone.

Like Griffin.

Fuck!

I couldn't bear thinking about Nickie *not being* in Marbury, because I knew what it meant. Maybe she was on that train, in a sleeper. Maybe she was hanging head down on a crucifix beside a liquor store.

Why did Conner do that to me?

It was making me sick.

Shaking and pale, holding on to the seats like a drunk as I passed them, I stumbled down the aisle to the toilet and threw up.

Welcome home, Jack.

And I stood there in front of the mirror, bracing myself on the steel sink with my arms locked against the rocking of the train. It felt like the whole universe was shaking apart beneath my feet. Everything was coming open, layer after layer, opening onto an image of a fucking kitchen floor and Little Jack.

Fun game, wasn't it?

I stared at my sick reflection in the mirror.

I looked like a crackhead.

I wanted to break something so badly, made a fist, and stopped myself from punching the glass.

I whispered, "Seth?"

Nothing.

A junkie, begging. "Seth? Please."

I ran the water and rinsed my face.

How could she see anything in me? I was hopeless and lost. I wasn't brave at all. And now I was acting like some desperate addict.

I'd do anything to get those fucking glasses back. I'd kill to get them back. I needed to see the end, to make the end come. But there was nothing I could do.

Don't let him turn into your enemy here, Jack.

You're dying.

I tried to get my head clear. Call home. My hand shook so badly I could barely open my phone. I thought I should try calling Wynn and Stella, didn't care what time it was there. I didn't care what time it was anywhere, except in Marbury.

Look at the photographs.

Jack flips through the pictures: Me and Nickie lying in bed together.

That was nice, wasn't it?

Do you remember that, Jack?

Jack's middle finger.

Fuck you, Conner.

Jack, naked in the shower in London.

The time when I came back from Marbury, and it was three days later.

Fuck you, Jack.

Wait.

Phone calls.

I look through the recent numbers.

There were those two calls yesterday morning.

Henry.

Jack calls.

"It's bad," I said.

"Where are you, Jack?"

"On a train. Fuck. I don't know. I'm on a fucking train somewhere."

I grabbed a piece of paper and wiped the sweat from my face.

Henry inhaled. He was smoking a cigarette. "Did something happen to Griffin and Ben?"

"I don't know."

"To you?"

"Something terrible is going to happen, Henry. I need to talk to you. I feel like I'm going to die."

"In Marbury?"

"No. Here. I feel like I'm going to die or something. And it's happening to me here. Right now."

He didn't say anything.

"I'm coming back to London. I need to talk to you. Tonight. I can be there at eleven," I said.

"I know where to go."

"Yeah."

Conner thinks you're crazy, Jack.

Freddie Horvath did something.

My hand shook. My stomach knotted. "I need to know one thing."

"What?"

"Tell me if it's real. Tell me if you're real, Henry."

He didn't say anything else.

"Henry? I'm sorry I fucked up."

I closed the phone.

When we got to Harrogate, Rachel said good-bye to me and Nickie. I was relieved when Conner walked her off, away from us. We sat in the lounge of the station and drank coffee, waiting for the next train to Leeds, where we'd catch another one down to King's Cross.

She covered my hand with hers. "Now, tell me what's going on, Jack."

I rubbed a hand across my eyes. I couldn't talk.

Nickie sat next to me. I felt her arm slide around my waist.

256

"Jack?"

I shrugged. "We got into a fight."

She flashed anger for an instant. "Did Conner hit you?"

"That part of it was an accident. It was my fault."

"What was it about, then?"

"Nothing," I said. But I could tell she was disappointed by my lame evasion. "Guy stuff. I wish it didn't happen. I feel like shit."

She put her hand on my leg. Suddenly, all I could think about was last night, being with her on the floor.

"I know how close you are. You and Conner will work things out."

"I don't know."

"Jack. I can't help you if you won't let me." I thought she sounded angry, frustrated. I couldn't fault her for it.

"God, Nickie." I pulled her into me so tightly and kissed her. I nearly tipped the small table over. I'd forgotten all about the cut on my lip until it hurt my mouth, and I recoiled from the pain. But Nickie held my face and kissed me so softly. And Jack howled inside because I could feel my eyes getting wet.

Jack doesn't cry.

"I'm sorry if that hurt you," she said, and I saw her blush. "I've been waiting for you to kiss me all day."

"I've been waiting for me to do it, too," I said. "I don't know what's wrong with me. I feel like I'm losing my mind or something. All these things that have been happening to me in the last couple of days. I feel lost, Nickie. And it's scary."

"Will you promise me something?" she said.

"Yes."

"Promise me you'll tell someone about what happened with that doctor. Talk to somebody, Jack. You need to stop letting this thing hurt you."

"I know."

"Will you?"

"God, Nickie. I'm such a fucking failure. I bring this shit on myself." I sipped my coffee, but it wasn't what I wanted, wiped my mouth, my puffed lip. "I feel bad about what happened last night. I told myself I wasn't going to do that."

Nickie looked down. I sensed she was hurt, and I was sure I'd said the wrong thing, that she didn't understand what I meant.

"I don't want to fuck up the lives of people who don't deserve it. And I've never fought with Conner over anything before today." And then I said, "I don't want to be like Mike Heath."

"Then don't be like him," she said. "Remember, I told you I believed you were all those things you want to be."

"I'm scared about stuff I don't understand."

She said, "You know what I think about last night, Jack? Last night, being with you, was the best night in my life. Ever."

"All I want is to be with you," I lied.

You're a fucking liar, Jack.

The truth was that she was only *most* of what I wanted. "I really love you, Nickie."

"You do?" She smiled.

"Yeah." I looked at my shaking hands. "See what you did? How could I not be in love with you? And I don't want to screw up your life. I really don't."

I put my arm around her shoulders.

Then she kissed me and whispered, "Jack. I love you."

"But what happens to us next week when I have to go back home? I wish I could stay. I'm coming right back, Nickie. I promise."

You're never coming back, Jack.

Not here. Not Marbury.

Ever.

A chair slid out along the floor from the other side of the table. Conner, looking dejected, pissed-off maybe, sat down and sighed.

Nickie straightened herself and patted his hand. "Did Rachel ask you back, Conner?"

She smiled, already knew the answer.

"She wants to meet me in York for a day before Jack and I have to go home."

"You'll have a lovely time there," she said.

"Yeah," he answered. He looked at me, I could see him at the edge of my vision, but I kept my eyes fixed on my hand and the stained coffee cup vibrating on the table beside it. Conner cleared his throat. "The train to Leeds is sitting there. We can get on it now."

We stood up to leave, and Conner pulled my shoulder back so I would look at him. "Come on, Jack," his voice was low, like he didn't really want Nickie to hear what he was going to tell me. She caught on, and took a few steps away from us.

"I'm really sorry," he said. "Especially about hurting you. Please tell me that we're still friends."

He held his hand out to me.

"Yeah," I said.

I took his hand, but I felt dead.

And I felt even worse when I had to say good-bye to Nickie in the Tube station at King's Cross. She promised to meet us for lunch on Monday. Then she headed off to Hampstead, while Conner and I took a very quiet and lonely ride to Great Portland Street.

It was late when we got back into our hotel room, but there were nearly two hours to go before I'd have to leave to meet Henry.

Conner threw his pack down on the floor. I kicked off my shoes and sat on the bed.

"It seems like we've been gone a long time," he said.

"Yeah."

"You want to get something to eat?"

"I'm tired, Con."

He tried to joke, "After last night, I bet you are."

I didn't say anything.

"Well, you want a beer, then?"

I shrugged. "Okay. Sure."

Conner brought two bottles over from the refrigerator and handed one to me. He took off his shoes, sat on the bed, and leaned his shoulders against the headboard.

"Are we ever going to be friends again, or what?"

I sighed, a long exhaled breath. "Conner, we're still friends. I just feel sick about this. It's, like, hurting me. I can't explain it. Like I'm lost, and I don't know whether I'm really here or there."

"That's why it's a good thing I got rid of them, Jack. Listen to me. You are really here."

I looked at the beer in my hand. When I swallowed some, it felt like there were needles inside it.

Something's wrong with you, Jack.

"Don't you think that other place really exists?"

"No. You need to forget about it."

"But there's something I still needed to do. You shouldn't have fucking done that, Con. Fuck!"

Jack doesn't cry.

"I said I was sorry."

"I'll get over it. I just feel shitty. Weird." I emptied my beer. "I'll get over it. I got no choice. What else can I do, anyway? I'm going to sleep."

I got into bed and Conner turned out the lights.

Jack watched the clock.

Conner must have been awake the whole time, too, because half an hour later, when I got out of bed and started getting dressed, he asked, "What are you doing?"

"Nothing. I need to go outside for a minute."

"You want me to come?"

"No."

And as I was on my way out the door, Conner said, "When are you going to give me a fucking break, Jack?"

forty-eight

"I lost the fucking glasses."

I said it as soon as I sat down. He was holding a beer to his mouth and had another full pint waiting on the table for me. He jerked like he'd been punched when he heard me say it.

Henry took a drink. "How?"

"My friend, Conner. He threw them into the sea." I pushed my untouched beer across to him. "I don't want this, Henry. I feel sick. I feel really bad."

Henry shook his head.

"Your friend didn't look through them, then?"

"He did. But I don't think he really knows what's going on. I don't think he really understood about, you know, us. And them. At least, maybe not until this morning; but that's when he got rid of them."

"But he threw them away? You saw him do that?"

"Yes."

"Are you certain?"

I didn't say anything.

Henry shrugged. "I never thought anyone could do that once you've been there. He must be very strong."

"Is there anything I can do to get back there?"

"I wouldn't know. No."

My forearms lay flat on the table. I looked at them. I was shaking so bad, just like I was getting shocked again.

Fuck you, Jack.

"It feels like I left part of me there, like there's something that's been ripped out of my guts. I'm scared because it's getting worse. The hole. I feel like it's really going to kill me."

"That's what it's like."

"I need to go back."

"I can't help you, Jack. I don't know what to do."

"Why did you do this to me?" I slapped the table, sounded pathetic. "They said I was your best friend."

Freddie Horvath did something to my brain and I need to get help.

"Here," he said, and he pushed my beer back across the table toward me. "You should have some of this."

I picked up the glass and drank. I could feel the cool slick of the liquid descending into my body. Then it felt like I'd swallowed shards of glass, like I was being ripped apart from the inside.

Fun game.

Henry could see the pain I was in. "I'm very sorry, Jack."

"Everyone's saying that to me today. Fuck this place."

"Will you tell me about Marbury now? Will you tell me what's happened?"

So I talked about everything I saw there since the first time I fell into Marbury: the boys, how Griffin saved me, Seth, the train, the crucified people, the slaughter on the mountain pass, finding the river in the canyon on the other side. Henry listened, and quietly drank three pints of beer while I told him the story. After that first taste from my glass, I couldn't take another sip, kept feeling weaker and sicker. And telling him what happened made me want to go back there even more.

I've tried to reason it out in my mind countless times, but I never understood what it was, or what combination of things there were, that pulled so hard on me and made me want to go back to that hell. Henry understood, though. But Henry was off the hook, too, because he couldn't go back. And the more I talked to him about it, the more strongly I became convinced that Jack really was dying here.

I was going to die.

I didn't say anything to him about seeing Freddie Horvath in Marbury, or how Nickie had looked through the glasses and seen nothing at all. I didn't want to tell Henry the entire life story of Pathetic Jack. It made me feel somehow guilty, even betrayed, too, that he was supposed to have been my best friend in Marbury, but here, on this side of the lens, I didn't like him very much at all.

Why did I bother coming to see him? I knew he wasn't going to be able to help me, but I was desperate. And hopeless.

Henry must have seen that I was fading. Maybe I was only tired, but I had my head down and my eyes were shut. It hurt. He tapped my hand. "You saw the same ghost from Marbury, and he was here? With you?"

"I saw him once. He told me he was scared. But he's been around here a lot of times. Mostly, he comes before I'm about to go back, he makes noises; and one time he moved stuff around in my room."

We were the only ones left in The Prince of Wales. The bartender began putting things away, signaling that he wanted to shut down.

263

Henry said, "There's a reason for it all, you know? I was there long enough to see that. And every time one of them helps you, a ghost, they get a little weaker, a little harder to see. Have you noticed that at all? But there's a reason for it."

I did notice it about Seth, and thought, maybe that was why he wasn't coming around anymore.

"There's no reasons for any of this shit. Not here, not there."

"I believe there are reasons, Jack," Henry said. "But what do I know?" Then he waved at the bartender, "Can I just have one more, then, please?"

The bartender shrugged, began drawing a pint.

"You know enough to have fucked up my life," I said.

"I didn't mean to. There was nothing else I could do, Jack." Henry sighed. "Look. I didn't have a choice. There were almost none of us left. You know that, a handful of people and hundreds of times more devils in that entire world. And you weren't the only one I cared about and trusted. You were quite simply the only one I could find here. When I got captured at the settlement, we had come all that way across the desert. We were trying to find more people — anyone. But everywhere we went, it was only them, devils, chasing us. I knew what they would do to me when they caught me, and then I saw you at Heathrow. You can't imagine how that made me feel, how it filled me with hope."

"Hope for what?"

"Balance, maybe. I don't know," Henry said. "All things balance out, don't they? They have to. But Marbury is out of balance. We have to save it, Jack, save those boys. There are things you can take with you, from here to there. There are things about you that can make a difference. I believe that. We have to save what is good."

"Or else what?"

"Everything tilts first, then everything falls."

264

"You know what I believe? I believe you're full of shit."

He looked at me, no reaction on his face. "To be honest, it would be a good thing if you were right. But I've spent a good part of my life there. You'll see."

I put my face in my hands, my elbows resting on the table. "I've never felt this bad in my life. Do you think losing the glasses is going to kill me?"

"Mind the gap," he said.

"What?" I was dizzy, didn't understand.

"If you do make it back, say that to Ben and Griffin. Mind the gap."

"Why?"

"I told them you would."

The gap. I had thought the gap between Marbury and here was disappearing. Now the gap was the only thing that existed, and I was stuck in it.

I winced, a knife in my guts. "When did you get the glasses?"

Henry smiled. "I was as old as you are. Ten years ago, when I was just a boy. Things were vastly different there at that time. It was just another place, simple and pleasant."

He leaned forward, trying to get me to look at his face. "I killed a man, Jack."

"What do you mean?" I bit my lip. Maybe he did know about me. Maybe he was some kind of fucked-up cop, like Conner said he was.

"I was a kid. I was stupid. It was an accident, but I still couldn't get over it. And nobody ever knew. No one ever found out," Henry said.

"What happened?"

Henry shrugged and shook his head. "It doesn't matter."

"It matters to me," I said.

"It was just that he . . . we'd had a fight. I didn't even know him before that night."

"What do you know about me?"

He shrugged, shook his head.

"I was sick about it," he said. "Perhaps a week passed. I remember it was raining. I had been on my way to school, and I'd missed the coach that all my friends had taken. While I waited, there was a woman who'd come up. She wore these glasses, and I was quite transfixed by them. She smiled and took them away from her eyes, and said, 'You're Henry Hewitt. You're there, too.' Of course, I had no idea what she was talking about, but she placed them in my hands and I stared and stared at them. I looked up, and she was gone. Just like that. At first, it was easy: going back and forth. But then the war, the disease, and everything came to a terrible stop there. What do I know about you? I've known you since you were a very young child. We were among the few who'd survived initially. And I knew who your mother and father were, while they were alive."

"Fuck them."

He shrugged. "You've seen how some people are different on one side. You're not, I think. That's why I had to get my glasses into your hands before I couldn't go back any longer."

"Even if what you say is true, it doesn't matter now, anyway," I said. "There's nothing I can do. Griffin, Ben, me, we're all probably dead already."

"If you were, you wouldn't be sick like you are right now."

"Did you get sick, too?"

Henry finished his beer. "Every time I came back. Except for the last time."

Darkness.

Conner was asleep when I got back.

266

I hurt so bad I couldn't stand up straight, couldn't take a full breath.

I got out of my clothes.

In the red glow of the nightstand clock, I saw that he'd left a note for me on my pillow.

Folded, on the top it said JACK.

I couldn't read it. I pushed it under the pillow and got into bed, curled on my side.

I knew I was dying.

Maybe it wasn't real. Maybe it was all just the shit Freddie Horvath shot into my veins.

Freddie Horvath did something.

Jack doesn't cry.

But fuck you anyway, Jack.

You deserve this.

I kept my hand on Conner's note, like it was holding me there, somehow making the pain a little more tolerable. I fucked up, I knew it. Everything was Jack's fault. Everything — from the moment I walked out of that party at Conner's to how I ended up in Freddie Horvath's house. And now I was a prisoner again — half in one world and half in another. Stuck in the gap. I hoped Conner would be okay. He didn't know what he was doing.

My chest heaved, but I don't cry.

Roll.

I knew I'd heard it, so faint.

Roll.

Longer now. Where?

Tap. Tap. Tap.

Conner stirred.

Tap.

Under the bed.

Tap.

Then the vibrating, winding sound that a spinning coin makes when it comes to rest.

Tap.

My muscles cramped, locked tight. I managed to get my knees over the side of the bed, and lowered myself onto the floor. Everything was soaked with my sweat. It smelled like the sea.

And when I looked beneath the bed, I saw the familiar white light shining upward onto the underside of the mattress through the oval of a single lens.

It looked like the eye of God.

And it was the same lens that had come out of the frames when Conner and I fought at Blackpool beach that morning.

I gasped, wondered if Jack was hallucinating.

My sweating hand snaked along the floor, fingers clutching the familiar glassy curve.

"Seth."

The Marbury Lens.

My hand closed around the lens, smothering the light, hiding the shapes I saw moving in that small window.

Think, Jack.

I grab one of my discarded socks from the floor at the bedside.

I need to be sure Conner doesn't find it again.

In the bed, he straightens his legs, turns onto his side.

Don't wake up, Con.

I crawl into the bathroom, whisper, "Seth. Thank you."

"Seth."

"Seth. Help me."

part five

SETH

forty-nine

They got Griffin Goodrich.

It was my fault.

When we went swimming, we'd left every one of our guns lying on top of the saddlebags, back by the cottonwood trees. It was stupid, and it was my fault. The boys trusted me to make the right decisions, to keep them safe, and I failed.

When I saw the Hunters coming toward us, I grabbed the knife I'd been using to cut the fish.

Both of them carried clubs that had been fashioned into pickaxes by lashing sharpened human femurs to the heavy ends, stained black with dried blood.

Conner and Freddie Horvath.

At first, they quietly moved through the cover of the trees, slowly, stalking, one of them pointing off at an angle to determine a method for reducing the odds that we'd be able to make an effective escape.

Freddie was gruesomely deformed, but I had no doubt it was him that I saw. The spots along his sides were glossy black. They mottled his skin all the way down to the outside of his knees. His hands were twisted claws with obsidian hooks for nails; and gray horns of bone jutted unevenly out from the flesh of his chin, curving outward from his lower jaw. The hair of the scalp he wore to cover his groin had been braided, so it looked like bouncing spider legs that danced from his crotch as he walked. The brand he showed was a fiery diagonal slash that started on his left shoulder and ended on the inside of his right thigh, like it was cutting him in half.

But I watched Conner, my eyes focused on that small fish-shaped cross above his groin; and I wondered if there was any part of him that could make a connection between this world, where we were enemies, and any other that we were part of.

When the Hunters separated, and Freddie Horvath began circling around behind the trees, Griffin made a run for our guns.

Conner sprang into the chase.

"Jack!" Griffin was terrified, unable to match Conner's speed.

And Freddie was coming toward me and Ben from the opposite side.

I froze. When I realized I was staring directly at Freddie Horvath, everything that had happened to me in that other place flooded my thinking and made me feel weak, captive.

Quit it, Jack.

I held the knife up in front of me.

I screamed, "Conner! Conner Kirk!" And just for a second, maybe, Conner slowed his stride and turned his face so he could look at me. Griffin cut to his right, away from our belongings, deeper into the cover of trees, but Conner was immediately on the boy's heels again, reaching out, so close he could almost grab Griffin by the hair.

Freddie hesitated, eyeing me and Ben cautiously from a distance of twenty feet.

"Ben, go for the guns," I whispered.

"Jack!" Griffin screamed from somewhere behind us.

"He got him, Jack! That sonofabitch got Griffin!"

Freddie started coming toward us, deliberately but carefully through the brush. I could hear twigs and branches snapping against his skin as he moved, holding that axe over his head. I glanced back and saw Ben running across the clearing by the riverbank to where we'd left our belongings, could see, through the trees beyond him, Conner sprinting out, deeper into the woods, carrying the scrawny boy, who was slumped helplessly over one shoulder. Griffin's arms punched and clawed, but Conner just kept running, unfazed. The dog chased after them, helplessly barking his high-pitched yelps.

Griffin kept screaming for me, wailing, "Jack!"

Frantic, I swung around to face Freddie, but he was gone.

Then all I could hear were Griffin's indistinguishable cries getting farther away from us. And soon, they became incoherent garbles, as though his mouth had been stuffed with something, or they were strangling the boy. Then there was no more sound at all, not even the yapping of the dog.

Silence.

"Fuck!" I kicked the ground and slashed at the air futilely with my knife blade.

Ben was behind me, sitting on his feet in the dirt next to our bags and holding a gun across his knee, pointing the barrel at the ground. His other hand masked his eyes. I could tell by the way his back pumped silent coughing motions that Ben was crying.

I walked over and pulled our wet clothes down from the willow tree, bundled Ben's into a ball, and threw them at him.

"Straighten up, Ben."

"Fuck this place."

"Get your clothes on and let's get moving. We're going to get Griffin back," I said. "We can catch them, even if they got horses, but you need to move. They aren't going to kill the kid yet."

Ben knew that, too.

They'd keep the boy until they got tired of messing with him, until he wore out and started looking more dead than alive.

273

Then they'd eat him.

The devils were on horseback, had tracked us over the mountains. I cursed myself that I'd made it easier for them to find us when I decided to double back after discovering that nun who killed herself and the old man; just so I could somehow protect Griffin from knowing what had happened.

And now Griffin was gone.

I tried not to think about what they'd do to him, or to guess how long they'd keep him alive.

They appeared to be making no effort to conceal the path they were following. They wanted us to chase after them.

Ben rode alongside me, trailing Griffin's horse on a line.

"I'm going to ask you something, Ben," I said.

"Okay."

"They can't be too far ahead. Probably not even an hour. When we catch up to them, no matter what's happened, I'm going to ask you to not kill that young one that carried off Griffin."

"No matter what?" Ben asked, his voice thick with obvious disbelief.

"Yeah."

"I can't promise that, Jack."

I didn't say anything.

So Ben said, "You're going to have to tell me why you want me to listen to you on that promise, before I can say yes to it first. 'Cause it's not like we're talking about some lunatic old lost person hiding up in the mountains. We're talking about Griffin now. And I think that no matter what, I am going to kill that one. Unless you do it first."

I nudged my horse ahead. I didn't want to look at Ben, but he was aware of what I was doing, so forced the issue by staying even with me.

"Are you going to tell me how you knew that one's name, or are you going to lie to me, too, 'cause you think I'm too much of a kid to tell the truth to?"

"Goddamnit, Ben."

"Well?"

"Mind the gap." I watched to see Ben's reaction, and immediately recognized that what I'd said meant something important to him.

"How did you know that?"

There is no gap.

"Henry told me to say that to you and Griffin."

"Is he okay?" Ben asked.

"Yes."

"I don't understand this shit. He told us that if you ever said 'mind the gap' that we'd know he was okay, and we'd know that we had to trust you, no matter how crazy you were acting."

"Okay."

Ben squinted, kept his eyes trained ahead of us, scanning. We had to be close now. I could almost feel their presence.

"So, that one who carried off Griffin, you know him, too, from that other place? Where Henry is?"

"Yeah."

"Who is he to you?" Ben asked.

"He's my best friend."

Ben glanced at me. "I have to trust you, like Henry said. But I want you to know that here is here, and if it means a chance to save Griffin's life, I can't promise what I'll do."

"I guess that's fair."

"How do you get there, Jack?"

I scratched my head. "I don't know. I get pulled. Back and forth. Part of me is there, where Henry is, and part of me is here. It feels

275

like it's going to kill me sometimes, it hurts so bad. It isn't good, but I can't stop it."

"Can you take me and Griffin?"

"If I could, I would."

"But Henry did it to you."

"He got lucky, is all."

"Lucky? How the hell do you figure that?" Ben said. "His head ended up on the same wall where they nailed up pieces of every last one of our crew except the three of us kids. And Henry tricked you into staying back with me and Griffin, because he must have known something about you. Otherwise some trophy of your carcass would have been up there next to Henry's. And me and Griffin'd probably both be dead."

I stopped my horse, extended a hand out so Ben would hold up, too.

Ahead of us, on a rise in a fissured pathway winding up the rock face of the mountain, I saw a flash of red.

Freddie Horvath.

We found them.

They were so close.

Then I saw another pale image, not five feet ahead of me. Seth stood there with blank eyes and an expressionless mouth. He was so faint, but as I looked directly through his outline, I could see another light, flashing and intense, growing more vivid, like a strobe coming from somewhere inside him, the epileptic shotgun blast of pictures through the lit windows on a train rushing past me, the flashbulb impressions of people alternating with emptiness.

I felt it pulling me back.

"No. Not yet."

"What the fuck is that?" Ben said.

He could see it, too.

"Goddamnit, no!" I screamed.

And a whisper, "Seth."

Fuck you, Jack.

fifty

A platform.

The Underground.

Night.

I'm alone.

The train rushes forward out of the yawning blackness beneath a tunnel arch and hisses to a stop. Doors sigh open with the suction of so many hungry mouths.

Welcome home, Jack.

I stagger back and fall against the dingy tile wall. The surface is damply warm, feels like every hot breath in the city adheres to it, makes me nauseous. I collapse onto a bench, head between my knees, eyes open. Try to concentrate: shoes (*white Puma tennis shoes. I don't own a pair of Puma tennis shoes*), concrete, I'm not wearing socks (*I don't go out without socks. Why did I do that?*), jeans (*ripped at the knee, they're dark and wet on the hems — it must be raining outside*), my hands hang down. They look gray, like there is nothing living inside me at all.

Jack's been dying a slow death ever since he got into that car with Freddie, and I'm sick of it.

Hold it, Jack.

Hold it.

I push myself up onto my feet and everything swirls around, floating, like I'm inside the biggest toilet imaginable.

Fuck this place.

I make it to a trash bin and empty myself into it.

I'm vaguely aware of the people trying to ignore me, pretending the sick bastard puking his guts out isn't even here, whooshing past me like particles in a wind tunnel.

Green Park Station.

What the fuck am I doing here?

When the train left, the cavern of the station became suddenly quiet and empty. I sat back down on the bench and tried to think. I felt so vacant, hollow, like I'd puked myself inside out, and hadn't eaten in days.

Days. I had no idea what time it was, or how long ago it was that I'd left Henry at The Prince of Wales.

I put my hands on my chest. I felt smaller, almost weightless. I couldn't account for how I was dressed, either. My hair was wet, and I was wearing a faded black T-shirt that didn't belong to me, that had a dime-sized hole on the belly and said THE RAMONES, with a rain-mottled tan canvas jacket that I'd never seen before. No socks, no underwear on, just the jeans — they weren't mine, either — without a belt. Definitely not the way Jack ever dressed when he was normal.

And how long ago was that, anyway?

I went through my pockets, nothing missing, checked my cell phone.

I opened it.

I didn't believe what it said.

I squeezed my eyes shut, closed the phone, flipped it on again.

It was Wednesday.

Conner and I were supposed to be flying back home on Friday, in just two days.

Four days had gone by since Seth brought the Marbury lens into our hotel room, on the night we came back from Blackpool and Conner and I had gotten into a fight.

All that shit was Jack's fault, too, and I suddenly felt so guilty about how I'd treated my best friend.

Four days, and I didn't have the slightest idea what had happened in that time, or how I'd ended up in clothes that weren't mine at the Green Park Station on a Tube line that came from nowhere I could imagine being, and headed in no direction I really wanted to go.

And I must have had fifty missed calls showing on my phone: Nickie, Stella, the last one from Conner just twenty minutes ago; voice mails and text messages I didn't have the guts to look at.

You fucked up, Jack.

Scared, I pulled up Nickie's number and called it. When I heard the connection ringing, I thought I would chicken out and hang up before she answered. I listened.

"Jack?"

"Hey."

"Where are you?" She sounded worried. Maybe disappointed. I knew from her tone that Jack really did fuck up again.

"Um. Green Park Underground."

"Is everything all right?" she said. I thought, maybe, she'd been crying.

"No."

Jack doesn't cry.

I swallowed. "Nickie. I really need to see you. I need to talk to you."

"I've been calling since you left."

She was obviously crying now.

279

"I know. Something's messed up. Bad."

"I checked for you at your hotel. Conner's been calling me, too, trying to contact you. Where've you been? He's worried, Jack. You should call him."

"Okay. But can I see you?"

"Oh, Jack." There was no hiding the hurt in her voice. "Yesterday afternoon before you ran off, you told me that you didn't want to see me again."

"What?" I couldn't believe what I was hearing, but then I thought, *Why the fuck wouldn't I believe it?*

"I . . . I don't know what's going on with me, Nickie. I need to find something. I don't know." I began feeling sick again, and images of the last four days began flickering dimly in my head, just like those flashing windows on the train passing by. Something about her brother, Ander. These clothes were his. I'd stayed at their home in Hampstead on Monday night, in a strange room. I thought about the lens, knew exactly where I'd put it — in the left pocket of these jeans. My hand absently rubbed the shape of it there.

"Please," I said. "Please can I see you one more time?"

Nickie waited. I could hear her strained breathing, and I knew she was trying not to let me hear that she'd been crying.

She said, "No, Jack."

"Nickie." I sounded sick. Pathetic.

"I can't help you. I can't do anything for you if you're determined to let these things happen."

She hung up.

I dropped my phone, heard it clatter down from the bench to the concrete beside my foot.

Maybe this is how it's supposed to be, I thought. Jack falls apart here, and everything falls apart in Marbury. No, not Jack falling apart:

I was willfully disassembling Jack here. Like Nickie said. Maybe that was why Seth made me come back again. I thought about taking the lens out of my pocket, but I was too disgusted with myself.

I picked up my phone and went across to the other side of the platform, waited for a train toward Oxford Circus so I could get back to the hotel.

I walked from the Tube stop in the rain. It felt good, warm and thick, like blood. By the time I got inside the hotel, I was completely wet.

The room was a mess. My clothes, the entire contents of my pack, had been scattered everywhere — on the floor, the furniture. Conner was gone. I remembered something about him telling us he was going up to York to be with Rachel. I ached, wished he was here so he could maybe help keep Jack from slipping away entirely.

I lay down on the bed and stared at the ceiling. I still had her brother's wet shoes and clothes on, didn't care. And, for the second time in the past few weeks, I seriously thought I wanted to die, to actually kill myself. I couldn't see any way out of the hole I was in, believed that nothing was going to get better or fix itself. Probably the only reason I didn't have the guts to off myself at that moment was that I was concerned about it being too much of a burden for Conner, Stella, and Wynn to deal with: my being over here, alone in London, and all.

How thoughtful of you, Jack.

But Jack doesn't cry.

So I drank a beer.

Let me tell you what Jack believes about Marbury and the Marbury lens.

I keep going back to this idea of Stella's nesting dolls: that there are things inside of things that, in turn, are contained within still bigger things. I can't guess how many times. I think there's something

281

called *M Theory*, in theoretical physics, that says eleven. Dimensions, or whatever you want to call them. I could go with that number, but I don't really care, either.

And I see Jack as a kind of an arrow shaft that shoots through every layer, simultaneously, the point directly piercing the exact center. I think everyone's an arrow like that, too, aiming into their own centers.

So the Marbury lens is a kind of prism, an elevator car maybe, that separates the layers and lets me see the Jack who's in the next hole made by the arrow.

And that hole is Marbury.

The one sure thing about Marbury is that it's a horrible place. But so is right here, too. And there's a certain benefit in the obviousness of its brutality, because in Marbury there's no doubt about the nature of things: good and evil, or guilt and innocence, for example. Not like here, where you could be sitting in the park next to a doctor or someone and not have any idea what a sick and dangerous son-ofabitch he really is. Because we always expect things to be so nice and proper, even if we haven't learned our fucking lesson that it just doesn't work out like that all the time.

Henry believed that Marbury was a world out of balance.

He needs to take a closer look at this one.

I opened another beer and sat back against the headboard on the bed. When I moved my pillow, I saw the note Conner had left for me the other night when I'd gone out to meet Henry. I turned it over in my hands, not really wanting to unfold and read it. It would be just like all those missed calls, I thought, just one in a series of messages about how Jack was fucking up his life and needed to get his shit together.

The phone vibrated in my pocket. I let it go for a while, and then, somehow, I got brave enough to fish it out.

Brave and considerate Jack.

I didn't look at the number.

"Hello?"

"Where are you now?"

It was Nickie.

"I'm at the hotel."

"Stay there."

"Okay."

"I can't stand this. I'll be there as soon as I can."

So the new, braver Jack decided to open Conner's note, too. But then again, I realized that it's fairly easy to be brave once you give up caring about how bad things can really be.

Hey Jack,

This feels really awkward — writing a note to you. Imagine me feeling awkward around you about anything. Anyway, you're closer to me than the people in my own family, so I have to tell you that there's something wrong, dude, and I think we need to do something about it. I'm not sure what we need to do, but we need to do it together. So you should think about it and let me know. And you know I'll be there for you. So if you want to go see someone about working things out in your head because of what that guy did to you, I'll go with you, just like I told you I would. And if you don't want to tell anyone else about it, you know I'm good with that, too. I'll even go with you to the cops and tell them the truth about what happened if that's what you need. But the main thing is I just really hope you find a way to stop letting this eat you up like it's doing.

I don't know what the story is with those glasses. It's like I said, that guy is just trying to somehow fuck with people's heads to see what they'll do about it. You have to admit that's the truth. There can't be any other way to explain it, but the way you were acting about those things was really kind of scaring me. 'Cause it's just some fucking glasses that you never even saw till you got over here, and I'd think you could just let it go. Jack, we've hung out together just about every day since we were pissing in paper diapers, so the only explanation I can come up with about how mad you are is that it's about what that dude did to you, or tried to do, I don't know.

I hope you don't get pissed off at me for saying it.

Anyway, Jack, I am really sorry. And this is hurting me, too. I hope we can forget about all this shit and just be like we used to be. I think you want that, too.

I have to tell you that after you left, I went out, too. I saw you at that pub, Jack. And you didn't even look at me. You were talking to yourself like there was someone there, but you were all alone, just staring at a pint of beer sitting on the table in front of you. It freaked me out, Jack. There was no one else around you.

Don't be mad about that, but it's true.

So, after I got back, I called Rachel and I'm going up to York for a few days on Monday morning, so I won't be hanging out with you and Nickie that day, not that you'd want me to, anyway. Don't worry, I can tell you're sick of me right now. If I don't make it back before then, I'll see you at the airport on Friday. It's really been a great time over here, even with all this shit going on right now between us.

Just so you know, I'll do anything you need me to do, and like I said, I love you, Jack. (I am not gay. Well, at least not as gay as you ha ha.)

Conner

He's lying to you, Jack.

He followed you.

Conner's turning into your enemy here, too.

Fuck you, Jack.

How did he not see Henry sitting with me? We were there until the place closed.

This is real.

But Conner had seen Henry before. He'd pointed him out to me in that picture of Nickie and me in the Underground.

My camera.

I dug through the stuff that was scattered all around the floor. I found my camera, turned it on, and hit the preview button.

This is real.

It said, "Camera contains no images."

I need help.

This can't be happening. Maybe none of this has been happening, and maybe Jack is still tied down, drugged out of his mind, rotting on some creep's bed in California.

Henry isn't real.

Conner isn't real.

Nickie isn't real.

Marbury is.

I kept playing with that lens in my pocket, flipping it over and over again through the thick denim of the jeans. But I was too terrified to touch it, knew that in my weakness, if I did, Jack would be gone again; and I'd completely destroy any slight chance I'd have of rebuilding things between me and Conner, between me and Nickie.

I couldn't help it. I wanted to go back to Marbury so bad that it was starting to hurt again, so I tried to do anything I could to distract myself. I folded Conner's note and put it inside my pack; then I started picking up the clothes I'd thrown all over the floor, shoving them into my pack. And all the while, I'd stop from time to time and just listen, because I was really expecting Seth to come around and tempt me with those little noises he'd make, to let me know it was time for me to go back to Marbury.

But he never did.

I tried to stop thinking about the lens in my pocket, to stop worrying about Griffin and Ben.

When I felt the sweat coming on again, I even opened another beer, forced myself to drink it.

Then I lay down on the bed and called Conner.

The brave Jack.

"Hey, Con." I know it's hard to really hear yourself, but to me, as I lay there on the bed, I sounded lifeless. Miserable.

"Jack! Where were you?" Conner seemed genuinely happy that I called.

Happy.

But I honestly didn't know where I'd been, so I tried to play my way around the question.

"At Nickie's. Hanging out. Nowhere, really."

"She told me you broke up with her."

Everyone knew more about Jack than I did.

"I must be out of my mind, Con." I tried to joke, but it didn't sound funny. "But she's coming over right now."

"That's better," he said. "Dude, I am, like, totally in love with Rachel. I'd marry her right now if I could. And we haven't even had sex yet, either. It's like, I can't believe I'm actually talking about me. Virgin Saint Conner. Ow! Okay, I'm sorry!"

I could hear Rachel laughing in the background.

"Where are you?"

"I'm at her parents' house. In Harrogate. It's really nice here, Jack."

"Are you coming back?"

"Tomorrow afternoon," Conner said. "So let's go out tomorrow night for our last night, Jack. It'll be fun."

"Yeah." And then I said, "Conner, I'm sorry about how I've been acting and stuff. And what you said in your note to me is right. I just don't know what's wrong with me. Maybe you can help me when we get back, okay? I'm fucking scared."

"We'll get it fixed, man. I promise."

"Con, do you know what happened to the pictures in my camera?"

"No, dude. What?"

"It's all empty. We took pictures, right?"

"Yeah." I heard him pause. "It's no big deal if you don't have pictures of St. Atticus to show off to Wynn."

"It was all real, right?"

This is real.

Conner exhaled.

I asked, "What are you doing right now?"

"Sitting here, watching TV with Rachel."

"Tell her I said hi."

"Okay." Then Conner cleared his throat. I guess he must have thought I sounded insane, because he said, "Jack. Don't do anything dumb, okay? Just relax, and wait for Nickie. Wait for me, tomorrow, and everything's going to be good, okay?"

"Okay." And I said, "Call me tomorrow when you're almost here and I'll come meet you at King's Cross. I miss you."

Conner laughed and said, "You are so gay."

"All right, Con. See you tomorrow."

Then it was deathly quiet, and I just stayed there, stretched out on the bed, waiting, like he told me to do. And I could feel that goddamned lens in my pocket like it was a living, pulsing organism, giving off heat. Whispering to me like Seth did. I knew that if I so much as touched the bare skin of a finger to it that I'd be gone again, so I just concentrated, saying, "Nickie, Nickie, Nickie," over and over in my mind.

And I watched the clock beside me until I fell to sleep.

Midnight.

Tap. Tap. Tap.

Fuck.

I opened my eyes, sat up.

Just the door. It was Nickie.

Dizzy, I got up from bed, me and the blankets, all damp from the rain, still fully dressed, wearing her brother's tennis shoes.

My hair hung down in front of my face when I opened the door. I didn't swipe it back with my hand; it was an old defense of Jack's when he didn't want to look Wynn or Stella in the eyes. And I was kind of embarrassed about seeing Nickie in my pitiful state.

She flashed a careful smile when she saw me. She held a blue nylon bag that she dropped at my feet.

"I brought your clothes back," she said. "I've laundered them all."

Nickie kept her arms straight down at her sides, waiting, just beyond the threshold. And I was so stupid and confused that I didn't really know what to do, so I kept my eyes down and said, "Thank you."

She turned to leave.

"Wait."

I went into the hallway after her, but she kept walking away from me.

"Nickie?"

"I really do think we should leave one another alone now."

I began to panic. It felt like everything was giving away beneath my feet. I stumbled toward her as she paused at the elevator.

288

"I don't know what's wrong with me," I said.

"Neither do I, Jack. And I don't believe you know how much I care for you, either. But I wonder what happened to the boy I was so taken with to make him turn so selfish and cruel. I'm tired of feeling like an idiot, and I'm scared for you. I can't be a part of your self-destruction."

All I could say was, "I'm sorry. It's not me, Nickie."

"Whatever it is, it's turning you into a monster."

The elevator opened and Nickie stepped inside. I wedged my hand against the door.

Her eyes flashed anger. "Let me go. I'm tired."

She meant it.

I moved my hand.

The door closed.

I leaned against it, holding myself up, wondering why I would just stand there doing nothing, and let Nickie sink away from me.

I couldn't remember anything about the Jack she met on the boat, about the Jack who told her she shouldn't see me again. And I couldn't come up with any reasons why I was letting this happen, here and now.

Why I was turning into a monster.

So I ran after her, flew down the stairwell, and caught her on the street outside.

"I'm so sorry, Nickie. Please come talk to me."

"I don't think I can help you."

"Nickie. I promise . . ."

"You promise *what*, Jack?"

"Please?"

"No."

She left me there.

I sat down on the side of the road and watched cars that drove past the hotel.

At that moment, I thought about the ways things could have been different, the other places I could have been — or not been. It would have been so much easier if I had simply said, "Yes, Dr. Horvath, I *do* want you to kill me right now."

But I fought back instead.

And now here I was, sitting on some rain-pissed road and arguing in my mind about whether I should go back upstairs and find my goddamned phone so I could call Henry Hewitt and ask him — again — if any of this was real; or if I could get up off my ass and try to find Nickie one last time.

I ached.

This is real.

The doorman stood there watching me.

He wore glasses.

Stop fucking looking at me.

I ran.

And with each step, every breath, I whispered in the back of my throat, *This is real this is real this is real.* I couldn't let her go, couldn't let myself push her away. Nickie was the only thing I could hold on to, the only thing that would keep Jack from floating into Marbury and never coming back.

Panting, miserable, wet, I found her sitting on a bench in front of Baker Street Station.

"Nickie?"

I scared her.

I didn't want to scare her anymore.

"I can't let you go like this," I said. "I can be the person you think I am. I am that person, but I need to hold on to you."

She'd been crying.

"Will you help me, Nickie? Can I talk to you?"

She nodded.

In the dark, we lay together under a single thin sheet. And I'd gotten up from bed to open the window so we could hear and smell the rain.

Nickie put her head on my chest, her hand stroked my belly, just like she did that first night we were together in Blackpool.

"I can hear your heart," she whispered.

"What's it sound like?"

"An angry little boy."

"Does it?"

"Well, he acts angry about all sorts of things, but to me it sounds as though he's hurt."

"How can you tell?"

"He's not a very good pretender. He's just afraid that it's not very manly to be hurt, so he cheats at acting angry."

"He should stop telling you things about me," I said.

I held her so tightly.

"I think I know why I told you that I couldn't see you again, Nickie."

I felt her hand tense against my skin when I said it, like she'd been burned.

"Why?"

"Because I don't even remember how I ended up wearing your brother's clothes. Because I don't know where I was the entire time between Saturday night and when I called you from the Underground in Green Park."

She was silent. I could feel her breath on my chest.

"There's something wrong with me, and I'm afraid."

Freddie Horvath did something to my brain, and I'm going to hurt you, Nickie.

I felt my throat constricting.

Jack doesn't cry.

I said, "I just don't want to hurt you. Because I really love you."

"You won't hurt me, Jack. Let Conner help you. I talked to him about it. He wants to help you work things out."

"I don't want to hurt him, either."

She inhaled. Her breath made a cool whisper of wind on my chest. "You were in Ander's clothes because you showed up drenched from the rain on Monday evening. You'd gotten lost trying to find your way. You looked quite pathetic. Not the best first impression for my parents, I'm afraid."

"Oh God."

She breathed a silent laugh. "They've since adjusted nicely to my American friend. And you stayed the night, as well."

"With you?"

Nickie drew a circle around my heart. I felt her face tighten into a smile. "What else could you do? You couldn't leave. I had every bit of your clothes. Ander gave you some pajamas, and you stayed in our guest room. I pouted when you told me you were too shy to sneak out and come to my room with me while my parents were home. But I think you were most frightened that Ander would be on his sister's guard."

"I remember him now," I said. "I'm sorry, Nickie. I know I shouldn't be doing this to you. I'm so messed up, and I feel so guilty about everything, not being in control."

"Shhh . . . ," she said, and pressed her finger onto my lips.

And I remembered how her brother had given me clothes and shoes, that the three of us had gone together for breakfast; and, later, how I'd told Nickie that I was afraid of things and, even though I didn't want to, I had to leave. She didn't understand. She started crying. And when I turned away to vanish into the Underground, I felt like crying, too, but Jack doesn't cry; I'd gotten onto one train after another, just trying to get lost somewhere in the darkness and the crowds beneath the city.

And I knew that I'd gone to see Henry, too; that he was aware that Jack wasn't really here. When I left him, I wandered around London overnight, aimlessly, until I came back to myself in the Green Park Station and phoned her.

She whispered, "Tell me how the story ends, Jack."

You mean the one where Jack kills himself?

You won't like it, Nickie.

"I don't think this thing ever will end."

"I mean the story about the boy. Seth. You promised you'd tell."

"Okay."

fifty-one

SETH'S STORY [4]

I found paying work in Napa City loading freight every day except Sundays. I wasn't as strong as the other fellows on the crew, but I tried hard, and got along with them, too. Of course, to be hired I had to lie about my age, but I didn't consider it a genuine lie, since I was never absolutely certain how old I was by any account.

Still, I believe that Mr. Pursely, who ran the freight office, knew I wasn't eighteen years old, because he did remark on a number of occasions how there wasn't the first sign of a hair on my chin nor chest. But every day, following work, I would sneak off and sleep in the woods or in some quiet barn, since it was still warm enough in the year to allow for that.

The other boys I worked with knew I was living away from home like an orphan, but they never bothered me about it; and I always did manage to keep myself reasonably clean and properly fed. From time to time, they'd go down the river to San Francisco to commune with the whore-women; they would frequently urge me to accompany them, but I believed I was already too wicked and sinful in my own heart, and so begged them to tolerate my abstinence.

Of course, they would regularly tease me about my youthful purity, them not having any idea what a black and loathsome thing I truly was. But I would never miss a day of church, even though, for all I'd attend and focus my mind on the words of God, I could never feel that I had truly come any closer to the light.

In November, I took a room at the Sutton House, which was a nice family hotel where I once again enjoyed the comfort of sleeping in a bed and having access to regular baths, which, although lacking a great degree of privacy, compensated for that shortcoming with an abundance of hot water.

I owned two books: a Bible and a copy of Longfellow, and I read from each of them every day. Neither book provided much comfort. For while one reminded me nightly of my corruption, the other only recalled to my mind thoughts of Hannah. I ached so desperately for her that I would sometimes lie in bed and cry, especially on those cold and silent nights when my loneliness became a particular frailty. I missed every one of the Mansfields.

December brought the darkest rains; work became an unpleasant labor for me. I had not brought suitable clothing for such weather, and scarcely earned enough to pay my board. But I remember that it was on the twelfth of that month, when I had retired to my room following supper, that I lay in my bed reading Longfellow by the smoky light of a lantern, and there came an unexpected knocking on my door.

I pulled the blankets up over myself, unsuitably dressed as I was, and said, "Come in."

And there, dripping in rainwater and coated to his knees in mud, stood my brother, Davey Mansfield.

He said, "Seth Braden Mansfield, what the hell do you think you're doing?"

At first, I scarcely recognized Davey, because the hat he wore hung so low across his brow; and his face was covered with a sparse amber beard, which I had never seen on him. But when I was certain it was him from the look in his eyes and sound of his voice, I tore the covers off from me and threw my arms around him.

"Davey!" I was overcome with happiness, having become so used to the drudgery of my sad life away from Pope Valley. Then I held him at arm's length and said, "Is something wrong at home?"

And Davey said, "Hell yes, something's wrong, Seth. Ma and Hannah are about sick to death from missing you, and Pa won't even talk no more except to tell me what jobs I ain't doing right enough to suit him."

Davey just stood there, dripping in my open doorway. I sat on the bed, suddenly aware that in my attempt to spare the family my wickedness, I had inflicted some degree of harm to them.

"I didn't mean to hurt no one," I said. "I was afraid, Davey, of what

I might do to you all if I didn't leave. You have to believe that I wouldn't ever do anything intentional to hurt Ma or Hannah, nor any of you."

Davey sighed. I reckon that he understood well enough the forces that drove me away from that home, but I could see he was determined to bring me back and make some peace there, too.

"Well, you're damned if you do or don't, I figure," he said. "But I came all this way looking for you and I aim to bring you back, too. So we can leave right now, or we can wait until the morning, either one that suits you is agreeable to me."

I wondered how strange my life was, because here I was, these seven years later, giving Davey clean clothes to put on, just as Ma did for me the day the Mansfields took me in and made me their son. I brought him downstairs and Mrs. Sutton fed him, even though it was not a regular thing for her to do once her lodgers had all retired. But since he was my brother, she said she didn't mind being put out; and told me he could sleep in my room, too, if he didn't have any other place to rest.

And that night, just before I fell to sleep, Davey told me, "Seth, the time is not right for you and Hannah. Understand me, brother. You're coming back home with me, and I aim to give Ma some rest in that. But you're going to see to it that you act like a proper man, now, and wait for the time to be right. You'll know it when it is. Do you hear what I'm saying?"

"I reckon I do."

"Good night, then."

The following morning, with my few belongings and one sturdy mule between us, Davey and I set off for Pope Valley in a light gray rain. It was Sunday, so I felt a particular foreboding about missing church; and my hands shook noticeably from my heart considering the prospect of touching Hannah once again.

I knew I was cursed.

The weather slowed our travel significantly, so it was nearly evening on Tuesday by the time we led that poor and tired mule into Pa's barn. Davey could see the relief on my face, I think, as I looked around inside that familiar shelter; and I was half-expecting to see Hannah there, waiting for me. I could sense her so strongly that I believed my knees would give out.

In the house, Ma cried and hugged me tightly, getting herself all wet from my sodden clothes; and she praised Davey for saving me once again. But Hannah stood back in the hallway, just staring at me, and I could see the tears on her anguished face before she whirled around and ran upstairs to her room without saying a word to me.

Pa extinguished his cigarette and stood over the both of us, kissing me on my wet hair, and he said, "Seth Mansfield, I reckon you've got quite a story to tell us about what you did, boy. Now run up and get some dry clothes on with your brother and Ma'll set a supper for the two of you. I reckon you just about killed them both, Hannah and Ma, with worrying over you, son; maybe Davey, too, for tracking you down in this fierce cold."

"I'm sorry, Pa," I said, and followed Davey upstairs.

In the dark of the hallway, I stood outside Hannah's door. Davey watched me. We both could hear her crying, and it made me feel terribly forlorn. I raised my hand to knock, and Davey said, "Don't."

So I put my hand down. And Davey held the door to our room open for me, and stood there, waiting for me to go inside.

Like he said, either way about it, I was damned.

At supper, Ma went and got Hannah so she could look at me. First, Davey seemed concerned when she hugged me around my neck and kissed me at least twenty times all over my cheeks and hair. Her lips and face were so wet from crying and it was all I could do to sit still and not put my mouth on hers and kiss her proper like I wanted to. My mouth watered for her tongue like I'd never been fed one time in my life. I turned red and shook, and was considerably attracted at that moment, and then Davey burst out hollering and laughing when his sister slapped me resoundingly across the back of my head and said, "Seth Mansfield, if you ever do a deed like that again, I'll come hunt you down myself!"

And Pa said, "I reckon you don't want to mess with that, boy."

He lit a cigarette and sat at the table, watching his two boys eat.

And I was so flustered I could barely speak, but I set my fork down and looked at Hannah and said with a wavering and sorrowful voice, "I truly apologize, Hannah. I promise I will never leave again."

Hannah blushed, but I don't think anyone other than me noticed.

And that night, when Davey and I went up to go to bed, we both saw how Hannah was waiting, peeking out her door at us. Davey put his hand on my shoulder. It felt serious, and I knew what he was trying to say without words.

"You go on in, Seth. I'm going to have a talk with Hannah."

I stood there, helplessly, and watched as Davey went in to his sister's room and shut the door behind him.

By Christmas Day, things had gotten back to normal, and it was almost like I'd never been away at all. In the morning, we all rode in to Necker's Mill and brought food to Uncle Teddy. We said prayers with him, and Pa allowed each of us to drink some hot cider, too. I enjoyed the drink, especially the way it made Ma and Hannah laugh and turn so red on their cheeks.

So before we left for home, Davey and I went out to get the wagon around for the family, while Pa stayed inside and smoked and had another drink with Uncle Teddy. I'd been waiting for days to get the chance to talk to Davey alone, but I just hadn't worked up the backbone.

"I need to ask your permission to do something," I said. "I've been making a present for Hannah and I want you to say it's allowable to you that I give it to her."

Davey said, "Why would I tell you no?"

"Well, I want to give it to her alone. Where it's just her and me."

He looked at me. I can't say that Davey didn't trust me, because our kinship went beyond that; and neither of us ever kept a secret from the other, which is why I asked him in the first place.

He let out a long breath of air. I watched it make a cloud in front of his face. "I expect you're going to remember to act like a man, Seth."

"Thank you, Davey."

And that was all we said about it.

So while Ma prepared our dinner, the rest of us sat in front of the fire admiring the coats and hats we'd received as gifts, and Pa told us stories about Christmas when he was a boy. I was uneasy because I knew Davey kept watching me and Hannah; and I felt especially sinful, it being Christmas and all, with the thoughts that kept plaguing my mind about me and Hannah out by the river's side last summer.

I finally worked up my nerve. I nudged Hannah's foot with mine and cleared my throat. "I have a present for you, Hannah."

"Well?" she said. And she watched me without blinking, which made me feel as though I would shrink to nothing under that stare.

"Well." I looked at Pa, and then at Davey. "I don't want no one else to see it until you do, in case you don't like it."

Pa shrugged. Hannah looked confused. Davey seemed like he

was maybe about to hit me. But he said go do it, so I gave him a stare like he better just leave me and Hannah by ourselves a bit.

"Come on." I pulled her up by her hand. "Put your coat on. I got it out in the barn."

And without so much as glancing back at Davey one time, I led her out into the cold.

I lit a lantern in the barn.

I closed the door behind us.

Then I slid the bolt through the handles. I was so nervous, I couldn't say anything, but I didn't want to, either.

I couldn't keep my hands away from her, she was so beautiful, and I had waited so long, tried to be good, but I didn't care about anything else once we were shut inside and finally alone together. Her skin was so cold and smooth. It felt like glass to my lips.

Her mouth tasted of cider, it made me alive; and I twisted my fingers into her hair and pressed myself so tightly against her hips. In honesty, I felt weak enough at that moment that I would have unfastened my clothes and thrown them entirely off without regard, but I tried to think about Davey and the family, so I softened my pull on her and held my face away.

"I love you so much, Hannah."

"Oh God, Seth. I thought I would die when you left."

She began crying, and I felt a tear in my eye at that moment, too, so I held her close and smelled her beautiful hair.

"Don't cry," I said. "I really do have something for you, my Hannah."

"I don't want for anything but you, Seth."

"Look."

I led her over to the work table by Pa's vice and anvil.

"I made this for you."

I'd carved a toy horse for her from walnut wood — a gray Appaloosa with black mane and glossy, striped hooves. The paint had just finished drying. It was slightly bigger than my hand; and I'd fashioned a kind of wheel from one of Ma's thread spools between his back legs by fastening a strand of rubber there. I showed her that if you pulled it backwards and let go of him, the horse would roll forward a few inches, and then, just when he'd stop, his front legs would rear up and stamp down three times.

Roll.

Tap. Tap. Tap.

Hannah laughed, and put her hands to her face.

"Seth!" she said. "This is the most beautiful thing I think I've ever seen!"

I didn't say anything. I only could watch her, I was so mesmerized by the look of wonder on her lovely face.

"Can I try him?"

I held my hand over hers and dragged the toy backwards along the surface of the table.

"Now, let go of him," I said. My lips were right against her ear, and I purposely caught a strand of her hair in my mouth.

Roll.

Tap. Tap. Tap.

She laughed again, so lightly, and then she threw her arms around me. We kissed.

Awkwardly, overwhelmed by my weakness, we nervously fumbled at each other's clothing and fell, tangled together, onto the floor right at our feet.

We brushed the dirt from one another's hair, hurrying, breathless; and Hannah clutched the horse to her breast beneath the folds of her coat, while I lowered the mantle on the barn lamp. We kissed

301

once more, swearing our love forever, and crossed the muddy yard back to the house in the rain.

And I felt like the most horrid and contemptible animal when we all sat down to Christmas dinner together. Pa said grace, and I believed it was going to cause my heart to stop on the spot because I knew I had allowed the devil inside of me. But Hannah shined and gleamed in her contentment, that little painted horse resting on the table between her and Davey, while she slid her foot across the floor and placed it so softly atop mine.

When I lay in bed that night, unable to sleep, I was overcome by my sinfulness. I felt certain that Davey was lying awake as well, that he was watching me, disgusted at my vileness, because he had to have known what I did to his sister out there in the barn. I was relieved he didn't ask me about it, too, because if he did, I would have confessed to him that I was weak again and could not stop myself from being with her.

I knew I would go to hell for it. But I decided that I'd rather go to hell for being Hannah's lover than go to heaven for not.

This is how it would be from then on.

I became resigned to my impurity.

The summer after we celebrated my sixteenth birthday was a turning point in all of our lives, I suppose. Davey got married; Pa and I helped build a house for him and his wife, just across the pasture from our own. And once Davey left, it was easier for Hannah and me to be together.

She was such a beautiful young woman at seventeen.

Sometimes, in our wickedness, she would steal into my bedroom in the middle of the night, and we would sleep together, saying promises, holding each other until the morning without anyone knowing. And I suppose that it was only destined to happen, in my cursedness, but in the second month following my birthday, Hannah informed me she was certain that she was carrying my child.

Of course, that was the most vivid day in my memory for a number of reasons.

On that day, Ma and Pa had gone visiting to Davey's, and I worked at stacking the pressed hay we'd purchased for the milk cows, sweating from the heat up in the haymow while Hannah watched me. When she said that she was pregnant, I had to stop what I was doing so I could sit down.

I wiped my face with my hand and ladled drinking water from a pail into my mouth, letting it spill down my chest, inside the overalls I wore.

"How can you be sure?" I said.

"I just know, Seth. I can tell."

I will admit that hearing her tell me about it brought a certain dizziness to my head. And I looked at her to judge the weight of what she was saying, but Hannah seemed to be happier than she'd ever been since I'd known her. I wasn't sure how I felt, even if I did recognize the thing was bound to happen after how recklessly we'd been carrying on.

Cautiously, Hannah walked across the floor and sat beside me on the hay. We held hands without talking for a minute, and all I could hear was my own breathing.

I looked out the open loft window at the perfect sky that hung over the trees, admiring the strength of the sight, the home I was fortunate enough to have been gifted.

"Well," I said. "I'm going to tell Pa. And I'm going to tell him today, Hannah. There's nothing else that can be done, and I reckon it's been a long time coming, anyhow. I don't believe it's going to come as a significant surprise to nobody."

"Are you pleased, Seth?"

I plucked a straw from a flat stack we were sitting on, and chewed the end. "Yes. I believe that I am pleased with this."

And Hannah said, "Thank you."

I put my palm flat on her belly and closed my eyes. "I do reckon I can sense him inside there, Hannah."

"So can I."

I kissed her face and brushed the soft hair away from the back of her neck with my fingers.

We made a bed by spreading all of our clothes out over the hay just inside the open hatch, where the breeze through the loft cooled our skin, and we lay together there, wrapped up in one another's arms, sweating, completely naked and unashamed in the humid stillness of the afternoon.

I always knew what Hannah and I did together was wrong and sinful. I knew it from the first day we lay together by the river, but I had surrendered myself to that immorality. I knew that there was nothing I could do to erase my wickedness. So, that day in July, we lay on the bed of our union, atop our scattered garments in the dimness of the shaded barn, while Hannah twirled her fingers in my hair and I closed my eyes, listening to the birds in the afternoon light outside. I held her tightly and pulled myself against her again.

Then a shadow fell across us both.

Hearing the sounds we made to each other, Uncle Teddy had come up into the barn looking for us, booming and cursing his proclamations, denouncing our evil.

"Flesh of your own flesh! Brother and sister be damned! Abomination!" Uncle Teddy wailed. He held a broken rake handle aloft and struck it down fiercely across my shoulders. I howled in pain, raising myself up so I might cover Hannah from his attack.

"Incestuous heathen filth!" Again, he raised his stick, and this time swung it squarely into the back of my head.

Everything went black in a moment.

When my eyes opened, my hand was pressed against my skull. I could feel blood all down my face, drying in my hair, and sticking to the pale hay beneath me. I was still entirely unclothed, and couldn't exactly remember what had happened to me. Then my thoughts began to clear when I heard Hannah crying and struggling beside me. Uncle Teddy had removed his belt and was thrashing her wildly across her legs and back with it.

I was so disgusted and enraged by what I saw the man doing to my Hannah that I forced myself onto my feet. Hannah turned her frightened eyes to me, but Uncle Teddy was only determined in having her submit to him. She tried to cover herself with our clothes, but every time she did, Uncle Teddy would slap her arm away and continue beating her bare skin. Her legs and arms were striped with bleeding welts.

"Whore! Whore!" he screamed.

I grabbed what was there — the handle of a hay hook — and when he raised his arm to strike her again, I swiped it at Uncle Teddy's side. I can't know that I intended to harm him, but the arrowed end of the hook went directly into his ribs, and I heard a sound like a spraying of gas and foam from his chest. I pulled him with the hook firmly swallowed inside his trunk, back, away from Hannah.

He straightened and dropped his belt over the side of the loft.

At first, Uncle Teddy didn't seem to register the magnitude of his injury. He looked down, first at the hook, which hung beneath his arm, rising and lowering with his strained gasps, then at me, with an expression of alarm and confusion. He staggered back two steps, began plucking impotently at the steel barb with blood-flecked hands. All the while, a hissing, gurgling sound emitted from the injury as blood spurted in rhythmic waves, running down his trouser legs to the tops of his shoes.

He kept backing away from me with the most puzzled and ridiculous look on his face. Eventually, he fell over the side and landed directly in the bed of Pa's buckboard, seated, with an attitude of resignation and defeat, like he was exhausted and waiting for a ride home. Both his hands clutched tightly around the hook, but he no longer pulled at it. His face had gone completely gray, and he looked up at me one more time, attempting to form words from lips that would allow no coherent sound to pass.

I dropped to Hannah's side. "Are you hurt bad?"

"No."

I would have flown down and killed him on the spot if she gave any other answer.

"We need to get help."

"Oh," she said. "Look at you, Seth."

She lightly touched my head where I was cut.

"I'm good, Hannah. We need to get help for him."

Hannah pulled her dress on over her head and soaked her undergarments in the pail of drinking water. Then she cleaned the blood away from me and kissed me.

"I'm so scared, Seth."

Uncle Teddy just sat there with his head slumped down, whimpering softly. His blood had puddled all around the boards of the wagon where he'd been sitting, and in the fall, the pointed end of the hook had erupted directly out his back, like the horn on a devil. I never imagined any man could contain so much blood.

I kept my eyes on him while I put my clothes on, but by the time

I'd gotten a foot into the first shoe, Uncle Teddy fell back, and stretched his legs straight out on the bed of Pa's buckboard like he was taking a nap.

He died there, just like that, in our barn.

"Don't look at him," I whispered.

We climbed down from the haymow.

I tried to pull the steel hook out from his side, but it was almost like he refused to let me have it back. I struggled fiercely, but finally the hay hook came free.

I wiped it on Uncle Teddy's shirtsleeve and tossed it back up to the loft above me.

When Davey and I left Napa City to go back to the Mansfield home on that raining December morning, I knew I was cursed. I chose my way in this world, though, and I chose to be with Hannah and give her my life. So the day I killed Uncle Teddy, I told Pa everything that was true about me and Hannah, and what happened in the barn. He listened to me talk, and he smoked a cigarette while I did. And I never begged him for his forgiveness, because I knew it was something no man could give me; but when I finished my story, Pa just put his hand on the top of my head and told me how much he loved me.

"Are you asleep?" I asked.

Nickie lay, so still, in my arms.

"No," she said. "I love that, Jack. I love hearing your voice, being here with you. What happened to them?"

"Terrible things."

"When you tell the story, I keep thinking to myself how it almost feels as though you were there."

"I was."

"How?"

"The boy is a ghost now. It's hard to explain. But he kind of gave me his life, I think. I don't know if I really understand it, myself." I stared up at the ceiling. "I know. That sounds totally crazy."

"I believe you, Jack."

I sat up and looked at her in the gray light that came in from the open window. I wanted to see whether she really did think I was telling her the truth, or whether she thought Jack was nuts, just like I do most of the time.

But she believed me.

I got up from the bed. "I need to show you something."

I kicked my feet around through the clothes we'd discarded on the floor at the foot of the bed until I found the jeans I'd been wearing. I picked them up, could still feel the shape and weight of the Marbury lens inside the pocket. I closed my hand around it and pulled the lens out, then I slid back into bed beside Nickie.

I held my closed fist in front of her and said, "Look at this."

Then I opened my hand.

I tried not to look, but immediately the room was washed in the pale, colorless light of Marbury. And it was suddenly like I was standing on the edge of the highest cliff imaginable, a hot, relentless wind pushing at my back, trying to force me down into the white abyss.

Don't look, Jack.

Not yet.

A flash of Ben Miller getting down from his horse. I saw Conner and Freddie Horvath. Griffin lay, curled on his side, on the ground between them. I wanted to go in. Something was happening.

I gasped, jolted, like I was shocked.

You made it longer than most till we got to this part, Jack.

Turned my face away, squeezed my fingers tight onto the lens, and shoved my hand under the sheet, made it stop.

"Did you see that?" I said, panting, wondering if I was still really here sitting beside Nickie. "Did you fucking see that?"

I tried taking deep breaths, could still feel the pull of that goddamned lens in my hand between us.

"You're shaking, Jack."

Nickie's hand, stroking my back.

Like Hannah when I was sitting in the cold tub on that first day.

"Did you see it?"

"You mean the glass?" Nickie said. "I saw the glass. Is that what you mean, Jack?"

I grabbed her shoulder with my empty hand, turned her face to mine. "You didn't see anything else?"

"No. What is it?"

I exhaled, fell back onto the pillow, shaking, sweating. I rolled over onto my stomach, eyes closed.

I need you to roll onto your stomach now. Do that.

I dropped my hand down from the bed and tucked the lens back inside the pocket of Ander's jeans.

Fuck you, Jack.

Nickie put her hands on my shoulders, began massaging me. "What are you so frightened of, Jack?"

"You think I'm crazy, don't you?"

"Shhh . . ." Nickie pressed her lips between my shoulder blades and kissed me. "Don't say that. Tell me what you saw, Jack."

She kissed me again, lay her body down on top of mine so I could feel every feature of hers as she pressed against my skin.

This is real.

"Terrible things."

309

fifty-two

I had to go back.

In the night, while we slept, Seth came.

Roll.

I woke first.

Tap. Tap. Tap.

I whispered, "Seth?"

I looked over at Nickie. Her eyes were closed. Then she breathed, so quietly, "Did you say something?"

"Listen." I whispered again, "Seth?"

Her eyes opened, met mine. I squeezed her hand and pressed it to my chest.

Roll.

Tap.

Tap.

Tap.

"It's him. Can you hear it, Nickie?"

"It's the horse, isn't it?" she said.

And then we heard that hushed breath of his: "Seth."

Sweat.

I'm shaking.

Nickie wipes her hand through the wetness down along my chest and says, "You're trembling again. You're sick."

"You heard him."

"Yes, Jack. I heard him."

"So it is real."

"It's really happening."

"I need to do something. Need you to help me, Nickie."

She rubs the side of my face gently, says, "Jack, I'm scared."

"I'm scared, too, Nickie. Don't let me do anything bad."

"Like what?"

I can't answer. For the moment, the shaking is too intense. Everything is wet all around me in the bed, and Nickie sounds so far away, but she's saying, "Jack? Jack, what's happening?"

Roll.

Tap.

"Jack?"

"Stay next to me. Please."

Tap.

She's crying. "What does he want?"

"Don't let me get lost."

I find it. The lens is in my hand and I roll onto my back next to her.

"Say you love me, Nickie."

She's crying. "Jack. I'm afraid."

I feel her face next to mine, her lips at my ear. She tells me, "I love you," and the breath carrying her words feels like a ghost against my damp skin.

Tap.

It's time, Jack.

Just a peek.

I open my hand and look.

They didn't see us, had no idea what we were capable of doing. And in the rush to get moving, I'd made Ben leave everything behind at that place by the river. Everything but the guns.

And Griffin's clothes.

We were going to get him back.

We'd left the horses a hundred yards from where we stopped. From there, we walked in, keeping a line of trees and scattered mounds of shale that had been washed down from the face of the mountains between us and them. Before we'd gotten too close, I pulled Ben's shoulder around so he'd look at me, know I was serious.

I said, "Remember. Don't kill that young one."

Ben didn't answer. He just glanced down at the .45s he held in each hand, as though he were saying it wasn't up to him to make that kind of a promise.

When we worked our way up the rise above them, close enough that we could see through the trees, Ben put a hand out to stop me.

"Something's going on," he said. He leaned his face around the trunk of a ponderosa, and they were so close to us, I could smell them.

Then I heard the sounds of a struggle, someone was getting hit, thrown around.

"They're fighting each other," Ben whispered. "It looks like they're fighting over Griff. Look."

He grabbed my shoulder and pulled me around to where I had a clear view of what was happening.

Griffin was on the ground, lying on his side. His hands were bound behind his back, and a rope trailed from his ankle.

Freddie works the same way here.

But he was awake and alive. I could see his eyes moving from Freddie to Conner as they fought.

Conner didn't match up well against Freddie Horvath. His face was bloodied; and I saw him reel back from a strike, grab one of the axes, and swing it wildly at Freddie.

They were trying to kill each other.

Ben raised the gun in his right hand, steadied it to aim.

"Wait." I held Ben's forearm.

When Conner missed with his swing, Freddie charged at him, arms forward, so the black spots down his side made him look more like a leopard than a man. Freddie threw himself into Conner, wrapping his arms around Conner's hips and burying his face into his belly.

Conner screamed — a horrible sound — as the horns under Freddie's jaw dug into his gut, goring him badly. It made me sick to watch. Freddie lifted Conner up over his shoulders and blood sprayed out, showering Freddie in coughing sprays of red. Conner kicked and cried, and Freddie looked like he was biting and tearing at Conner with his mouth. Then Freddie threw him down on the rocks where Griffin was lying.

I shook my head and looked away, my hand still held tightly on to Ben's arm. I could feel him tense at the sight of what Freddie had been doing.

Conner lay on his back, painted with his own blood, eyes fixed upward, staring. His hands and feet were moving, but I knew he was not going to ever get up from that spot.

Freddie lifted up Griffin in a hug, began licking his face, smearing spit and blood all over him as the boy tried to shut his eyes and mouth and turn away. Griffin whimpered when Freddie grabbed him by his hair and turned the boy over in his grasp like he didn't weigh anything at all. Then Freddie pushed Griffin's face into the pooling blood on Conner's belly and pried the boy's mouth open with one of his black clawed fingers.

"Drink it! Drink it, you sorry little bitch!" Freddie said, grinding Griffin's face into the wounds. I heard the boy gagging in the blood, struggling to breathe.

"Drink!"

313

I raised the rifle.

"Fuck this place."

One shot. So fast, but I could see the spray and smoke come out through the other side of Freddie's head.

Fuck you, Freddie.

You're dead again.

He let go of Griffin's hair, and dropped the boy on top of Conner. Freddie, startled, looked up to where I'd fired from, then sat down on the ground, leaned forward, and died.

Ben rushed through the trees as soon as I pulled the trigger, holding those .45s out, both of them pointed at Freddie.

Griffin spit and blew red cords of snot from his nose, trying to wipe Conner's blood away from his face, onto his shoulders, struggling against the bindings on his wrists while he rolled away from the gore.

"Griffin!" Ben called.

"What the fuck did you wait so long for?" Griffin said, and spit again.

I followed Ben into the clearing. I didn't say anything as I walked up to them. Ben worked at untying the ropes from Griffin's wrists, and Griffin kept spitting and blowing out snot all over himself and Ben.

I stood over Conner. His eyes were wide-open, those soulless black-white polished stones, staring at me. He gurgled and moaned with shallow, quickened breaths. That mark, shaped like a fish, the scalp fastened around his genitals on a strand of dried gut that had been threaded through blackened and dried human fingers, a chain of adult molars, spattered pink and red with Conner's own blood, dangling around his neck.

Fuck this place.

"Conner?" I said. I was looking straight into his eyes. "Conner Kirk?"

He blinked, and whispered, "Jack."

Fuck you, Jack.

Hearing him say my name was like getting kicked in the balls. I stepped back, saw just the faintest image of Seth standing on the other side. He vanished, and once again Conner mouthed my name.

"Jack?"

"Jack?" Nickie says it again, shakes my shoulder.

I'm lying down in the tub. In a bath.

Ice.

Jack doesn't take baths. Ever.

The water is freezing cold; and the light I see coming from beyond the open door shows the color of morning. Traffic sounds from the street, through the open window.

I close my eyes tightly. There are images burned into them: people I've never seen, but I know who they are — Hannah and Davey, laughing at me while Ma bathes me in the well house. Freddie Horvath, forcing Griffin's face down into a pool of Conner's blood, making him drink it.

Conner.

Freddie Horvath.

Seth.

"Fuck!" I throw my arms out in front of me and pull myself upright, my knees breaking the surface of the water. "Goddamnit!"

I slap my fists down into the icy water.

I'm freezing, shuddering, muscles locked in protest against the cold, but I can feel the sweat coming. The sickness.

Nausea.

Nickie grabs a towel, tries to wrap it around my shoulders, and my wet feet slip on the floor when I attempt to get myself out of the tub.

Just like being born.

You're going down, asshole.

It doesn't matter.

Nothing matters when you're puking everything that's alive out of you, watching it drown in a goddamned toilet.

Shivering.

"Jack?"

I'm collapsing. Every layer, imploding, compacting into that black, painful piece of scabrous nothing that makes a perfect heart for Jack Whitmore. And she's rubbing my back with the towel, making me warm, and it feels so good — like Hannah's hand.

But I give up.

I'm tired.

Jack begins crying.

First time in his fucked-up life.

"I am so tired, Nickie," I said. "I am so tired of this shit."

I couldn't understand it at all. I never felt like this once in my life, and I couldn't control the flashbulb images of all my messed-up thoughts machine-gunning through my brain: Conner dying in Marbury; worrying about Griffin and Ben; thinking why the fuck Nickie would put up with my shit for even one minute, but I loved her so much. I loved her so much. My stomach was tightening by itself, my throat locking up, and tears — goddamned tears — were coming out of my eyes.

"Shhh . . ." She rubbed the towel into my hair, all down my back, making me feel so small. "It's going to be better, Jack. You're going to be okay, now."

She stood. I heard the sink running, and Nickie held a glass of water out for me.

"Here. Drink some," she said.

When I set the glass down on the floor, Nickie gently put her arm around me and said, "Come on, now."

She helped me stand and led me back into the bedroom. She dried my body with the towel, and I stood there numbly, like a patient. Then she covered me with blankets and sat down in a chair beside the bed, stroking my hair, her voice, like a song, as she said, "It's going to be all right, Jack. It's going to be all right."

I didn't believe her.

As I lay there, sensing her touch on me, I felt so stupid about the wetness on my eyes. But I didn't want to wipe it away, either, because I didn't want Nickie to notice it, even though I knew she did.

I told myself that I wouldn't go back to Marbury again, but that made me feel stupid, too.

You're a fucking liar, Jack.

I felt so sad about Conner. He knew who I was, I was certain of it, and I was afraid to go back and see the waste of it all.

But more than that, I was afraid to not go back, to always wonder about Griffin and Ben, or to ask myself, constantly, if there was some reason, like Henry believed, for me — for us — to be there, as though I could make some kind of difference and help those boys.

I was an idiot to think I wouldn't go back again.

I'd die here if I didn't go back to Marbury.

Fuck you, Jack.

Nickie's fingers ran through my hair.

I closed my eyes.

Nickie sat by my side while I slept. She never took her hand away from me. It made me safe.

I woke before noon.

She kissed my forehead and smiled. "You look better."

I was embarrassed, felt so weak. I combed my hair back out of my face with a hand. "Thank you for staying, Nickie."

"I can ring down for breakfast if you'd like."

I sat up, realized I still didn't have anything on. "What happened last night? What happened to me after we heard Seth?"

"We went to sleep. I woke up and you were gone. You'd gone into the bath. I thought you were sleeping. You were so cold."

The lens.

I jolted, suddenly awake, and glanced over at the clock.

"My phone." I looked on both nightstands. Nickie reached down and grabbed it from the floor, where it had fallen among our clothes.

I had two missed calls from Conner, and one from Henry.

I got up from the bed, holding the blanket in front of my waist. I don't know why I acted so dumb and fragile, standing there in front of her, could feel myself turning red.

"Conner's probably at King's Cross," I said. "I forgot all about it."

I looked away from her, dropping my covers and quickly pulling on the jeans I'd borrowed from her brother. I should have worn something else, but I didn't want Nickie to see that I was most concerned about making sure the lens was still in my pocket. I felt it there as I buttoned the jeans. I looked at her then. She had been watching me get dressed, and that made me feel renewed embarrassment.

It was good to get out. The rain had stopped, and the city was clean and smelled like the sea. On our way to the Underground, I called Conner. His train was ninety minutes out, so Nickie and I ate breakfast and had coffee at the station.

"I don't want to go home tomorrow, Nickie."

She sipped her coffee, dabbed her lips with a napkin. "I wish you could stay."

I held her hand. She said, "Promise me that you will fix that angry and scared boy inside here."

She smiled and rubbed my chest.

"I promise."

And we kissed.

"Then perhaps before you come back to England for school, I can come to California for a visit."

I looked into her eyes to see if she was joking.

"You could move into my bedroom and Wynn and Stella wouldn't even notice."

She laughed.

"Jack," she said. "Tell me about this."

She reached across my lap, clearly making no effort to avoid brushing her fingers slowly over me. Her hand closed around the lens inside my pocket.

I was stupid to have fooled myself into thinking she didn't know what I was trying to hide.

"It's a lens," I said.

"It was from those glasses, wasn't it?"

"Yes. They broke that day Conner and I got into a fight at Blackpool."

"What does it do?"

"It shows me things in another place. Most people can't see it, though, I think."

Because most people are dead there, like you, Nickie.

"Is it a good place?"

"No."

Nickie took another drink. "I can't see it, but Conner can, right? Is that why you fought over it?"

I took a deep breath, sighed. "I guess so. He didn't want me to see it, and I needed to keep him away from it."

"Why?"

"It's a terrible place for Conner. That's all. I guess I was trying to protect him, or protect our friendship. But he didn't understand." I shifted. I was uncomfortable, and I was so distracted by her touch at that moment. "Do you think I'm crazy?"

"I don't think that, Jack. I saw what it did to you last night."

"And you heard the sounds. You know I'm not just imagining this."

"I don't know what to believe," she said.

"I'm sorry. Neither do I." I cleared my throat, and nervously, hurrying the words out of my mouth, said, "Will you spend the night with me again tonight?"

"I think Conner would be very jealous if I did." She blushed, smiling.

"Please?"

She rubbed against my leg. I wished we hadn't left the hotel so early.

Don't hurt her, Jack.

Don't be Mike Heath.

But I wanted her so badly at that moment, and I was so caught up in being disgusted with myself for how weak and unreasonable I felt.

Nickie leaned against me, put her head down on my shoulder so her hair fell against my face and spilled, coolly, inside the neck of my T-shirt.

"Okay. So tell me the rest of it," she said.

"I'll tell you whatever you want me to."

"Tell me the rest of the story. About the boy."

But I didn't want to do that.

Seth didn't want me to.

"There isn't much to it, Nickie. And it's not nice."

"I want to hear it. I want to hear it like the boy who made that horse, and played with it under our bed last night, was telling it to me and nobody else."

fifty-three

SETH'S STORY [5]

I came to find out from Pa that it was he who'd sent Uncle Teddy over from Davey's house to fetch me and Hannah so we might come to supper there. And Pa felt sorely terrible for doing that, so blamed himself for everything that happened after. He told me that, in the darkness of the barn, before we left with the preacher's body.

I only saw my beautiful Hannah one more time after that morning when Pa and I dragged Uncle Teddy out into the ditch and burned him. I believe we both felt sick about what we did, but we also knew we had to do it for Hannah's sake, and that's all there was to it. And Pa was mad enough at me, and rightfully so, but we swore to each other we would never mention Hannah and what had happened to her, no matter what.

On our way back home, Pa stopped alongside the river, and I used a bucket of water and a brush with lye to try and get all that preacher's black blood out of the wagon bed, but it hardly faded at all. At least, not to me it didn't; and every time I looked down at those splintered and dismal boards, I could see by how the stain had taken shape exactly where Uncle Teddy had stretched out to die.

So I couldn't help but think that he was following me around, making some kind of telltale mark to illuminate my wickedness and lead anyone with a pure soul to me, so he might kill me and do God's just work.

"It ain't coming clean," I said.

Pa sat by the river, smoking. "I didn't believe it would, Seth."

He rolled up another cigarette and handed it to me. "Here," he said. "I been meaning to ask you one day if you'd care to sit and smoke with me, and I reckon today's a proper time for it."

So I sat down next to him and watched the river rush past us while we had our cigarettes.

The house was deathly quiet when we got back, and I felt so terrible for the suffering I had brought into everyone's lives there. I went into the kitchen first, and kissed Ma; but she didn't say anything to me, and kept her eyes fixed downward on the dinner she was fixing. I figure it was too much for her to take in all at once, and I couldn't expect that she would ever forgive me for what I'd done to her daughter.

I left Pa there and went upstairs. He knew I was going to see Hannah.

She sat on her bed, admiring that horse I'd made for her one Christmas before. It seemed like such a long time ago to me.

I left the door standing open. Hannah understood that I swore no more disrespect to Ma and Pa.

"Hello, Hannah."

She raised her eyes. I could see she'd been crying, so I went over and sat down beside her. I combed her beautiful hair with my hand and she said, "You smell like smoke, Seth."

She put the toy horse down in her lap.

"Pa and me smoked some cigarettes."

She smiled. "Pa don't mind your wickedness any more than I do, I reckon."

"I want you to know that everything I ever did in my life, I did because of how overcome I am by loving you, Hannah. And now I believe things are going to be the way we always dreamed."

We embraced and kissed.

"Does it hurt much?" I asked.

"The baby?" she said. "No. He regular don't hurt."

"I meant your arms and legs."

"Oh. That'll heal." Then she put her hands around mine and said, "And I want you to know that everything I ever did in this life, I did because I am so taken by loving you, Seth."

We kissed again, and during that kiss I heard the urgent knocking against the door below of the men who'd come looking to take Pa and me away.

The women cried.

There was nothing we could do; Pa and I weren't about to fight, and there wasn't any sense in trying to run, either.

When they took us outside, they put irons on our wrists. I was scared so bad I was shaking, but Pa didn't show any feelings at all. I turned back only one time and Ma and Hannah were holding one another on the porch.

That was the last time we'd ever see each other.

They were vigilantes from Necker's Mill: five of them, men we knew by little more than name, because we'd see them at church and Davey worked at the mill alongside them, too. They drove us away from home in a wagon, three of them following on horseback.

The big man, Mr. Russ, drove the wagon, and he was irritable enough.

"Dumb sons of bitches, the both of you are," he said. "Alvin Hanrion sat there and watched the whole murderous deed from start to finish."

Hanrion was on horseback, so I saw him nodding like a puppet while Russ spoke.

"What you could possibly been thinking defies my reckoning," Russ said.

And Pa said, "I suppose it does, Russ."

"Ain't no sense in taking you two all the way, thirty mile, into Napa City for what'll be done."

"Ain't none," Hanrion said. The other riders stared at us with grim, unshaven faces.

"This'll be good right up here," Russ said.

Ten miles away from our home was the spot they chose to hang Pa and me.

Russ brought the wagon around under a redwood tree, looking up and back, alternately, to judge the height of the wagon bed to a suitable branch.

He stopped the wagon just there, and set the brake.

Then the men took me down. I couldn't stand anymore I was so scared. They left Pa in the wagon and Russ said, "Let's put the boy up after his pa."

"Ain't no need for you to harm the boy," Pa said. "It was my doing."

"Hanrion saw different, I reckon," Russ said.

Two of the riders grabbed me and made me stand between them. I was shaking so hard, like I was freezing from cold, only I knew it was summer.

Hanrion tossed a rope over the tree branch. The loose end spilled down into the wagon bed.

Russ said, "Put it in closer to the trunk, so there's room out that-away for the boy."

Then Russ tied a simple slipknot on the end and put it around Pa's neck. He and the other driver made Pa stand. Pa looked at my eyes, but I couldn't stand it and looked down. He didn't say anything at all. I watched his legs. He wasn't shaking or knee-buckled at all. I just watched his feet.

He went up on his tiptoes when Hanrion secured the rope tight to a second tree.

I heard the brakes unlock.

The wagon lurched forward.

I watched Pa's feet.

He didn't struggle at all when the wagon went out from under him, but I heard the heavy creak inside Pa's body just at the moment when he died.

I can't move on my own.

Three of the men lift me into the wagon.

Pa's feet hang weightless, dragging along the bed boards.

Everything is so loud. My breathing becomes a screaming gale in my head; I feel as though I'm underwater. It seems the universe has reduced down to nothing that isn't within five feet of me.

The men hold me up next to Pa.

I still don't look at him. I'm ashamed because what happened to him was all my doing.

I realize my hands are clasped behind me. I think about a prayer, but no words come to me, outside of my own voice telling me, *Why would God care to listen to me after what I'd done on His world?*

When the men let go of my arms I fall down.

They say something, and cuss at me, but I can't hear over the roaring in my ears.

With angry hands, two of them prop me back up to my feet.

Russ tosses the rope up over the branch, and I feel the soft weight of the end hit me between my shoulders where it comes down. They hold me.

I see Hanrion ahead of me with both his hands at the rope's end.

The other man stands beside him, looking at me while he pisses on the same sapling they use to anchor me and Pa.

Russ forces the loop down over my ears. It scrapes them, and I can feel the needle end of every single whiskered burr of that hemp jabbing my skin as he tightens the knot.

It makes me dizzy even before Hanrion begins to secure his end.

When he tightens it to the tree, I do like Pa did. I am forced, stretched out as far as I can go, up on the narrowest tips of my feet.

The men get down, the sounds their boots make on the wagon boards is like a thousand simultaneous eruptions of thunder. The brake lets go. Wheels loosen, and the wagon moves forward.

I fix my eyes off in the distance through the trees.

I have never seen colors as spectacular.

I imagine my Hannah, and how she smells, but there is no more air, and I am floating in it, besides.

I feel myself kicking and kicking at the empty air.

My shoes come off.

Kicking.

My britches are even slipping down my waist, I am kicking so hard.

I keep my eyes fixed on the distance.

I have never seen anything so perfect.

I hurt.

It made me sick again.

"Fuck." It was all I could say, that one word. I pressed my head down, so the heels of my palms squeezed my eyes shut. There were tears in them for the second time that day, and again, I said, "Fuck."

I felt Nickie's hand, resting so softly on my leg, her fingers barely squeezing me, like she was scared.

I said, "I'm sorry, Seth."

And I didn't pull my hands away from my face until I felt Nickie's arms slip around me. Then she put her face against my neck and cried.

Everything is so loud: my ears, roaring just like Seth's must have.

I have to touch the lens, but I can't move my hands yet.

Nickie whispers, "There must be a reason he chose you, Jack."

Who? Freddie or Seth?

Or Henry?

I try to get a breath, feel strangled.

"He knew who I was. Whitmore. She gave his baby that name."

I know I need to go back, and Nickie says, "I love you."

fifty-four

"Jack!" Conner saw us before we realized he had already gotten down from the train.

He smiled and threw his arms around me. Then he looked at Nickie, hugged her, and gave her a kiss on her cheek.

327

He looked good, healthy, like I wished I did.

"Damn," he said. "You look like you lost twenty pounds. And, dude, what's up with the ripped jeans?"

Conner never changed. I liked that.

We walked back along the platform together toward the Underground, and that's when Nickie said what I was hoping she wouldn't.

"I think I'd better be going home now. I likely am going to find myself in a bit of trouble when my parents realize I didn't come home last night."

Conner slapped my butt. "Dude."

"It's our last night here, Nickie," I said. My voice sounded dumb and whiney. "Me and Conner are going to go out. Please come with us."

"Ooh. Threesome," Conner said.

"Shut up."

"I don't know," she said. "I'll phone you later. If I can't make it, I promise to go to Heathrow with you both tomorrow and see you off."

I sighed.

And as soon as I kissed her good-bye at the Tube station, Conner patted me on the shoulder and said, "And in case you're wondering about me and Rachel, the answer is *Yes, we did, too.*"

I rolled my eyes. "I am so relieved."

"Not as much as me, dude."

We went on a run for the last time through Regent's Park. I tried not to think about the distractions — the lens, Marbury, Nickie, going home — but I couldn't stay focused. Sweating, we walked back in toward the hotel along Marylebone Road; and Conner just couldn't seem to wipe the beaming, gloating look from his face.

"You look different," he said.

"You already said that." I wiped my hand through my hair. "I'm skinnier."

"No," Conner said. "I don't mean that. Just your face, I think. Dude, see what sex does to you?"

"Whatever."

"Do you love her?"

"I am totally in love with her, Con."

"You still pissed at me?"

"Not even close." I said, "What about you and Rachel?"

"Yeah," he said. "I am ready to check out of Glenbrook and get back here before it's even close to the beginning of the term."

"Me too."

When Conner was in the shower, I began sweating and shaking again. I sat there on the vinyl-covered desk chair, the bare skin of my legs and back adhering to it, just staring at those ripped jeans that were balled up on my side of the bed.

Don't do it, Jack.

Just get through one night without pulling that shit on the people you love.

I felt sick, looked at my phone, trying to will it to ring so I could hear Nickie's voice. Maybe it could anchor me down.

I went to the refrigerator bar and opened two beers. I stuck my arm into the shower and said, "Here. Party time."

Just trying to do anything to keep myself away from the Marbury lens.

Conner clinked his beer bottle against mine.

"And hurry up and get out. I want to get ready, too," I said.

I hated times like this; times when I'd just carry my phone around in my sweaty hand, waiting for a call, checking and rechecking the empty screen.

It began buzzing when I was in the shower. It spun a half circle on the marble countertop beside the bathroom sink.

I shut the water off and shook what I could from my arms and legs.

I picked up the phone.

It wasn't her.

"Henry," I said.

"I wanted to see if you'd come back," he said. "You weren't exactly *here* when you came to my flat on Tuesday, were you?"

"I don't remember it."

Jack doesn't remember anything.

I grabbed a towel and wrapped it around me, tried to keep my voice down so Conner wouldn't come. I could hear the television. It sounded like an English version of *The Amethyst Hour*.

"Is everything good, then?"

"The boys are okay now."

"And you?"

"As usual. Fucked," I said. "I'm going back to the States tomorrow."

Silence.

"I see."

"Yeah."

"Jack? Sometime, will you tell me how it ends?"

"Sometime," I said. "Bye, Henry."

I closed my phone.

I wondered if maybe Henry still hurt about Marbury. He said he didn't, but I didn't really believe that, either. I imagined him, at that moment, holding his guts and shaking somewhere in his dirty flat, all alone, wishing.

And I didn't care anymore if Conner couldn't see Henry that

night, or if he couldn't hear him on the phone. Or if he was ever real in the first place, because I knew when I hung up the phone that I was never going to hear from Henry Hewitt again.

I dried off and pulled on a fresh T-shirt and underwear. It actually felt good, like I hadn't been clean in days, and I tried to just keep my head focused on going out with Conner for our last night in London. But I still carried the phone in my hand, waiting for her, when I walked back into the bedroom.

Conner was sitting, one foot on the floor, one leg stretched out on top of the bed. His shoes were on. He looked, as Conner usually did, like a guy you'd see in some trendy clothes company print ad, like he was forever on his way out to some club or party or something. He was talking on his phone, and just when I came in I heard him say, "I love you," and he closed the phone, looked at the screen, then slid it into his pocket.

I cleared my throat. "Pretty serious, Con."

"Dude." And I could tell he was going to say something sarcastic: "That was a surprise voice mail message I was leaving for *you*."

Crazy Jack would probably think it was from Henry.

"Okay. Sure."

Conner's smile faded. "Is something wrong?"

"Nah. It's okay."

I began digging through my pack, looking for something to wear. "All my shit's thrashed," I said.

"Well, if you didn't live like a drug addict, it wouldn't happen."

Then I remembered Nickie had actually left a bag of laundered clothes that she'd taken from me on Monday. It was still sitting by the door. When I opened it, it was almost like going back in time. And everything I'd worn that day was in there, perfectly folded, and clean. Even my socks. I took them out, sat on the bed, and pulled them onto my feet.

Then I saw that she'd left a small square of paper inside. On it, she'd written *I love you*. I took the note out and stared at it for a while.

Conner leaned over my shoulder and said, "Is that for me?"

"She washed some clothes for me," I said.

I pulled out the jeans that were in the bag. They looked like she'd pressed them or something, like they were brand-new. They smelled like Nickie's house.

"That," Conner said, "is called *folding*. Some people do it to their clothes so they don't look like fucking newspapers you'd find at the bottom of a trash can. Observe, numbnuts."

Then he grabbed Ander's balled-up jeans from the bed and shook them out to give me a lesson.

That's when the Marbury lens dropped out of the pocket.

I don't know if Conner said, "Holy shit!" before I said, "God-damnit!" or if we both blurted out our curses simultaneously. But it was like a floodlight being shot out into every angled corner of the room; so overpowering that I could instantly smell and hear every-thing in Marbury. I looked down at the lens as it sat there, blasting a hole through the rumpled sheets, opening up on some other forever.

Conner saw it, too, said, "How the fuck did this get here?"

I looked at him. His eyes were stuck on the lens.

"I can see you there, Jack."

I looked down, saw a black bug the size of my forearm crawling on the bed.

Then, I don't know.

fifty-five

That sound.

Chewing.

My stomach, twisting, as I looked down at Conner, wondering what he was seeing, what this felt like to him.

"Here," Ben said. He handed a water bottle to Griffin, and the boy poured it out over his head, bathing the blood away from his face and chest.

"And put these on." Ben held Griffin's fatigues and gun belt in the other hand.

I'd been kneeling beside Conner. His breaths were faint, gurgling rasps.

The harvester I'd seen was chewing its way inside Freddie's skull through the exit wound from my bullet. Another had already slipped inside a fresh, perfect circle just below his sternum. There were maybe a dozen more on the ground, working their way beneath his body.

Chewing.

But none on Conner yet.

I leaned over him, looked right into his eyes.

"Hey. Jack," he whispered. "It hurts pretty bad."

"What the fuck, Jack? What the fuck?" Ben said.

He took one step toward me. I put my palm up, warning him back.

"No, Ben. I'll tell you about it some time."

"Put him down, Jack," Griffin said. "Just shoot him in the fucking head."

I turned and looked at Griffin. "I can't."

Conner moved his hand, tried to touch me.

I grabbed on and held it.

Jack doesn't cry.

Seth had been watching us, back at the edge of the trees where I had taken the shot at Freddie.

"Come on, Jack," Ben said. "Either do it, or let's get out of here. We left a lot of shit back there at the river, and I vote we go get it now."

He raised his hand.

Griffin's came up, too. "So do I."

I got up onto my feet. "Well then go ahead and leave me."

"We can't do that, Jack. You agreed to always do what we vote on. We all did. You agreed," Ben said. "Fuck you if you're going to break that now."

Fuck you, Jack.

I looked back at Seth. He was so pale and dim.

"Seth," I said. "Can you help me? One more time? You know what I'm asking. Can you do it?"

Seth vanished, then immediately reappeared between me and the boys.

Two of the harvesters abandoned Freddie Horvath and scuttled across the ground toward Seth. They were after the ghost. He disappeared again, then faintly stood above Conner's head.

Then Seth spoke. It was the only time I'd ever heard his voice clearly, not in a whisper. I mean, I could hear him in his story, but this was actually audible. Real. The clear and confident-sounding voice of a boy.

"I believe I might not see you again, Jack." He faded, moved beside me. I could feel him. The harvesters came across the ground toward us. "You love that girl, don't you?"

"Yes."

"I reckon you do." I could see his mouth twist into a grin. "I understand about this one, Jack. You love him, too, I suspect."

I looked at Conner.

"You know who I am, don't you, Seth?" I said.

"Ever since you were born. Well. I just might not see you again, Jack. So, thank you for carrying my story."

Then I saw that small gray fog, and Seth vanished inside of Conner Kirk.

The harvesters stopped, moved along the ground back toward Freddie, their jointed legs clicking like plastic.

Conner convulsed, doubled forward like he'd been stung. He curled up onto his side, panting, his eyes closed tightly, arms locked across his midsection where Freddie had stabbed him. He stayed there crumpled in pain, breathing fast, like an injured animal.

"Jack." Ben was impatient.

Griffin pulled on his pants, his guns hanging low, arms folded across his bare chest.

I grabbed Conner's knee and rolled him over, onto his back. He groaned, eyes still shut tight. I put my hand around his wrist and pulled his arm away from his gut.

"Let me see," I said.

The bleeding stopped. The gore wounds had closed up to narrow slits, like they'd been glued shut; and that small fish-shaped mark above Conner's groin had gone dark, faded to nothing more than a pale scar, like some souvenir of a burn, or a birthmark.

His body shook everywhere.

"Con?"

Ben stepped forward. He held a gun in his hand. It was pointed down, and he swung it right up in line with Conner's face.

335

I jumped. I tackled Ben around the waist, driving my shoulder into his belly. He grunted, and I felt the wind being knocked out of him as he fell back. The gun swung up into the air and fired as his finger clenched around the trigger. It rang so loud in my ears that for a moment I wondered if I'd been shot.

We hit the ground. I snaked my hand up along Ben's wrist and pinned his hand against the ground. He was gasping for air, but his lungs didn't work. I sat on his chest and brought my right hand up into a fist.

Before I could punch him, Griffin launched himself into me, catching my swing on the back of his shoulder and rolling me away from Ben.

He sprang onto his feet like a monkey, ready to jump at me again.

"Cut it the fuck out!" Griffin snapped.

Ben sat up. He'd dropped his gun in the fight, and reached to grab it again.

I stood between the boys and Conner. I swung my rifle behind my back.

"Go ahead, Ben," I said. I put my arms out. "Go ahead and shoot me, too. I don't fucking care anymore."

Ben's hand shook.

Griffin screamed, "Stop it!"

Cautiously, Ben put his gun away and stood up. He brushed himself off. He never took his eyes from me.

When I turned around, Conner was sitting up, taking deep breaths, his head was lowered between his bent knees, arms folded across his ankles.

He looked up at me. I saw his eyes. It was him, the black and white eyes were gone, and I could clearly see that it was really Conner Kirk who was sitting on the ground, right there in front of us.

"What the fuck is going on, Jack?" he said.

I looked back at Ben and Griffin. Their mouths just kind of hung open like they couldn't understand what had happened.

"He's just a kid," Griffin said. "Just like us."

"You okay, Con?"

Conner looked down, jolted, shocked when he saw the scalp and dried human fingers that were strung around his hips.

"Fuck!" he said. He tore at the cord around his waist and tossed it away into the dirt. The bugs were immediately on it, chewing. Then he pulled at the necklace, scattering teeth everywhere. He brushed his hands all over his body, like he'd been covered with ants, or was putting out some kind of fire; and when he saw Freddie lying right beside him, Conner crab-crawled back toward the edge of the clearing and sat there, panting, with his knees hugged up to his naked chest.

"What the fuck is this shit?" Conner looked at each of our faces, eyes wide.

He didn't remember.

"It's okay, Con. It's going to be okay," I said.

I stepped over toward him, but Conner scooted back, like he was afraid of me or something.

I put my hand out to him. "Come on. You're okay now."

He stopped backing up and sat there, shaking, out of breath, while I kneeled beside him.

Then I saw the fog, like the mist your breath makes on a cold morning, swirling around Conner, taking form once again: the faintest, gray outline of Seth. And they all saw it, too.

There were harvesters everywhere on the ground now, moving, column after column, into the clearing, picking and chewing away at Freddie Horvath, at the scant coverings Conner had torn away from

337

his own body, the sound of their mechanical clicking, buzzing of wings, chewing, growing louder all the time.

And they were on Seth, too, at the outlines of his shoeless feet; it was as though they were actually holding him down to that spot.

Then the noise started. It was low at first, distant-sounding, but then it grew into a painfully loud, jangling din that sounded like metal being torn apart. I heard screams of pain; and the black bugs held on to Seth; and I could tell the terrible wailing was coming from inside him.

Seth began to pulse and flash, the same way he did when I'd seen the subway through him. All of us could see those same images through him: a spastic kind of movie reel of poorly focused and faded film clips. I saw Seth, a tiny boy, shivering, sitting in the freezing water in a steel trough while Davey and Hannah laughed at him; then I saw Glenbrook, and Freddie Horvath driving his Mercedes by the Steckel Park basketball courts at night; Conner and me fighting in the cold water at Blackpool; I saw us in our hotel room, Conner dressed to go out for the evening, me standing there in my underwear, holding a bottle of beer and staring at the gaping doorway that blasted through the middle of the bed; the dead people inside the train; two bodies hanging beside one another from the branch of a redwood tree; the little wooden horse — *Roll. Tap. Tap. Tap.* And I could see other places, too — places I'd never seen before — a city built entirely upon stone bridges; a dense jungle with flocks of birds so thick it was like standing inside a tornado while they swirled around and around, and I could feel the beating of their wings in the millions; huge mountains covered with ice and snow; endless, storm-tossed black seas. Endless.

Then I heard gunfire.

The boys had begun shooting the harvesters that were ripping Seth apart. The black things spun and flipped into the air, spraying arcs of foamy orange and yellow innards as they disintegrated under the storm of bullets. I swung the rifle around and began firing as well. The images inside the ghost blurred, faded.

Then Seth was gone.

And we all stood frozen in the ringing deafness that followed the firing of our guns.

I looked from Ben, to Griffin, then back to Conner, who had gotten to his feet and was standing, half-hidden, behind the trunk of a pine tree. When my ears stopped buzzing, I heard the chewing of the harvesters again.

"Spot!" Griffin yelled. His little dog came back from where we'd left the horses, hunched down like he was walking on ice. The dog whipped his tail when he saw Griffin, but as soon as the boy bent to touch him, the dog curled his shoulders and tucked his tail between his legs. He smelled the blood on the boy.

"Awww," Griffin said. "It's okay, boy."

I walked over to where Seth had been. I noticed something moving on the ground. It glinted and wriggled, like the reflection of the moon at night on a windblown lake.

"Is something there?" Ben said.

"I don't know."

I stood back just as I could see what it was Seth had left behind.

"Fuck!" I said. I scooped my hand along the ground blindly and closed my fingers. I tucked it into my pocket.

"What was it?" Griffin asked. The dog sniffed his bare feet.

"Nothing," I said. "It doesn't matter." I sighed, and glanced at Conner. I was sure he'd seen it, too, could tell by the look on his face that he knew I was lying.

It was easy to convince myself I was saving the boys from something they wouldn't want.

I looked back at Freddie's body. It was moving by itself, a puppet, twitching on invisible strings, as harvesters crawled inside, just below the skin, chewing.

"Let's get out of here."

"Is he coming with us?" Ben said. He looked once, warily, over at Conner, who was still standing behind the tree.

I raised my hand. "I vote he comes with us."

Griffin did the same. "Me too."

"He would have killed you, Griff," Ben protested.

"Not him," Griffin said. "Look at him. He's just a kid, like us. And if Jack says it's okay, that's good enough."

Ben nodded. "Well, then, let's get out of here."

fifty-six

Two discs of glass — perfectly blue, dark as lapis, flawlessly round. Lenses. And when I saw them lying on the ground at the spot where Seth had vanished, I could see tiny images of people and things swirling around on the other side of them, just like I'd seen in Henry's glasses that first time I noticed him watching me in London.

I kept them hidden. What else could I do? I tried pretending they weren't there, but the pull was, at times, too much to take. It made me sick in Marbury, too: the same obsessed Jack who'd shake and sweat his cravings on floors and toilets in that other uncertain world.

Conner began seeing it in me, too.

And both of us found ourselves wondering about how we'd get back to Marbury next time. If there was going to be a next time.

Two days later.

Riding north, we came to the shore of an endless lake — maybe it was the sea.

I couldn't tell which it was. It didn't matter. Of course it wasn't endless. There was no horizon in Marbury, no reference for anything, beginnings or endings; only that infinite screen of heat and white fog that constantly got farther and farther away, no matter how desperately we pushed ourselves on toward it.

The dog followed Griffin everywhere. He ran along with the horses, kept his paws just inches from the edge of the water.

And that morning, we walked the horses slowly out across the sand, past the wreckage of a pier. The immense wooden supports jutted up from the beach and broke the surface of the water like irregular teeth, rotten and crooked. Here and there, the posts hoisted random spans of crossbeams and asphalt that formed little islands floating in the colorless sky above the dark chop of the waves. We stopped there, and I tasted the water. It was gritty and piss warm, salty.

"What is this?" Griffin asked.

"I don't know," I said. "A pier, I think. It was a place where people —" I trailed off, wondering if there was any purpose in telling the boy what piers were.

I glanced over at Conner. It could have been Blackpool at some other time, in some other form.

The additional horse that once belonged to Freddie Horvath carried most of our gear now. And Conner wore an extra set of fatigues Ben had taken from the suitcase of one of the dead soldiers, with the boots that Griffin refused to put on since the first day after we'd abandoned that train. And I gave him my gun belt, too; twin 9-millimeter semiautomatics hanging at his sides.

The boys had grown accustomed to my friend, but it was a cautious acceptance of him. Still, they realized there was something more to us than they knew. At least Henry had prepared them for that in some ways, once he'd seen me in London.

So, that morning, when we came to a point where we could discern the faint silhouette of a walled city that had been built right up against the water's edge, we stopped our horses on the beach. We tied them inside a shallow canyon notched in the face of the tall gray bluffs that followed the contour of the shore.

There were a few birds here, and they made nests of mud high on the rock walls. I noticed Griffin watching them in wonder as they flew in and out of the dark yawning mouths of their homes; and I thought how lucky it was to be able to experience seeing birds for the first time in your life.

We sat together, quietly, on the beach and watched the distant city for hours.

We waited.

I knew each of us was afraid to commit, out loud, to passing some kind of judgment about whether we were in a good place or not.

"The way I see it," Ben said, pointing up the shore to the wall of the settlement, "is we can either go that way, or we can turn around and follow the shoreline south. I don't know how much longer you're planning on waiting, Jack, but we can't sit here forever."

"There might be people there," Griffin said.

"We might be better off without them," I answered.

"I'm tired of always running." Griffin shifted in the sand, where he sat, cross-legged, and looked at Conner. "I suppose Conner's going to get a vote now, too. That could mess things up. What if we tie? Are we gonna split up?"

Conner shrugged and looked away. "I won't vote if you don't want me to, little man."

Griffin said, "Which way would you vote if you did?"

"Not telling."

"Okay, then. Don't vote, in that case. I'll let you know when you can vote."

"You can't be like that, Griff," I said.

"Sure I can. He's new. We have to see how he's going to work out."

I shook my head, and Ben got to his feet and said, "I think we're going to have to hold off on the election, anyway. Look down that way, Jack. Someone's coming."

Griffin's dog began barking nervously. Then he ran off, back toward the bluff where we'd left the horses.

Silhouetted in dust, they came; three of them, running toward us awkwardly over the sand from the south. One of them fell down twice, and each time, the others would turn back and scoop up arms or hands, pulling, running; something frantic in their movements.

Our guns were already out before any of us could clearly tell who they were. We spread out across the beach, kneeling or lying down in the sand, watching.

I could hear them before I saw they were people. They grunted and gasped, one of them was crying, a woman, saying, "Papa, are they people? Are they people?"

I looked over at Griffin, lying so flat in the sand he was almost invisible, biting his lip, squinting to aim. Conner got down onto his belly, holding the guns in front of him, level. I could feel his leg against mine, and I knew he was scared.

"What the fuck, Jack?"

"Just hang in there, Con. It's going to be okay." I patted his back. "Do what I do."

Ben was watching us, off to my left.

"Are you people?" a man's voice called out. They stopped running, fifty feet away, but their gasping breaths sounded like more footfalls on the sand.

The boys waited.

"Answer them," Griffin whispered.

A man and woman stood at the front. They wore rags, and the man looked as though part of his scalp had been removed, from near his left eyebrow across his skull to the side of his ear. The wound was rough and crusted with dried blood that spattered the torn sleeve of the shirt he wore.

The third one was just a kid, a boy, wearing nothing more than shorts that were so tattered they looked like a skirt. I guessed he was about the same age as Griffin. He stood just beside the woman. His eyes were crazed and hollow, looked like he'd eat us if he could.

I stood up. "We're people."

The man's shoulders heaved, and he almost fell forward in relief. "Thank God," he said.

His boy stared at the guns we held. I suspected he had no idea what we were capable of doing with them.

Griffin got up next, followed by Ben and Conner.

We must have looked like we were springing up from graves in the sand, I thought.

"What is that place?" I said, pointing at the walls of the city behind me.

The man twitched his chin in the direction I'd pointed. "It's called Grove." He looked at me like he couldn't believe I didn't know. "Security is not sold for any kind of gold. You know, Grove. We thought you were soldiers from there."

"No. We're not from there," I said.

He looked puzzled, glanced quickly at the woman and boy. "Everyone who came with us is dead. We have to hurry. They're coming for us. We have to hurry to Grove."

Then he coughed. It didn't sound like much, just a quick hiccup, but he fell forward onto his face and I saw that a black arrow had buried itself just below his shoulder blade, and another was sticking straight up from his lower back.

Instantly, more arrows rained quietly down at us, whooshing into the sand. It seemed like there were dozens of them.

"Fuck!" Ben said, but Griffin had already started shooting in the direction of the attack before the word was fully out of the older boy's mouth.

By then, we could make out the dim shapes of the devils who'd been chasing the refugees across the sand, and we all started shooting. And as the attackers fell, the woman and boy got behind us and crouched, pressing their hands to their ears, moaning and crying.

Griffin screamed. An arrow appeared, as if from nowhere, sticking entirely through his arm. He fell back into the sand.

"Griff!" I shouted, moving across the beach toward him. "Griff!"

He twisted in the sand. Already, his blood was everywhere.

"Oh my God, Griff!" I scooped him up and started running back toward our horses. "Ben! Conner! Get to the horses! Griff's hurt!"

The hail of arrows thinned as Conner and Ben continued reloading and firing in turns. I tripped, fell forward into the sand. I tried not to land on top of Griffin, and he moaned when I did. The point of the arrow snapped off in the sand beneath him, and I realized that my shirt was covered in the boy's blood.

"Jack," he said. "Jack. Am I going to die?"

"No," I said. "Don't say that, Griff."

They were still shooting behind us. I squeezed my hand around the arrow shaft, and gripped Griffin's bicep with the other. My fingers nearly wrapped the entire circumference of his upper arm, he was so small. I pulled the arrow out quickly and tightened my grasp over the holes, trying to slow down the bleeding.

Griffin screamed, but he never cried.

When I tried to stand up, I realized that I'd fallen because there was an arrow through my calf. I couldn't move.

"Shit!"

I sat down in the sand next to Griffin, and propped my rifle on my knee. I watched the end of the arrow shaft bob its feathers up and down beside my shaking leg.

The shooting stopped.

Quiet.

I lay back in the warm sand and stared up at the sky.

I could see where the sun was: an indefinite circular blotch that was brighter than the rest of the endless nothing hanging above us. I reached over and put my hand in Griffin's hair and rubbed his head with my thumb.

"You okay?" I asked.

"Shit."

"We're going to be all right, Griff."

"Goddamn it hurts."

"Who's going to doctor us? Ben'll get scared if he sees us bleeding like we are."

346

"If he's not shot up, too, he's gonna have to toughen up, I guess. Him or your friend."

I heard footsteps through the sand, moving in our direction. I moaned when I sat up.

Ben and Conner were coming. Conner had his arm around Ben's shoulder, and the other boy followed behind like a prisoner. Ben was hurt. When they got closer, I saw an arrow shaft sticking straight out from the right side of Ben's chest. They stopped, stood over me and Griffin. The boy sat in the sand and watched us blankly, like he was bored. He carried an arrow and drew circles with it between his legs.

"Hell," Ben said. "Are you two okay?"

"Ben?" I said. I pointed at the arrow in his chest.

"It didn't go in anything. I can feel it rubbing next to my ribs. I'll be okay. I don't think I should sit down, though. Someone's going to need to help me pull it out. Shit."

Conner's face was twisted into a grimace. "What the fuck is this, Jack?"

"I don't know, Con." I looked at the arrow sticking through my leg. "Did you get hurt?"

Conner said, "No."

"How many'd you kill?" Griffin asked.

"All of them." Ben spit; and looked back at the kid sitting in the sand. "But the woman . . ."

He didn't have to finish.

"There's a med kit with the horses," Griffin said. He just lay there, facing directly up at the sky, one arm crossed over his bare chest, so he could squeeze the spot where he'd been shot.

Conner started off in the direction of the bluffs.

"Don't leave without me," he said. He tried to smile at us.

"And bring my dog, too," Griffin said.

"Soldiers!" I heard them calling out the word when we rode through the gate into Grove that day, like we had come to save them or something; when we could hardly get ourselves down from the horses, we were so battered.

They were careful at first, keeping back in the shadows or entry-ways of the buildings, but once the word spread about the boys who had come back from the war, we were surrounded by people, thousands of them, all trying to help us. They brought out food, water; there were instantly doctors and nurses making their way through the press of bodies.

"Henry promised you'd get us here," Ben said. He was pale and bloody.

Griffin sat straight on his horse, his little arm wrapped tightly around with bandages. His eyes lit up at the sight of all the people there who'd blocked the street and stopped our horses from carrying us any farther.

"There's girls here, too," he said.

"Don't go grabbing any of them now, Griff," I said.

A struggle broke out around Ben's horse. I saw Ben raise his foot and kick at a man who'd come to his side. Then another came up and Ben smashed his boot squarely into the man's mouth. As he spun away from Ben's horse, I could see him spitting blood and two of his teeth.

"Get the fuck off my guns!" Ben had his gun in his left hand, was waving it at the crowd, who pushed back.

"Jack!" Conner yelled.

"Get the fuck off me!" Ben threatened again.

"Jack!"

I saw Conner striking at reaching hands with his pistol's butt.

"What the fuck, Jack?" Griffin tried to pull his gun with his good hand.

"Don't!" I screamed.

"Jack!" Conner again.

I tried to jab my toes into my horse, get him to back up, but the pain sent a jolt through me and I nearly fell. And when I looked down at my bloody pant leg, my vision blurred and I saw a flash of white, a light reflected on sheets of water smearing down a cold pane of glass, the pale yellow of a streetlamp.

Fuck you, Jack.

fifty-seven

Just like being born.

I want to go home, but I don't know where that is anymore.

I'm covered in water, and I'm staring at a light.

My legs are stretched out in front of me. I see my shoes, my Vans, wonder how they got so wet.

"Goddamnit!"

I kick my heel into the ground. It takes a while for me to feel it.

Jack is very drunk.

Hey, kid. Kid. Are you okay?

Fuck you, Jack.

Fuck you, Freddie.

I'm cold, shaking, and my clothes are soaked, as though I'd just crawled up from the sewer. The rain comes pouring down; and Jack sits on the sidewalk like some fucking bum, just watching the blur of light on the dark windows across the street.

A car whirrs by as I roll around onto my hands and knees.

I can feel the spray when it passes, smell the nauseating stench of tires and exhaust.

I lower my face and vomit.

I stretch out, flat, onto my belly. My face hangs over the curb. It's like lying down at the bottom of a cold shower, but I suddenly feel good, can sense every nerve in my body pressing down against the earth through my wet clothes; and I think about Nickie, how much I want to be with her.

Something moves in my pocket.

My phone.

I spit.

It's nearly midnight.

Conner's calling me.

"Con."

"Where are you?"

"I don't know. On a street somewhere."

"Where?"

"Con? Are you here?"

Silence.

"Yeah."

"But you were there with me."

"Yeah."

"And Griff and Ben, too?"

"Yeah."

"What was the last thing you saw?"

"I'm fucking sick, Jack."

"Where are you?"

"I'm in the toilet. At that pub. Can you find it?"

I stood up, had to steady myself against a bus kiosk. I almost dropped the phone, fumbled to get it back up to my face.

"I'll find it."

I checked the calls before putting it away, and saw that I'd spoken to Nickie two times that night.

And I wondered if I fucked things up again.

I stumbled along on the sidewalk, and found the Warren Street Underground. I wasn't too far from Conner, but I had no idea how I'd ended up here, either.

I had to know.

I phoned her.

"Jack." She sounded tired, like she'd been sleeping.

"Nickie. Is everything all right?"

"Yes. I told you, Jack. I wish I could help you to stop being frightened about things. You know I love you. I'll see you tomorrow."

"Did I do anything stupid?"

She laughed. "I think you and Conner have had a little too much beer, Jack. You should go to sleep."

"I love you, Nickie."

"Good night, Jack," she said. "I do love you. I promise. Now go to bed."

The rain stopped before I got there.

I stood in the doorway to The Prince of Wales, dripping, embarrassed to go inside because I was so wet and so drunk. The bartender eyed me, but promptly ignored me. He was closing down. I wondered if I'd done anything bad.

"Your mate's come back." The bartender nodded toward the rear of the room.

Conner left some money on the bar and came out to the street.

"You look like hell," he said.

I shrugged. "You don't look so good yourself."

We started back to the hotel. Conner put his hand on my shoulder and squeezed. "Did you fall in the river or something?"

"Dude, I have no idea. When I came out of it, I was just sitting on the side of the street. Where were you?"

"I was standing at the bar watching that guy fill a pint glass of beer for me," Conner said. "I'm fucking drunk, I know that."

"Me too." I began shivering. "I need to get dry."

We walked.

"So, do you remember the last thing you saw?"

I heard him inhale. "I was just sitting there with you guys. And I saw this winking light in the window, and the next thing I know I was looking at a glass of beer."

We had come to the front of the hotel. The doormen looked suspiciously at me. I dripped water all over the floor.

Don't fucking look at me.

We walked through the lobby.

I said, "You were with me and Griff and Ben?"

"And that kid, too. In that hospital."

"What kid?"

"The boy on the beach. He said his name was Max, but that's all he ever said. Max."

"I don't remember how we got there."

The elevator doors yawned open.

"Ben started a fight because he thought they were going to take his guns away. He was crazy, I guess. Nobody wanted to hurt us, Jack, but we were all scared of them. Then everyone started fighting. It was pathetic, a bunch of bloody crippled kids trying to fight. Finally, Griff let off a few rounds in the air and everyone ran back. So they brought you all to the hospital and they left you guys in all your clothes because they were scared to touch you, and thought I'd do something crazy if they tried to take your guns off." Conner looked at me. "So they put five beds in there and let me stay with you."

"And everyone's okay?" I asked.

"Griff threw a fit because somebody took his dog home. You had to talk him out of shooting everyone at the hospital over it."

I began to feel warm again once I'd changed into dry things. Conner was already in bed, and the lights were out; but I had other things to take care of.

I had to be sure.

And I began tearing through everything I owned.

"I know what you're doing, Jack."

I froze.

"What the fuck do you expect me to do, Con?" I don't think I'd ever been so angry at him, didn't really understand where it was coming from.

I heard him sit up in bed.

"I know what you're doing because I already looked for it, Jack. It's right where you left it, inside one of your socks. Want me to show you?"

I sat down on the bed. "I'm sorry, Con. Sorry."

I put my face in my hands.

Jack doesn't cry.

"I'm sick of this shit, Con, but I can't stop it. I don't think I'm supposed to stop it. I know that sounds fucking crazy."

"I kind of get it, Jack," Conner said. "I almost wish that we really did get rid of them that day at Blackpool."

"You did. Seth brought the lens back."

"I know."

"Do you know everything? About him? Who he was?"

353

"Yeah."

I swallowed. "I know this is crazy, Con, but Seth was there, in Freddie's house with me. Way before I ever ran into Henry. Like, somehow, it was all supposed to happen, anyway."

"You were right, Jack. He wasn't just fucking with our brains. There really is something there."

"You sure of that, Con? You sure that guy was ever really here, on this side of the lens?"

Conner shrugged.

I got up, dug my hand down inside the backpack. I just had to know it was still there. I found the sock and Conner said, "And those other two blue ones are in there, too. I saw them, and I'm scared of 'em, Jack."

He turned on the light.

I found the sock, could already feel the additional weight of the other lenses inside it. I balled the sock up tight, slipped it inside another. "I'm going to leave it alone, Con. I promise." I sat down again. "I saw something in those lenses that night I picked them up."

"So did I," Conner said. He got out of bed and stood in front of me. "And, Jack? I think maybe things are happening to me."

"It's not our fault what happens."

"I'm scared, Jack."

fifty-eight

Jack was going home.

We met Nickie at Paddington Station and caught the train to Heathrow.

It was depressing. We held hands and said little more than how slow time would pass until we could be together again.

Conner had already phoned Rachel. He sat across from us, glumly watching the places that passed by outside the window.

An American soldier walked down the aisle through our car. His name badge said STRANGE. Conner noticed it, too. He shifted in his seat, looked at Nickie, then me, and whispered, "This is fucked up."

I could see it in his eyes. He was feeling sick.

So was I.

Conner stood up. "I got to go to the toilet."

"It's going to be okay, Con."

He started to walk away, and I said, "We'll be back soon."

He turned around and just nodded his chin upward.

He knew what I meant.

I wasn't talking about here. I wasn't talking about California, either.

We had to say good-bye at the check-in. Conner and I were nearly late by the time we walked what seemed like an endless path of corridors and sidewalks from the train platform to the terminal.

Nickie kissed Conner and gave him a hug. She smiled at me, but her eyes were heavy and wet. We embraced, kissing so deeply I didn't think I'd be able to let go of her. Then she said, "I think what you did was beautiful, Jack."

I didn't know what she was talking about.

She opened her bag. A painted wooden horse with a thread-spool wheel between his back legs.

"It was next to my bed this morning," she said. "I can't imagine how you did it, unless you enlisted Ander as your confederate. But he's lovely, Jack. Thank you. And it was a beautiful story, too."

We kissed again.

I lied to her. "You're welcome. I'm happy you like it. Remember me."

"I need you to remember something, too."

I knew what Nickie meant.

"I promise I will."

Don't lie to her.

And Nickie said, "Things are going to be better, aren't they?"

"Yes."

"Then take care of yourself."

Conner watched.

He knew.

And, later, he kept his eyes on me, nervous, trembling, when I checked my pack in at the counter. He'd seen me shut it with those lenses inside. I must have opened it to be sure they were still there a dozen times or more before I finally let it go.

"Are you sure you can do that, Jack?"

"It'll be okay, Con."

fifty-nine

Glenbrook.

The day after we came home.

We're both pale and sweating. We sit in Conner's truck while he drives around.

The windows are up and the air-conditioning blows against my bare chest, but it doesn't help.

Summer's end is so hot in Glenbrook.

"Maybe it will only be for a minute," he says.

I'm shaking so bad I can hardly get the words out. "Park over here, man."

Just a peek.

It's a joke, right? I notice we're sitting in the lot at Steckel Park.

Everything comes back to this, doesn't it?

"Come on, Jack. I'm really sick. I feel like I'm going to die or something."

"I know."

I look up. "I need air."

I open the door. "Get out of the truck, Con."

I am holding the sock. I never once opened it since we left London, but I can feel what's inside it like it's vibrating in my hand, a buzzing insect, tickling me to open my fingers and set it free. Conner doubles over beside his door. I can hear him trying to throw up, but nothing comes.

"Let's go over there," I say.

He follows me and we sit down in the grass beneath a tree.

"This really is happening, isn't it?" he says. "I didn't want to show you this. I was scared. Look what happened to me."

Conner leans back and pulls down the waistband of his shorts. There is a small scar, a burn on the skin a few inches below his belly. It is shaped like an incomplete figure 8, sideways, like the outline of a fish.

"This wasn't here before," he says. "Never."

I shake my head. "I don't know what it means, Con."

Two boys are playing basketball.

Conner bends his knees and puts his face between them.

I unroll the socks, try not to look at what's inside.

There.

I have the Marbury lens in my hand, close my grasp around it. But I can feel it, and I am happy.

Jack is happy.

"I have it," I say. "You ready?"

Conner lifts his face. He looks like he's been crying, but I know

357

it's only the sweat. I take a deep breath. I wind the sock up and put it into the Velcro pocket on my shorts.

A basketball rolls up and hits Conner's feet.

"Hey. A little help, please?"

Two boys, shooting baskets in front of us. Ben Miller and Griffin Goodrich.

Ben asks, "You guys want to play?"

Conner grabs my wrist. "Holy shit, Jack."

Griffin says, "Hey, do you speak English, or what? Can you throw us the ball?"

I look at him.

And seeing Ben and Griffin in the park gives me some careful sense of relief. But it makes me wonder, too, about Marbury, Henry, the gap between here and there.

Conner says, "It's them."

"This is real, Con. I need to be sure it's real."

Conner is breathing hard. I can see him shaking. "Don't do it, Jack. Let's just quit."

We can't quit.

He picks up the ball and fires it at Griffin.

"Thanks. So, you guys want to play two-on-two?"

Shakily, Conner pushes himself to his feet, but he looks sick. "We'll play. Get up, Jack."

I open my hand.

Griffin stares at the lens, and behind him, Ben stands frozen at the edge of the court, watching us.

In their eyes, I can see a pale reflection.

Something big.

A colorless sky.

acknowledgments

Thanks to my friends Craig Morton and Dean Shauger, who were willing to talk me through some of the tricky parts I had with this story. Thanks, also, to fellow authors Michael Grant, Brian James, Bill Konigsberg, Yvonne Prinz, and Kelly Milner Halls; as well as to blogger Adam DeCamp; and friends Nora Rawn, Andrea Vuleta, Nevin Mays, and Lucia Lemieux — all of whom gave me their input when I asked for it.

As always, my warmest thanks and appreciation to my agent, Laura Rennert.

One more thing. My great-grandfather on my American side lived around the same time as Seth Mansfield. He was a foundling, too.

SQUARE FISH

THE MARBURY LENS
by Andrew Smith

Discussion Questions

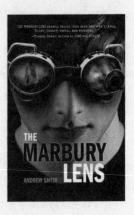

1. Violence is a major, recurring theme in the book. Jack's story begins with brutality; and the cruelty inflicted on innocents by others resurfaces again and again—in Seth's story, and in what happens to everyone in Marbury. What are Jack's feelings about the brutal nature of his universe? What does Conner think about it?

2. One of the ideas Smith explores in *The Marbury Lens* is the dynamic found in relationships between males. We see this in the way Jack interacts with Ben and Griffin in Marbury, how he and Conner get along throughout the book, and even to some extent through Seth's relationship with Davey and Pa. Compare and contrast Jack, Conner, Ben, Griffin, and Seth. When Jack's in Marbury with the boys, who's in charge? Who's in charge when Jack's with Conner in England or at home in California?

3. Jack, Seth, and Henry all have one terrible thing in common. What is it? How is this similar/different between the three of them? "It's no wonder I became a monster, too."

4. Jack keeps coming back to his idea of being at the center of the universe. Discuss the importance of this image as it relates to the entire book.

5. Along with that image mentioned in question 4 (above), Smith once wrote that *The Marbury Lens* reveals layer upon layer. There are worlds within worlds, stories inside of stories, the past trapped in the present, and monsters inside of people. How many examples of these layers can you find?

6. In *The Marbury Lens*, there is enough room for readers to make their own decisions about what is real. What do you think? Is Marbury real? Is Henry real? What clues are you given that Henry really exists?

7. There are many turns in the book that deal with being or feeling trapped, and then escaping. Is Marbury a trap for Jack, or does he escape something when he goes there?

8. So much of what we learn about Marbury comes only in bits and pieces throughout the story. Discuss the boys finding the train, the passengers, the soldiers. What might have happened there?

9. Based on the clues provided in the novel, what explanation could you give for what's going on in Marbury?

10. Jack endures so many profoundly powerful events through the course of the novel. How does he change by the novel's end? How does Jack mature over the course of his story?

11. Everything in Marbury seems to be without color. There are no stars at night, and the sky never gets completely dark, but contrasts are sharp there. Why all the "colorless" imagery?

12. Discuss the role of setting in the narrative (California, London, Blackpool, and the locations in Marbury).

13. What do you find out about what happens to the boys after they arrive at the walled city of Grove in Marbury? How has Ben changed by the end of the book?

14. How would you describe the "voice" of the novel? Is Jack an empathetic character, despite his obvious anger and frustration? Give examples of Jack's tone in his narration.

15. In the beginning, Jack seems uncomfortable and inept at telling lies. He fumbles over explaining his injured ankle to Stella. But the Marbury lens has some major effect on Jack in this regard. Discuss the lies Jack tells later in the book.

16. Discuss the wooden horse Nickie shows Jack and Conner at the airport. Where did it come from? What is its significance? Do you think Seth may have intended it as a message to Jack? How do the boys play off Nickie's finding the horse, and what does it tell you about Conner and how he may have changed?

17. In the beginning of the book, Jack mentions that the things that happen turn him into a monster. In fact, the only people Jack finds in Marbury that he knows from this world are monsters. Do you think Jack becomes a monster by the end of the story?

18. In the final lines of the book, Jack makes a decision to do something. What does he do? Is it the act of "a monster"? Is he doing the right thing? Can Jack help himself?

19. AND THE FINAL QUESTION: Would you go there? Even for "just a peek"?

GOFISH

ANDREW SMITH

© Kaija Bosket

Is Marbury real?

In truth, most of what I write has a very strong connection to reality. When I'm writing a book, I usually have vivid dreams that help point the way to solving certain problems and making the vital connections between what is really a part of my experience and what I fictionalize as an author. When you dream, what you experience is just as real as anything could ever be. I had dreams about a place called Marbury when I started writing this novel about Jack's abduction. In my dreams, I could see people I knew, but they appeared as monsters—and I kept hearing this title over and over: *The Marbury Lens*. I don't feel as though I made any of this up. I was shown and told it. I guess that makes it as real as anything.

Did you do any travel or research for this novel?

I did travel to London while writing the book, and again while writing the sequel, *Passenger*. I spent a lot of time in the UK when I was young. My brother had a house in North Yorkshire, in Harrogate, which is where the character Rachel lives, and I'd been to Blackpool a number of times. Also, I made those same train trips from Harrogate to Leeds to Kings Cross a lot. I also did some research into physics and cosmology because I had this idea of how Jack's layered universe worked, and I wanted to see if there was any basis for this architecture in theoretical physics—which I stretched to fit my own concept of Jack's reality. I also have a London Tube map application on my iPad and iPhone, so I wouldn't get lost. Oh . . . and I spent quite a number of hours submerging myself in heavy research at a pub called the Prince of Wales.

What was your favorite scene to write and what was the most difficult to write?

My favorite scene to write was the one where the boys—Jack, Ben, and Griffin—find the anomalous train sitting in the middle of a salt flat in the Marbury desert. I think the qualities that appeal to me most in that scene are the dark mystery of the train and the sense of wonder and discovery at all the cool and horrifying stuff the boys find inside. I had always intended to write the backstory about how that train got there and what happened to the passengers inside it. Needless to say, this is an important element in *Passenger*.

The most difficult scene to write was what happened to Seth and his adoptive father, Blake Mansfield. That scene upset me for a long time. It still bothers me to go back and reread it.

Up until now, your stories have taken place in the here and now. What was it like to write about another world for the first time?

In some ways, I would argue that all my books are actually about other worlds, so writing about a place called Marbury was not really much different than writing about the New Mexico desert or the Pacific Northwest. Although setting plays a major role in what I write, the real connective tissue of my novels are the relationships between rather complex characters, so dropping them in the middle of an environmentally ruined wasteland was no more laborious than putting them on horseback in the Sierra Nevadas. (Notice how I worked in references to just about every book I've ever written?)

What can we expect in *Passenger*, the sequel to *The Marbury Lens*?

I think the bridge between these two books is this: *The Marbury Lens* is ultimately about how one tragic event can have rippling consequences over the timeline of an innocent's life. *The Marbury Lens* is about how Jack tries, arguably with varying degrees of success, to deal with that issue despite his obvious flaws and predilection toward blaming himself. *Passenger* examines the effect of Jack's traumatic past on others—the people who love Jack. This book is about Jack finally being "okay" with where he finds himself (wherever that is), who he really is, and what he means to the people who love him.

What did you want to be when you grew up?

I think I always wanted to be a writer when I grew up. The problem was, growing up when I did, most families were overly concerned about having stable futures and working in industries that would always expand—like warfare and stuff. After all, I am a child of the Cold War. So, my parents were not very enthusiastic when I revealed my future aspirations to them. In fact, I think I recall them saying something like, "But what do you *really* want to be?"

When did you realize you wanted to be a writer?

I always liked it when my teachers would give creative assignments that dealt with writing stories or illustrating things. And I actually am a pretty decent artist, although I really wish I could paint better. But becoming a writer probably became a certainty for me when I was in high school.

What's your most embarrassing childhood memory?

When I was in kindergarten, I sat next to a boy named Chip. Chip had to pee really bad, but he was too afraid to ask the teacher, Mrs. Bailey. So Chip just peed under the table, all over the floor, and, of course, he denied it was his. I was ethically torn by the situation. We were sitting two-to-a-desk, Chip was my friend, and I had an irreconcilably feverish crush on Mrs. Bailey.

As a young person, who did you look up to most?

When I was a kid, I looked up to my brother Patrick the most. He was older, and we shared a bedroom (there were four boys in my family) until he enlisted in the army—when he went off to fight in Vietnam. Patrick drove a 1959 Cadillac—a gift from our aunt—and he used to drive the three of us younger boys around with him and his tough-guy high school friends on their crazy adventures, and we listened to AM radio stations and daringly used words like "bitchin'" when we talked.

What was your first job?

My first real job—where I actually collected a paycheck—was writing for a local newspaper in Southern California. Beginning reporters are called stringers, and in those days, stringers got paid by the inch of copy we wrote (newspaper columns, typically two inches wide, had about fifty words per inch). I often say that getting paid for writing by the inch is very likely the origin of my predilection for big words and long sentences.

How did you celebrate publishing your first book?

It honestly wasn't much of a celebration for a couple reasons: First, publication takes such an interminably long time. From the time you get an offer to when you actually sign contracts may take several months. Then, when the book is actually in the stores is usually more than a year after that. But the biggest reason for a non-celebration was that I wrote—and continue to write—in secret. Nobody knew what I was up to, so my family and friends really didn't believe much of anything had actually happened. In fact, I didn't tell my wife that I had written a book until after I received an offer for representation from my agent. And when I finally told her, she was so relieved because she thought I was having some kind of online affair due to the hours and hours I'd been spending quietly working on my computer. Now, I think my writing is more of a bother to my wife and kids. Maybe they'll want to celebrate when I decide to quit.

Where do you write your books?

I write my books in my upstairs office at home. It is a perfect writing place. It has a deck and lots of windows looking out at mountains and trees and my horses. When I travel, I carry a laptop with me and I work on my writing by emailing bits and pieces of my work back and forth to myself.

Where do you find inspiration for your writing?

Inspiration is a moving target. If you sit still, you'll never find it, and you'll get really old waiting for it to bump into you.

Which of your characters is most like you?

Well, to some extent, all my protagonists are part "me," but if you had to isolate one individual character, I think there'd be no doubt about it: I am most like Simon Vickers, from *In the Path of Falling Objects*. He always takes risks without seriously considering the consequences, and I think he has an attitude—maybe due to naiveté—that nothing bad will ever happen to him. He likes to push buttons and then acts indignant when the people around him get pissed off. Yeah . . . that's me.

When you finish a book, who reads it first?

When I finish a book, I read it first. That's when I try to read it like I didn't have anything to do with it having been written. I am not a writer who shares what I write with friends and family, though. So, when I finish a book, I usually send it directly to my agent and my editor. Then, immediately after that, I get sick and start asking, "Why did I send that to them? Why? Why? Why?" and I start calling myself every version of stupid I can think up. Then I get really grumpy until I hear back from them—an interminable and agonizing wait, even if it's only a few days long.

Which do you like better: cats or dogs?

I am entirely a dog person. Still, we do own four cats who are all very good at keeping down the rodent population around the house and then making little shrines of death on our front walkway.

What do you value most in your friends?

I like my friends for their intelligence and sense of humor. I also truly value the fact that my friends understand that I am a fairly quiet and reserved person who can go for long stretches of time rather quiet and isolated.

Where do you go for peace and quiet?

I live in a very peaceful, quiet location—and I really couldn't have it any other way. Although there are certain cities that I absolutely love (Los Angeles, New York, Chicago, Boston, London, to name a few), my ideal getaways usually take me to secluded places that are not very crowded.

What makes you laugh out loud?

I most often find myself laughing out loud at things we say when I'm hanging out with my wife and kids—or when I'm joking around with my very funny friends: John, Casey, Brian, Steve, and Jeremy.

What's your favorite song?

I wonder how many people can confidently answer that question. My favorite song changes about every other week. But I can offer, as a means of getting around the question, that if there ever were perfect "soundtracks" made for *Ghost Medicine* and *In the Path of Falling Objects*, I would like to have the following artists contribute: The Felice Brothers, Bob Dylan, Bon Iver, and Johnny Flynn. Now, if there were a soundtrack made for *The Marbury Lens*, I would like to hear what Radiohead, The Cure, and maybe a reunited Pink Floyd would come up with for that monster.

Who is your favorite fictional character?

"My" favorite fictional character is, naturally, one of my own—a kid named Stark McClellan. He's in a book I wrote called *Stick*. But the reason that I like him so much is that he has this really dry (but definitely not cynical or sarcastic) sense of humor in the way he looks at things, and he has this remarkable ability, I think, to see a kind of wonder in everything—even if he's surrounded by cruelty and ugliness. I admire people who are like that.

What time of year do you like best?

I definitely prefer summertime. Still, there is a lot to be said for sitting by a fire while snow falls outside, reading a great book.

What's your favorite TV show?

I do not watch television at all. I am incapable of sitting still and having information, noise, and visuals pumped into my skull. I know this is a shortcoming on my part and that I am missing out on something, but I just don't ever do it. My friends think I'm a snob, but it has nothing to do with my looking down on the medium. They're all dumb, anyway.

If you were stranded on a desert island, who would you want for company?
A television. Just kidding. There wouldn't be anywhere to plug it in. This is a trick, right? You left out the phrase "besides your wife," right? Okay, so if I couldn't have my wife OR my kids with me, then I'd probably be just fine by myself. I am an incurable loner at heart.

If you could travel in time, where would you go?
I would very much have liked to live in California during the 1880s. I know that's a random choice, but I've always had a fascination for that time period, which is only part of the reason why I set a portion of *The Marbury Lens* in California during that decade. There were so many interesting political, social, and religious movements in America at that time, and those tremendous transformations in the ways that people looked at themselves and the universe—coupled with the anxious feeling of being right on the razor's edge of this incredible twentieth-century future—really made for some potentially amazing adventures.

What's the best advice you've ever received about writing?
People who make it a practice to give advice about writing tend to give the *worst* possible advice. Here are my top three pieces of idiotic nonsense people will tell you about writing:

1. You have to have a thick skin.
2. "Show" don't "tell."
3. Don't quit your day job.

Those are all really wrong and meaningless, in my opinion. The only rule in my writer's code is *there are no rules.*

What do you want readers to remember about your books?

I want my readers to find some personal connection to what I write. It's hard for me to say just how much it means to me when I get letters or email from readers telling me how they've been impacted by one of my books. That's the greatest thing in the world, and it seems like every one of those letters always tells me something different about how that connection was made.

What would you do if you ever stopped writing?

I would probably be an inconsolable grump, the worst neighborhood grouch in the history of neighborhood grouches. I can't see myself quitting.

What do you like best about yourself?

I'll tell you what I like *least* about myself: I take everything personally. I know that's a critical weakness for someone who writes professionally because everyone in the business seems to repeat this *you-need-to-have-a-thick-skin* mantra (see above), but I can't help it. I actually lose sleep over the littlest things people say or do.

What is your worst habit?

Evasiveness. When I don't want to talk about something, I'll craftily change the subject. My sixteen-year-old son, who is afraid of insects, is far braver than I am when it comes to riding on roller coasters.

What do you consider to be your greatest accomplishment?

Here we go again with the "bests" questions. I think I am a good father. I believe my kids will look back on some of the things we've done together as a family as some of the greatest memories in their lives. That said, I am also very proud of all the books I've published—as well as those that will be coming out in the future.

Where in the world do you feel most at home?

Oddly enough, I feel most at home *at home*. I am a bit of a recluse, I suppose, and I greatly prefer the quiet of the countryside (where I live). I have never been able to understand the "dream" of living in a house that sits in a tight row of clone houses, surrounded by row upon row of other houses, in a neighborhood where you constantly hear the sounds of traffic and sirens.

What do you wish you could do better?

I wish I could speak Italian better. When I was a child, my mother could not speak English, and I spent many years in Italy, so I naturally picked up the language when I was young. Now, it's difficult for me to form the words although I still can understand them very well.

What would your readers be most surprised to learn about you?

When I was a little kid, my family lived in a very old house that was actually haunted. And to be completely honest, I frequently saw the ghost of a little boy in it, but never told anyone until after we moved away, and then my mother told me that she saw ghosts in it all the time, too.

Jack and Conner thought they had escaped Marbury, but their obsession draws them back into the unresolved war there. Even after they try to destroy the lens, the dark world will not leave them alone.

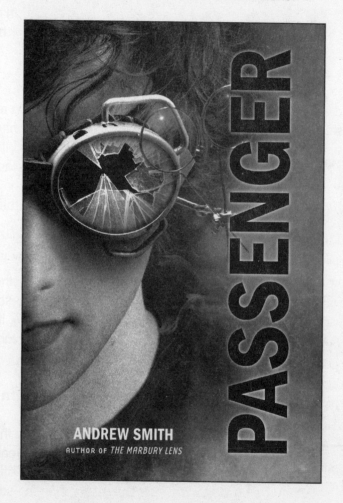

Re-enter Marbury in Andrew Smith's

PASSENGER.

This is it.

Of course it wasn't over.

Things like this never end.

It has been two and a half months since Freddie Horvath kidnapped some dumb fucking kid who was too drunk to find his way home.

You can't possibly believe things just end, dry up, go away, can you?

Sometimes, when I look at myself, I see the likeness of Wynn, my grandfather, in my face. And I wonder if I'll still be carrying all of this around when I'm his age.

It's not like a sack of garbage you can just drop off at the side of the road and then keep going, pretending you had nothing to do with it in the first place.

Sometimes, it makes me very tired.

————

All this time I thought it wasn't me, it wasn't me.

But it was.

I need to tell you a story.

The garage steams with the smell of cat piss and something dead. The reek hangs in the still press of late August heat.

Every one of us is sick and scared.

I tell them, "We said we'd do it, and we're going to do it, okay?"

My best friend, Conner, shrugs. "We got no choice."

I would die for Conner Kirk. Sometimes, I think I have died for him dozens of times, over and over again.

Conner looks at the other boys, as if his words are spoken to convince himself more than the rest of us. "Jack and me are leaving for St. Atticus next week. When the four of us split up, you're going to go crazy if you don't have the lens, and we can't just leave it here."

Among all of us, Griffin looks the most scared.

"It's okay, Griff," Ben says. "As long as we're together in this."

I watch a bead of sweat as it arcs up and over Griffin's collarbone, then streaks down his bony chest. And he says, "Well, what are you looking at me for? You were the one who said it was a good idea."

I wonder why I did this to them—Ben and Griffin—and I answer, *They asked me to, they asked me to.*

"The only idea," Conner says.

I squeeze my hand tight. "I don't have nothing better. It's getting late."

We're all soaked, but we're afraid to open the doors. We even put a canvas painter's tarp over the only window. Conner pulls his shirt off and wipes his face and armpits with it.

I can hear him swallow. He closes his eyes and inhales deeply.

"Keep your eyes up," he says. And then he looks at me. "Jack? You know."

He grabs my wrist.

I say, "I know, Con."

"If we get lost or something," he begins, but he knows I don't want him to say any more. Not now.

A ball-peen hammer rests on the table next to the vice. There is a lidless Mason jar with some cloudy paint thinner; the stained handle of a brush tilts against the lip of the inner rim. The things belong to Griffin Goodrich's dad—Ben Miller's stepfather.

No one else is home, just the four of us—standing around that workbench, sweating like junkies inside the boys' unlighted garage.

It is suddenly so loud when Ben cranks the vice open.

One turn.

He lets the knob-ended metal bar drop through its catch hole, and the steely clang makes Griffin twitch like he's been shocked.

Half an inch.

The Marbury lens is in my hand.

I know what I'm doing, don't have to see anything.

When I open my hand, it's like we all gasp for the same short-ened mouthful of air—and it's not enough.

The familiar dull purple glow, like an aquarium filled with smoke and creatures swimming just below the surface of our blurry vision; writhing shadows like pendulous scythes that sweep across the stalks of our legs, asking us to fold before their blades, wanting us to go down into that swirling light.

Conner's eyes are locked on mine.

"Don't look," I say, and my voice sounds ridiculous.

Fingers feel the toothy edge of the vicemaw.

Griffin is shaking, his eyes shut tight. I don't know if it's tears or sweat I see on his face.

No. Griffin never cries.

Like Jack.

"Don't look," I say again, more to myself than anyone else.

I tighten the vice, let go of the lens.

The swimming shadows boil below us, urgent, pleading.

Just a peek.

Blindly, I reach for the hammer, line it up with my thumb.

I swing.

The lens cleaves. The upper fragment, freed, spins jaggedly through the air and I see flashes like I'm thumb-flipping through a book of unrelated photographs taken by strange hands at different times and places. I feel the broken piece as it lands with the weight of a dead bird on top of my foot.

Screams. Sounds like a slaughterhouse running at full tilt, a jangling of machinery: agonized, pained cries coming from somewhere, everywhere; and I'm thinking, *It's not me, it's not the kids, it isn't Conner;* and I can't see the garage anymore.

Nothing.

No Conner. Nobody.

I fall backwards through the slithering monochrome shapes that writhe up from the floor. I thrash my arms, try to grab hold of anyone, try to shout the names of my friends—I forget how to make the words leave my mouth.

My hand slides over something slick. It is Griffin's arm and I squeeze a grip on the boy and together we fall and fall through the forever of passing images. Endlessly slow and silent, like we are descending; downward through lukewarm pudding.

And I feel my fingers passing through Griffin's arm, like the boy has turned into steam, and all I can feel is a moment of moisture before my hand is empty.

Then I hit.

And I know only two things.

My eyes are closed.

And I am alone.

In time, I gave up worrying about whether I'd lost my mind. It didn't matter. Because my best friend, Conner Kirk, had been dragged beside me into hell. Ben and Griffin, too.

Now they were gone.

It's time to take things apart.

Monsters make monsters make monsters.

Ten weeks before, a man named Freddie Horvath kidnapped me. He was a monster, and I was something like a little bird that nobody gave a shit about.

I fell out of my nest.

Poor Jack.

Since then, all of the horrors that stacked and stacked, layer after layer—the killing on Nacimiento Road, being pursued by Henry Hewitt when I was lost and sick in London, stumbling and falling into the nightmare of a place called Marbury that made me feel more at home than I'd ever felt at any other time in my regrettable life—it all turned me into a monster, too.

I could not stop myself from having Ben and Griffin fall with us into Marbury. It was what they told me they wanted, and I believed every sound I'd ever heard in Marbury. So after Conner and I returned from England and found them playing basketball in the park, we could not help ourselves.

Nobody could.

The four of us became willingly trapped.

Now we straddle the gap of nowhere, between this world and the not-world called Marbury. And Marbury is what we need more than anything.

I can't explain it; that's just how things are.

Freddie Horvath made me into a monster.

I made monsters of my friends: Conner Kirk, Ben Miller, and Griffin Goodrich.

And before Conner and I could leave Glenbrook, California, for the coming school year in England, the four of us monsters must divide our pathetic kingdom.

Here, in this piss-reeked garage.